LAKE HOUSE

Sally Faubel

WestBow
PRESS
A DIVISION OF THOMAS NELSON

WestBow Press books may be ordered through booksellers or by contacting:

WestBow Press
A Division of Thomas Nelson
1663 Liberty Drive
Bloomington, IN 47403
www.westbowpress.com
1-(866) 928-1240

Because of the dynamic nature of the Internet, any web addresses or
links contained in this book may have changed since publication and
may no longer be valid. The views expressed in this work are solely those
of the author and do not necessarily reflect the views of the publisher,
and the publisher hereby disclaims any responsibility for them.

ISBN: 978-1-4497-4742-8 (sc)
ISBN: 978-1-4497-4743-5 (hc)
ISBN: 978-1-4497-4741-1 (e)

Library of Congress Control Number: 2012906946

Printed in the United States of America

WestBow Press rev. date: 5/9/2012

To our ancestor—the Gehls, the Karstens, the Wernekes, the Pfeiffers—who had the courage to flee the oppression and tyranny of the powerful few. To those who seized the opportunity to built a new life, in a new world, with nothing except their trust in God, hard work, dedication to family, and the help of their neighbors and friends. To those who passed down that Spirit and 'moral code' to the next generation.

PREFACE

Lake House and the property surrounding it are factitious. Like Brigadoon it rises from the mist and hovers between the real and the unreal, the past and the present. Except for the obvious historical figures such as the kings of England and the French missionaries, no character in the novel—past or present—represents an actual person. However, in some cases a character is a composite of an array of people known to the author. The Indian community that Will and his friends joined is fictitious; however, information about the Indians of that era is based on historical information. Most of the written history, regarding the Indians in the 1600s and 1700s, is from diaries and journals of missionaries, fur traders, and explorers. Each brings his own cultural background and bias to his account; sometimes, this is admitted by the writer.

Some episodes in the story are based on true events in the life of the author's family—Sarah's golf tournament, Samantha and Sarah's dancing lessons, Abby's adoption . . . .

A sincere effort has been made to research the historical background and present it as accurately as possible. The geography and information about Michigan, particularly the northwestern part of the Lower Peninsula, is as precise as possible. Most places are just described; few are given names—most are fictitious. The reader may enjoy trying to detect the actual place.

Sally Faubel

❧·CHAPTER 1

Each is given a bag of tools,
a set of rules.
Each one makes, as life is flown,
a stumbling block or a stepping stone.

Adapted from poem by R. L. Sharpe

In the same week in June, Samantha Sophia Schwerin celebrated her 22nd birthday alone, graduated from college, and had 77 million dollars bestowed upon her through unfortunate circumstances. At the age of eighteen years and two months, she had been left without parents, siblings, or close relatives. Finally, all had been settled, and she did, indeed, have 77 million dollars in an account or two in her name. The money was of little comfort in her great loss and loneliness, and it was perhaps a great burden and greater responsibility for someone so young. For the past four years, she had been beset by attorneys, investigators, bankers, and questionable friends. She had been getting glimpses of part of a world she'd never imagined and was becoming a bit cynical and suspicious of people. Now, with 77 million dollars, could she trust anyone's motive for friendship, financial dealings, or anything?

She had managed to attend college (the University of Michigan in Ann Arbor) in spite of everything and graduated with honors. The original plan had been for her to attend the small university her parents had attended. She'd wanted to enjoy campus life.

1

Needing the anonymity she could find in a large university, all that had changed.

Absorbing herself in her studies had helped immensely to take her mind off the madness in which she was immersed. She'd lived at home, commuted, and kept to herself as much as possible. She'd majored in math. She was good at math. It was an orderly subject where everyone played by the rules. She knew the rules and where she stood. But now, how was this going to help her? What were the rules now? Should she have majored in something more practical—something to suit her circumstances? Accounting? Business? Maybe psychology? Maybe philosophy— maybe not! She was suspicious of professors who spent a lot of time quoting Nietzsche—scary!

It was mid-June—daylight came early. At 5:30, the air was already warm and steamy because of a heavy rain during the night. Samantha knew she had to start her daily four-mile trek soon. Walking was her exercise of choice. For a nanosecond, she'd thought of taking up jogging. After picturing herself in a state of sweaty exhaustion, the idea disappeared as fast as pressing the "delete" key on her computer. With all the complexity in her life, a brisk walk was simple: no new skills to learn, no decision about what equipment to purchase (a good pair of walking shoes was all), no risk of injury, no getting into the car and going to a gym. It got to be a habit like brushing teeth.

Since walking outside was her preference, planning around the weather was necessary—signs of lightning meant definitely no walking; otherwise, any other conditions would do. Since today promised to be hot, very hot, she knew she had to get out there *tout de suite*. Preparing for the trip, she drank a few swallows of water and then a glass of half chocolate soy milk and half skim milk—to mellow the earthy taste. She didn't think she could make the usual four miles without a little hydration and a few calories kicking in after awhile. She always went the same way so she could think about a math problem or another class problem or just enjoy the day without having to divert any mental energy to decisions about an itinerary.

She finally ventured out at about 6:45. The route was pleasant enough: along the sidewalks of her neighborhood subdivision, past a long stretch of wooded area, two laps around a large park with a dramatic fountain (and a few splashes of water to cool off), and then back along neighborhood sidewalks. During her time on the university campus, she'd frequently walked the distance between classes if she'd had the time and the weather hadn't been too horrible.

As it was Saturday, she was not the only one out early. Husbands were beginning to emerge in their weekend attire—khaki shorts, polo shirts, Nike shoes, and white socks—starting the Saturday-morning duties of homeowners. Fortunately, due to the rain the night before, the grass was wet, and the roar of lawn mowers and blowers had not started.

Aah, a quiet walk! she thought. This gave her time to contemplate seriously her circumstances—no studies to mull over any more. After slightly more than four years, she was still in her parents' home in a modest subdivision, but she didn't know the neighbors. The homes were neat and well-cared-for; however, it wasn't a friendly place. The properties turned over frequently as families moved on to bigger and better things. Being a young woman alone, she was out of place. The over-scheduled families around her were absorbed in their day-to-day struggles, tedious jobs, and the never ending activities of their children.

Since it was summer in Michigan, half the neighborhood had gone "up north," and in the winter, the snow and cold tended to isolate people. Her parents had subscribed to a yard service that included snow removal. She just kept paying the monthly bill, and—whatever the season—they kept showing up to do their thing. As a result, she was rarely in the yard. Unless someone caught a glimpse of her exiting or entering the house or the car slipping into and out of the garage, no one would know the house was occupied.

She and her parents had moved to this neighborhood after she'd finished high school and they'd retired. Her parents had wanted to be near their grandchildren. No one around her knew of her circumstances, and Samantha was not one to talk about her situation. Instinctively, she was aware that the less people knew, the safer she would be.

As she started the walk, she tried to focus; she had to get serious. *A woman with a fortune . . . Samantha with a fortune . . . me, me, me—I have a fortune! What now? Where do I go for guidance? Who can I trust? I need to set goals—maybe, just one—maybe just one for today.*

Her mind wandered. She laughed, remembering the Jane Austen novels she'd read when she was fourteen. Her goal then had been to read all six, and she'd accomplished it in a few months. Was there any wisdom there for her current situation? In the world of Jane Austen and her character Mrs. Bennet, "It is a truth universally acknowledged that a single man in possession of a good fortune must be in want of a wife."

No help there! I'm a single woman in possession of a good fortune, she thought as she amused herself in her reminiscing. *I wonder how 10,000 a year, Mr. Darcy's fortune, and poor Jane's fortune of 5,000 a year when she married Mr. Bingley would translate into today's dollars? A single man with a fortune naturally inclined to be on the hunt for a wife may have been "a truth universally acknowledged" in England in 1813. But, wow! The 21st century in the U. S. of A. is indeed a different place.* She was grateful that her scope of life and possibilities were significantly greater. Yet, she admired Miss Austen's heroines—their instincts when it came to men. She wouldn't have to compromise when it came to marriage and settle for an irksome, silly, senseless man, in order to attain security—as did Charlotte Lucas in *Pride and Prejudice*.

She did admire Elizabeth Bennet's loyalty to her family (with all its shortcomings) and her initial rejection of Mr. Darcy's proposal because of his unfortunate attitude toward the Bennet family. It grieved Samantha deeply no longer to *have* a family. Also, Elizabeth did not jump at the chance to marry a wealthy man in spite of the societal pressures to do so. She came to love him when his honorable character was revealed and he was willing to admit his mistakes. What a man! Her favorite Jane Austen character was Fanny Price in *Mansfield Park*. In spite of Fanny's poor-relation status in the household of her uncle, she stood firm and was not pressured into marrying a man of better social circumstance whose character she judged to be weak and defective. Fanny knew she would be accepting an intolerable situation for too long a duration. Samantha wondered, *Will I be discerning enough to marry wisely? No hurry about that now!*

*   *   *

As she entered the house, she noticed a message on the answering machine. "Hello, dear, this is George Reynolds. We are long overdue to discuss your financial plan. Give me a call as soon as possible to set up a time."

The great Financial Planner calling me in person, and this early on a Saturday, no less. What a go-getter, she thought. *And, "Hello, DEAR," isn't going to send me rushing to speed-dial his number. An unfortunate attitude to overcome, and he doesn't sound like a Mr. Darcy. I wonder if his plan is to separate me from as much of my money as he can. Oh dear, I shouldn't become suspicious and cynical. Get a grip, Samantha! Don't let this get you down. Set a goal—one goal, just for today. Go to library—get books on money management!*

She decided she would go to the main library downtown, as it was close to a large bookstore with a Starbucks. Maybe she could peruse some books and after that treat herself to a café mocha latté. Then it dawned on her. *I don't have to worry about spending a little extra on an expensive coffee drink, and I could buy the books I want, take my time and use them for reference. This is a whole new mindset to get used to.*

Until now, she didn't have much money—just a modest allowance determined by a judge. This was doled out by "dear George," who had been appointed by the court as temporary trustee. She had to scrimp and take out loans to pay her tuition. Fortunately, the house had been paid for—no large mortgage payments to make. There were two paid-for vehicles in the

5

garage—her mother's silver Buick Century (now six years old) which she had been driving, and her father's very large truck, which she had never driven.

She hadn't let herself think she would actually receive the great sum of money that the courts had mulled over. She was too sensible to go into significant debt on a hope, and she was naïve about the whole process. Fortunately, her brother had chosen a reputable law firm for his business, and the lawyers had the situation in hand. Of course, there was a lot in it for them, but as it turned out they did their job well.

Tired after her walk in the warm, humid weather, she sat for awhile at her father's desk in the dark maroon office chair the family had given him for his birthday several years ago. It gave her some comfort, just sitting there surrounded by the soft leather high back and padded arms of the chair. Memories of her father spilled over her. She started going through the file drawers in the lower part of the desk, shredding some papers, reading others. This was a task she had avoided. The size of the task and the emotional strain were overwhelming—a lifetime of personal and family records. Perhaps there were items he had never intended her to see.

She was engrossed in sorting, shredding, and reading for several hours. It was about three in the afternoon when the phone rang, startling her and bringing her back to the present. Ordinarily, she would not have answered it, having been inundated with unwanted calls over the past few years. Nevertheless, hardly thinking, she picked it up quickly.

A young woman's voice said, "Hi, Samantha?"

"Yes."

"This is Betty Ann Doyle." She was a student in one of Samantha's math classes. They had commiserated only a few times between classes or on the way out of an exam.

How did she get my number? Samantha wondered. *I had it changed and unlisted. I'm sure I never even told her what city I live in or my last name.* Nevertheless, she did not ask, but engaged in some simplistic conversation.

6

"I didn't see your name in the commencement bulletin," Samantha commented.

"I need six more credits. I'm taking classes this summer—then I'll graduate," Betty Ann replied.

"Oh, I see."

"How about meeting for coffee?" Betty Ann suggested.

Samantha was not keen on pursuing this relationship, but she couldn't think of an excuse. It was too late today. She was preoccupied and not in the mood to go downtown. "I'll be going to the library Monday—"

"We could meet at the bookstore next to it," Betty Ann interjected. "The Starbucks there would be a good place to have coffee and a chat. How about one o'clock?"

"Okay," Samantha replied hesitantly.

After she hung up, she reflected on what she knew about Betty Ann. *Betty Ann is pleasant enough, and heaven knows I needed a friend. But, I'm sure we're not kindred spirits nor have the potential to become "bosom friends for life" (or was it "as long as the sun and moon shall endure?") like Anne Shirley and Diana Barry, in Anne of Green Gables.*

The only thing she really remembered about Betty Ann, the one thing that bothered her, the one thing that always seemed to be on her mind when she talked to her: her initials: B.A.D. What parents would give their little newborn sweetie initials like that? Betty Ann could have dropped the Betty or the Ann, and it would not have been obvious. Samantha would have definitely dropped the *Betty*. But, Betty Ann insisted on being called *Betty Ann*. What was that about? What sort of statement was *she* trying to make? Betty Ann and her parents may have been amused, but Samantha was not.

*   *   *

A hasty breakfast had been her last meal, and she was plenty hungry. There was little to eat in the kitchen, but she could not face going out on a Saturday afternoon to fight the crowds at the supermarket or a fast-food place. She rummaged through the few items in the cupboard—flour, sugar, boxes of cereal. She found one can—ravioli. It had been there awhile, but the can wasn't bulging, and the date on the label assured her it should be safe. She found some fruit and milk in the refrigerator and quickly ate her little feast.

Feeling revived, she returned to the library. Emotionally drained from her previous task, she could not face resuming it, so she started surveying her parents' collection of books. The walls were lined from floor to ceiling with built-in shelves filled with books—no knick-knacks, no plants, no decorative items of any kind—just books. Samantha had been an avid reader all her life. However, as a child and teenager, her tastes had been immature. She saw the books she had enjoyed as a young child on the lower shelves. Her mother had saved these for her granddaughters to enjoy when they visited. This broke Samantha's heart into a thousand pieces. Remembering two beautiful little girls sitting on the floor with the books spread out around them, she began crying uncontrollably.

⚜·CHAPTER 2

"God of grace and God of glory . . .
Grant us wisdom, grant us courage
For the facing of this hour . . .
Grant us wisdom, grant us courage
For the living of these days . . ."

Henry Emerson Fosdick (1878-1969)

By Monday, her profound grief had subsided, and she was ready to start her first goal. It was good she had made the appointment to meet Betty Ann; she needed that push to get her out of the house.

Wanting to look at books before she met Betty Ann, she arrived at the bookstore around noon. She was surrounded by neatly dressed, prosperous-looking men and women from the nearby courthouse and banks. Some were portly, middle-aged men with their well-cut suit jackets concealing their spreading waistlines; some were smartly dressed women with perfectly styled hair and the ever-popular manicure; some were young men whose workout builds looked good in cheap suits, but their shoes gave away their less prosperous status. For some reason, Samantha always looked at the shoes; they were telling about a person. The older men had highly polished, expensive shoes, probably polished by someone in the locker room of an exclusive country club. The shoes of the young men were cheaper and older, with a self-polishing job. The women's shoes were simply new and in the latest style.

In contrast, Samantha's clothes were ordinary—white sneakers (the lace-up kind); no socks; jeans; a light blue shirt; a nondescript, medium-sized, beige canvas shoulder bag; and no jewelry except for a cheap watch. Her hair had not been styled and was long overdue for a trim. She had no fingernail polish, no makeup except for a soft pink lipstick hastily applied, and no pierced ears—or pierced anything. She wore glasses—small, plain, oval ones with gold-tone rims—which she used for distance. These were tucked into her shirt pocket as, unlike most people, she took off her glasses to read. With minor variations, this was her everyday appearance. She had no iPod or BlackBerry, only an outdated, rarely-used cell phone tucked into the designated pocket of her shoulder bag. She carried this out of habit, for convenience, and in case of emergency; no living person knew her number.

Samantha looked young. She was tall, slender, and had pretty blue eyes, a charming smile with naturally straight white teeth, shiny dark brown hair with natural highlights a beauty salon could never reproduce, and regular features. She had a natural prettiness about her. Nothing suggested that she was anything but an ordinary college student or a poor, struggling 22-year-old. As it was a Monday in the business district, she looked unemployed; actually, she was.

A nice-looking man about 35 was looking at books in the personal finance section. Being on the shy side, she never started conversations with strangers; however, she decided to overcome her apprehension. After all, this was the first day she'd set out to accomplish her first goal.

She spoke in a pleasant, soft voice with proper grammar and the generic accent of a network anchorperson. (In spite of going to school in Florida intermittently, she avoided the southern drawl of the natives and had intentionally escaped the Midwestern twang prevalent in the culture where she spent the rest of her time.) "Excuse me. I'm looking for something on personal finance and investing. Any suggestions?"

"Sorry, I know almost nothing about money. I'm a criminal attorney." They exchanged three or four sentences of meaningless conversation before he excused himself and left the store.

It was getting close to the time she was to meet Betty Ann when an attractive young man approached her. "I couldn't help over hearing your conversation with the lawyer," he began. "I might be able to help."

She was astonished and muttered something like, "Well—well, thank you."

"I've seen Suze Orman on TV. Try her books. I think they might be good. You might like to watch her program sometime," he suggested.

"Thanks," she replied.

He walked away and disappeared behind the shelves labeled *Mystery Books* on the other side of the store.

She saw at least half a dozen books by Suze. *The Courage to be Rich* caught her eye. *Well, now, doesn't that sound appropriate?* she thought. *Why has this responsibility been given to me? Why me?* She felt an obligation to seven unfinished lives; she was the beneficiary of the life's work of her parents, the hard work of her brother and sister-in-law, and even the lifetime work of her brother's father-in-law. It was overpowering; she wasn't taking this lightly.

She paged through the books, reading Suze's personal story and her narratives of how others had taken responsibility for their financial problems and turned their lives around; she was impressed. They were different from hers; nevertheless, she admired their courage and conscientiousness. She picked up a book entitled *You've Earned It; Don't Lose It; Mistakes You Can't Afford*. It was for retired people; even so, it pretty much fit her situation. After purchasing the book, she went directly to the coffee shop counter and ordered a café mocha latté. This was definitely more potent than her recipe for Café Mocha Lite she occasionally fixed at home. Steaming hot beverage in hand, she selected one of the high tables with a good view of the main entrance and sat down. She started reading, glancing up from time to time to check for Betty Ann. The café *was* where she said she would meet her, so she stopped looking and started reading more intently. Absorbed in the book, she was startled when a voice that was not Betty Ann's interrupted her. "How's the book?" It was the young man who had suggested it. Then Samantha realized that Betty Ann was already 45 minutes late.

She hid the title page and replied, "Good. Good basic information. Easy to read."

"Do you mind if I join you?"

All the tables were filled. Insecure about the possibility that someone might want to sit with her because he liked her looks, she wondered about his motives. Was there no place else to sit? Was he presuming on their short acquaintance, or did he like her looks and manner and want her company? "Please, sit down," she responded politely.

With a cold drink in hand, he sat across from her. He had no books, no backpack, nor any other paraphernalia. He introduced himself as Joe Morton. She gave him her name— only Samantha—no last name. They engaged in small talk about the hot weather—"It would be nice to go to the lake" (Lake Michigan, that is)—"It's usually ten degrees cooler there"—and so on. From what Joe told her and his appearance, she guessed he was in his mid—to late-twenties. He was about 5' 10" (an inch or so taller than she was). He had sandy colored hair—neat and conservatively styled. He had a clean-cut appearance—no tattoos or piercings. And, his clothes were neat and pressed—unusual for their generation.

He volunteered quite a bit of information about himself; Samantha volunteered none. She remained evasive to anything he asked about her, and he did not persist. He said his mother had died when he was young. He had taken care of his father, who had suffered from cancer for a year and a half and died about three years ago. He was left with some inheritance that had allowed him to finish college (pre-med). He wanted to go to med school, but an opportunity to go on a humanitarian mission to Africa had presented itself through a doctor friend. He'd felt compelled to go and thought it would be a good experience. He had just returned a few weeks ago.

The time passed quickly, as Joe related some of his African experiences.

Samantha said almost nothing except for polite, intermittent responses: "Oh, really!" "Wow!" "Isn't that interesting?"

She thought she might like Joe—charming personality, engaging smile, seemed sincere and noble.

Joe looked at his watch and remarked, "Wow! It's late. Gotta go! Nice getting to know you." He made some other comment and said goodbye.

She said she enjoyed their conversation too. *Getting to know me?* she thought. *Oh, well.* Actually, she had enjoyed hearing about his adventures. She couldn't remember the last time she'd had a conversation with anyone in the past four years that lasted that long. In fact, she noticed her face hurt a little from the polite, fixed grin she had maintained during the one-sided conversation. She wasn't used to smiling that much.

I must have looked like a simpering idiot, she thought.

She was, however, glad he didn't know anything more about her than her first name. As reserved as she was, she certainly wasn't apt to pour out her personal story to a total stranger. It was now 2:45; it was apparent Betty Ann wasn't coming. Samantha felt it was just as well and thought no more about it.

♱·CHAPTER 3

She decided to stay among the books for awhile; some of her best friends were in their pages. Also, in a strange way, it felt good to have people around her, even if she didn't know them. It reminded her that she was still among the living. What she knew about life, for the most part, was from her sheltered family life and from books; none of that had prepared her for the past four years or what was ahead of her. She had slipped in and out, and back and forth, through the stages of grieving. Isolation had been the first and most persistent obstacle to overcome. A daze had been its companion, perhaps numbness. Intermittent bewilderment haunted her. *Unreal, bad dream—wake up! wake up! It's impossible! Can this be true?*

She passed a display of the new translation of *War and Peace.* Her college courses had been demanding; time was at a premium, and there were other intrusions. For the most part, she'd read what was required. Last summer, being alone and not having any money or the inclination to go on a vacation, she'd decided to read all of Tolstoy's novels. She hadn't realized that even though she was a fast reader, this was way beyond her abilities. However, she had made it through *Anna Karenina* and *War and Peace*. Leafing through the new translation, she recalled the story and searched for some lessons to apply to her current situation and the life challenges ahead.

Women in Russia at that time were as limited as women in England, she thought. *Interesting. But what about their personal relationships? Did they draw a parallel?* That reminded her of the young, naïve Natasha, who paid a heavy price for her impatience and was taken in by a too handsome, smooth-talking man with a roving eye. Natasha didn't value a man of noble character and good reputation; she was taken in by the superficial excitement of the attractive con-man's deception.

Samantha, beware of a charming, handsome, smooth-talking man with a roving eye for women! she warned herself. *Don't miss the signs of a good character—someone who may have a few flaws but has a teachable nature and a basic kindness.*

Reading the introduction, she was interested in how much influence Tolstoy had on the Russian people in his era. *What a mind boggling job of writing all those pages by hand—not even an ever-sharp pencil! No wonder there were a few inconsistencies as to time and place. Well, his wife helped copy the final pages. Imagine what he could have done with a computer and Microsoft Word,* Samantha mused.

She picked up a nearby copy of *Anna Karenina* and reviewed the chapters. She especially liked *Anna Karenina*—the book, not the woman. She thought Anna was a pitiful person. Somehow, Samantha could not feel sympathy for her while reading the book. Bored at home as wife of a prominent but dull man and the mother of a delightful boy, Anna took up with a dashing young military officer. *Another charming, handsome, smooth-talking man with a roving eye for women,* Samantha reiterated to herself. *And this one, willing to take up with a married woman (actually, I think Natasha's nemesis was married, too)—a faulty character, for sure. Beware, Samantha!*

She couldn't imagine herself like Anna. Samantha had her insecurities, but losing herself and becoming that emotionally dependent on a man was inconceivable. Wanting to spend every minute with him, Anna suffocated Vronsky. Samantha always liked her own space, pursuits, and alone time. As she saw it, the plight of the upper-class women in those days was boredom. Outside of having children, they didn't do much. Samantha thought it would have been a great story even without Anna and Vronsky. She especially liked Kitty and Levin (as they were called in her translation; those Russian names were a bit much—most characters had four long names). Levin was a semiautobiographical Tolstoy (part autobiographical and part wishful thinking).

If they had just shortened the names to initials, the book would have been at least 200 pages shorter, she mused with a slight grin.

There was a lot of info on Tolstoy's thinking about workers and their masters in the narrative about Levin and Kitty running their estate. At that time, upper-class children were educated by tutors. Peasant children were educated by their parents, the church, or whatever experiences they could glean from their surroundings. Unlike other landowners, Tolstoy (like Levin in the story) had a school on his farm for the worker's children. However, locked in generations of a class system, most lacked a sense of purpose, and were burdened with myths and misconceptions. Tolstoy found educating these children frustrating. Nevertheless, putting the minds of the children in the hands of the central government, as was being deliberated at the time, was troubling to him.

Samantha and her siblings' education had been rather unconventional. Since her father was in the golf business and they lived in a resort town that just about folded up in the winter, the family had always set off for Florida before there were snow flurries in the air. Her parents' friends, also in the golf business, had kept the same routine. There were various places where the pros gathered, playing golf and spending endless hours talking about and searching for the perfect swing. Her father was a class-A PGA professional and an excellent teacher. His pupils would come from miles for lessons. Their southern location was determined by the arrangement their father could make with a local pro for permission to teach and play golf at his course.

One year, their father arranged with the owner of a driving range and par-3 golf course for unlimited play and use of the driving range for his family in exchange for golf lessons for the owner and his wife. Most evenings found the family hitting balls or playing nine holes on the lighted course. Her brother, Michael, became a scratch player, which came in handy later as he built his business. Her sister, Sarah, also became an excellent player, winning tournaments from a young age. She had attended a small college which had no golf program for women, but Sarah had entered the National Intercollegiate Golf Tournament on her own in her second year and won. Samantha could play a respectable game, but she lacked the drive, concentration, and perseverance for it. Sarah had it—she was competitive!

Samantha had followed her in several state tournaments and watched her deliberation and determination. Sarah could be several holes down (these tournaments were match play) and come back to win. One time, Sarah was one down going into the 18th hole. In the same number of shots, her opponent was on the green, and Sarah was in an enormous sand trap below the green, where she could not even see the flag. Analyzing her predicament, she walked down the fairway toward the green, paused, and then stepped into the trap. Fortunately, the ball wasn't buried; it had rolled in and was resting on top of the sand. She studied the situation with her cool, determined look, and then set her stance at the ball. She wiggled her feet into a firm position, drew the wedge back clearing the fine white sand, and blasted away, the sand flying. The ball arched over the huge, grassy lip of the trap, landed six feet from the hole, slowly rolled toward it, and with that familiar hollow "plop" dropped into the metal cup. Her stunned opponent, who'd been daydreaming about how the trophy would look on her fireplace mantel, two-putted.

When the restrained kudos ceased (they had been taught that golf is a polite game and good sportsmanship is paramount), the players headed down the 19th hole of play. They were followed by family and friends of the players, and a couple dozen spectators collected as they made the clubhouse turn. News spread fast, and more people, on foot and in golf carts, joined the parade down the fairway. Sarah had won the hole and the tournament. Samantha could hardly restrain herself. She wanted to let it all out, jump up and down, and shout for joy. Nevertheless, she did not.

Her family had politely shaken hands with the loser at the appropriate time, offering their condolences, saying all the right things about how well she'd played and what a good match it had been. Win or lose, Sarah had always been gracious; she'd never displayed anger or anything inappropriate. Their parents had instilled this in them from early on.

After the tournament, for the first 15 or 20 minutes in the car on the way home, there had been laughing and chattering. Then, Sarah and her dad, as was their custom, critiqued the match shot by shot. Samantha found this a total bore, but Sarah and her dad were in serious conversation having a grand time. The rest of the family politely and quietly let them have their moment—coach and star pupil.

*   *   *

The three children would start school in Michigan, and the first of November they would head for Florida. Some of the time, they had enrolled in school there; however, for various reasons, it had never been the same school twice. It had been hard for Samantha to make friends, knowing she would leave and most likely never see these classmates after March, when they would return for the opening of the golf course in Michigan and her original school. This had made her withdrawn and dependent on her family. A few winters, their parents had tutored them from their Michigan school books, and couple of winters they'd gone to a private school where they also were tutored. She had liked this better; however, she'd always finished the books by March. Then she'd had to sit though all the same stuff in March, April, and May in the Michigan school.

She and her siblings had been close. Michael was older and protective of his little sisters. He was always interested in computers and had patiently shown Samantha how to navigate the programs. She'd been interested partly because of her analytical mind and partly because she'd reveled in the attention her big brother was giving her. She'd been attentive to everything he showed her so as not to disappoint him, and he'd been remarkably patient.

*   *   *

It was just after five when she left the bookstore. Knowing the traffic would be heavy and having not had a decent meal in days, she decided to find a nice restaurant and order filet mignon (which she could afford now), a baked potato, broccoli, and a Caesar salad. Perhaps she would indulge in an appetizer and, later, a decadent dessert and a pot of tea. Looking in a large front window, she saw crisp white linen tablecloths, white linen napkins fanned out neatly in oversized wine glasses, and place settings with expensive-looking tableware. It was Monday and early for most diners. Only one table was occupied by two middle-aged men and a woman casually dressed, so she felt safe to venture in. She followed closely behind the hostess, who led her to a quiet table for two next to the wall away from the kitchen, the cash register, the dish bussing station, and the threesome.

How lovely! she thought.

Within minutes, a young, perky waitress greeted her cordially with the usual, "My name is Christy, and I'll be serving you this evening." They exchanged pleasantries. Christy—pleasant enough for both of them—then took her order.

While she waited, Samantha picked up where she left off in Suze's book and started reading through the chapters. Suzy seemed honest, sincere, and knowledgeable. Samantha wished she were making her fearful appointment with her instead of "dear George." She thought Suze would be sympathetic to her dilemma and understand her sense of responsibility for what had been entrusted to her.

George Reynolds had been her parents' broker and financial advisor. She had overheard them talking about watching out for his suggestions to switch mutual funds or stocks too frequently for little apparent reason. This seemed to benefit him, as he received the fees to sell the old and buy the new. Still, they felt he was useful. She really didn't know what that was all about. She had dealt with George several times over the past four years. It *was* urgent that she set up a cash flow, pay her debts, and organize the inheritance. She needed help getting this consolidated and tying up the loose ends. George Reynolds was competent, but she didn't want to be bullied into doing something risky.

She stayed at the restaurant nearly two hours reading, enjoying her meal, and lingering over a pot of Darjeeling and the anticipated decadent dessert. Since the restaurant never became very busy, Christy was able to chat with her intermittently. Samantha learned the girl was working her way through college and admired her resolve. She wanted to leave a generous tip, but not so much as to draw unwanted attention. The food was excellent, and she thought she might want to return sometime. After analyzing this a bit, she settled on an amount she thought generous but safe. Paying for the meal with a credit card, she left the cash for the tip on the table.

❧·CHAPTER 4

The day dawned with sunshine somewhere, but as Samantha woke, the gloomy, cloudy morning hardly produced enough light to differentiate day from night. After procrastinating for several days and eating every item of food in the house, she had nothing remotely resembling the makings of even a meager meal. She really needed to get serious about eating better; she was losing weight. Hunger motivated her to start off for the Whole Foods Market. Now that she could afford them, she would buy a few of her favorite foods. *Olives—the green olives—the super colossal grade green olives, each stuffed with an almond or a giant garlic clove. They are most excellent!*

The store was several miles from her house. As she passed an affluent suburban district of impressive-looking office buildings, she remembered that "dear George's" brokerage firm had a whole floor of offices there; his was a spacious corner one in a suite of offices occupied by several associates and assistants under his title.

On a whim and in spite of being hungry, she decided to stop; perhaps she could see him or make the dreaded appointment. She pulled into the parking lot and rummaged around for the business card she'd thrown into the armrest compartment. She studied the card, more to focus her thoughts than for information as, no doubt, it was irrelevant to her objective.

George Y. Reynolds, CIMA, CFP, CFM
Senior Vice President—Investments
Wealth Management Advisor

Then, there was the address and *Global Private Client.*

Studying the card, she wondered about his middle initial. *Y? Must be some family name—can't think of any regular first name that starts with Y. How many vice presidents are there? And who is the president? Global Private Client—what's that? Do I qualify as a "Global Private Client?" Sounds impressive, I suppose. Makes me nervous!* Inside the folded card were the names of seven underlings with various titles. She had dealt with them all briefly and intermittently over the past years. For the most part, George had handled the details. After all, she, perhaps, would turn out to be one of his biggest clients; she didn't know how much money was a lot of money compared to other clients. Did he have her interest at heart or his? She was sorry to have developed a suspicious attitude, but she had been learning cold, cruel lessons. She wanted to like George; he had always been kind to her. She wanted to trust him, but . . . .

After reading Suze's book, she felt armed with some knowledge. She rehearsed, *I can say, "I'll have to think about what you suggest." I won't be pressured into making a hasty decision. I'll at least give myself time for deliberation and consultation with Suze—her book, that is. I can do that! I will do that! I must, at least, do that!*

She walked into the building's spacious entrance. She was looking about the same as usual—hadn't gotten her hair cut yet, but it was clean and shiny and as neat as she could manage. Her clothes were simple—plain, in muted solid colors, but as always clean and pressed.

She walked over to the elevators, entered one, and pushed button number 6, labeled with the name of the large world-famous brokerage company. She rode to the top floor. There was a new receptionist, Ms. Allison Jackson, according to the shiny brass name plate on the counter above her chair. Looking a little surprised, perhaps at seeing someone so young and dressed as she was, she asked, "May I help you?"

"I'm Samantha Schwerin. I would like to see George Reynolds," she blurted out in a matter-of-fact monotone.

Ms. Jackson asked in rapid succession, not giving her a chance to answer between questions, "How do you spell your last name? I don't see your name on the list. Do you have an appointment? Would you . . . ?"

"No, but would you tell him I'm here?" Samantha finally interrupted.

"Well, I can see if his assistant is available to make an appointment for you."

"Please! Just call Mr. Reynolds. Tell him I'm here." Samantha wasn't one to be pushy or aggressive, but she was becoming annoyed, although she had no right to be, since she had barged in unexpectedly. Also, hunger made her edgy. Nevertheless, she had made up her mind to do this; she was determined to see it through.

"Are you a relative?"

"No."

Just then, Jan Harris, one of George's assistants, walked briskly past the reception desk like a woman on a mission. Recognizing Samantha, she stopped abruptly, greeted her cordially, and invited her to come back to her office. Ms. Jackson looked stunned.

Jan ushered her into a conference room and offered her, "Coffee, tea, soft drink, ice water?"

Being nervous, her mouth was dry and feeling her face flush, she settled for ice water. There were 12 large, high-backed, black leather executive chairs strategically positioned around a highly polished table; Samantha sat in one of them.

The beverage was delivered shortly, and Jan assured her, "I'll check with George and be right back."

Samantha swiveled a bit and tipped back and forth a few times to get the feel of the chair, then settled down to some gentle rocking to sooth her nervousness. The table was so shiny and spotless, she was afraid to touch it for fear of leaving a fingerprint. She drank some of the ice water but kept holding the glass. She didn't want to spoil the gloss on the table with that, either. The thought of entering the world of finance overwhelmed her—people buying and selling shares of everything all over the world with a few chosen letters on a computer. Amazing!

She had watched the business channels on TV a few times, trying to get a sense of what was going on in the financial world. Now, she was thinking, *All that jargon—stagflation, recession, inflation, the CPI, the S&P, the Dow, commodities, stocks, bonds, mutual funds, ETFs. Steve and Rick arguing about the bond market, and Neil, Liz, Charlie, Joe, Carl, Becky, Maria, and endless guests hashing over the economy—Keynesian economics, Fredrick Heyak's* The Road to Serfdom, *Milton Friedman's* Capitalism and Freedom *and* Free to Choose, *Yergin and Stanislaw's* Commanding Heights: The Battle for the World Economy .... Samantha had seen these books in her parents' library. As worthy as they were, she wasn't ready to take on The Battle for the World Economy. This was too much; it was all spinning in her head. Suze's book was what she needed right now—practical information.

She was a little lightheaded from not eating and reproached herself for taking this on under these circumstances. How was she going to keep her mind focused when her stomach kept grumbling? Just then, Jan came back and led her into George's office. By then, she was looking pale and thin.

"How are you? Are you taking care of yourself?" George asked with concern.

"Oh, just fine, thank you." She staggered over to the chair and sat with a plop. Her stomach grumbled loudly.

"Have you had lunch? When did you eat last?"

"I'm not sure."

George picked up the phone and said, "Cancel my appointments for the rest of the day." He turned back to Samantha. "I'm taking you out to lunch."

Too weak and hungry to protest, she responded faintly and pathetically, "Okay, thank you."

*   *   *

They drove along a shady, tree-lined street to the edge of town, passed though the impressive entrance to a private country club, and drove under the spacious portico. The valet opened her door, and she stepped out onto the red carpet. An attendant opened the heavy, ornate door, and they went in. After walking down a long, green plaid carpeted hallway with wood-paneled walls adorned with pictures of the past presidents of the club and polished brass plaques engraved with the names of the club champions, they arrived at a casual dining area. The clubhouse was on a hill overlooking the course. Through the floor-to-ceiling windows, one could view the green expanse of the tree-lined fairways, the manicured tees with precisely positioned pots with appropriately colored flowers for markers, and the terrain dotted with water hazards and the white silica sand of the traps. Today, the flags on the hole-indicator poles were snapping in the brisk wind.

It was still early, and most of the golfers who would occupy this area were still on the course. She was used to the hum and buzz of the golfers' jargon. Now the chatter of past days took over her thoughts as the players talked about "if only . . . I would have . . ." scenarios, or about how the greens were fast or slow or something about the pin placement and the putts, always the putts. "I missed that putt on number nine—can't believe it!" or "I've got to do something about that slice. I think it's the grip."

She had been to private clubs many times. The atmosphere was more subdued than at her parents' public golf course. The clientele was different, but basically golfers were the same. At the public course, people came from all walks of life, and being on vacation, they seemed happier and more relaxed.

Fortunately, she had not worn jeans that day; jeans and collarless shirts were definitely not appropriate attire at a country club of this class. By chance, she had worn a golf shirt and khaki-colored slacks. Actually, this was what she'd worn while working at her parents' golf course. She'd put this on, as she was behind in her laundry.

As they were escorted to their table, the club house manager approached them. "How are you, Mr. Reynolds? Glad to see you."

"Hi, Dave—things are looking good," George responded.

George introduced Samantha as one of his clients. Dave addressed her as "Ms. Schwerin." She was amused, as she wasn't used to being addressed as "Ms. Schwerin." As they progressed to the table, George greeted and exchanged pleasantries with people along the way.

When they reached a table, the hostess pulled a chair out for her. Seated, she and the hostess made a cooperative effort to scoot her to the table. The waiter took their drink order. She ordered an Arnold Palmer (half iced tea and half lemonade), and so did George. The beverages came immediately, and she sipped hers while she studied the menu. No prices were listed on her menu. With three children and a risky business, her parents had been careful about prices, and so had she, until a few days ago. But, she'd had this experience before of no prices on the menu. All of her family had been the guest of a member at a private club a time or two, and her father had explained that the guests of a member received menus without prices for obvious reasons, and she *could* figure that one out. Samantha quickly finished her drink, and another was on its way. The tea and sugar revived her, and she felt more alert. However, all the ice water and tea made it necessary for her to find the ladies' room.

"Excuse me, I'll be right back," she said. George stood and pulled out her chair. He anticipated her next question and gave her directions.

*   *   *

After washing her hands, she dried them with an individual snow white cloth towel from the neat stack on the shelf above the sink. Alone in the room, she lingered at one of the little dressing tables with all the niceties available. She combed her hair, still too long and shaggy, and with irregular curls from the summer humidity, and spritzed on a squirt or two of hairspray, which ordinarily she never used. Checking out the lotions, she selected one for her hands. At that time, someone came in and gave her a polite greeting. Samantha responded pleasantly, then returned to the table. George stood and helped her with her chair. She thanked him and started on her second Arnold Palmer. George asked her what she would like; she told him, and he gave their order to the waiter.

That old custom of the gentleman giving the order to the waiter is still in effect here, or maybe it's just George, she thought. *That doesn't bother me. It's nice for a gentleman to be a gentleman. It makes me think he's considerate—maybe he is. I must be observant—don't make any social blunders. I don't want to stomp on his gentlemanliness. It's sort of nice—a little comforting, to have someone looking out for me for a change—feels like a fatherly thing, I guess.*

Next followed another one-sided conversation, with Samantha uttering her usual profound rhetoric: "Yes," "No," "Oh, really," "That's interesting."

He asked about college, how she was doing, her plans now that she had graduated and the like.

Her brief answers continued: "Good," "Fine," "I don't know," "I'm not sure."

"If you need anything, let me know," he assured her. Then he moved on to the matter at hand: her investments and cash flow. "I've worked out a diversified investment plan for you. We can

27

go over it when we get back to the office. Currently, you have the money in several bonds and Money Market accounts, earning about 3% interest."

Samantha quickly calculated in her head: *$77, 000,000 times .03 equals $2,310,000, divided by 365—hummm—wow—that's over $6,000 per day. Well, that's not bad,* she thought. *Why do we have to get risky? Even after taxes, this would be a lot, and if I buy some tax-free municipal bonds—remember Suze's book!*

"There is the issue of taxes, and quarterly payments to the IRS and the state. You need to start this immediately," he said. "We can handle all of that for you. We can talk about that when we get back to the office, where you can sign the necessary forms."

Signing forms started to sound a tad scary. "Okay, I can take a look at it," she said.

They stayed awhile longer; she finished dessert and a third AP. By the time they returned to the office, it was two in the afternoon. She thanked him sincerely for his thoughtfulness and assured him she felt much better.

*   *   *

Reading the fine print, she noticed fees involved mainly for sending in the tax payments and maintaining a portfolio of stocks and bond. All would be on a percentage basis. She wondered if she could take on the IRS thing. It seemed like a small amount of work for a lot of money. She didn't need to scrimp, but she didn't need to waste money, either. After all, she had the time and ability to do it. She could set up a spreadsheet using Excel and keep track of the checking on Quicken, which she already did. She definitely needed an accountant to help her with the taxes. That was the big issue, and that's where she directed the conversation. He halfheartedly went through her requirements in that area. Okay, she would take care of that for the time being.

So, there it was: a tax-friendly portfolio with dividends and interest—some flowing into her checking account, some being reinvested. She also signed up for a credit card—monthly outflows listed on the same statement. She had a credit card from a bank and decided to keep it as a backup. She also needed to continue giving at least 10% to a church and charity, as her parents had. She knew they would want that. She had gotten out of the habit of going to church; the church the family belonged to was in Florida, and they hadn't decided on a church in their new community. Besides, she couldn't face people, even well-meaning people. Well, now she was in business—but what business? An accountant would be next. George recommended one (this made sense, as they would have to coordinate the assets). The secretary set up an appointment with Fran Marshall, the accountant, for Monday. *That was fast enough. Well, it is after April 15th—maybe this is her off season*, thought Samantha.

*   *   *

Monday morning at 10:30, Samantha gave her name to the receptionist and asked for Fran Marshall, who appeared immediately to greet her. After the preliminary introductions and niceties, Fran led her back to her comfortable office and offered her the usual. Again, Samantha settled for the solution that seemed to calm her nervousness: ice water. Fran did not appear to be much older than she was; perhaps she looked young for her age. The pictures of grade-school children on her desk and a narrow gold band adorning the appropriate finger made Samantha think that perhaps Fran was in her thirties. A gold band set with a spectacular solitary diamond next to the plain gold one suggested there was a prosperous husband about.

Samantha felt comfortable with Fran and thought they would get along well. She was organized and efficient; that impressed Samantha. George had sent Fran the information needed, and she had calculated the quarterly payments Samantha would need to remit. She had the instructions and the forms with the dates. That seemed easy enough, but what large payments! Nevertheless, Samantha had ample funds flowing into her checking account and with the tax-free assets—no problem. However, with such large payments, Fran told her it would be unwise to send checks through the mail and suggested some alternatives for automatic deductions.

"Wow," remarked Samantha. "I'm not used to so much money."

"I'm here to help," Fran responded. "I can set that up for you."

"Well, maybe you should," she agreed. "George offered to do it through the broker account, but the fees were awful—not that I have to pinch pennies, but it's the principle of the thing,"

"I know," she said. "I can find you something more reasonable."

Their business concluded for the present, and with Fran promising to keep her informed, Samantha left the office.

That done, she needed to give some serious thought to what she might do with the rest of the money. For now, since all was settled and she had significant cash flow, she decided a change of scene would be of benefit—someplace with regular meals. There were many appealing places in Michigan. Mackinac Island had always intrigued her. She Googled "Mackinac Island" and got all the information she wanted. The Grand Hotel looked lovely, and meals were part of the deal, but the prices . . . . Wow! Calculating that four nights would be considerably lower than just one day of her income and overcoming her initial misgivings, she chose four nights and five days in July—well after the 4th. That suited her—arrive Monday, leave Friday morning. It seemed best to avoid the weekend crowds. July in her part of the state was often hot and humid. The temperature chart for Mackinac Island stated that the highest temperatures of the summer were in July—average high 75 degrees, average low 60 degrees. *I can handle that*, she thought. *Wonderful!*

She called. There was room. She decided to spend the extra for the lakeside view. The reservation was made! The ferry schedule, baggage tags, and confirmation would be coming in the mail.

❧·CHAPTER 5

"There is a tide in the affairs of men,
Which, taken at the flood, leads on to fortune:
Omitted, all the voyage of their life
Is bound in shallows and in miseries.
On such a full sea are we now afloat;
And we must take the current when it serves,
Or lose our ventures."

Shakespeare: *Julius Caesar*

She spent much of Tuesday morning reading books from her parents' library. This was their legacy to her—the books that they enjoyed and that reflected their way of thinking. As she read, she felt she was sharing interests and insights with her father or mother.

After reading most of the morning, she needed some exercise and diversion. It was a cloudy day but a pleasant temperature, so she headed out the door for a walk. She started thinking about her family. Their family had had disagreements, like most families; she could be a pesky little sister at times, pushing the patience of her senior siblings beyond their limits. Samantha was not going to probe around in her memories to irritate any minor unpleasant events. These became dimmer and dimmer and faded, leaving a wealth of warm wonderful episodes and images of these precious people.

Due to their peripatetic life style, most of the time, the siblings had only each other for playmates, particularly during the months in Florida. However, Michael was older and had Jenny, his forever-girlfriend, but Jenny was in Michigan. Jenny's mother had died when she was fourteen. She was an only child, but her father, a successful businessman, didn't have much time or interest in a teenage daughter. She had no other family—both parents were only children, so she had no aunts, uncles or cousins, a circumstance she'd shared with Michael. Jenny's grandparents lived in California and Florida, so she rarely saw them. It seemed she was always part of their family, especially after her mother had died.

Michael and Jenny had gone to the same high school in Michigan. Jenny had lived in a larger non-resort town about ten miles away, and Michael had traveled there when he was in Michigan. They'd commuted to the same college, majored in the same subjects (business administration and computer science), and graduated early (at 20) with honors. They had married immediately after graduation and had set out to build the business Michael had already started in his room at home and to take a mega market share in their niche of the computer world and cyberspace. They'd seized their opportunity and made a fortune.

During the high-school years, the months when Michael was in Florida had been difficult for them. Besides the phone calls, occasionally a tear-stained, scented letter or card would arrive for Michael. During Christmas vacation, Jenny and her dad would come to Florida and rent a condominium near wherever they were. The week had been a reprieve from their pining.

Jenny's dad liked golf, and the dads played frequently. They all took advantage of the pool and game room at the condominium complex. Jenny's dad took time out to visit his frail parents in a nursing home; Michael and Jenny went along.

*   *   *

Samantha remembered her parents as thoughtful, encouraging, and patient. They'd never put her down or made her feel inadequate, even though she didn't have any particular talent. She couldn't play golf as well as Sarah and Michael. She didn't have musical talents like Michael. For one week every summer when he was in his teens, he'd gone to Interlochen, a prestigious music camp in the northwestern part of the Lower Peninsula. He would arrange to go the same week as Jenny. Jenny played the piano, and he'd learned so he could play duets with her—anything to be with Jenny—but the trumpet was his thing.

Jenny's dad would take them to camp. Then on the final day of their session, Samantha's family would leave the golf course in the hands of the hired couple and drive to the camp to pick them up. This was the only day during the summer the whole family left the golf course, and Samantha enjoyed the trip immensely. That final Sunday afternoon, the students always gave a concert. It was an amazing performance—exceptional teenage musicians from all over the United States and other countries coming together to make such beautiful music. It was wonderful, sitting outside with a glimpse of the lake behind the stage of the Interlochen Bowl. She never remembered rain there; it was always a mild, sunny, pine-scented day. It was absolutely thrilling—not only because the students were so talented and the music awesome, but because Michael was playing. Her eyes were focused on him.

They routinely arrived at the camp early and meandered along the paths through the pines, past the cabins and the tiny practice buildings. Music came from everywhere. A melody from a flute would be faint then louder as they strolled past a practice hut, then briefly mix in some discordant sounds as it mingled with the tune of a clarinet in another little building. The flute faded as the music of the clarinet became stronger. Walking along, the clarinet tune became a trumpet tune, the trumpet tune a piano sonata, the piano sonata an oboe solo.

One year, when Samantha was about seven, Michael had begun the piece with a five-measure fanfare solo. She was as proud as she could be as he executed it perfectly. Being less inhibited and more impulsive at that tender age, she whispered to the stranger next to her, "That was my brother."

The stranger had smiled politely. Her mother had immediately put her finger across her lips and given her "that look." Her parents did not tolerate anything but total silence and respect for anyone's performance—musical, speech, during a golf shot.

Her mother loved to hear the organ, the hand bells, the choirs, and all the music at church. Michael was occasionally asked to play with the organ, timpani, and other musical instruments on festival days like Easter. Her mother had a quiet temperament and not much upset her, but she often vented after church when a couple of old ladies would be chattering away while the hand bells rang, the choir sang, or any other part of the church service took place. "If the ladies are hard of hearing, they should not be rude," she would complain. This was strictly forbidden in her family. It had to be an emergency of major proportions for them to say a word. Even a cough might get "that look" from their mother. Another thing her mother had insisted on at church was that her daughters dress modestly—covered from the neck to below the knee, and no tight clothing. "I don't want my pretty, shapely daughters leading a young man's, or any man's, eye astray," she would insist. Sarah and Samantha were okay with that; they hadn't built up a significant peer group. They usually went along with "Mother's rules" without resistance. If they didn't, there would be Dad to contend with; he always backed her up. If there were a question about something, her mother would say, "Your father and I will take this under consideration and let you know."

Their circumstances were different from most families; their parents' work had not required them to daily disappear for nine or ten hours; they were available all during the day. This had given them the unique experience of having their golf swings under the continuous scrutiny of their father—any swings out of line would be corrected immediately.

They all worked together in the same business. From early on, Michael, Sarah, and Samantha had work schedules and were paid minimum wage. Nobody showed up from Social Services, claiming abuse of child labor laws, and they certainly did not feel misused. Their mother always excused the girls from work and took on their duties if a social opportunity arose. Michael's schedule was not as flexible, especially when he was older. He had more responsibility with golf course maintenance. At one time or another, all the children dusted, swept, washed tables, washed dishes, waited on customers, took green fees, sold golf balls and tees, made sandwiches, made coffee, prepared ice cream sundaes, loaded the pop cooler, and made the ever-popular Black Cow (root beer and vanilla ice cream). On the golf course, Michael operated the machines and tractors when he was older, and Sarah and Samantha weeded the flower beds and trimmed the bushes. Only her father sold the golf clubs, to ensure a proper fit for the golfer, and threw in a few tips for the perfect swing. There were also a few college students working; the ones on golf teams usually applied, since unlimited golf on off-hours was part of the deal.

*   *   *

As she returned from her daily walk at about one o'clock, she noticed a car parked half a block down the street with a woman in it. It had been there earlier when she'd taken out the trash and when she'd left for her walk. She wondered if the woman had been sitting there all that time. She reminded her of Betty Ann, but as Samantha drew closer, the woman turned to get something out of the backseat. Samantha went into the house and thought no more about it.

Since she was out of food and hungry, she decided to go to the Whole Foods Market again. In particular, she was out of olives. Not fond of eating out alone, she resolved to get some nourishing food and prepare a meal. Most recipes were for six or eight, so she picked a couple she thought she could freeze in individual microwave containers; she would have meals for weeks! After writing down the ingredients, she headed out the kitchen door.

As she left the house, she noticed the same car was still parked in the same place. It pulled away from the curb as she backed her car out of the garage.

*   *   *

At the store, she chose a shopping cart and headed straight for the olive bar to make her selection. She scooped up an ample portion of the almond-stuffed olives, placed them into the container, and safely tucked them into her shopping cart. Having her primary objective accomplished, she began wandering up and down the aisles, stopping now and then to read the label of some intriguing package and look for the items on her list. She picked up a can of minestrone soup. *No trans fats—that's good. Only one gram of fat—that's good,* she assessed. It joined the olives in her shopping cart.

As she was reading a cereal box label, someone said, "Samantha? Is that you?" She turned; it was Joe Morton, from the coffee shop. "Nice to see you again. How are you?"

"Very well," she responded, extremely surprised to see him.

They slowly wandered up and down the aisles, chatting and picking up items as they went. Joe said he was in a hurry, but perhaps they could arrange to meet again.

"The same bookstore café?" he quickly suggested. "Three o'clock Friday?"

"Okay," she agreed hesitantly, at a loss for any other response.

*   *   *

When she arrived home, her mind took her to the past again as she stared at the books. Her interests gravitated toward American history. She picked out *John Adams* by David McCullough and read until the sun was coming up and a bird was chirping near the window. She realized she had been reading all night. She sat quietly, gathering her thoughts as more birds joined in to form a lively glee club. *Remarkable woman, Abigail!* she ponder. *She was definitely a smart, gutsy, early-American woman. What's more, her husband knew it and respected her abilities. She was devoted to her short, portly, brilliant soulmate. She ran the family farm, raised their children, and managed everything while her husband was away for long periods of time. They wrote such interesting and descriptive letters to each other!*

Do John and Abigail have lessons to teach me? Samantha thought. Abigail had liked to quote Shakespeare; Samantha was particularly impressed with the lines from *Julius Caesar* about seizing the moment or losing it that she had quoted to John. *When John's task of forming the new nation caused him to become weary and discouraged, her letters sustained him and encouraged him to preserve and seize the moment. Would I take the tide that leads to opportunity? Would I recognize it? I don't want to be "bound in shallows and in miseries." Who is there to encourage me? Who is there to trust and help me sort things out?*

Due to her analytical nature, she had a history of getting bogged down with the paralysis of analysis. When she thought she wanted to buy something, she thought about it for a long time, fretted over the model, the color, how much it cost, how long it would take to save the money, how hard she would have to work for that amount. Would she really like it in a month, two months, next year? She went on and on—'round and 'round. Cornered family members listened patiently while she went though her tedious scenarios. They would make suggestions, which added to the information spinning in her mind. In the end, she'd relied on her mother to help her sort it out. Nevertheless, more often than not, she couldn't decide and did nothing.

✤·CHAPTER 6

"To be, or not to be: that is the question:
Whether 'tis nobler in the mind to suffer
The slings and arrows of outrageous fortune,
Or to take arms against a sea of troubles,
And by opposing end them? To die; To sleep;
No more; and by a sleep to say we end
The heart-ache and the thousand natural shocks
That flesh is heir to . . ."

William Shakespeare: *Hamlet*

Wednesday passed uneventfully—more sorting, shredding, and rearranging. Exhausted from no sleep the night before and the mental strain of sorting the family documents and possessions, she fell into bed early. After a good night's sleep and a substantial breakfast from the foods she'd purchased Tuesday, she was drawn to the library again. Her eyes fixed on the extensive DVD collection of Shakespeare plays on the shelf and three volumes that made up *The Complete Works of Shakespeare: The Histories, The Tragedies, The Comedies.*

Her mother had liked Shakespeare. *What did Mom like about Shakespeare?* She tried to remember. She'd warned Samantha *not* to read or see *King Lear*, as it was entirely too gruesome—mentally and physically—not worth the psychological torture for the lessons it might impart. "There are hideous images I would not want invading a young mind," she remembered her saying. *She said something about King Lear's regrets in the end, one being he wished he had treated his subjects better.* But, *Hamlet* interested them both. *There certainly is a great deal of violence. By the end of the play, at least half the characters are wiped out. However, poison in the ear and poison in the wine seem neater, and sword-fighting and stabbing are tolerable,* she thought. Samantha wondered what was so awful about *King Lear.* In spite of her curiosity, she still wanted to take her mother's advice; her emotions were fragile, and she trusted her mother. She didn't need anything gruesome disturbing her mind at this point.

Samantha recalled one evening when she and her mother had watched *Hamlet*—the Laurence Olivier version. She saw the video on the bookshelf and picked it up—155 minutes, B&W, 1948. And then, on another occasion, late into the night, she and her mother had watched the Kenneth Branagh version—the every-line-recited version (Kenneth as Hamlet had 1500 lines alone). She took that video off the bookshelf—color/242 minutes, 1996. *Hummm,* she contemplated, *Four hours! I knew that was long!* They had taken many hours and several breaks, discussing parts as they went along. Her sister had started watching with them, but early on she'd fallen asleep and eventually gone to bed. She remembered, it had been well past midnight on a Friday, and *she* hadn't gotten sleepy. She'd enjoyed watching it with her mother; it had felt special—just the two of them. Enjoying snacks now and then, especially ice cream, had made the long-winded parts less tedious. She was glad now that she and her mother had shared that time together—their time, their thoughts.

Somewhere along the line, much later, they'd watched the Mel Gibson version. That "to be or not to be" speech set in a crypt and was her favorite: "sling and arrows of outrageous fortune . . . take up arms and by opposing . . . ." That sounded apropos; she was without a doubt feeling "the slings and arrows of outrageous fortune." How was she going to take up arms, oppose them, and end them? That was her question!

She seemed to catch her mother's fascination for *Hamlet.* Samantha liked the Laurence Olivier version best—not so long and tedious, and the acting was good.

Overwhelmed by the commission of his ghostly father and his dysfunctional family, Hamlet was contemplating suicide. But, he hesitated.

> *"For in that sleep of death what dreams may come*
> *When we have shuffled off this mortal coil,*
> *Must give us pause. There's the respect*
> *That makes calamity of so long life;*
> *For who would bear the whips and scorns of time,*
> *The oppressor's wrong . . .*
>
> *To grunt and sweat under a weary life,*
> *But that the dread of something after death,*
> *The undiscover'd country from whose bourn*
> *No traveler returns, puzzles the will*
> *And makes us rather bear those ills we have*
> *Than fly to others that we know not of?*
> *Thus conscience does make cowards of us all . . ."*

Hamlet was about my age, but his family role models were rather pathetic, and he was definitely confused, she thought. For some reason, a Spirit within her gave her strength to go on. She wanted to be a credit to those who loved her and those she loved. She continued to puzzle over the meaning of why she was still on Earth and why they were not. She did feel a sense of purpose, and somehow she would find it. She definitely was not about to go to "the undiscover'd country" yet. She had things to do, but she was still regrouping and reorganizing the pieces of her life to build a new direction. *Shakespeare had a thing about ghosts showing up to give his characters instructions and guidance. I need guidance, but I sure don't want any ghosts showing up for that duty! No, thank you!*

Being in the golf business, one did not take summer vacations; however, she remembered one summer her mother had taken her to Stratford in Ontario, Canada, to the Shakespeare plays. They'd had a wonderful time, just the two of them. Sarah hadn't been interested, and Michael hadn't wanted to go any place where Jenny wasn't. Her mother had called Samantha "my little Shakespeare pal."

*   *   *

It was Friday, the day she planned to meet Joe at three o'clock. In the morning, the mail arrived with the information and conformation for the Grand Hotel. Finding her Guest Information booklet, she turned to the first page. There was the layout of the Grand Nine (the nine-hole course across the street); she hadn't played golf since they'd moved. *Perhaps I'll rent some clubs and try a round*, she thought. On the opposite page was an impressive picture of the hotel with high, white pillars lining a porch that seemed to go off into infinity, American flags flying from long poles stretched over the broad driveway, and parked at the entrance, a carriage drawn by two horses; the driver was wearing a top hat. It did indeed look *grand.*

Turning the page and reading on, she found that the hotel had 385 guest rooms. On most of the following page was a description of devices and accommodations for the handicapped—next came babysitting arrangements and children's programs. *All very nice*, she thought, *but is this for older people and families with children?* Somewhat apprehensive, she reassured herself that she didn't plan to fit in, just to enjoy the pleasant surroundings. Next, "Guest Attire" caught her attention. Was she going to have to buy some appropriate clothes? She wanted to blend in—blend into the crowd—not stand out or bring notice to herself. She continued to read: "During the day, casual resort-wear is the generally accepted style. Every evening at the Grand Hotel is an occasion. Most of our guests dress in their finest."

Their finest, she thought. *The last "finest" dress I bought was a bridesmaid's dress for Michael and Jenny's wedding. That won't do. I looked like a flower girl—a pink marshmallow! Besides, I'm taller and have filled out since then. Maybe there's something in Mom's closet. No, I don't want to go there. I guess it wouldn't be the end of the world if I bought a nice dress and some stylish contemporary clothes, and maybe even had my hair styled.*

41

Although she'd been in this city for several years, everything was relatively new to her; she hadn't gone anywhere or done anything.

Reading on, the booklet stated: "Ladies: Slacks and Bermuda shorts are acceptable throughout the Hotel during the day. After 6:00 p.m., dresses or very nice pantsuits for women are preferred." *This doesn't sound like my era*, she thought. *Pantsuits? Bermuda shorts?*

"Gentlemen: Traditionally, sportswear, shirts with collars, and Bermuda shorts are acceptable in the Hotel public areas before 6:00 p.m. In the evening, gentlemen 12 years and older are required to wear a coat and necktie." She was getting the idea. *This is similar to private-country-club attire. I know about that.* However, prior to last week, she hadn't been to a private county club since she'd been in high school. Venturing out to buy new clothes and getting a proper haircut were not what she had anticipated having to do for her modest vacation. On the other hand, it might be good therapy and brighten things up for her—force her out of her routine. She would get a new look! It would help her move forward. In spite of her apprehensions, all in all, she thought this trip was turning out to be a good idea.

She didn't even know where there was a mall with clothing stores. And who could cut her hair? When she'd gone to Fran's office, she'd admired her style. It must have been particularly outstanding, as she usually didn't pay much attention to those things. Mustering some courage, she decided to call Fran, who had seemed personable enough and wouldn't mind a minor intrusion in her day, as it *was* after April 15. She punched in the numbers and left a message with the secretary. Fran called her back in about 15 minutes. Samantha explained her predicament and why she'd called *her*. Fran thanked her for the compliment and gave her the name of a hair stylist, Mr. Dan, and told Samantha to tell him she was a friend of hers. Then, she gave the name of two stores where they had saleswomen who could help her find the proper clothes and where alterations could be done, if necessary. Fran said she was happy Samantha had called and to call her anytime she needed anything. Samantha felt relieved and was actually looking forward to her expedition into the world of fashion.

She read on in her booklet: "Grand Picnics: Tasty box lunches or a luscious Special Picnic Basket for Two can be ordered prior to 9:00 p.m. on the previous evening. Concerts in the Parlor during Afternoon Tea at 3:30 p.m. to 5 p.m. and also during Demitasse each evening from 8:00 p.m. to 9:30 p.m. Bicycles, Carriage Tours, Croquet, Garden Tours, Hiking/Jogging/ Walking (Mackinac Island offers over 60 miles of roads, paths and trails), Historic Points of Interest."

Fort Mackinac looks interesting. I ought to be able to fill up five days. I could walk on every mile of road. I could up my four miles per day to fifteen. She laughed. *I think I'm going to enjoy this.*

She had whiled away the time anticipating her trip, and it was now after one o'clock. She needed something to eat before meeting Joe. She wanted to go early to look for a map and information she might use for her trip. After a hasty lunch, she quickly changed her clothes.

Arriving at the bookstore, she purchased a map, bought a cold drink at the café, headed to a nearby table, and started planning her route. Engrossed in studying her map, she didn't see him slide into the chair across from her.

"Hi there," he said. "Planning a trip?"

She was somewhat startled and simply answered, "Hello!"

Excited about her trip, she couldn't help spilling out her plans and relating the activities that appealed to her as listed in her little booklet. Listening to her with his full attention, he caught the spirit of her enthusiasm.

"I've been there several times—just for the day—never stayed overnight. It's interesting—the Grand Hotel—its history—the Island in general—the fort and all."

"I thought so too," she replied.

"I was there once during the Port Huron to Mackinac race. Fantastic sight—sailboats with full sails and colorful spinnakers billowed out, coming into port one by one."

"Sounds wonderful!"

"It's one big party—all sorts of boats side-by-side along the docks—what they call rafted. The dockside boats are trapped until the outer boats leave. People step from one boat to another to get to where they're going."

Since she didn't like crowds very much, this part certainly did not appeal to Samantha, but Joe seemed impressed with all the imbibing and camaraderie.

He talked another five or ten minutes about himself. Samantha didn't ask questions—she didn't need to—however, she wasn't sure where he lived or what he was currently doing. She didn't want to venture any questions, as he might want some reciprocity, and she wasn't comfortable answering questions about herself. She really didn't know him at all, except what he told her.

Being inexperienced in social situations, she was surprised Joe was interested in spending time with her. If she were honest with herself, except for her enthusiasm about her trip, she'd hardly said anything and hadn't been particularly interesting. Perhaps she'd been a good listener and he enjoyed talking about himself. That was okay with her, as she was not a loquacious person, outside of her family, on even the best of days.

Beginning to emerge from the depths of grief, she had no emotions left for any close relationship. In high school, she was popular enough with her classmates from her northern school, where her most consistent friends were. She'd had dates and even a couple of short-term, steady boyfriends. With the five-month Florida interruption, a relationship was too hard to maintain. Due to her self-imposed isolation for the past four years, she had not dated anyone; she had missed out on that part of her youth. She wasn't sure what impact this had on her, one way or another. Right now, she enjoyed Joe's friendly voice and stories interrupting her days of solitude; perhaps they would become friends. She had no romantic leanings; perhaps her emotions were wrung out, and there was no room for another right now. She hadn't made any indication he was any more than an acquaintance on the verge of the first step of friendship.

Joe continued talking. He asked her, "What dates will you be there?"

Her mind had wandered a little. "What dates?"

"The Mackinac Island dates," he said.

"Oh, of course." In the process of trying to regain her concentration, she responded automatically, "The third week in July, Monday through Friday."

"How about if I come up on Wednesday, stay one night, and go back on Thursday? It would be great to have someone to explore the island with," he said enthusiastically.

Flabbergasted at his suggestion, hoping he wasn't suggesting he stay with her, and hoping her face wasn't turning red (this idea definitely made her nervous), she said halfheartedly, "Oh, ah . . . uh, well, that might be nice." Quickly she added, "Do you think you can get a room?"

Struggling to regain her composure, she reached for the cold drink and gulped some down—crushed ice included. Fortunately, she didn't choke. *What next?* she thought. *How do I handle this?*

He was not put off by her less-than-enthusiastic response. "It's settled, then. I'm sure I can get a room. I'll meet you in the lobby at ten o'clock Wednesday. Is that too early?"

Samantha sputtered, "No—no—not at all . . . ."

"Good!" he hurriedly interjected. "Have to go now. See you then."

She weakly made a response: "See you then?"

Sipping her drink, she remained at the table, mulling over the previous events. *Is Joe independently wealthy? He did talk about inheriting some money when his father died a few years ago. He doesn't seem to have a job—never talks about having a regular job or any job, but he usually leaves abruptly, as if he has an appointment.*

⚜·CHAPTER 7

"The year's at the spring
And day's at the morn;
Morning's at seven;
The hill-side's dew-pearled;
The lark's on the wing;
The snail's on the thorn:
God's in his heaven—
All's right with the world!

Robert Browning (1812-1889)

The sun woke her up early, and being rather excited about the trip, she hurried with last-minute preparations. Before long, having packed the day before, she tossed her suitcase with the new clothes into the car and headed north. It was a pleasant drive. The highways of the upper part of the Lower Peninsula were beautiful as far as highways went. The southbound lanes were often not visible to those going north as they wound through the woods and hills of northern Michigan. There was still dew on the undergrowth and the shady side of the hills, and as she observed birds flying in an out of the treetops, she thought of Robert Browning's dew-pearled hillsides and lark on the wing. But, here it was, on a grander scale and less refined than his English countryside garden.

She began to think about the boat ride to the island. Going out onto the water of the great lakes would be a test. Could she deal with it? How would she react? Would it cause her to conjure up horrific thoughts as she imagined the last moments her family had experienced? She had already struggled with that, and she didn't want to let her mind go there. She knew she had a choice: slip into a destructive state of mind, or keep a grip on her mental stability. She would prepare herself to think of good and pleasant things. In spite of everything, she would focus on: "God's in his heaven—all's right with the world!" *It will be all right. All will be better,* she thought.

She arrived at one of the ferry docks in Mackinaw City at about ten-forty—plenty of time to catch the eleven o'clock boat. With her tag for the Grand Hotel securely fastened to her luggage and the stub with the matching numbers safely tucked into her pocket, she let the attendant load her suitcase onto the cart. She parked her car in a huge, grassy lot among the motor vehicles forbidden to go farther, walked back, stepping around the water-filled ruts of the dirt road to the white-washed ferry station, and purchased a round-trip ticket. As she walked down the long dock and got in line, she noticed all the interesting things around her: the variety of cargo being loaded: numerous bicycles, strollers, pieces of furniture, a small tree, cartons with all sorts of labels, and of course, the mountain of luggage. After making her way across the gangplank in a crowd of passengers and a few pets, she climbed the steep steel stairs and headed for the open upper deck. The deep, full sound of the air horn echoed across the water and signaled the departure. Soon the boat surged ahead, toward the open water. The sky, the clouds, the bright sunshine, the birds, and the vastness of the water made it easy to appreciate the beauty of her surroundings, and she felt happy.

Since the brisk wind was chilly and she'd packed her jacket, she reluctantly retreated to the enclosed protection of a lower level. During the 25-minute trip, the only other boat she saw in the open water was one with SYSCO painted on the side. She realized that all the food for the 130,000 meals per year at the Grand Hotel and the food and supplies for other hotels, restaurants, stores, and especially the fudge shops (they needed tons of sugar and ingredients for the ever-popular fudge produced on the island) had to be delivered by boat and horse-drawn wagon. Food companies had to have their own boats to accomplish this.

As they approached the island, she was overwhelmed by the magnificent sight of the Grand Hotel and the three—and four-story Victorian "cottages" perched on the side of the cliffs. All the energy of the blue sky, the sunshine, and the water seemed to be distilled in the clear air that poured over the island, making it green with abundant vegetation.

Fort Mackinac, strategically placed by the British to protect the harbor in 1870, dominated the bluffs to the right. *I will definitely check that out*, she thought.

As they approached the harbor, the variety of boats and quaint buildings of the town made a charming sight. The ferry was expertly maneuvered to the dock, and the crew began their routine preparations for the disembarking of the passengers and the unloading of the cargo. As she crossed to the landing, Samantha became one of the one million tourists to visit the island that year. Like the village where she'd grown up in the summers, it had 600 year-round residents. Her village, without a doubt, had a lot of tourists in the summer but didn't come close to one million. Unlike her village, there were over 500 horses.

Since her luggage would be taken to the hotel and the weather was sunny and cool, she decided to walk. She meandered through the narrow streets, taking in their charm, lingering now and then to glance at the array of colorful memorabilia in a shop window, studying the alluring cottages, and enjoying the flowers. A block or two from the main street, she passed massive lilac bushes with thick, twisted branches. Some extended to the cottage eaves, spread over the tiny lawns, and reached over the fences above the passersby on the sidewalks. There were no sweet-smelling purple flowers among the small leaves today. *It must be breathtaking in May*, she thought.

Pedestrians, bicycles, and horse-drawn vehicles, passed her as she walked up the hill. There were no automobiles. There was no mistaking where the Grand Hotel was—it was grand as it rose up between the cliff-side and the sky. She arrived just after noon. Although check-in time wasn't until later, the room was ready, and she was allowed to occupy it early. On the third floor, she found her room. It was well-maintained and tastefully decorated in the bright summer cottage colors of green, white, and yellow, with delicate geranium designs here and there—on the dressers, the headboard, and the toiletries in the bathroom. She had a magnificent view: ahead, the sparkling water of the Straits of Mackinac, and to the north, the great bridge connecting the two peninsulas.

Her luggage had not arrived, so she decided to walk around the hotel and grounds to get her bearings. Walking down the long hall was like walking on a boat; the hotel had been built in 1887, and the floors seemed to undulate. She strolled through the main lobby, across the carpet with its black, green, and red geranium motif. Then she stepped out onto the world's longest front porch and looked up and down. Two hundred and sixty white flower boxes containing super-sized, bright red geraniums were positioned evenly along the white railings. Buttressed to a procession of white pillars were sturdy poles bearing patriotic red, white, and blue flags floating gloriously in the light breeze. White rocking chairs placed in a line along the wall of the porch looked tempting, but she decided to save a rocking-and-viewing session for another time. Instead, she descended the rosy-red carpeted steps of the grand entrance and crossed the street.

Next, she started down a long flight of wide, battleship-grey wooden steps with white supporting posts and handrails. High, overgrown bushes lined the sides, hiding chirping birds and scurrying chipmunks. She climbed down the first 33 steps and reached a landing and an outlook. There was a choice, right or left. She chose right. After a series of alternating three to five steps and short walkways, she took a 45-degree turn and descended the remaining 20 steps, rounded the dense hedge, and emerged onto the expansive lower lawn. Positioning herself where she could view the entire area, she sat on the thick grass to enjoy the sun's warmth in this area sheltered by the steep cliff along one side and a substantial growth of trees and bushes on the other. An abundance of overachieving flowers in colorful gardens adorned the lawn and outlined the edges of the paths. The extensive lawn was also decorated with a topiary of a full-sized horse-drawn carriage. A fountain—appropriately scaled for the area—spewed a mist of sun-colored water.

She observed several groups of children playing while parents carefully watched. She was reminded of her little twin nieces. Becoming less sensitive to the pain of loss, she could almost take pleasure in those memories while watching these children. She particularly enjoyed studying a little girl about two and a half years old, dressed in a cute pink outfit with a charming matching hat and pink canvas shoes. *Looks as though she went shopping for new clothes for her vacation, too,* Samantha reflected.

The toddler was holding her mother's hand and appeared mesmerized by three boys, about eight or nine, engaged in a game with a large ball. They seemed to be making up the rules as they went along. They, of course, were totally oblivious to the tiny tot, straining on the mother's hand. The little vision in pink, coveting a place in their activity, started perseverating, "My turn! My turn, my turn, my turn . . . !" Her mother, as gently as possible, pulled her in another direction, talking to her in a sympatric voice and engaging her in another activity. Soon, she toddled off to do some heavy lifting with the Bocci balls.

* * *

When Samantha returned to her room, her luggage was there. She carefully unpacked, admiring each new item and finding a convenient place for it. As it was nearly five o'clock, she selected one of the two dresses she had purchased for evening—a simple black dress with a modest neckline and a slight suggestion of puffy sleeves covering her shoulders. The costume jewelry the sales lady selected gave it the simple, understated elegance that made her comfortable. She had plain black shoes in the latest style, but with sensible, two-inch heels, not the five-inch stilettos with the severely pointed toes that in no way resemble feet. She definitely did not need the extra height, nor did she want the extra length in the toe to trip over. She wanted shoes, not weapons. Besides, she wasn't used to wearing high-heeled dress shoes and didn't want to embarrass herself the first night by falling off her shoes. After an hour of relaxing and preparation, she was ready to step out in her "finest" and ready for "an evening at the Grand Hotel is an occasion . . . ."

The shoes were surprisingly comfortable, but she had to concentrate to keep her balance as she traipsed over the uneven floor of the corridor. Then she took on the two flights of steps, clutching the handrail for fear she would misplace one of those heels, catch it in the carpet, and tumble down the stairs. After all, her goal was not to bring attention to herself. Being airlifted to the mainland after breaking her neck would be a bit much.

Making it safely to the lobby, she saw a line forming at a wide door some distance to the left. She assumed that was the place for the five-course dinner. *A five-course dinner—what will that be like?* she thought. *Five decisions—the biggest decisions of the day—wonderful!*

The sign over the door, *Salle à Manger,* confirmed it. She knew enough French to know this was the "Large Room for Eating." When her turn came, she showed her identification booklet to the waiter at the door and was directed farther and farther into the room by a series of waiters. At last, she was ushered to a small table for two close to the windows. A pleasant-looking, elderly gentleman was sitting alone at the next table for two. Although at separate tables, they were close and were seated facing each other. It was hard to divert the eyes, as it usually is when one is sitting alone, and she smiled faintly a time or two when they made eyes contact. He smiled back.

After several minutes of studying the menu, she looked up and caught his eye. He spoke to her. "Are you alone?"

She couldn't say anything but, "Yes."

He said she reminded him of his granddaughter, then asked her if she would sit with him and keep him company, as he was alone, too.

I don't mind—he does look lonely. I know how that feels! she thought. *He will probably do most of the talking. I'm a pretty good listener. I know how to be evasive, and I've perfected my "profound" responses: "Yes. No. Really? Isn't that interesting?"*

She got up and moved toward the empty chair across from him. Surprisingly, he got up and held the chair for her. He was tall for his age, a little taller than she was in her two-inch heels, and slightly underweight. He had a full head of white hair—neat and well-cut. In spite of the slightly rounded shoulders that came with age, his clothes fit perfectly.

"I'm Samantha," she said with a slight smile. Looking straight into his tired blue-grey eyes, she held out her hand; his gnarled, wrinkled hand with clean, well-manicured nails shook it with a firm grip.

"I'm Edmund," he said with a smile and looked *her* straight in the eye.

Throughout the meal, she noted that he had impeccable manners. He was attentive when she spoke, looked at her, and showed interest. His grammar was perfect. She didn't mean to be a language snob, but it just happened that her tutors and her mother had instilled it in her. *It's like a tune that keeps repeating in your head*, she thought. *I can't help it.* Her mother had always made sure the children used correct grammar. Also, in her private school education, her tutors had been very particular about grammar. She'd been required to write out answers; true or false and multiple-choice questions on tests were not used. The classes were small, and teachers had time to correct essays; every wrong word and punctuation mark, or lack of one, was circled in red and sent back for correction. As she remembered, early on, there had been lots of red marks and notes on her papers. She still could hear her mother, adding to the chorus, correcting her and explaining the proper use of words; that was probably why she noticed people's grammar. Joe slipped up in this area from time to time—more frequently than she would have expected. He gave her the impression he'd had a proper education, and having been in pre-med, certainly he was smart enough.

For dessert, she ordered one of the 55,000 pecan balls to be served that summer; Edmund ordered applesauce. *Applesauce?* she thought. The applesauce set Samantha on one of her analysis sessions. To her, the meal was quite an event, and she wanted to try new and special foods. She surmised that to him this was an ordinary restaurant meal, something he had been used to for years. She didn't think this was due to dietary problems, as he had eaten a variety of foods one might not imbibe if one possessed a touchy GI tract. He seemed used to an opulent lifestyle—money provided things, expedited things, made navigating through life easier, and she supposed it all became quite ordinary, something taken for granted over a long span of time. Samantha wondered if that would happen to her over time; she hoped not.

But, then again, it put material things into perspective. He had worked hard to build up a business, but in the end what mattered was his family. Now, he was alone. His beloved wife had died recently, and he'd come here because they had come here when they were young and occasionally, when time allowed, throughout the years. It had been a time they could be together without the intrusions of business. He was hoping to recapture some of those memories. His son and daughter-in-law had been in Australia for years and rarely came back for visits. When they did, they had his daughter-in-law's family to visit; that took up most of their time.

His granddaughter, who had been dear to him, had just finished an internal medicine residency program in California. Now, she was in a three-year fellowship program in nephrology in Oregon. Her demanding exhausting life has left little time for even a phone conversation with her grandfather. His grandson had graduated from MIT. He had remained in Boston and had recently finished an MBA from Harvard. He was still in Boston working for a company. He seldom visited. The little time he had was spent with his fiancée. Edmund's grandchildren had grown up at his estate on Lake Michigan. They had all lived there at one time—his mother, father, brother, sister-in-law, son, daughter-in-law, grandchildren, and he and his wife. His only sibling,

Robert, had died last year. Robert's wife had died young; he'd never remarried and had no children. Not only had Robert been Edmund's business partner and older brother, he'd been his best friend. Now, they were all gone.

She sympathized with him. "Perhaps we take our families for granted, thinking they will always be there. We don't realize until they're gone how important they were."

"That's a wise observation for someone so young," he responded.

For some reason, she felt she could trust him with her feelings and situation and felt an impulse to confide in him; however, she resisted. She couldn't get the words out; she was on the verge of a total meltdown. She quickly composed herself and started talking about something else; the *Salle à Manger* at the Grand Hotel, among a hundred or more diners, was not a good place for a hysterical sobbing episode.

By now, they had finished their dinner and lingered over pots of tea. "Well, my dear, this has been very pleasant," he said.

"I enjoyed it very much, too. I'll no doubt see you around. I'm staying until Friday. How long are you staying?" she ventured.

"I'm scheduled to leave Thursday, but I may stay longer."

He got up from his chair and helped her with hers, and they walked out together. After saying their *au revoirs*, he went to an inviting overstuffed chair at the far end of the lobby and picked up a newspaper. She wandered over to the ballroom. As she walked, she reviewed their conversation and came to the conclusion that she liked Edmund very much. *My dear,* she thought. *Somehow, when Edmund said, "My dear," it sounded grandfatherly and endearing and made me think he really liked me. I rather liked it.*

George's just plain "dear" sounded condescending, as if he didn't take her seriously; she definitely did not like it. George had been kind to her, and since he had daughters—one about her age and one younger—his fatherly mode was probably transferred to her. Nevertheless, she needed him to take her seriously in her undertaking to manage her inheritance. She was determined not to be taken lightly.

☙·CHAPTER 8

When you do dance, I wish you
A wave o'the sea, that you might ever do
Nothing but that, move still, still so,
And own no other function.

Shakespeare: *The Winter's Tale*

Guests were seated on sea-green velvet high-back settees arranged along opposite walls of the lobby just outside the ballroom. Covering the wall space above the settees were mirrors repeating images and lights back and forth into infinity. Enjoying the music coming through the open entrance doors, people watched finely dressed men and women wander in and out of the ballroom and pass through the crowded lobby. Gradually moving toward the music, Samantha ascended four semicircular steps, crossed the rosy carpet through the crowd, climbed three more steps, and entered the ballroom. She stood there a few minutes. While her eyes were adjusting to the darkness, she saw only sparkling points of light and phantom dancers floating past her. Soon, a middle-aged-plus gentleman approached her and asked her to dance. She didn't see any harm in it; the music and surroundings were intriguing. So, somewhat hesitantly, she responded, "Well . . . all right, thank you."

He introduced himself; they engaged in some brief small talk, and as the music started they glided across the floor. There was no talking on his part after that. He was serious about his dancing and they whirled on in silence, which suited Samantha. He was an excellent dancer and had probably worn out a couple of ladies previously. Samantha had not had an occasion for dancing since the last high school prom, but she knew how to dance very well. Actually, most of the couples in her small school had known ballroom dancing, and unlike most proms of her generation, it was incorporated.

Samantha had learned the steps and rhythms from Louis and Loretta. Among the summer cottagers where she'd grown up was a family from New York. The parents, Louis and Loretta, were professional dancers who worked in New York during "the season." During the summer, they ran a dance school in town, mostly attended by the locals who didn't have such opportunities. The cottage children from big cities were on vacation from such things.

As it happened, Louis was an avid golfer—a regular at the course—rain or shine.

One day, Samantha's father had announced that his daughters would be taking dancing lessons. Beginning immediately, ballet, tap, acrobatic, and ballroom dancing would be added to their repertoire of experiences. Their father had made an arrangement with Louis that his daughters would have dancing lessons in exchange for a golf membership and golf lessons. So, over many summers, the girls had danced and danced, and Louis had played golf to his heart's content. Even Michael had gotten in on the ballroom dancing for two or three summers. You guessed it—Jenny wanted to do it, and he'd obliged.

Samantha and her sister were definitely not launched into careers as prima ballerinas, and Samantha was not destined to be the next Shirley Temple, tapping her way to fame and fortune. Yet, their dancing lessons still brought a smile to her face. Samantha almost laughed out loud, remembering one episode. They had been dancing for about two or three summers in the soft black slippers, learning all the basic positions, twisting their small feet into unnatural positions with arm movements to correspond and endless *poses* and *plies*. They'd learned the moves—the *tour jete*, the *arabesque*, the *glissade*, plus the spotting and turning technique that was supposed to keep them from getting dizzy. Now, it was time for the dreaded pink toe shoes. The shoes had been ordered and had arrived. The children opened the boxes and saw the long, narrow, pink satin shoes. Upon further investigation, they'd found long, wide, pink ribbons and a huge chunk of coarse wooly stuff—the lamb's wool. The shoes felt as if they had wooden blocks at the tip; the lamb's wool was to soften the blows and reduce the pain of the dancing on tippy-toes.

She vividly pictured her skinny, long-legged sister stuffing the wool, slipping into the shoes, and wrapping the ribbons to her knees, then launching herself from the chair. After a few instructions from the teacher, she'd made it up onto her toes. Awkwardly, she'd clomped, crunched, and careened with unsteady, quick little steps, trying to keep her balance. Breaking new ground for dance positions, she'd worked her way across the floor. The Tulip Time Dutch Klompen dancers in their wooden shoes were far more graceful. Her ordinarily straight legs were bent into the most bowlegged position possible; hands were in the curved first position but definitely expressing pain. The teacher was calling orders to the students: "First position hands—straight legs—straight legs!"

The younger Samantha, in the midst of preparing her own shoes and launch, had been falling off her chair and hold her sides laughing. Sarah had peered back and responded with a painful half-smile. She'd known this was a hysterical moment and was quite good-natured about it. In the midst of this, the teacher had continued to order, "Hurry up—hurry up—straight legs—straight legs . . . ."

Samantha had wiped her tears on the short sleeve of her leotard, completed her own ritual, and started her painful *pas seul* to join the other "dancers," the new shoes squeaking with every step. She'd thought she would need about twenty summers before she was ready to dance the part of Clara in the *Nutcracker*. By then, she would be too old.

After being spun around the dance floor by her energetic partner for about half an hour, she thanked him, and they complimented each other on their skills. As she left the ballroom, she noticed that he had quickly moved on and was gracefully ushering another young lady to the dance floor.

Feeling warm, she wandered out onto the long porch and sat in one of the white rocking chairs. She was comfortable and content in the twilight as she gently rocked. The surroundings were breathtaking: the sparkling water of the great lake in the fading light; the deep, royal blue sky of a clear, cloudless sundown; and a full, orange moon just coming up over the trees. Then a sense of loneliness came over her—there was no one to share this spectacular evening. She watched the couples stroll by, some hand-in-hand. One woman, about in her forties, was walking slightly behind her husband, silent and looking more alone than she was—an expressionless face, head bent forward, and shoulders slumped. She and her husband gazed in opposite directions—never looked at each other or touched. He strolled on at his own pace and direction, and she kept pace behind him. Samantha was reminded of the saddest lines of literature describing such a marriage: "the atmosphere of stale familiarity . . . carried along like a nimbus."

Wow, Thomas Hardy described it well, she remembered. *"Preserving the perfect silence for fear of conversation that might be irksome to him. The woman enjoyed no society whatever from his presence . . ." And, the saddest of all, "No other than such a relationship would have accounted for the atmosphere of stale familiarity."*

No other relationship except husband and wife would have tolerated such coldness. He seemed oblivious to her, the glorious surroundings, and the magnificent evening.

Body language is supposed to be 88% of the communication, but maybe I'm reading too much into this, Samantha admonished herself. *Maybe they aren't even together—Oh, but, they are! I do remember seeing them sitting together at dinner. He has a wedding ring on his finger, and so does she! I wonder what makes a marriage that stale and cold. How sad. Maybe she wanted to come and he didn't, and now there's hell to pay. Why did he come? Was it out of a sense of duty or guilt?*

His pursed lips, annoyed look, and body language gave the impression that he truly didn't want to be there. Samantha wondered where he wanted to be. Her imagination wandered on, and she wondered if perhaps there was another woman—maybe that was where he would rather be. People-watching wasn't something that usually caught her attention, but for some reason this couple sparked her curiosity. She thought that if the opportunity presented itself, she would attempt to strike up a conversation with the woman—but, that wasn't like her. Nevertheless, she felt sorry for her. Maybe she'd find out that her imaginings were totally erroneous.

❧·CHAPTER 9

"Blessed be the tie that binds
Our hearts in Christian love;
The fellowship of kindred minds
Is like to that above.
We share our mutual woes,
Our mutual burdens bear,
And often for each other flows
The sympathizing tear."

John Fawcett (1749-1817)

The next morning, she woke up with the sun and wandered over to the window to enjoy the high-priced view; it was worth it. For some time she stood there, taking in the spectacular sights of nature and an achievement of man: The Mighty Mac. She had read it had been built over 50 years ago and was five miles long; each of the two towers was 550 feet above the water and 300 feet below. Even from the distance of the island, it had a commanding presence. *Wow! About four million vehicles cross each year. That would have been quite a challenge for the ferry service if the bridge hadn't been built,* she speculated.

In her reading, she took particular note of how to access the Drivers' Assistance Program for people who are afraid to drive over the bridge. Being afraid of heights, she would, without a doubt, need to call for help if she ventured that way. The Timmies, as they called them, ranged from little old ladies to motorcyclists, truck drivers, and 22-year-old heiresses. Many passengers were visible exiting the bridge with their heads covered or on the floor of the vehicle. Samantha thought, *Head covered and on the floor. That sounds good. I could do that.*

* * *

It was early; there were few people at the *Salle à Manger* when Samantha arrived for breakfast. She again had a table for two with a good view. Reading the extensive menu, she noticed grits listed there. This brought back memories of her Southern days. On their drive to Florida each year, they'd known they were in Southern territory when grits appeared on the breakfast menu. This had been a favorite of the whole family. This was the first time in the North she had ever seen grits on the menu for breakfast.

"May I take your order?" asked the waiter.

"It will be two sunny-side eggs, grits, and whole-wheat toast."

When the breakfast came, the grits were in a cereal bowl. *I wonder what part of the world they serve grits in a cereal bowl*, she thought. Well, she knew what to do. The grits being thick, she slipped them out of the bowl and onto the plate, to their rightful place next to the eggs. Then she plopped on a large pat of butter and thoroughly enjoyed her breakfast.

After breakfast, she walked down the hill to the village. The clip-clop rhythm of the horses' hooves was unfamiliar to her. She noted the quick rhythm of the classy carriage horses, and the slow, heavy sound of the stocky work horses, as they pulled the loaded wagons up the hill. She explored the lower part of the island: the village, the harbor and the path along the water. She had lunch at a pleasant restaurant adjacent to the marina, with a good view of the boats and the water, then headed back to the hotel.

As she reached the top of the red carpeted front steps, she noticed Edmund sitting in a rocking chair to the left at the far end of the porch. Pencil in hand, he seemed to be writing. She decided to join him and quickly walked the 330 feet." Hello, Edmund! How are you?"

He greeted her with a smile and a friendly, "Good afternoon. Won't you sit down? I need some help with the crossword puzzle. There are some questions that seem to be from a different generation—yours, I think."

She agreed and sat in the rocking chair next to his.

Each morning, a five-page paper with excerpts from the *New York Times*, including the crossword puzzle, was slipped under the door of each room. He had most of the puzzle finished, but she was able to help with three or four questions, which wasn't too hard, since he had already filled in several letters.

With the puzzle finished, they sat and rocked, talked, and even shared a few jokes; he had a good sense of humor, and it had been awhile since she'd shared a bit of wit with someone. The time passed quickly. Despite the age difference, he seemed to enjoy her company as much as she enjoyed his. She felt honored that he would trust her and share his feelings with her. She thought of Joe sharing the events of his life with his family in a rather cool and matter-of-fact way. She couldn't empathize with Joe like she could with Edmund. Her heart couldn't go out to him the way it did when she was listening to Edmund; there was something quite different. Maybe Joe had not had the same closeness with his family as she had. Her family had consisted of people who knew each other's faults and shortcomings, who'd loved each other in spite of them and because of them. It was a place where she'd felt safe and loved, no matter what. She could thank her parents for instilling in them a commitment to family—always nurturing it, honoring it, respecting it. They'd built each other up and recognized their strengths and individuality; they hadn't tried to make them into something they weren't. She would have to hold onto that, if she ever had a family of her own.

It was apparent that Edmund adored his wife and family; again, he talked about how he missed them. Then, unexpectedly, she deviated from her guardedness and volunteered, "I'm alone, too. I lost my family in an accident, and now I have no one."

"I'm so sorry, my dear. It must be difficult for you, especially at such a young age," he said with genuine concern. "I hope *we* can be friends."

"I'd like that very much," she responded.

It was late in the afternoon; he said he was getting tired and wanted to take a nap before dinner. However, if she would like, he would enjoy her company for dinner. She was pleased to accept the suggestion.

They arranged to meet at the entrance to the dining room at six o'clock. After sitting for so long, Samantha decided to walk for an hour.

Arriving at the dining room about six, she did not see Edmund, but she got in line anyway to reserve a place for them. The door attendant drew her out of line and asked, "Are you Samantha?"

"I am."

He motioned to a waiter, who said, "Follow me, please."

They walked through the double doors to a lovely table for two on the porch, where Edmund was seated. He got up and greeted her. The waiter helped her with her chair.

He said with a shy smile, "I got here a little early and arranged for us to eat out here. It's a lovely, warm evening and I thought you would enjoy the view from here."

"How thoughtful," she responded. "This is wonderful! It's beautiful!"

They chatted like old friends about everything from art and books to politics. She found him well-read; he suggested books she might like to read that were not in her parents' library. Nevertheless, his philosophy of life, political, and social views were similar to those of her parents. He had well-thought-out answers for questions she raised. His knowledge was remarkable; she had always been eager to learn and found him interesting. He liked her bright, alert mind and thoughtfulness.

Their conversation reminded her of time with her family, especially in autumn in Michigan and winter in Florida, as they had more evenings together. In particular, Sunday after church

63

was set aside for family time. Their mother would organize a special dinner, and everyone had a modest job to do. They would sit down to a hearty meal, then linger at the table and engage in lively discussions. Their father would often read articles from the newspaper and ask them what they thought. Michael, of course, would fetch his laptop and overwhelm them with facts and figures, and their parents would help sort them out and arrive at proper conclusions.

With the long daylight in the summer and customers playing golf until they couldn't see the ball anymore, they had limited family time; besides, after working from sunup to sundown, all they wanted to do was get a good night's sleep. They rarely had time to even sit down for a proper meal, and by no means could they eat together.

Edmund reminded her of her father, who had been skilled at using the Socratic Method to evoke critical thinking from his children. Even so, he'd definitely had a goal as to where he wanted to direct their thinking. With social problems, Sarah had tended to be sympathetic, and Michael'd had the "tough love" solutions, saying, "I think people should learn from mistakes. Other people shouldn't be forced to bail out irresponsible people." Then their father would start with his "What if? And suppose . . . ?" scenarios. Samantha would just listen and observe most of the time. Occasionally, her father would ask her a question he knew she could answer to bring her into the conversation and build up her confidence. As she'd gotten older, she'd ventured into greater participation. Eventually, they would move into the living room. Michael would continue offering a barrage of facts and figures, and their father would check a few sources of his own. Samantha would often curl up on the sofa next to Michael so she could watch him look up information.

The still air was balmy and comfortable, and this kind pleasant friend made her feel safe and relaxed, like being wrapped in a cozy blanket on a cool night. Taking a moment to appreciate the surroundings, they fixed their eyes on the sun moving toward the horizon and sending a glorious glow in all directions. They remained awhile and, as with her family, eventually moved to the more comfortable chairs of the lounge and chatted on into the evening. Despite their gender and generational differences, they seemed to be kindred spirits.

She told him she was meeting Joe Morton the following morning at ten o'clock, how she'd met him, and that she felt apprehensive about it, as she really didn't know him very well.

"If our paths crossed tomorrow, I'll introduce you."

"That's fine. Just call me Mr. Jones—or Smith," he said, with a chuckle. "I'm trying to maintain anonymity."

"I understand completely," she assured him.

It was getting late when they parted. Samantha went out onto the porch for a few minutes of rocking and stargazing. The stars made her think of one of her nieces decorating the Christmas tree. The mild evening surrounded her, and she was able to experience a happy memory devoid of sorrow. She envisioned the charming three-year-old in her midnight blue velvet dress with a white, lacy collar, white tights, dressy white shoes, two necklaces, sunglasses, a red balloon in her left hand, and a purse over that arm. She did like to dress up! Taking her decorating duty seriously, she'd daintily placed each ornament until she'd heavily decorated the lower three feet of the tree. She had stayed with the task until it was completed: no ornaments remained in the box, and the tree was spectacular. Smiling, Samantha got up and went to her room.

❧·CHAPTER 10

"You can discover more about a person in an hour
of play than in a year of conversation."

Plato

Arriving in the lobby at the agreed-upon time, she wondered
if Joe would really be there. Mostly expecting he would not, she
started thinking about alternate plans for the day. To her surprise,
she saw Joe coming from the lower level where the check-in desk
was located. They greeted each other; he even gave her a hug and
commented on how much he liked her new hairstyle, how well
she looked, and other pleasantries. Subsequently, he asked her
what she would like to do. She made three suggestions: a hike
over the island, a bike ride around the island, or a visit to the fort.
He settled on a hike over the island. Expecting that one way or
another she would like a picnic lunch, she had ordered one the
night before, and they went off to pick it up from the designated
place. After tucking it into a backpack along with a couple of
bottles of water, Joe picked up the supplies and arranged the pack
in a comfortable position. They started off on their hike. They
went down the steps to the lower level and entered the long hall
that led to the side exit. Stopping now and then, they looked at
the historical memorabilia arranged along the walls. Outside, they
found the road leading to various hiking trails around the upper
part of the island.

For the first hour Joe said little, which was rather unusual. This gave Samantha time to analyze what she knew about him. *He seems to be interested in noble pursuits—going to Africa was a worthy endeavor,* she thought. *There's something about it I can't quite figure out. What is it? He seemed so mechanical talking about it. Wouldn't he have more emotion, excitement, passion, sympathy, or empathy with the people, and satisfaction for their accomplishments?* Nevertheless, Samantha, being somewhat reserved by nature and withdrawn the past few years, found his good looks and outgoing nature appealing and his little jokes amusing.

They both enjoyed the birds flitting around the treetops and small critters scurrying through undergrowth. As he spotted hawks and eagles, he pointed them out to her. She was glad the nature sounds were not interrupted by human conversation; perhaps Joe felt that way, too.

Listening to the sounds around her, she thought of the time she'd walked with Jenny and Michael through the tall pines at Interlochen, on a windy day near the lake. She remembered Jenny telling her that nature often sings in a minor key. Being students of music and, in particular, with Jenny having perfect pitch, they were aware of and immersed in the sounds around them. Jenny had told Samantha that she had been reading a book by Dr. W. A. Criswell, a theologian, in which he said that according to the Bible, angels never sang. The Greek word some translations record as singing actually means "saying" or "speaking." He says music is for this world; the moans and groans in a plaintive minor key reflect the travail, wretchedness, hurt, despair, and agony of a fallen creation, the wretchedness of a lost race in a dying world. The sound of the wind is a wail; the sea moans in its restlessness and speechless trouble. The many bird songs are in minor keys. Holy angels cannot understand this hopelessness. Somehow it's the sorrow, the disappointment of life and anguish that make people sing in their sad hour or in the joy of redemption. Music is a language that speaks at a deeper level than words can reach.

"I was intrigued by the thought and have been trying to analyze it. This is the perfect place to do it. I haven't come to *my* conclusions yet," Jenny had said.

True or not, this thought suited Samantha's mood. She missed them terribly and wished they were here instead of Joe. She was comforted, knowing Jenny and Michael were redeemed and she would see them all again. Yet, how would she manage the next ten, twenty, forty, sixty or maybe even seventy years without them?

The trails through the woods were well-worn and led past neatly kept cottages (some very grand and some small, but all charming) and stables, some for horses and carriages instead of garages for cars.

It was afternoon, and finding an old, worn log in a small clearing, Joe suggested they sit and have their lunch. As they ate, Samantha was curious to see if Joe had any opinion or demonstrable passion for anything. So, she cautiously ventured a question. "What do you like to do? Do you like to read? Do you have a favorite author?"

"I don't read much. I like football and soccer, baseball, most sports—not golf—too slow."

"What teams do you follow?" she pursued. He rattled off various popular teams and went on to tell her about the accomplishments of the star players. Now here, he showed some passion, and even some disgust and criticism for the coaches and players. Well, by now, she was pretty sorry she had asked. She had no interest in sports *except* golf. Nevertheless, she got more insight into what made Joe tick and was able to see more of his personality. In spite of his being agreeable, attentive, and polite, she sensed something about him that unsettled her. Perhaps it was his annoyance with one of the hotel staff, a little thing that had occurred in an instant—a snappish encounter followed by his charming smile and a joke to smooth it over and dismiss it. Nonetheless, she was having a good time; she was in harmony with the glorious day. Surrounded by a light, cool breeze; clear sky; warm sun; the pungent scent of pine trees; industrious, tiny forest creatures; and the sparkling expanse of water, the uneasy sensation dissipated.

When they returned to the hotel, they entered by way of the front steps. She saw Edmund in the same place he'd been the previous day, working on the Wednesday crossword puzzle.

"There's someone I'd like you to meet," she said to Joe.

"You make friends fast," he replied.

"Not really, but he's a very charming gentleman—quite special."

They walked down the porch, unobserved by Edmund, and as they approached, Samantha said, "Good afternoon. How's the puzzle going?"

"Good afternoon, my dear. I'm just getting started."

"There's someone I'd like you to meet."

After the introductions, Edmund invited them to join him and help with the puzzle. He and Samantha methodically went through the clues and became engrossed in the task. Joe suppressed a yawn. Oddly, considering his educational background, didn't offer any help. They tried to bring him into the enterprise by asking him from time to time, "What do you think, Joe?" Unfortunately for Joe, there were no questions about sports.

Edmund and Samantha bantered about ideas with cheerful and pleasant quips that evoked frequent smiles or chuckles and finally zeroed in on the solutions and finished the puzzle. Joe continued with an uninterested, somber expression and appeared relieved when the mental exercise ended. Forcing a pathetic smile, he congratulated them and suggested he and Samantha continue their excursion.

They politely excused themselves. Joe wandered off a bit; Samantha stay behind a moment. In a soft voice out of Joe's hearing—for a reason she could not determine, she did not want Joe to hear her plans—she informed Edmund that Joe was leaving in the morning, and she would be hiking around the island the rest of the day. She expected to return to the hotel late in the afternoon. Edmund smiled slightly and nodded his acknowledgement; she smiled back, then turned and walked briskly past the white rocking chairs to join Joe. He was almost to the hotel's carpeted entrance. He made a half turn, looked at her, and forced a smile.

*   *   *

She and Joe had a late dinner in the *Salle à Manger.* Initially, the intermittent conversation was polite and cheerful enough; nevertheless, Joe seemed pensive. His slightly knotted brow and tight mouth suggested he was deliberating on something. Samantha was not about to question his mood and open that subject. Sporadically and somewhat unnaturally, Joe would break the brooding look shadowing his face, flash a grin, and resume some trivial conversation. They finished dessert and remained at the table for awhile; by now, Samantha was looking over his shoulder and studying the wallpaper pattern while she sipped her lukewarm tea and he drank his second cup of coffee. After a short stroll on the veranda, she wanted to put an end to it and said she was worn out, wanted to go to her room, and would see him for breakfast at eight o'clock. They parted at the bottom of the stairs.

*   *   *

The next morning Samantha walked with Joe to the ferry and they parted uneventfully. After the boat pulled away, she paced back and forth and then walked to the end of the long pier and stood until the craft looked like a toy on the water.

She hurried back along the dock. Her pace slowed as she came to the main street. With a change of mood, she sauntered past souvenir stops, boutiques, and art galleries. Drifting in and out of the numerous fudge shops, she indulged in the aroma of warm chocolate. That was all the fudge she considered after the meals at the hotel. She followed the paved road up the hill, walked by the fort and then passed the towering cottages above the harbor that fascinated her. *What sort of people live with a view that seems to encompass the top of the world?* she wondered.

She hoped they never tired of this magnificent scene or took it for granted; she hoped they paused by the window for at least a few minutes each day and perhaps were inspired to say a prayer. Moving on, she found a steep wooden stairway with periodic platforms, and as she worked her way down, it seemed like a descent from a tree house. She was again on the main street, now crowded with tourists. Since it was way past noon, she entered a fairly deserted restaurant next to the harbor and enjoyed a leisurely lunch, watching the boats come and go. Fortified from a hearty meal, she resumed her hiking.

When she returned to her room there was a handwritten note on the bed. It was from Edmund, inviting her to join him and his friends. It instructed her to go to the head waiter at the *Salle à Manger.*

How kind of him, she thought.

As she headed toward the queue at *Salle à Manger,* the waiter, recognizing her, left his station and with rapid, long strides approached her. "Good evening, Miss Samantha. Please, follow me."

She smiled at his calling her "Miss Samantha." He led her to a private dining room. As they entered, Edmund moved from a small group standing by the windows on the far side of the room to take her from the care of the waiter. He greeted her warmly, escorted her across the room, and introduced three couples to her as old and dear friends. They had arrived that afternoon by private plane. He didn't exactly explain to them who *she* was, just "a new friend and fellow crossword-puzzle fancier." She trusted that Edmund had been discreet about her circumstances. She had a feeling he might have mentioned something to them about unfortunate circumstances in general. If they knew him well, they probably knew this wasn't the first time he had taken some waif or lost soul under his wing.

They were kind and attentive to her and filled her in when the conversation drifted to "old times" with Edmund. They were

71

socially astute. Although Samantha had a sense they were quite wealthy (arriving in a private plane was her first clue), they never talked of a rich and famous lifestyle—yachting around the islands of the Caribbean, vacationing in the south of France, ski trips to Switzerland or Aspen, or the trips to Monte Carlo she had read about in books. Actually, she doubted they were interested in those things. Another clue that they might be very wealthy was the expensive jewelry the women were wearing. It wasn't that they had a gaudy display—no garish ring on each finger or series of heavy gold bracelets to mid-arm. They seemed to have simple but eclectic tastes. The older woman was wearing a necklace that consisted of a basic gold chain of substantial strength to accommodate a crescent-shaped gold pendant. Sparkling in the light of the chandeliers were three beautifully cut diamonds resting within its curve.

Stunning! Samantha wasn't much interested in jewelry, but this elegant piece could not be ignored. This provoked some self-analysis: was she inadvertently using this display to evaluate this woman? What signals did people send by the way they dressed and talked? She decided that if she got married, she would just want a plain gold ring—no diamond engagement ring. She didn't want anyone sizing up her husband by the size of the diamond she was wearing. And, she knew from her limited experience people did that. That was just personal. Now that her financial situation had changed, she was overly sensitive about flaunting wealth and attracting attention. Actually, she didn't think any more or less of the lady because of the diamond necklace.

Soon, they were ushered toward a round table, the right size for eight, and sat as Edmund directed. This intimate circular format suited Samantha quite well, as everyone could connect with the conversation and it excused Samantha from having to talk to the person next to her. She was content to listen and answer with her usual rhetoric reserved for strangers. Her lack of participation wasn't noticeable in this arrangement. The conversation focused on some charity work that interested them. To acknowledge Samantha's presence and keep her interested,

Edmund intermittently addressed her with brief explanations and comments.

Eventually, the conversation turned to their grandchildren, and they exchanged pictures—cute little sweeties! Children and grandchildren seemed to be irresistible topics. Samantha politely examined each picture as it was passed to her with comments like, "So cute!" She had her own pictures, those of her precious nieces, which she treasured in her heart and couldn't share. Edmund glanced her way with a questioning look to see how she was handling this. As they made eye contact, she responded with a slight smile and nod, giving him an I'm-okay-with-this look. She was able to manage the situation graciously with pleasant and less painful memories.

She felt flattered that Edmund had included her in his intimate party with such personal friends. As the gathering ended, Edmund thanked her for coming. She responded by letting him know how honored she was that he had invited her. He informed her he would be leaving early in the morning with his friends. She reiterated her plans to stay an extra day then went on to explain her extended plans to go to Old Mission Peninsula, the Leelanau Peninsula, visit a lighthouse or two, and perhaps stay at a bed-and-breakfast winery. After that, she was planning to drive to Petoskey, Traverse City, then along Lake Michigan, and arrive home late Monday or Tuesday.

He seemed almost relieved to hear her plans. "I'm very pleased to hear it—very good plan—excellent! Excellent! You will enjoy that very much."

She was a little surprised at his tone, but she didn't think much more about it. They exchanged a few pleasantries about how much they had enjoyed their time together and hoped they would meet again. She shook hands with the other guests and made her parting remarks, expressing her delight in meeting them.

❧CHAPTER 11

"Know your enemy and know yourself
and you can fight a thousand battles without disaster."

Sun Tzu: *The Art of War—c. 512 B.C.*

When Samantha returned home Tuesday morning, she went to her computer and Googled "Edmund Paul Jones." Several sites came up. Following the links, she discovered that all he had said was true. His biography was indeed exceptional. He had been modest in regard to his accomplishments; they were extensive. She found the estimate of his net worth staggering; it made her fortune seem like a pittance. He was much-admired in the business world and a revered philanthropist. The picture that accompanied the text showed a man probably in his early sixties; however, it was unmistakably the same face that had become familiar to her.

Restless from the long early-morning drive, she decided to go for a walk. She noticed two cars parked some distance apart across the street; they had not been there earlier when she'd pulled into the garage. One was the same car with the woman she'd noticed several days before she'd left. The other was a plain black SUV with heavily tinted windows. Just as she opened the front door, her cell phone rang. Startled by the unfamiliar sound, she tried to ascertain the source. Locating the phone, she hesitantly spoke into it. "Hello?"

"Samantha?" a man questioned in a firm voice.

"Yes."

"This is Edmund. My dear, are you all right?"

Recognizing his voice and noting the concern, she replied nervously and stammered, "I—I—I'm fine, I'm okay."

"I know you're about to leave the house. Don't go out, and don't say anything!" he said in a steady voice.

She was distressed by his urgent tone and the nature of his instructions; her heart started beating fast.

"You may be in danger," he said urgently. "It's a long story, and I'll explain later. For now, I assure you that this is a serious matter, and I've taken steps for your safety. I hope you will trust me."

"I—I—I do . . . I will," she responded, confused.

"Your house is probably bugged, so don't say anything," he instructed emphatically. "Go outside onto the back patio. Close the door behind you."

She wondered, *How did he know about the back patio and the door?* With much agitation and a thousand questions running through her mind, she took a deep breath and tried to composed herself. She responded quietly, "Okay." Then she did as he had instructed.

Edmund persisted, "There's a man in a black SUV across the street. He will drive into your driveway, get out, and come to your door—the garage entrance. Let him in. He's a bodyguard. I sent him."

Alarmed, she asked, "What's wrong?"

"Everything will be all right. Don't worry! You will be safe with him," he assured her. "He will tell you his name is Ben, an old family friend who has come for a visit. Do what he says! He will explain."

She went back into the house, through the kitchen, and into the garage. As they were speaking, she saw the black SUV drive up close to the garage. The man Edmund had described got out. "Is he coming to the door? Just say yes or no—no more," he instructed.

"Yes," she replied as steadily as she could manage.

"Very good, very good. I'll talk to you again very soon. Goodbye for now, my dear, and don't worry. You're in good hands."

Bewildered, she said with a rote response, "Okay, goodbye."

She watched the athletic-looking man in his mid-thirties, a tad more than six feet tall and with short, neatly cut brown hair, walk up the driveway. The bell rang. In spite of expecting him, the shrill sound caused her to jump. She hesitated a moment, then opened the door.

Succinctly, he said in a normal voice, "Hello, Samantha. I'm Ben, a friend of your brother's. We talked earlier."

Continuing the deception, she responded in a low voice, "Oh, yes. Come in. I'm glad to see you."

They walked into the kitchen, where he handed her a note that read: "House and cars probably bugged—can't talk openly. Be careful—guard conversation."

Exhibiting an astonished look but remaining silent, she nodded and continued reading: "You're in danger from the person you know as Joe Morton." Now, the blood drained from her face, and she went limp. He supported her, opened the sliding glass door, and helped her to the chaise lounge on the patio, then closed the glass door.

"I'm sorry. I shouldn't have been so blunt," he whispered with embarrassment. "Let me get you something."

"Oh, I'll be all right," she said weakly. She was shocked and embarrassed for being so frail. There were questions spinning in the back of her mind, but she felt so groggy and sick that she couldn't formulate any. Recovering a bit, she explained in a low voice, "Being alone, I have a bad habit of going without eating for long periods. I'm usually not this much trouble."

"It's no trouble—no trouble at all—it's my fault," he apologized profusely. "Let me fix you some food, and I'll explain when you feel up to it."

While they were recovering from their uneasiness and apologizing, he helped her into the house and into a chair in the kitchen. He gave her a paper with instruction for a conversation between them designed to mislead the listeners and explain his presence at the house. They engaged in this dialogue intermittently for about 25 minutes. In the meantime, he rummaged around the refrigerator and cupboards and found ingredients to make a tuna sandwich, then poured chocolate soy milk into a glass. He heated water, found some English Breakfast Tea, and made a strong brew. She ate slowly. Gradually, the food and the caffeine-laden tea started to take effect; the foggy, queasy feeling lifted, and color came into her face.

"You're looking better," he whispered with relief. "How do you feel?"

"I'm feeling much better, thank you. Thank you very much," she responded in barely a whisper, but with a revived, alert expression.

He wrote, "I'll be taking you to Mr. Jones' estate for safety."

They continued their misleading conversation while Samantha organized some things for their departure.

He handed her a piece of paper and started carefully picking up things and looking around the house. "I'm looking for bugs. I'll leave them. Tell you more later. Can you sell that truck in the garage? Do you know where the title is?"

She didn't understand but felt he must have had his reasons for asking. She was in no position to question him, and actually, it was fine with her. She nodded and found the necessary paper. They announced that they were going out to dinner. He wrote, "Truck bugged. Don't talk."

He gathered all the papers with their writing, put them in the fireplace, and set the little heap on fire—they went up in flames quickly. They found a dealership and sold the truck. They called a taxi and proceeded to the post office. Ben had the taxi wait while they collected Samantha's mail that had been held and left a forwarding address for a post office box. When they returned, they noticed the car across the street was gone. With the garage door opener from the truck, Ben opened the door, drove the SUV into the garage, and quickly closed the door. Once inside the house, Ben said with a mischievous smile and in a normal voice, "Too bad the truck broke down." Ben had seemed all-business and seriousness, so this impish little grin surprised Samantha. Yet, this tiny speck of humor in this tense situation was a welcomed relief.

She went with the scenario by saying, "Lucky we could find a garage nearby. I hope it doesn't take too long to fix."

He looked at her approvingly and nodded.

The original car was not across the street when they arrived; however, another car pulled up and parked a half-block away shortly after they returned. "They've come back. Must have heard us," he whispered.

She packed her computer, clothes, files, and anything else she thought she might need to function away from this place for an extended period. *I guess the lawn service people will keep doing their thing,* she thought.

They loaded the rear space of the SUV with Samantha's necessities, which were minimal. There was room to spare. Samantha drew the curtains, locked the house, and they left.

Ben headed for Detroit—the opposite direction from their destination. Samantha started to ask questions, stammering, "Who—what—ah . . . ?"

He interrupted, "Well, for starters, my name isn't Ben—it's Steve. You can drop the Ben and forget it forever, I hope. Mr. Jones called me when he became suspicious of Joe and asked me to check out the situation. Joe Morton is an alias of Bruce Albert Doyle, from a family of con artists. Bruce has been in prison for some minor stuff but suspected of some serious crimes, including one murder. The police haven't been able to close the case on him."

Things started to click with Samantha. "Interesting initials—B.A.D. I know someone else with that last name and those initials: Betty Ann Doyle."

"Interesting!" He spoke with slightly raised eyebrows. "That's his sister. She does the setup—finds out personal things about the victim—then he moves in."

"Victim? Is that me?

"I'm afraid so."

"Sounds awful! I think she was watching my house and following me."

"Yep, that sounds about right. I think the Doyles are working on a plan B in your case. I take it, from Mr. Jones, Bruce's romancing efforts weren't progressing well with you. Apparently, you aren't as naïve and vulnerable as some women. You'd be surprised how easily he has charmed a series of women—usually rich widows a little older than he is. Mr. Jones didn't want you to be alone—those people having malicious designs on you. So, he sent me to take you to his estate. You'll be safe there. We don't want them to trace you—you have something they want badly. Mr. Jones didn't say."

"That's incredible!"

"They can be persistent."

"What can I do?"

"They haven't broken the law—no grounds for an arrest."

"Oh, thank heavens for Mr. Jones! How did he know?"

"He's pretty perceptive. There was something about Joe that caused him to be suspicious. He asked the hotel manager to keep an eye on him and alerted some of the waiters. When you went to the ladies' room, you left your small purse on the table. Joe took a key out and made an impression in some clay or waxy substance. Mr. Jones reported it to me, and I called a detective I know up there. Mr. Jones gave us a detailed description of Joe. We knew the ferry he'd be on. The detective waited for him, saw him get into his car, followed him, checked the license plate, etc. Then we made an interesting discovery—Joe was Bruce Doyle. The detective watched for you when you left the ferry the next day, and we knew no one was following you. Since your plans were random and the Doyles didn't know them, they would most likely be waiting for you when you got home. Sure enough, there they were!"

Samantha thought, *They must be after the money! Who would've thought? How did they know? I've been so careful—well, I thought so. Edmund is definitely a trustworthy friend. He didn't reveal that I'm worth a lot of money, even to his chief security officer. I can't believe he went to so much trouble for me! He's certainly not after my money. Money changes things in ways I would never have expected.* She started to cry.

Perplexed and apologetic, Steve started in a concerned voice, "I'm very sorry. I thought you were better and up to this . . . ."

"No, no, no, it's fine," Samantha interrupted, recovering a bit. "I'm just overwhelmed and touched by Mr. Jones' kindness and concern for me." With the stress from the events of the day, crying *was* an emotional release. Nevertheless, she didn't want to mention that to Steve. He seemed worried enough about her emotional stability.

"That's the sort of person he is. He's been more than a good employer. I try to do my best for him."

"You must be very good at what you do. Mr. Jones is a kind man, but I have a feeling he doesn't suffer fools or incompetence."

He flashed her a slightly modest, knowing smile.

They continued driving toward Detroit, and Steve remarked that they *were* being followed. As they entered the city, Steve pulled into a large parking ramp—just to the point where the car didn't set off the ticket dispenser. They watched the car following them pass by and turn the corner. Steve backed out quickly, went two blocks, turned left, then right, and drove through the city streets until he found an entrance ramp to the expressway going north. He drove north for half an hour and seemed satisfied the car was no longer following them. He took an exit and headed west on a two-lane highway. They traveled about forty minutes, and as he was going down a hill, he turned onto a dirt road and slowly drove down it, constantly checking his rearview mirror. He turned and slowly returned to the same highway, then turned back the way they had come. Totally satisfied they were no longer being followed, he took the next two-lane highway north and then took a highway heading west. They reached Lake Michigan, turned north, and followed the magical miles of M22. The winding, hilly road was streaked with shady patterns as the sun spilled through the trees; occasionally, to their left, glimpses of Lake Michigan flashed brilliantly in the light of the late-afternoon sun.

They entered a small village and stopped at a local restaurant on the main street. "Sorry I haven't fed you sooner, but I felt it was best we keep going. Hope you aren't too weak from hunger. Don't faint on me," he teased.

"I'll try not to. I *am* terribly hungry."

It wasn't long before they were eating heaps of the home-style food the sign advertised.

"We'll be there soon," he assured her as they exited the restaurant.

Eventually, they came to a fork in the road; the main road veered to the right, a paved back road to the left. They took the northwest road, which had no yellow or white lines of pavement markings and wound through a forest of pine trees. They traveled several miles and came to an area where the left side of road was cleared of trees and brush to a high, chain-link fence. "That's the start of Mr. Jones' property," Steve commented. "There're about forty acres on the west side of the road. The house overlooks a very nice stretch of beach and Lake Michigan."

Finally, they turned into a driveway. About 60 or 70 yards from the road was a massive iron gate attached to two huge, concrete pillars with some attempt at an architectural design. Design seemed to have given way to function. In keeping with the previous landscape, all the trees and brush had been cleared along the driveway up to the gate. It wasn't a grand entrance or approach—no flowers, no shrubs, no lush grass or manicured lawn, just scrubby beach grass.

"There's a security camera on the gate and a beam across the driveway. That'll let the gate guard know we're approaching."

Amazed and taking it all in, Samantha sat quietly and said nothing.

A large man came out and recognized Steve. They exchanged a few good-natured remarks, and the man returned to the gatehouse. Shortly, mechanical devices started moving the heavy iron gates, slowly separating them in the middle. Steve waved his thanks as they passed through. They drove on a narrow road winding through tall pine trees, then came to a wider road lined with maples whose canopy obscured the last of the daylight.

No ordinary drive up to a house, thought Samantha as the driveway emerged from the leafy tunnel and continued through an abundance of flowers and other plantings tastefully decorating an expansive, manicured lawn, which was in proportion to a massive house now engulfed by the rays of the setting sun.

"This is Lake House, Mr. Jones' home."

❖·CHAPTER 12

Break, break, break
On the cold gray stones, O Sea!
And I would that my tongue could utter
The thoughts that arise in me.

Alfred, Lord Tennyson (1809-1892)

After a long, restless night with intermittent, troubled sleep, Samantha heard the first chirp of the early bird just before dawn. Staring at the fabric in the ceiling of the huge canopy bed, she listened to the sounds around her—the strange sounds of a different house, the sounds outside the French doors, and the sounds in the trees just outside the window. As the sun rose, light started brightening the window shades. The early bird was joined by the chorus, and the antiphonal calling of the various species began. Before long, she got out of bed, pulled up the shades that covered the tall windows, and moved toward the French doors leading out onto a narrow balcony. From her vantage, her gaze quickly moved across the green lawn and the beach following the early-morning colors of water and sky as they met at the horizon.

She inhaled the clean air—especially clear after the rain during the night. It was a beautiful day, and if the enthusiastic sound of those feathery, flighty friends ushering in a fresh start was a prelude to the rest of the day, it should be a better one. However, due to the stress of recent events and time on her hands in a strange place, the coping skills she had been building were slowly being displaced with restless disorientation. Where was the library? Where were the books she trusted to take her out of herself? Where could she go for her daily walk and feel safe?

It was midsummer, and daylight came early; she saw no one. She wandered out onto the lawn and followed a path to the wind-worn but sturdy switch-back stairs that led to the beach. Along the side of the steps, rooted in the sand, were rugged, gnarled, undernourished shrubs scattered sparsely among the abundant swatches of yellow-green beach grass. The lake was unusually still; there was only a hint of a breeze. Small waves were washing gently onto the sand, leaving their wet curves in artistic patterns at the water's edge. Soon the wind strengthened, and dark clouds started to form in the distance, casting inky shadows miles wide near the horizon. Closer, the sun pierced the billowing grey-white clouds, creating bright turquoise-green expanses of water.

She sat on the cool sand with a massive piece of driftwood at her back. As she stared over the water, the memories of that horrible day were pressing hard against the gates of her mind. She struggled to keep them securely locked away. The optimistic mood with which she'd started the day began to give way. If only she could get up and move to another place . . . but she was situated in the sand like one of the massive rocks the waves were starting to pound. If she could see another person, if she could talk to Edmund, especially Edmund, or even a maid, the gardener, a stranger on the beach—anyone—she could break this trance. No one was in sight on the miles of empty, wide beach. She couldn't take her eyes off the horizon; the mounting whitecaps were hypnotizing.

The scene in her mind was changing to the one on that frightful day when she'd seen the fury of the lake—white waves, larger ones rolling on top of smaller ones, gathering together, breaking into geyser-like sprays, creating a towering aura that engulfed the lighthouse at the end of the pier. The monstrous waves were rolling down the channel, spraying and swallowing whatever was in their path and obliterating the current of the river that flowed out to the lake.

Her defenses gave way, and like a great flood the memories flowed into every corner of her mind. In every nerve and muscle of her body, she felt the sensation of that horrible day when she'd become aware that her family was missing. She relived the agony of waiting. Waiting was the worst. Paralyzing! Sickening! Agonizing! Nothing could be accomplished. Her family was missing; the coast guard was searching. The long drive in the storm—the cold, dimly lit, lonely motel—trying to eat breakfast, trying to remain optimistic. Lunchtime had come and gone with no word. Afternoon had crawled by—no word. The sun had set—still no word.

Now, sitting on the beach, she was shaking, partly from the cold front that was moving in and partly from the overpowering memory, and she broke down in a flood of tears. This broke the trance. She came back to herself in the present time and place, and like all floods, the memories subsided. She pushed out the remnants and bits of debris and barred the gates again.

By then, the waves were smashing hard upon the rocks, and thunder was rumbling in the distance. The mood of the lake had changed as rapidly as hers that morning. She sought the safety of the house.

Wandering through the enormous house, searching for some comfortable spot, emotionally and physically, she found a library—a huge library! The floor-to-ceiling bookshelves of cherry wood lining the long south wall were filled with books— no nick-knacks, no plants, no decorative items of any kind—just books. It was the same as at her parent's house, except on a grand scale. The ceilings were high, very high. There was a ladder that could be moved along a track to access the higher shelves. The room was tastefully decorated in a traditional style. There were sofas, chairs, and a massive table in the middle of the room that could accommodate as many books as a person needed to spread out for a research project or, she imagined, a business meeting.

On the north wall were two narrow alcoves containing desks equipped with computers and related paraphernalia. Perfectly placed portraits, almost life-sized, occupied most of the available walls space; they were like those she had seen in English movies set in ancestral homes or museums. The background of each picture was particularly interesting, as it depicted, she presumed, small scenes highlighting the life of the individual standing or sitting in the foreground. On the west end, overlooking the lake, were tall window sections forming a curve that protruded from the room and provided a well-lighted reading area. The view was lovely: blooming bushes, colorful flowers, a green lawn now with sparkling raindrops reflecting the sunlight emerging from the dissipating storm clouds and, beyond that, the spectacle of Lake Michigan. In spite of its grand scale, Samantha felt something familiar and soothing about this room. She knew how to lose the pains of the here and now among the books.

Perusing the books on the shelves, she found a series of book-like containers. She removed the first one and settled into a comfortable upright upholstered chair in the reading area of the high west windows. The storm had subsided, and it was bright, warm and cheery there. She opened the box and found several journals stored there for preservation. She felt she should be handling them with white cotton gloves. She cautiously opened one and found it difficult to read. Some of the writing was smudged, and some parts looked as if they had been written with berry juice and were faded; also, the writing was in an old English style.

Upon further investigation, she discovered that the books next to the boxes were printed copies of the journals—someone had translated the old English into 21st century American English. Taking care, she placed the original journals in the box precisely as she had found them and repositioned the little safe on the shelf. Returning to her cozy spot, she started reading the printed copies. The preface told of the life and times of the English Jones family, in particular, Will Jones, who left home in 1631 at the age of seventeen.

Samantha gathered from her reading that the Jones family had a long-established ancestral home in England. Will was the youngest son in the family, and his four older brothers were quite hardy and in excellent health. According to English law, the oldest son inherited the entire estate to keep the wealth and land intact. His siblings hoped he would be benevolent. This seemed like a dreary prospect to young Will. The political turmoil was heating up, and the notion of going into the family business seemed a bit daunting and risky to a shy, peaceful boy just turning seventeen. In spite of parental protesting, he set off, seeking adventure, he crossed the Atlantic.

Curious about what was happening in England around 1631, Samantha searched the shelves for a history timeline; she found one that suited her. She wanted to back up a bit in history to set the scene for the family circumstance. The Jones family had been of the noble class and members of Parliament for as long as it had existed. Besides the running of the estate, government seemed to be the family business.

Since the death of Queen Elizabeth I (the clever daughter of Henry VIII) in 1603 was a turning point in English history and was shortly before Will made his way to the "New World," she decided to start her investigation at that point. This was the end of the age of the Tudors—Henry and Elizabeth had reigned most of the 1500s. These monarchs were extremely careful to cover their absolute power with constitutional legality; due to their powers of persuasion, they were able to manipulate members of Parliament into rubber-stamping what they wanted, thus making it official. For the most part, the people just wanted security. In the journal, Will noted that his grandfather was under the thumb of the king and his family was disgusted with the king's control.

Will rather nostalgically wrote about the conversations at the dinner table while he was growing up. Since there were only boys in his family and his mother was quite liberated, politics was not a forbidden subject. In fact, the boys' tutor lived with the family and ate his meals with them. After all, the boys were being prepared for some role in government.

With the end of the Tudors, Elizabeth's distant cousin from Scotland, James Stuart (son of the unfortunate Mary Queen of Scots), became the king—James I of England[1]. He had good intentions and was very well-educated—he had a plethora of theories. However, he did not bother to read the laws of England; nor did he study the traditions and nature of the English people. Thus, his methods were useless. Also, being a poor judge of character, he surrounded himself with incompetent fools. Morals were not their strong points, either. One of James' theories was the "divine right of kings,[2]" which he took to the extreme.

It seems James forgot to check his actions with the source of his divine right, Samantha thought. *It looks like he was setting the stage for the exodus to the New World.*

Will was born in 1614, in the midst of James' reign, and was well aware of European history, what was making history in England, and how it was affecting his family. His father and uncles were dealing with James' failing administration.

She read on in the history books and found that one of the first things James did was set up a policy of opposition to the Puritans[3]. He suspected them of wanting a democratic church government like the Presbyterian Church in Scotland,[4] which had already caused him trouble. James wanted control of the state church in order to maintain an absolute monarchy. He swore he would make the Puritans conform or "harry them out of the land."

In spite of oppression in England, some of Will's ancestors maintained their Catholic heritage. They had a chapel, as was common in the manor house of an estate, and unnoticed by the

---

[1] James I of England, king 1603-1625.

[2] Divine right of kings: kings receive their authority directly from God; opposing the King was opposing God.

[3] Puritans: Loosely used label affixed to various groups of Protestants who wanted a simple church service, adhere to Scripture, and move away from the "High Church" Anglicans who maintained Catholic rituals. Although similar in this respect, each group had its own opinion on doctrine and church government.

government, held worship services there. Catholicism had been outlawed during the reign of Henry VIII, when the pope would not annul his marriage so he could marry another woman. Henry solved that by making the Protestant Anglican Church the state church. Catholics were persecuted if they refused to denounce the pope and change to the state religion. Initially, things weren't quite so severe in James' rule; he lifted the fine on those who didn't attend the Anglican Church. However, attendance dropped so much that he reinstated it. An angry group of Catholics concocted the famous "Gunpowder Plot" in November 1605 to blow up the Parliament buildings. It was unsuccessful but resulted in a fear and hatred of Catholicism. (Later, in Will's time, all of his family had converted to the Anglican Church.)

James persisted in ignoring English sentiment, and from 1619 to 1623 he tried to arrange a marriage between his son Charles and the daughter of the King of Spain. The thought of a Spanish Catholic Queen did not go over well with the English people. They protested violently, and Charles came home a bachelor.

*　　*　　*

Suddenly, Samantha realized that she was extremely thirsty and hot. Reluctantly, she abandoned her books to search for a beverage. Recalling a narrow butler's pantry off to the side where she'd entered the library, she walked that way. It was well-stocked with an assortment of snacks and beverages. She found an eight-ounce bottle labeled "Lemonade," found a large glass, filled it with crushed ice from the dispenser, and poured in the pale yellow contents of the bottle.

Fortified, she returned to her reading—back to the unpopular James, failing in both domestic and foreign policy. James being in a vulnerable position, some of the members of Parliament took courage and tried to assert themselves. Having put up with a long subservience to the previous reign of the Tudors, Will's family, and other members, were now appalled by the royal government's extravagance, the incompetence of the king's favorites, and the court's immoral reputation. The opposition was, for the most part, from the Protestant gentry. Some held borough seats representing city merchants. When they expressed their concerns, James showed no tact. He lectured them on the subject of divine right.

James' insistence on the "divine right of kings" seemed like a dangerous philosophy for him, mused Samantha. *It seems if God put the king in place, then only death could remove him—natural or otherwise. James must have realized that there were enough people lurking in the political wings who had no qualms about breaking the fifth Commandment[5]: "Thou shalt not murder." They were a trifle picky about which laws of God they thought mattered.*

Reading on, she discovered the people were insulted and shocked by the lectures and began a strategy to assert legal power over the king. The king's spending beyond the royal revenue was their best weapon. He indulged his friends with lavish gifts and tolerated wasteful, corrupt ministers. Parliament threatened to withhold consent for more taxes unless he took their grievances seriously. Over and over again, James dismissed the Parliament and never resolved its requests.

James died in 1625, leaving his discredited monarchy to Charles I, who was still not married. The son carried on his father's legacy, especially the theory of divine right. He also continued with the same inept fools and added new favorites. He had an even more zealous opposition to Puritanism. Charles was kind and loyal to his friends, well-mannered and well-educated; however, he apparently inherited his father's lack of perception, wisdom, and statesmanship. In spite of being brought up in England, he made no effort to understand the English people. He had even less understanding of Scotland, which came under his rule.

---

[5] Fifth or Six Commandment: Depends on how a particular denomination numbers the commandments. For Catholics and Lutherans this is the fifth; for other Protestants it is the sixth; also for the Jewish religion it is the sixth. Exodus 20:2-17 and Deuteronomy 5:6-21 provide no guidelines for enumeration.

There wasn't much hope for cooperation between Parliament and Charles. The cunning Duke of Buckingham, perceived as intelligent and well-educated, was the power behind James and Charles until he was assassinated in 1628. No loss there, as the Duke's recklessness had thrown England into a series of useless and humiliating political fiascos, domestic and foreign.

Some people, Samantha thought, *are so smart there's no room for wisdom and common sense. Beware of too smart, unwise people, Samantha! Edmund seemed both smart and wise—that's rare. Maybe wisdom comes with age and experience. I'd like to be wise. I hope I have common sense.*

She read on in the history book. Charles repeated his father's tactics of dismissing one Parliament after another. Desperate to fund his wars, he tried forced loans. In 1628, Charles had no options and reconvened Parliament. Its members took this opportunity; they would cooperate in raising taxes if he would accept their Petition of Rights. They confronted the king with the illegal exercise of absolute power on four important points: martial law, the billeting of soldiers on civilians[6], arbitrary taxation, and arbitrary imprisonment. This petition would eventually become the cornerstones of British freedom. Charles accepted it, got what he wanted, promptly broke the agreement, and didn't call Parliament for eleven years.[7]

It looked as if Will's family business had folded—no Parliament. Also, Charles distorted the law and imposed heavy royal taxes on the property of the gentry and burghers. At this point in the power struggle, young Will didn't see much hope for his future and the future of the people, and so he left England.

Mulling over the character of the kings in light of what she had read, Samantha thought, *Within the court, all had impeccable manners and social graces, but the kings secured loyalty and friendship by bribing them with privileges and extravagant gifts (oblivious to or thoughtless of at whose expense). It appears that no matter when you lived, you don't know who your real friends are if you're rich and powerful. The contrived*

---

[6] Billeting: Forcing civilians to provide room and board for soldiers.

[7] Eleven years: 1629-1640.

politeness was a façade! James and Charles showed their true character in their actions: greed, dishonesty, and disdain for Puritans, Catholics, peasants, and even Parliament. Apparently, they felt they were above any law (including the Ten Commandments or the Golden Rule) and held fast to their "divine right of kings" theory. In other words, the king with his divine right assumption thought he was God's gift to the "little people," sent to them from heaven, and the "little people" thought he was the king from the other place. It seems this theme sure has repeated itself throughout history, just the names and places change. I'm glad our motto is "In God We Trust" and not "In the king We Trust." I can see why some people risk everything to get out from under a seriously flawed regime of the few doling out hardly any, if any, basic rights to the many, looking down on them as somehow inferior and incompetent. Ironically, it says in 1604, James I convened the Hampton Court Conference to authorize the translation of the Holy Bible[8]. If he read it, he certainly didn't take it to heart or skipped over the parts he didn't like. It seems kings, like others, start out with good intentions but are often corrupted by the people surrounding them. You would think the king would set the standard. Moral: choose your friends and colleagues wisely!

Returning to the journal, she discovered that Will joined up with some English fur traders and made his way to Quebec. However, after a treaty returned Quebec to the French in 1632, he left with a small, implausible group of rugged adventurers—two Englishmen, two Frenchman (brothers and army deserters), and a Huron[9] Indian. An unlikely, but genuine, friendship developed amongst the group.

---

[8] Holy Bible: Now known as the *Authorized King James Version*, it first appeared printed, named this way, in 1884. An earlier version called *The Great Bible* was issued during the reign of Henry VIII; however, the Puritans and others detected problems with the translation and the Church pressed for a rewrite. Over a seven-year period, 47 scholars worked on the new translation.

[9] Huron: French name for the Wyandot. The original territory of the Wyandot was in the St. Lawrence Valley in Quebec; however, they fled to Ohio and Michigan after being crushed by the Iroquois. The homeland of the Iroquois was in Ontario, above Lake Erie and Lake Ontario, and in New York State, but war parties went as far west as Michigan. Early on, Indians in the Great Lakes area were divided into two groups based on language and culture—Algonquin and Iroquois. Later smaller groups spun off from the Iroquois—the

They were probably kindred spirits, she thought, *since they left their families, heritage, and traditions in quest of a new experience and a better, mostly peaceful life.* Totally immersed in the 17th century and the saga of Will Jones and his companions, Samantha lost track of time. As she came to herself, she realized she was having difficulty seeing the words on the pages. The light coming through the west windows was waning; dark clouds were gathering again, obscuring the late-afternoon sun; the day had passed away. Not having eaten all day, she was now aware of hunger pangs.

A man entered the library as she was returning the books to the shelves. "Good evening," he greeted her as he walked over to shake her hand. "I'm Neville Ryan, the General Manager of Mr. Jones' estate. Welcome to Lake House. I'm sorry I left you unattended today. A minor emergency required that I leave early this morning. I've just returned and set out to find you. One of the security guards said he saw you in here most of the day. As I asked, he has been keeping an eye on you. He said you looked content and absorbed in your reading, so he left you in peace. Did you find my note on the refrigerator?"

"No, I haven't thought about eating all day."

"You must be famished. Since Mr. Jones has been away, most of the staff have taken the opportunity to take some of their vacation—including the cook and her helpers. I've come to remedy that and invite you to have dinner with my wife, daughter, and me at our cottage. We can leave immediately."

"Thank you very much. I'd like to take a quick trip to my room. I need a couple of minutes to regroup. I'll be right back. How long will it take to get there?"

"About two minutes," he responded with a reserved smile. "It's on the grounds of the estate, just down the path to the north. I'll wait here for you. This evening, I'll fill you in on news of Mr. Jones and try to answer any questions you may have."

Huron, Seneca, Mohawks; the subgroups of the Algonquin are the Ottawa, Chippewa, Menominee, Pottawatomic.

❧·CHAPTER 13

In cases of defense 'tis best to weigh
The enemy more mighty than he seems.

William Shakespeare: *Henry V*

When she returned to her room, she noticed that the bed had been made neatly; she had hastily thrown the spread over it when she'd left in the morning. The wet towels were gone, and the dirty clothes she had left in a pile on the closet floor had been washed, neatly folded, and placed on the dresser. *Oh, dear, what little genie came and did all this?* she thought. *I will at least have to make my bed neatly every morning. I don't want to cause extra work.* She quickly completed some minor ablutions, changed into something more presentable for the dinner, and returned to the library.

The air was warm and still. It seemed more like nine or ten in the evening than 6:30 as dense dark clouds continued to form over the horizon. They entered a path lined by lights, which led through a mixture of deciduous and evergreen trees to a well-lighted, charming two-story cottage. Upon entering the foyer, her eyes moved to an appealing great room with a large, natural stone fireplace. The raised hearth provided ample space for sitting; she could imagine people seated on the soft hearth cushions, roasting marshmallows or hot dogs or popping corn. Thick logs of real wood were laid strategically with the proper kindling below so that a roaring fire could appear instantly if desired. It was an inviting room. She wished the weather were cool so they might be enticed to light the fire, but alas, it was July.

Her gaze drifted across the room to a modern, open, well-equipped kitchen. The table that divided the kitchen from the great room was attractively set for four. A woman in her late forties hastily emerged from the kitchen, welcomed her, and introduced herself as Mary, Neville's wife. Mary had an attractive, ready smile, bright blue eyes, and short, well cut-hair with natural streaks of a mixture of blonde and white strands. She looked athletic; maybe she played tennis or something like that.

Suddenly, a petite (and soon to be discovered as precocious) Asian girl of about six or seven bounced into the room and introduced herself. "I'm Abby Gail Ryan. Everyone calls me just Abby," she said with a huge smile.

Abby's smile was contagious, and Samantha responded with her own huge smile. "Well, how do you do? I'm Samantha, and I'm very pleased to meet you."

"Me, too, Samantha," Abby responded.

At dinner, Samantha ate as slowly and as politely as she could, restraining herself from eating like a famished farmhand on a lunch break from harvesting. She was anxious to hear of Mr. Jones and had a barrage of questions for Mr. Ryan, but she restrained herself here, too. With Abby and Mary there, it was not the time. It was clear that Abby's parents doted on her, and she was the joy of their life. The conversation centered on the little girl's curiosity. She was full of questions and chatter; surprisingly, these were not directed toward the dinner guest. Her parents had probably instructed her that it was not polite; Samantha was grateful for that. She found the atmosphere and the little girl refreshing, a relief from the events life had been throwing at her.

A reprieve, she thought.

It was quite late; Abby was allowed to stay up way beyond her bedtime, as it was summer and they had a "special guest." Samantha was honored to be considered a "special guest." In fact, it was way past everyone's bedtime. Samantha, satisfied from a good meal and feeling comfortable and safe with people she felt she could trust, was relaxed and sleepy. She thanked her hosts profusely for their hospitality and with all sincerity complimented them on their delightful home and family.

Mr. Ryan walked her back to the main house. On the way, they passed a security guard, one she had not seen before, making his rounds. He and Mr. Ryan exchanged the pleasantries of long-time acquaintances.

Then the guard addressed her. "Good evening, Miss Schwerin. I hope all is well." He even pronounced her name correctly.

"Very well, thank you," she responded, being polite and stretching the truth a bit. Actually, things *were* better and were "very well" at the moment.

Mr. Ryan took this opportunity to explain to her, "There is an extensive security system throughout the grounds, with guards on duty 24/7. I know Steve has explained some of this to you and will give you additional information later. The guards wear khaki pants and jackets. Their shirts and sweaters are light blue. There are a couple of women security guards. Most of the guards carry concealed weapons."

"Oh, dear," she commented.

"Unfortunately, it's necessary these days," he lamented. "You should know that besides protecting Mr. Jones' property, there's a business here—in the lower level of the main house. It requires security. You may have noticed the special windows in that area."

She hadn't.

"You can see out but not in, no matter what time of day or night. So, note that if you are on the lakeside lawn, people may be watching you. They can only see to the end of the lawn. They're too low to see the stairs or the beach."

"Well, that's definitely good to know," she said, a bit surprised.

Unresponsive to her comment, he carried on methodically, "You may see some young men coming into the house at the south entrance and taking the stairs to the lower level. They work there. They wear white shirts and black pants, and sometimes black sweaters. They don't come into the other part of the house. You may have noticed them."

She hadn't.

"I'll introduce you to or make you aware of all the people who are employed here, so you, like everyone else, can be aware of any strangers. I'll also show you how to alert security. The maintenance staff wear navy blue pants or jeans and medium-blue shirts, jackets, and sweaters. The housekeeping staff wear navy pants and light yellow shirts."

Thank heavens I don't look good in navy, Samantha thought. *He must think I'm going to be here quite awhile.*

Neville went on. "The dress code helps with the security and organization. Don't worry, we have never had any serious problems. I should also tell you that there are security cameras located throughout the grounds and around the outside of the house, as well as some places in the house, mostly the halls. You can see them if you look carefully. Only one security guard at a time monitors these, so you're not on general display."

By now, they were at the front door; he slid a card through an entry box and the door opened. "The doors are locked after dark and opened again at dawn. You can always get out but not in. I'll get you an entry card tomorrow. A security guard can always let you in. Here is the call box by the door. Regularly, a memo is sent out, notifying staff of guests and new employees. All staff carry identity cards. Guests do not, as security is aware of all guests."

"Did you send out a memo about me?"

"Yes, Mr. Jones told me to report that you were in trouble, through no fault of your own, and that we are to take care of you and keep you safe. Steve probably has more details. We operate on a need-to-know basis. Mr. Jones is strict about confidentiality. Well, I'll give you a tour tomorrow and give you the additional information *you* need to know. As Steve told you, Mr. Jones was called away on pressing business and is still in Davos, Switzerland. It's consuming his time, and with the time difference it's difficult to talk to him in person. We keep in touch through his staff and by e-mail. He should be returning in a few days. I know you're anxious for details from him, but we'll do our best until he gets back. Try to get some rest. I'll see you at ten tomorrow morning, if that's agreeable with you."

"That's fine. Thank you again. I really do appreciate everything all of you are doing. Good night."

"Eat some breakfast! The kitchen is through those doors. Just help yourself to whatever you want. We can't have you getting sick on us!" he commanded.

"Yes, sir," she said with a friendly smile.

*   *   *

After no sleep the previous night and a long day, and in a calmer, more secure mood, she fell asleep immediately. She woke suddenly the next morning shortly after nine to what she thought was a banging door. She hadn't set an alarm, as she didn't have a habit of sleeping late. Not wanting to be late for her appointment with Mr. Ryan, she jumped out of bed, showered, and dressed hastily. Nevertheless, she did take time to make her bed neatly and tidy up her things; then she made her way to the kitchen. She thought Mr. Ryan might ask her if she had eaten; she didn't want to disappoint him.

She entered the kitchen. It was like no kitchen she had ever been in before; it was a large, commercial kitchen like one might find in a five-star restaurant. It was spotless with white tiled walls—tile from floor to ceiling. The terracotta tiled floor had a drain in the middle. The rest was stainless steel: huge box-style refrigerators and freezers, gleaming counters, work tables with drawers and shelves underneath where pots and pans rested. There was an area marked "BAKING PREP" with large bins on rollers marked flour, sugar, oatmeal, etc., and on a rack above the counter large containers of spices (not the little two-ounce bottles she had above her stove).

I just want an uncomplicated breakfast, she thought. *Where do I start?* She started on a systematic tour of the kitchen, opening and closing stainless steel doors. She found a refrigerator with covered pitchers of milk labeled skim, 2%, whole, and buttermilk; next to the milk was a large bowl of assorted summer fruits. *Good start.* She selected a pitcher of milk and some fruit and set them on the counter.

Moving on, she found a pantry; it was more like a small room. There were two aisles and three rows of wire shelving—one along each wall and one down the middle. Like the freezers and refrigerators, it was about 80% empty, but there were boxes of dry cereal on the shelf near the door. She picked one she liked, then started searching for a bowl, spoon, and a glass. At the end of the kitchen she found a dishwashing area with carts and a tall rack on wheels—more stainless steel. These contained clean bowls, plates of various sizes, cups, glasses, and cone shaped containers with the utensils.

She placed the items she needed on a tray and made her way to a large, round table to the left of the kitchen door where she had entered. She saw a microwave on a long, narrow table against the wall. *Now, that's something familiar. I can operate that,* she thought. There were mugs, tea bags, and the usual accessories next to it, as well as a small sink where she could get water. Breakfast prep was accomplished. When she finished, she took the dishes and set them on the counter by the dishwasher, along with a couple of other cups with the remnants of coffee in the bottom. *This must be the place.*

She returned to the beverage station and made herself a second cup of tea. Not having been given a location for their meeting, she sat at the table and stayed put. *With all those cameras and security people, he probably knows my whereabouts within a few yards at any given time.*

Sure enough, precisely at ten, he entered the kitchen. "Good morning, Miss Schwerin. Are you significantly fortified for our tour?"

"Good morning, Mr. Ryan," she replied. Then, with a sense of accomplishment, she added, "I am. This is certainly a big kitchen."

"It's like a small hotel. There have been many guests and events here in years past when Mr. Jones and his brother conducted the major part of their business from here. Now, it's done with computers," he explained. "In the early years, when this place was remote and not everyone owned a car, many of the employees lived on the grounds. They needed to be fed. Mr. Jones even entertained a United States President and his wife here many years ago, and, of course, they came with their entourage."

Samantha's eyes widened a bit. "Everything is so empty now."

"Things change, but as usual, by the end of the summer and after the harvest at the farm, the freezers and storage areas will be full," he explained, then gave her the promised entry card and started with a tour of the house. "Mrs. Andersen manages the house and the housekeeping. She's been here for years. She keeps to herself, but she's efficient. Currently, she's away. Her mother passed away—lived about 70 miles from here. Mrs. Andersen needed to arrange the funeral and settle her estate. She should be back in a couple of weeks. In the meantime, some of the Lake House staff and I are trying to fill the gap. Things may not be running quite as smoothly as usual. Mrs. Andersen is hard to replace."

"I don't need much. I'm sure everything will be fine," she responded.

"Are you comfortable in your room? It's not the largest of the guest rooms, but most guests enjoy a view of the lake."

"It's lovely—just perfect. It's plenty big enough for me." She was coming to terms with the lake, and she did indeed enjoy the view.

"If you need anything, just let me know. If you can't get me directly, you can leave a message by house phone or the in-house computer system. I'll show you how."

If that is a "smaller" guest room, she wondered, *what are the other ones like?* Her assigned room was large enough. There was a short passageway within the room to the private bathroom, with ample walk-in closets off the passage—one of equal size on each side.

She'd chosen one; the dimensions overwhelmed her few clothes hanging there. *If this is a guest room,* she wondered, *who would come with that many clothes? Maybe guests came for the whole summer or something like that.* Next came the dressing room and then the private bath—beautifully tiled. There was a modern shower on one side and a spacious whirlpool tub at the end, with windows just above it overlooking the lake. *I'll have to check to see if those windows are the same as the lower level,* she thought with an amused smile unnoticed by her tour guide. They did not tour the other guestrooms. *Well, guestrooms are guestrooms. When you've seen one . . . .*

In spite of the apparent age of the house, it seemed solid and had modern fixtures. The rooms were tastefully decorated. The furniture, paintings, and art objects had an eclectic look, as if they had been collected over a long period of time. One might have expected that in an ancestral home with items collected over generations. All appeared well-cared-for—nothing shabby or run-down. They only toured the common spaces—sitting rooms, dining rooms, sun room, small rooms, large rooms, and on and on. They did not go to the lower level or any rooms on the second or third floor.

"Mr. Jones' suite and those that are maintained for the family are on the second and third floors overlooking the lake and in another part of the house from the guest quarters. In the back of the house on the third floor are the employees' quarters, with a small kitchen and eating space. This was an addition a few years ago." He informed her that all staff, except security, had Sundays off.

"Alice, the cook's assistant, is back from vacation," he continued as they entered the kitchen. He introduced her and instructed her to show Samantha where things were. They could arrange a time later.

He showed her how to use the house phones to contact security or anyone in the house or on the grounds.

This is astonishing, Samantha thought. *What an operation!*

"There is a fence around the grounds. There are various roads within the property leading to maintenance buildings, some staff residences, and guest quarters. There is a paved road just inside the perimeter of the property but not in view of the road on the other side. The road on the outside of the fence, the road you came down that leads to the entrance, dead-ends at a creek that flows into Lake Michigan. It's a private road that leads to a farm house down that way on the east side of the road. If you like walking or jogging, there's plenty of room for that—feel free to do that. Of course, stay inside the fenced area. Steve has an apartment in that building. The security office and my office are in that building over there. I'm taking you to the security office, and Steve will fill you in there."

They entered the building, and Steve greeted them amiably.

"I'll leave her with you, Steve. See you later."

"Thank you," Samantha responded.

"How's it going?" Steve asked when they were alone.

"Okay, thank you."

"Are you ready for some instruction?"

"Yes."

"I'm going to give you a security device, and we'll program it regularly for you. Keep it with you at all times. However, let us know if you go walking on the grounds—call the security office, and the guard will program in new numbers. We can do that automatically from here. My number is also in the device. Feel free to call any time—push this button to talk to me, this one to leave a message. If you go to the beach, stay in front of the property. Stay clear of strangers. Beach-walkers rarely venture this far. If they approach, come up to the house. I know all this sounds like a prison, but we take our responsibility seriously. It won't be for long. I hope you are agreeable with this."

"Oh, yes, of course, thank you," she responded, overwhelmed by the place, the attention, and the concern.

As they made their way back to the main house, he continued with information about the security system and introduced her to several of the guards.

"Would you like to rustle up some lunch together in the main kitchen? If we're lucky, Alice will be there to help. Otherwise, we'll be on our own."

"That would be great. I'm rather hungry and haven't quite figured out the kitchen and the meal situation yet."

"With Juanita gone and a lot of people on vacation, there's been a fend-for-yourself directive," he informed her.

*　*　*

After lunch, they went their separate ways, and Samantha sought out the library. She had been fascinated with the saga of Will Jones and was looking forward to finding out how things had turned out for him. However, at that moment in the quiet of the library, Mr. Ryan and Steve's instructions dominated her thoughts. She was trying to make sense of it all. *Are Joe, or Bruce, and his family that dangerous? Surely, they wouldn't be able to find me here.* Her mind started formulating scenarios. *I suppose if they try to kidnap me from here, they'd have someone who cares about me to threaten. Up to now, who would they have dealt with for the ransom? I wonder what scam they conjured up for me. I wonder if they're still going to try the scam angle or if they think it's going nowhere. Do they know we're on to them? Probably not. That's a little comforting! But, Steve must think they've abandoned plan A and gone to plan B. That's pretty scary! Steve must have found out they're a pretty evil bunch. Now, that is scary!*

Looking back, she thought, *The scam seems to have something to do with Joe's attempts at romance. That wasn't working. Neither was his gaining my confidence. The romantic part had to be obvious. My confidence . . . ? Was he so arrogant to miss that? Maybe so. What an astounding string of lies: pre-med, humanitarian trip to Africa, clinic for the poor in the inner city, taking care of a dying father, dead mother, an inheritance, alone without family. It's almost laughable now. No doubt, he was trying to evoke some empathy with me. But where was he going from there?*

She couldn't clear her mind enough to return to the 17th century. She sat in her favorite chair and stared at the portraits. Joe came again to her mind. *He was certainly a smooth talker—con men are. He was certainly attentive—con men are. He was certainly attractive and charming—con men are. He was definitely interesting. It all sounded so interesting. I suppose he could make things interesting when he could make up anything. He appeared so altruistic—what a fabrication! Well, at least I had my doubts—unconsciously or consciously. I'm not sure. He didn't fool Edmund. It didn't take long for him to size up the situation.*

She consoled herself, *I did have the uneasy feeling. He seemed too self-centered to be so noble. He claimed to have a heart for the poor, but there were glimpses of irritation with people, especially the staff at the hotel. It always seemed he was keeping himself in check somehow—restraining some inner self. Maybe he was working up to my investing in his so-called clinic for the poor. He did mention that "vision" periodically.*

❧·CHAPTER 14

One generation shall make known Your truth, Your faithfulness, to the next.

Isaiah 38:19

And these words, these commands, which I entrust to you this day, shall be in your heart. You shall teach them diligently to the children, and shall talk of them when you sit in your house, and when you walk along the paths, and when you lie down, and when you rise up.

Deuteronomy 6:6-7

She sought a way of disrupting her mental confusion. Sliding the library ladder along the track and ascending it from time to time, she examined the vast, high shelves and familiarized herself with the organization of the books. She wondered who had assembled this substantial library. In spite of the electronic information age, someone felt compelled to maintain a library of books.

Finding the history book and timeline she had consulted the day before, she pulled it off the shelf. Then she found a pencil and a tablet of paper, spread her project out on a section of the massive table, and jotted down the following:

1604   England: James I convened the Hampton Court Conference, which authorized the start of a new version of the Holy Bible (now known as the *Authorized King James Version*).

1606	England. First Charter of Virginia granted by King James I.
1607	Jamestown, Virginia: First permanent English settlement in North America; set up commerce and community under laws of England. Canada: Henry Hudson explored the Hudson River for the Dutch Republic.
1608	Samuel de Champlain[10] started a new trading post where the city of Quebec on the St. Lawrence River is now located. In his search of rivers leading to North America, he found no other large enough to handle the growing fur trade.
1609	Florence, Italy: Galileo constructed a telescope that would magnify by 30 diameters.
1610-1614	Virginia: First war there with the Indians; colonists prevailed.
1610	Étienne Brûlé, 18 years old, was commissioned by Champlain to live with the Indians and learn their language, customs, way of living, and the nature of their land. With a party of Ottawa and Hurons, friendly to the French, he left for their home territory.
1611	Brûlé returned, having done what was asked. Champlain asked him to continue his endeavor to learn more.
1611	England: The *Authorized Version of the Bible*[11] was first published by the Church of England.
1614	Canada: Catholic missionaries started coming to Quebec, set up a mission in what is now Midland, Ontario, and began their work among the receptive Huron Indians in Huronia. This became a missionary and a fur-trading center.

---

[10] Samuel de Champlain (1567-1635). Navigator, cartographer, soldier, explorer; served as governor/administrator of New France.

[11] The phrase *King James Version* did not appear in print until 1884.

I think I'll insert Will's dates into the history, she contemplated. *If I can visualize it, I might get a better understanding of his motives for leaving England. This will give me a better appreciation of the world in which he functioned. It's awesome to think about the advances in technology we take for granted, besides the independence and freedoms we have.* She stopped to review her outline and then returned to her task with renewed interest.

1616	England: William Edmund Jones I was born.
1615	After four years with no communication, Champlain met Brûlé in Huronia. Brûlé displayed a nugget of copper and, among other things, told of a great sea that lay far to the west. He may have been the first white man to have seen Lake Michigan.
1618	Europe: Start of the Thirty Years' War.
1619	Virginia: First representative government established in the New World (quickly lost autonomy and reverted to a crown colony).
1620	Plymouth, England: Funded by the Virginia Company of England, the Pilgrims set sail in the Mayflower for the New World. Blown off their course to Virginia, they landed on Cape Cod. Being out of the Virginia Company's jurisdiction, they set up their own constitutional document, which became the model for the government of the New England colonies and the new nation. The Mayflower Compact: *In the name of God, Amen. We whose names are underwritten, the loyall subjects of our dread soveraigne Lord, King James, by the grace of God, of Great Britaine . . . haveing undertaken, for the glorie of God, and advancemente of the Christian faith, and honour of our king & countrie . . . doe by these presents solemnly & mutualy in the presence of God, and one of another, covenant & combine our selves together into a civill body politick . . . .*[12]

---

[12] Mayflower Compact: The words in this text are not misspelled but a printed rendition of the original 17th-century British English handwritten text.

1622-1632	Virginia: Second war with the Indians; colonist/Indian cooperation deteriorated and hundreds of settlers died—30% killed by Indians, hundreds more due to destroyed livestock, inability to plant, and disease in the crowded forts where they were forced to seek protection.
1623	England: William Shakespeare's play Macbeth plus 16 other plays published in the *First Folis*.
1624	Manhattan Island: Dutch colony founded.
1625	England: Charles I becomes king.
1631	England: Will Jones left for America.
1632	Quebec, Canada: Will arrived; French gained possession from English; Will left with the adventurer friends.
1633	Rome, Italy: Galileo Galilei arrived to defend his position that the earth revolves around the sun.
1634	Michigan[13]: Jean Nicolet of France, guided by the Wyandot, passed through the Straits of Mackinac and followed the southern shoreline of Michigan's Upper Peninsula searching for a passage to the Pacific.
1636	Massachusetts: Harvard College founded; in the 17th century, half of graduates became ministers.
1642-1648	England: Torn by civil war—a struggle to transfer full authority from the king to Parliament.

This straightforward exercise helped Samantha take her mind off the "what if . . . ?" scenarios of her predicament. She picked up her outline, walked over to the shelves, removed a printed copy of Will's journal, and again began to read. According to Will's journal, the group got on quite well. As young men have a habit of doing, giving nicknames that is, Will called the Indian "Tom," and Tom called Will "Big English." Will wrote in his journal, "I nicknamed the Indian Tom, as his five-syllable Huron name is a

---

[13] Michigan: The Algonquin word mishigama or meicegama (French), meaning great water, described Lake Michigan and the Michigan territory long before the white men came. Later, it was part of New France, the Northwest Territory, the Michigan Territory, and then, in 1837, became the State of Michigan. Hereafter, the territory now known as Michigan will be called just "Michigan" to ensure easier reading.

bit cumbersome. Tom nicknamed me Big English. Maybe he is used to more descriptive names with more syllables. I look more like a Swede—big-boned, muscular, and 5 feet 11 inches tall; the others come up to about my lower lip.

"Geoffrey and Clive are the typical English weedy type and never can put much muscle on those scrawny frames, but they do hold their own, no matter what we encounter. Jacque and Pierre are a trifle weedy, too, but quite agile and used to working with their hands. In France, they worked on farms and later had army training. The Huron is quite well-built, strong and agile. He has a full head of black hair and does not sport the usual haircut of his tribe. That probably comes from living at the mission. In spite of his years at the mission, he knows what he is doing when it comes to living off the land and surviving in the wilderness.

"Tom is teaching us a lot, including the Huron language (well, me, anyway) and how to communicate with other Indians—as well as which ones to avoid like the plague. I come from a large estate—a manor house full of servants and farmhands who tend to the horses, animals and crops. I never knew how to work with my hands. I can say for myself, with all honesty, that I am quite strong, good-natured, and willing to learn and do my share. They are at least ten years older than I am. I feel lucky they took me along!

"Growing up, I had good tutors and learned French well; I think my grammar is better than theirs. I keep that to myself. Learning Huron is a struggle under these conditions. I am used to pen and paper—something I can see. Learning Huron is my goal, and I am working hard at it. Tom does not talk much in any language. He knows French from living at the mission, so four of us communicate in French, and I translate for Geoffrey and Clive—their French and Huron are minimal. They do a lot of gesturing. We have developed a sign language amongst us. There are plenty of times we need to be silent and become part of the vegetation, then quietly move to accomplish a task or avoid a situation."

Samantha skimmed through several pages and then read, "Jacque and Tom seem to have emerged as leaders, alternating positions depending upon the circumstances. I step forward when we encounter the English, as I seem to have a way with words. The Frenchmen and the Huron stay mute and pretend to be English. That is a trifle hard for Tom; we jest with him about it. As we leave, he imitates our English mannerisms and says a few English words he knows, with a French accent, no less. Then we all have a good laugh." Samantha paused a moment, trying to visualize Tom, and giggled a trifle herself.

"In spite of being in the army," Will went on in his journal, "the Frenchmen are quite civil and even-tempered. They do not swear or use coarse language. I attribute this to their mother (now dead; father dead, too) rearing good Catholics. She was quite strict about this. The Huron was reared by his mother at the mission and is, by nature, self-controlled. His tribe, including his father, was slaughtered by the Iroquois when he was a young boy. He and his mother escaped and found their way to a Jesuit mission at the head of Georgian Bay. After his mother died, he went exploring with two missionaries. We English gentlemen are just too polite and instilled with manners to be offensive."

Flipping through the pages and arriving at entries from about a year later, Samantha was impressed with Will's entry: "A noble friendship has developed amongst us; all are honorable men. We might have been enemies under other influences. However, we all seek peace in this new land. As we encounter various people, we move by them like a stream, sometimes encountering smooth, peaceful water; sometimes a rocky, rough, irritating environment; sometimes into a stagnant, sickly pool along the edges. The Frenchmen were weary and sick at heart over what they perceived as the senseless bloodshed over this territory. I find no blame in them. It seems there is plenty of room for anyone who wants to venture here. What a greedy, vain bunch of Europeans, fighting over the fur trade. If they were really aware of all the killing for domination of the fur trade for the wealthy of England and France, they might have other thoughts about wearing them.

How many fur coats or wraps, does one need? We all have fur coats—made them ourselves. One is enough. We enjoyed the meat, too . . . ."

Samantha had read somewhere that Henry VIII[14] had owned a particular ensemble of clothing that had cost a year's wages for a peasant, and he had an extensive wardrobe, paid for with taxes. The members of the royal court also had furs and fur trimmings to keep them warm, but these seemed to attract fleas. They wore them, anyway. And the extravagance of the French kings[15], queens and aristocracy at the expense of the peasants is common knowledge.

"I doubt if the army will ever catch up with the Frenchmen," she read, "as one of their army mates, sympathetic to their feelings, agreed to report them drowned and washed away. He would have gone, too, but he had a wife and family back in France and was hoping to see them again someday. Now, with their grizzled beards, they look quite different from the day we met."

Will reported that they subsisted on fish, game, wild rice, berries, occasionally waterfowl eggs, and whatever else the land provided. As the group moved into the northern part of the Lower Peninsula, they had no contact with other Englishmen, no contact with the French this far west, and saw no Indians. No one was very interested in this part of Michigan at that time. Remarkably, they survived the first two relatively mild winters, wildlife (including mosquitoes and biting flies), and swampy terrain without any record of mishap or illness. "The Huron mixed some concoction of bear grease we smear as armor against the biting flies and mosquitoes; nevertheless, somehow those miserable things manage to find an opening to penetrate and attack a patch of skin now and again."

Later, he continued, "The Huron is learning English remarkably well. We have more conversations now in English.

---

[14] King Henry VIII (1491-1547)

[15] Louis XIII (1601-1643) was partial to a beaver hat as a personal adornment in his drafty palace.

His English is better than my struggles with his language. He is exceptionally bright and eager to learn about the rest of the world. He is a valuable asset to the group. In spite of being separated from his tribe at an early age, he was an apt student of his tribe's knowledge of the wilderness. His uncle was what we might call a medicine man. The young boy tagged along, absorbing every instructive utterance his mentor passed on to him. His uncle taught him the laws of the land—the laws of nature—and how to overcome its cruel ways with understanding and wisdom, and to use its benevolence to his advantage. He instructed Tom on how to use all his senses to the fullest. 'You are the most intelligent of all the life in the forest,' he would say. This is a departure from the general Indian superstition that animals are spirits or controlled by spirits and sometimes possess supernatural powers. His time at the mission purged the tribal incantations and remnants of Indian superstitions. He is exceptionally thoughtful and analytical and does not accept things without thinking them out. He would have made a good tribal leader, head man, or whatever they call them . . . ."

Will had been totally ignorant of the vegetation and survival skills and had paid close attention to Tom, who showed them which plants were poisonous. He could then recognize the three-leaf crown of the poison ivy—one side of one leaf had a distinctive jagged edge. He also was alerted to the twisted vines that warned of the poison oak. Tom showed them which berries were edible. Will liked the blueberries, and Tom pointed out that different areas of bushes had different flavors. Blueberries with a cinnamon-like flavor were his favorite, but rarely did they have the luxury of being selective. Tom also showed them how to make a tunic-type buckskin garment with fringes and to color them, making a pattern that blended with the vegetation. Today we would call it camouflage. This was a technique he acquired not from the Indians but from the woodsmen that passed through the mission. Making the buckskin or doeskin soft, pliable, and suitable for sewing into a garment was a long, tedious process. When the snows came, they chose white or silver furs.

In the third-year diary, Samantha found an interesting section that described their dilemma during a severe winter. About the middle of January, Will wrote, "The winter started early and has been, cold, cold, cold, wild and windy with snow, snow, snow. We were half-frozen, half-starved, lumps under a blanket of snow that had covered us during the night. I did not move, as I wanted to avoid encountering a colder spot on the ground. The snow on my fur garments did offer some protection from the wind. The wind had subsided a tad from the day before, but any sharp, icy wind still nipped about the edges. I heard Clive, about three arm-lengths from me, whisper my name and then tell me to look up slowly. Around us stood a group of Indians. They were heavily dressed in furs, and I did not know what tribe they represented. We were outnumbered more than two to one. I saw the Huron get up cautiously and walk over to the leader. They seemed to be able to converse adequately. As they were quite a distance from me and spoke calmly and quietly, I only caught a few words. I could not understand any. Nevertheless, they appeared friendly, and the Huron seemed to be doing a good job of conveying our situation. After the leader and Huron were finished, the Indian in charge spoke a few words to the others. They picked up our gear, and the Huron gave us orders to follow them, explaining that they were taking us to their camp. We did as we were told. Not having enough energy to speak and somehow sensing it inappropriate, we trudged on through the snow in silence. We trudged; the Indians marched easily over the snow in snowshoes. The snow had been light the previous winters, and we walked about without difficulty, but this winter the snow was deep, and every step took effort and concentration. We TRUDGED on for a mile or two (it seemed like twenty) and arrived at the Indian village . . . ."

As they would learn later, they were in the camp of a group of Ottawa and Chippewa Indians who had fled to the eastern part of the Lower Peninsula of Michigan and combined forces to avoid and repel the hostilities of the Iroquois. Then they'd moved west and south along the lakeshore. Few Indians ventured here, due to the difficult journey across the Great Lakes and the inhospitable nature of the territory—heavy forests, swamps, biting bugs, and endless streams, rivers, and rapids to cross. This was a small, relatively newly formed tribe of survivors from various Iroquois massacres in western Ontario. Apparently, the tribe was used to picking up strays, as there were a few Huron refugees in their midst and refugees from other tribes.

"We entered a large dome structure covered in the distinctive patterned white birch bark. Various animal skins also covered the structure. It felt warm; I had not felt that much warmth since the last mild day in October. They brought us a strange, warm drink and food. Regularly in the winter, Tom had brewed a similar bitter concoction of pine needles, leaves, twigs, and roots. He insisted we drink it and explained that it would ward off a dreaded disease. If we resisted, he threatened that if we did not, we would break out in sores, have sunken eyes, bleeding gums, loose teeth, broken bones, and ruptured blood vessels under the skin and die a painful death[16]. Well, after that gruesome lecture, we gulped it down like Christmas wassail, deferring to his knowledge of surviving in our circumstances. This drink was similar, but it tasted rather good . . . or maybe anything would have been scrumptious in our situation."

They stayed with the Indians. It was difficult to understand all the superstitions and rituals, but Will perceived that this particular group of Indians had an ethical tradition—the Moral Commandments similar to the Ten Commandments. However, they did not observe a Sabbath and had about twenty guiding principles. Will was grateful for the precept that commanded, "Always feed the hungry and the stranger," and he particularity liked, "Honor the grey-headed person," and, "Do not mimic or ridicule the cripple, the lame, or deformed." He liked them not

---

[16] This is a description of scurvy, a vitamin C deficiency common, at that time, among the British and Europeans, especially sailors, when their diets were deficient in fresh fruits and vegetables. Indians in North America may not have known about a vitamin C deficiency, but they knew this was the cure and prevention for the manifestations of the sickness.

because he was grey headed or crippled, but because he thought they were just plain nice.

They believed in a Great Spirit who saw all—day or night. One's actions could not be hidden. Any transgression would eventually be revealed, causing shame and disgrace to the perpetrator. In this tribe, it was not up to them to avenge. They were not to engage in revenge. Vengeance toward their enemies belonged to the Great Spirit. If they respected the guiding principles, they would be blessed and protected.

They didn't have a written language, but it sounds like they read Deuteronomy[17] or the end of Ecclesiastes,[18] Samantha thought. *What ancient history and oral tradition was preserved that made theirs correspond with the Israelites'?*

The Great Spirit, creator of all things, was over minor regional spirits. These spirits seemed to have certain powers and were in charge of particular areas of land, water, forests, islands, and so on. Will compared them to angels but was grateful that angels were commissioned to watch over humans. He recorded, "It reminds me of the passage from Hebrews: 'Are angels not all ministering spirits, sent forth to minister for them who shall be heirs of salvation?' Well, we sure have been keeping the angels busy."

His parents had insisted that the new translation of the Bible be part of the education of their sons. Like Will's parents, the parents of the Indians had passed down their moral code to their children. The children of the tribe were perpetually taught the guiding principles. Honesty and honor were at the top of the lists, strictly observed and instilled into the offspring. One's word was of high value—one's reputation for honesty.

Samantha thought of this as being a strong value amid the people of England, especially at that time. Remembering James

---

[17] Vengeance is God's business, not ours: Deuteronomy 32:35 *"It is mine to avenge; I will repay. In due time their foot will slip; their day of disaster is near and their doom rushes upon them."*

[18] Ecclesiastes 12:13-14: *Now all has been heard; here is the conclusion of the matter: Fear God and keep his commandments, for this is the whole duty of man. For God will bring every deed into judgment, including every hidden thing, whether it is good or evil.*

and Charles, she thought the royals were an exception. She thought of Shakespeare writing many times in his plays, calling one's reputation and word of honor the "jewel of the soul" and "the immortal part" of the self. In the play *Othello*, Cassio laments, "Reputation, reputation, reputation! O, I have lost my reputation! I have lost the immortal part of myself, and what remains is bestial." And, in *Richard II* Shakespeare wrote, "The purest treasure mortal times afford is a spotless reputation." Maybe Shakespeare wanted to stress the importance of honor, honesty, and reputation and hoped the royals would get the message. The people longed to have a king who would keep his word and treat them fairly.

Recalling the attitude toward cheating by many of her peers at the university, it was disconcerting to think that honesty was out of vogue in much of American culture these days. *I'm definitely keeping honesty at the top of the list of qualities I'll endeavor to maintain, even when no earthly creature is looking. Edmund, Steve, and Mr. Ryan seem to value integrity in their work and honesty,* she thought, and she felt honored to be in their midst.

Reading further in Will's description of the Ottawa and Chippewa, she discovered that profanity was not even a part of their language; she hoped it remained so today. They seemed quite self-controlled and did not have outbursts of frustration and anger.

He recorded, "The same principles do not apply to all Indians. The refugees tell of the savagery and ruthlessness of the Iroquois. They saw them torture captives, burn enemies at the stake, and inflict other cruelties. The Iroquois and some other tribes live by a code of revenge and hold ancient grudges. Revenge is considered their honor and duty. They indulge in hero-worship, trickery, and magic spells. They have a strong belief in evil spirits and try to appease them and gain their aid and favor by appalling measures. One newcomer heard tales of cannibalism within some tribes, but he did not actually witness it."

The six, after regaining their strength, worked with the Indians, particularly hunting and fishing and preparing for hunting and fishing. The major occupation was obtaining food. These were not simple, neat activities. Workmen spent hours making suitable clubs for killing, bows, arrows, and fishing equipment. They chipped chert[19] for arrowheads, spear heads, and knives, and they made canoes. Canoes were used not only for transportation and carrying supplies, but also for fishing in the lakes and rivers. Being the major food item, fish were caught in every way they could think of—in nets, on sinew lines with bone or copper hooks, shot with bows and arrows, driven into shallow water and scooped up with the hands, or speared. Hunters seeking larger game—elk, deer, bear—had to cover great distances. Large game was not that abundant, due to the dense forests blocking out sunlight and inhibiting the growth of small plants. Large and small animals sought the vegetation found along the shoreline of the great lake, inland lakes, rivers, and streams. From spring through early autumn, the men hunted waterfowl.

To take advantage of as much daylight as possible, all in the encampment rose with the first rays of the sun and worked hard all day. The women worked around the village and in the wigwam. When the men killed a deer, the women dragged it to the camp, dressed it, and cooked it. Women gathered the wood to keep the fires burning, carried water, gathered wild rice from the marshes, gathered berries, braved the bees for wild honey, and searched for waterfowl eggs. They gathered nuts, but these had to be shelled. They tanned deerskin (a complicated and strenuous process) and sewed the clothes. From reeds, they wove mats to sit on around the campfires; they wove baskets. If the camp needed to be moved to find a better hunting area, the women disassembled the wigwams and packed up everything they could carry. The work was hard; by 40, the faces of the women were haggard and their hair—once shiny black—had turned dull gray. They did not do laundry, as clothes were not washed, and they did not do dishes. They made dishes of birch bark, which they used again and again without washing. When the light faded, they

---

[19] Chert: Hard stones similar to flint found along Lake Michigan.

retreated to the campfires—outside in mild weather, inside the wigwams or lodges when the weather turned bitter cold, or when the wind and rain were severe.

Due to the reports of Iroquois cruelty from the victims in their midst, the influence of Hurons who had spent time at a mission, and the heritage of the Ottawa and Chippewa Indians, this band sought a kinder, more peaceful way of life. Nevertheless, they prepared and trained for war. All the Indians and white men in the camp practiced hand-to-hand combat frequently.

Will wrote, "The Frenchmen, having been soldiers, have a few tricks to teach us. They also pass on some organizational tactics, and we work out strategies of our own. The European version of "stand up like a man and shoot at each other" seems absurd to all. We English and French concur. I have no qualms about taking protection behind a tree. The Indians are very skilled with the bow and arrow and depended on it for hunting. We all make bows and arrows, which is delicate work. At first, I was clumsy at it. After much practice, I can use the bow and have the arrow hit the mark quite regularly. The Frenchmen have muskets from the army, but the gunpowder is long gone. Nevertheless, in the forest, a skilled warrior with a bow has an advantage over an enemy with a musket. An accurate, silent arrow finding its mark does not betray the location of the warrior with a bang, a plume of smoke, and the smell of burnt gunpowder. Although damage from a single musket shot could be more deadly, a warrior can fire off several arrows in the time it takes to reload a musket."

* * *

Will and his friends proposed to the Indians that they all trap for furs to trade in the spring. They would be able to acquire things that would help the tribe, and they could use a good pack horse, tools, guns, ammunition, and gunpowder. The Europeans especially wanted some metal dishes and eating utensils, and perhaps an iron kettle for cooking. The Indians agreed, and they had an exceptionally successful trapping season.

Will noted: "Unfortunately, Indians are regularly cheated in fur trading, with white men, so we suggested that the Frenchmen would be able to make the best deals, as the trading posts are in the hands of the French. The three Englishmen and the Huron will go along to help with the supplies and protect them. One of the Ottawa will go, too, as we will need a guide, especially over land on the way back. We have gained the Indians' trust, and they agreed to the plan. We have heard that the French are trying to regulate fur trapping and trading by issuing licenses in the territories, mostly in Canada, but this far west, people do pretty much what they want."

Several pages later, Will wrote: "The weather has been decent, and for several days now we have been traveling the water trails of the upper Great Lakes in the canoes the Indians provided. I helped build one—a big one, too—over four times my length. In spite of its light weight, it is remarkably strong. It carries men and supplies easily. We used a tree called giiqhikg [white cedar] to make the frame, ribs, and sheathing; wiigwas [white birch] covers the hull; gaagaaiwanzh [black spruce roots] were cut into long, thin strips and used for fastenings and stitching the sheets of bark; seams were sealed with a mixture of some tree gum. The canoes frequently need repairs, more gumming, which we try to do after dark, so as not to slow us up too much. It has been a long trip, but we made good progress once we were able to travel along the shoreline."

And, a later journal entry: "As we approached the trading post, it was our turn to pretend to be Frenchmen; three of us said nothing (the Indians stayed with the canoes). Although my French is good, I cannot get rid of my accent. Jacque did most of the talking and was able to strike an exceedingly satisfactory settlement for the furs. We were able to trade for most of the items on our list at the trading post. It took us two more days to find the rest. We loaded the supplies into the canoes. We traveled south and again crossed the open water between the two land masses without difficulty. Proceeding southeast for a short distance, following instructions obtained at the trading post, we were able to obtain two fine horses. Then, leading the horses, Pierre, the Ottawa, and I tagged along on the shore as long as we could. As the canoes headed across the bays on the western shore, the Ottawa guided us to the inland trails. The weather continues to be favorable to our endeavor . . . ."

Just then, Mr. Ryan came into the library, greeted Samantha graciously, and sat in the chair next to her (by then, she had moved to one of the wing-backed chairs by the windows). He asked her how she was getting along. She asked about Abby. They chatted about her reading and Will Jones.

"I'm glad you're finding something interesting to do," he said. "I imagine it's lonely for you, confined to this place."

She thanked him for his kindness and reassured him she had been quite absorbed in the reading, was enjoying it, and was not lonely or bored.

"You might be interested in meeting Dr. Howard Tyler," Mr. Ryan suggested. "He's the archivist who comes occasionally to update the family records and 'treasures.' He knows the history of the Jones family from England to Michigan. He's quite a storyteller. Perhaps, we can get him to come for dinner some night and tell us some of his stories about the Indians and the early settlers. It's fascinating. Abby loves it."

"I think I would love it, too," Samantha said with a little laugh, thinking of Abby's enthusiasm.

"I came to tell you that Mr. Jones sends his regards and regrets. He will be gone for at least another week. His son in Australia has been taken ill, and he's going there from Switzerland. He hasn't seen his son and daughter-in-law for quite sometime."

"I'm sorry to hear his son is ill. I hope it's not too serious."

"We don't know, but I'll keep you informed. Well, must get back. I have an appointment. I'll be away for a couple of days. If you need anything, contact Steve. The cook is back and will fix you what you like. Just let her know a little in advance. She will be cooking for some of the staff, but they eat in another area.

Just go into the kitchen anytime during the day, except around mealtime, and work out with her what you would like. Her name is Juanita. She's very agreeable. You'll like her."

Samantha expressed her gratitude for his kindness and for keeping her informed about Mr. Jones and his son. Subsequently, he hurried out of the room.

She started to leave the library when she was captivated by a particular painting. She was entranced by the compassionate blue eyes staring down at her from one of the portraits. She recognized Will Jones, the adventuresome young man who had left his family home in England to explore the land where she was now living. Her heart beat faster, and her face flushed red as she was struck with admiration and affection. He looked incredibly handsome and strong, dressed in the tanned, fringed camouflage skins the Huron had taught him to make. The artist made a perfect fit for his muscular body. She wondered if Will's cutting and sewing had been that precise and attractive. She thought the artist had captured his honorable nature, or perhaps she was imposing her value of the young man on the portrait. It was a remarkable painting, almost life-size, with miraculous detail depicting in the background events from his life. In the distance, the six friends sat around a campfire on the lakeshore at the edge of a Michigan pine forest. In another small portion of the background were the Indians and his friends, paddling canoes heaped with furs along the shore of Lake Michigan. Samantha stood a long time, studying the painting, mesmerized by the eyes and the man. Reading his intimate thoughts for these many hours, she felt she had peered into his young heart and soul. Now, all of a sudden, staring at the portrait made it seem as if he had become flesh and blood. It felt as if he were trying to say something to her. She wished he could; she surely wished he could.

☘·CHAPTER 15

In his devout reverence for the LORD a man has strong confidence;
and his children have a place of security.

Proverbs 14:26

With specialized communication device in her pocket, programmed for all events short of the Second Coming, Samantha ventured out for a brisk walk and exploration of the grounds. In some ways, she felt like Will and his friends, going into the unknown territory of the pine forest—maybe they'd walked on this very ground. Stepping onto the paved road put things into perspective. Nevertheless, carrying on the mood of the explorers, she imagined, *Maybe some of these mosquitoes and bugs that are starting to pester me are descendants of the ones that bit Will and his friends.*

One August, every page of Will's journal mentioned methods of coping with and complaints about mosquitoes and flies painfully nipping at patches of exposed skin. He explained the blood spattered on one page: "An aggressive mosquito sucked up a pint of my blood. I swatted the miserable little extractor just as she finished her dirty deed . . . ."

Will's journal was beginning to take on a new dimension of realism as a large, nervy fly with big, shiny, dark green eyes circled noisily, landed on Samantha's bare lower leg, and took a bite out of her. A light wind was coming up off the lake, so she headed in that direction and left the critters to enjoy the pine forest alone. Mercifully, she reached the beach unscathed, except for the chunk of flesh taken by the fly. There was just enough wind to keep the flying menaces off the beach today. She couldn't walk far without leaving the beach in front of the house. So, after walking back and forth a few times, she sat on a log.

After a few minutes, she heard someone behind her. Lost in thought, she hadn't been paying attention to her surroundings and was startled when a voice said, "Hi, Samantha." She was relieved to see it was Mary. "Mind if I join you?" She'd been out for a jog and had encountered the attack of the creatures in the woods and was rerouted to the beach.

"How about a walk down the beach?" Mary said.

"I'd like that very much. But just a minute."

She removed the communication device and pushed a single button. Steve answered, "Is all well, Samantha?"

She replied as instructed. "Yes, *very* well. I'm on the beach with Mary Ryan."

"I know," he said.

"Of course you do—how silly of me," she replied sarcastically. "Would it be all right if I walk down the beach a ways, if I am with Mary? The flies and mosquitoes are so bad in the woods, we escaped to the beach. I really need a good walk. There's no one in sight on the bea—oh, I forgot, you know that."

"Of course I do," he said with a teasing and friendly tone.

"I know," she conceded.

"Well, we can arrange it. Go ahead—walk to the north. Keep the communication device in your hand."

She wasn't sure what he meant by "we can arrange it," but she didn't ask, and she and Mary started walking north. Mary didn't ask any questions about the conversation, and Samantha didn't volunteer an explanation; she really couldn't explain. She was happy for Mary's company; she was the first woman Samantha had met in these past years with whom she felt comfortable enough to trust. Nevertheless, the past was still locked to strangers, and she wasn't going to go there now. Edmund was the only one she had confided in about her family.

Samantha directed the conversation to Abby. That was safe, as mothers always liked to talk about their children. Abby was visiting cousins today and tomorrow, and Mr. Ryan was away on business, so Mary had the day to herself. "Abby is a precious child. How blessed you are to have her. Is she Chinese?"

"Yes, she is. When we considered adoption, Mr. Jones suggested that we adopt a Chinese girl. He insisted on paying for everything. He had spent some time in China on business and couldn't get the plight of Chinese girls out of his mind. He said he was happy that someone could make a better life for one of these girls who otherwise would have had a hard future—an orphan girl with no family, no realization of her potential. Can you imagine that?"

A young girl alone in the world with no family, no place of refuge, and security provided by an honest, caring father and mother who would pass on the "precepts" to the next generation . . . no loyalty that brothers and sisters can provide . . . I can imagine that. I did have 18 years with my family. Still, it's hard without their continued support and encouragement, Samantha thought. She just replied with a sad half-smile to the rhetorical question.

As she and Mary were walking along, enjoying the day, the exercise, and the companionship, for some reason Samantha looked back. She noticed someone following them about 20 yards behind. She was a little startled; then she recognized him as one of the security guards. He was wearing a light jacket and long pants, which seemed a little unusual for such a warm day.

I wonder if he has a gun under that jacket, Samantha thought. *I guess that's what Steve meant when he said, "We can arrange it." That's awesome that he would go to so much trouble, just so I can go for a walk with Mary.* Overwhelmed by his consideration, she wanted to cry, but she checked herself and resumed her conversation with Mary. She was definitely fascinated by the account of their adoption process. "How old was Abby when you got her? Where did you go?"

"Abby was 13 months old when we went to Guangzhou, the capital of her home province. Guangzhou also happens to be the city where all the U.S. adoptions from China pass through before returning home, because that's where the consulates are located. We traveled with a group of eleven adopting couples from the agency that arranged the adoption."

"Oh, that was nice, being with other couples. How was it decided that Abby would be your child?"

"Honestly, I'm not sure. It was supposed to be randomly decided by the Chinese government—the branch in charge of adoptions."

"You were fortunate to get a bright, healthy, well-adjusted child."

Mary laughed a little and sighed. "The child then was *not* the same as you see now. At 13 months, she was physically and emotionally underdeveloped. She was only fed a thin rice mixture from the bottle, which the orphanage passed on to us for her feedings. The nipple was cut wide open to allow the watery gruel to flow quickly, and Abby swallowed it as fast as she could, sometimes choking, but she persevered—sucking and gulping. It was as if she had only minutes to get an adequate share. Usually, babies at that age are well-acquainted with soft foods and accept them from a spoon. Abby had no concept of this, or anything like crackers or solids that easily dissolve in the mouth. She just smacked and sucked—no rotary chewing motions."

"Wow," responded Samantha. "How long were you there?"

"We spent two weeks in China. Most people who adopt spend the majority of the time in their child's home province, and then go to Guangzhou for only a few days at the end to finalize all the official paperwork. By the way, did I mention that the paperwork for the whole processes—almost two years—was horrendous?"

"No!"

Mary went on. "The city of Guangzhou is in Guangdong Province, which happened to be the same province where Abby was found, so we spent the entire time in Guangzhou."

"What do you mean, 'Where Abby was found?'"

"Well," Mary said sadly, "she was found at a train station on the darkest day of winter. She still had the umbilical cord attached. It's against the law in China to abandon a baby, so they are left without any identification in a busy place so that they will be found quickly."

"Sounds cold and cruel," Samantha responded. "Why do they do that?"

"They have a one-child policy in China. Most couples want a boy. It's a cultural thing. If the first child is a girl, well . . . . This seems most likely, since almost all the abandoned children are girls. Then, there's the issue of forced abortions—I'm not sure how that figures into it—and poverty—many terribly poor people in China."

"I never realized . . . ."

"Yes, it was an eye-opener. Well, back to your question about our stay. In Guangzhou, everyone stays at the White Swan Hotel— nice, but small rooms. It did have a fabulous breakfast buffet with American foods and Chinese foods. Neville particularly liked the *dim sum* selection."

"What's *dim sum*?"

"Technically, well . . . *dim sum* is sort of like the English high tea or cream tea or afternoon tea event served with little sandwiches and bite-sized sweets. *Dim sum* is also served with tea. However, in China, it's usually served in the morning—usually until noon, and in restaurants rather than in homes. In restaurants that specialize in *dim sum*, typical dishes are served all day. Where we were, at the hotel, there were *dim sum* items on the breakfast buffet. In China, some families like to gather for *dim sum* on special occasions, such as Chinese New Year. Some families like to meet with grandparents weekly in the morning—some bring newspapers and discuss current events."

"Sounds like a nice custom."

"I think it may be a relatively recent custom."

"What are the *dim sum* foods like?"

"Typically, most are like little dumplings, or dough I should say, wrapped around various fillings—meat, seafood, vegetables, fruit—then steamed, I think. I'm not sure. They're usually served in little steamer baskets or on small plates. Actually, they were quite good, and I liked them too, but my favorite was the wonderful selection of tropical fruits and the omelet bar at the hotel's breakfast buffet."

"Ooo, that sounds good, too."

"Actually, *dim sum* is quite popular in the U.S., especially in big cities. Would you like to go to a *dim sum* restaurant sometime?"

"Oh, that sounds nice! Where would we go?

"There is a good *dim sum* restaurant in Grand Rapids. If we left early one morning, we could be there in about three hours. We could have an early lunch, then go to a couple of museums and shopping, and be home before dark." Mary paused; caught up in the anticipation of showing her young friend a new experience, she suddenly became keenly aware that there was something in Samantha's situation that might prevent her from leaving the estate.

Samantha, enjoying her new friend and anticipating the day, had also forgotten her situation. As she caught a glimpse of the security guard following them, she returned to reality. Sadly and slowly, she responded in a low voice, "I don't think I can leave here right now."

Mary's mood changed from carefree to concerned. "Oh, I'm sorry. I forgot. I'm *so* sorry!"

"Oh, no, no," Samantha responded, thinking of the time when she might have done something like that with her mother, Jenny, or Sarah. "It was wonderful to think about it. I really appreciate your wanting to take me. I haven't had anyone to do that sort of thing with in a long time. We *can* go when all this is over."

"Yes, yes, let's do that," Mary assured her in a sympathetic tone. "I hope it will be over soon."

"Me, too. I think so—I think it will," Samantha faltered in a meagerly hopeful tone, then changed the subject. "Tell me more about your time in China and Abby."

"The hotel and area cater to foreign adopting parents. There are shops with baby clothes and accessories. And we encountered many Caucasian couples with Chinese infants wandering around.

Although we had Abby within a couple days, we were required to stay the two weeks to complete all the paperwork, as I mentioned before. Once we received Abby, China became a little tedious, and we were anxious to return home."

"What was China like? Did you go outside that hotel area?"

"Yes, the first day we went exploring other areas of the city with another couple from our group. We saw endless markets selling medicinal products like ginseng, ginger, dried seahorses, dried deer bones, dried frogs, and a whole assortment of dried things we couldn't identify. There were street vendors selling food. We didn't take a chance of getting sick on that. I wasn't sure what all the items were. Then, there were the uncooked food items—every kind of organ you could imagine, not to mention live ducks in cages, live turtles in barrels, live scorpions in tubs, live eels in tanks, live snakes in cages. Then, the dead things—gutted goats lying on the sidewalk and so on."

Samantha grimaced. "You have to have a strong stomach just to go shopping."

"I guess so! It was interesting, but definitely a culture shock. Later, when we walked through the city with Abby, we were somewhat of a 'tourist attraction' for the locals. Heads would turn in our direction constantly. Fairly often, someone would come up to us, touch Abby lightly on the arm, and smile, or if they could speak some broken English would say something like, 'Lucky child,' or, 'Very good.'"

"Oh, that was nice—must have made you feel good."

"It did. We were surprised. We didn't know what to expect."

"What was it like when you got her?"

"It was an exciting moment they called 'Gotcha Day.' Exciting for us—scary for Abby. It was a rough couple of days for her. We were prepared for this from our classes, expecting something from catatonic to unwaveringly clingy. She was mostly catatonic. For the first 24 hours, she wouldn't look at us. When we carried her, she tried to face outward. If she happened to be facing us, she would keep one arm up between us and her, like this." Mary raised her arm across her chest with a clenched fist up to her cheek. "It was heartbreaking when we first received her. At the hotel, we put her on the bed next to an open window. It was barred, and she would clutch the bars for dear life and stare out the window for long periods of time until we were able to gently pry her loose and coax her away. Neville had a chance to ask the nannies about her. They told him she was afraid of strangers. When a stranger came to the orphanage, she cried the whole day. It was obvious she was absolutely terrified. She soothed herself by rocking on her hands and knees. We just patted and rubbed her back, and that helped. We worked hard to comfort her and find little games and gestures that amused her, and eventually we found a happy child under the dismay and fear."

"It must have been bewildering to you as new parents."

"Yes, we did all the usual things new parents do—watched her sleep, checked her breathing, got little sleep . . . ."

"That's sweet," Samantha commented with a little smile.

"It was obvious that she had not experienced the outside world. Everything was new to her. She hardly knew what to do with toys. She carefully examined everything—just kept feeling all of the different textures on everything. She looked intently at the sky, felt the grass as if she had never seen it before, and was puzzled with the wind on her face and blowing through her short cropped hair."

"A whole new world was opening to her."

"Yes, it was. These children came to Guangzhou from an orphanage about six hours southwest. We were offered the opportunity to visit the orphanage and site of abandonment. We decided I would stay with Abby. Only three fathers, Neville included, made the trip. Neville reported that the orphanage was bare-bones and seemed cold and unfeeling."

"How sad."

"Yes, and when he told me about it, he was in tears, and Neville is rarely moved to tears. He couldn't bear the thought of Abby spending her first year there, not to mention the other children *still* there. We tried to adopt another child, but adoptions after that were closed."

"Oh, that's too bad. How was it when you got her home?"

"Pretty tough—many adjustments. Overcoming her fears was a long process for her and definitely challenging for us, trying to think up ways to help her. We think she probably spent the first 13 months of her life in a crib. She had almost no torso strength, was nowhere near walking, and didn't crawl very well or do other things one would expect of a 13-month-old. You could tell she had never really been held before. You know how kids usually hold on when you pick them up?"

"Yes, I know what you mean. My two nieces did that. They liked to hold on tight or balance on my hip. I spent a lot of time with them. They liked to be carried at that age."

Mary didn't question her on the subject, which was consistent with Edmund's directive. She just smiled in acknowledgment and went on. "Abby didn't do that. She was always tipping away from us at first. But, we weren't used to holding a one-year-old—she felt so heavy to me! I remember trying to comfort her one night, and Neville and I having to trade off several times because our arms got so tired. Moms and dads starting out with a seven-pound newborn have time to warm up. Abby was about 20 pounds! The beginning was a little scary for us, too. We were told to expect a one-month development delay for every three months she was in the orphanage, but she was much more delayed than that. We worried that she might not be normal. But, we worked with her, and she caught up fast."

"That's amazing. Seeing her now, no one would suspect she had a slow start and such a traumatic adjustment."

"Not at all," Mary affirmed.

By now, they were headed back toward the Lake House beach. When they returned, Mary invited her for lunch; Samantha was pleased to accept. Mary wanted to show her an ancient poem she found that partly explained the persistent cultural attitudes toward girls in China. She handed her a book with a marker protruding from the top. Samantha opened the book and read:

When a son is born,
Let him sleep in the bed,
Dress him in fine clothes
And give him jades to play with.
How lordly is his cry!
When he is a man, may he wear crimson
And be the lord of the land and the clan!

When a daughter is born
Let her sleep on the ground,
Wrap her in plain cloths
And give her broken tiles to play with.
May she have no faults, nor merits of her own;
May she attend well to food and wine
And bring no dishonor to her parents!

—traditionally attributed to Confucius

"How sad," Samantha said. She was not able to say anything else for several minutes. They looked at each other without speaking. Yet, as their eyes met, the expression on their faces spoke volumes. There were no words to explain such a thing, only a deep compassion that could be felt to the bottom of the heart.

☧·CHAPTER 16

*Elijah went before the people and said,
"How long will you waver between two opinions?
If the LORD is God, follow him; but if Baal is God, follow him."
But the people said nothing.*

1 Kings 18:21.

Early the next morning, Samantha returned to the library and the portrait of Will. It was easy to fall in love with Will, since she knew he was dead and gone; in a strange way, she didn't have to be afraid of losing someone she loved. She could fantasize, fill in the gaps of his personality. He would never say a harsh word to her; he would never get angry or lose his temper. All she knew of him was what he wrote. There were no writings criticizing him or pointing out flaws in his character—only those *he* chose to reveal. *How critically do we look at ourselves? How honest are we about our faults?* To her, at this point in his saga, he was cheerful and pleasant; he was a good comrade; he was young, strong, intelligent—overcoming all situations, solving all problems. To her, he would be protector, kindred spirit, soul mate. *Well, for the moment, anyway*, she thought, trying to cure her obsession with a dose of reality.

Samantha found Will's journal of the fourth year. They had been with the Indians for over a year. She turned the pages and was intrigued. "Tom carried a small Bible written in Latin, which I observed him reading once in a while. How he came by such a

132

rare possession, I do not know, and for some reason I have not gotten around to asking. I know it is in Latin, because he asked me one time if I could read Latin. He did not know a word and asked me. I told him I studied Latin. He showed me the word. It was *philos*. I told him it was not exactly a Latin word, but a Greek word explaining that the New Testament Bible was originally written in another language—Greek. He did not know that. I explained to him that *philos* was the Latin way of spelling the Greek word, and Greek had a different alphabet and symbols. In the sand I drew: φιλος. I speculated that the translator probably did not like the Latin version and used a Greek facsimile to convey the original meaning from the Greek. I told him that *philos* was a Greek word that meant brotherly love. He looked surprised, maybe pleased, and then a slight smile crossed his face. I smiled back, and our eyes connected and communicated—*philos*. We sat and talked awhile. He was interested in the different people and languages of the world. I told him what I knew. He learned to read and write French and Latin at the mission. The priests must have considered him an apt student; perhaps they were training him to be a priest—we did not talk about it. I have seen him cross himself a few times when things were tough—the Frenchmen, too. Tom is unusually smart. He can calculate figures in his head, figure out how to build things, and make things work. He is able to grasp things quickly and has plenty of common sense. Apparently, the tribal leaders recognize his intellect and wisdom, because occasionally he is asked to sit around the council fire of the elders. What they talk about I do not know; they do not ask me and that is all right. What could I tell them? My experiences with government have not been anything I would want to recommend. Tom says almost nothing to us about his discussions with the council members. He is getting quite involved with the Indian community.

There is a very pretty girl of about 16 who turns Tom's head and produces a grin; well, I detect a grin, as I know him better than anyone. No one else would be likely to notice. If she catches him looking at her, she smiles back. He turns his eyes away quickly, and I suspect a blush would be noticeable if his skin were a different color. I think he wants to stay with these people permanently; the rest of us talk about leaving one day. In spite of everything, I have found English family life is in my nature."

Later, she read, "Tom does not talk very much about what he is reading in his Bible. However, on one occasion, possibly because of the influence of the seven Hurons from the missions who seemed to hold to Christianity, the cruelty others experienced at the hands of the Iroquois and the heritage of the Ottawa people, he did. Some tribes indulge in cruel sacrifices and detestable rituals to appease, what they perceive as, evil spirits; the Ottawa and Chippewa leaders of our group have abandoned such things, or they were never part of their beliefs. However, there is one disgusting ritual practiced by a small group of refugees. These Indians are not fully integrated into the ways of this community. To ensure good fishing on the Great Lake, they take a puppy, bind its legs and tie its mouth shut, paddle a canoe some distance into the darker water, and toss the poor creature to the lake god or as an offering to the devil spirit of the lake—a sacrifice so he will allow for good fishing. To say the least, the Europeans find this practice disgusting. We do not mind eating dog from time to time when things are really tough, but this is too much. Heaven knows, Indians from various tribes cling to dozens of harmless little ceremonies and customs they never can really explain or that my grasp of the language is too poor to understand, but this is hideous. I think that in some council meetings, Tom tried to resolve this problem—do away with it, to be precise. He is not making progress. Knowing our concern, this struggle he shared with us. It seems he is trying to make a bigger point—there is no god or devil of the Great Lake to appease. Tom wants a cohesive way of life for this community and some form of government, using principles from the Bible and the Moral Commandments of the Ottawa and Chippewa (which are not inconsistent with the Ten Commandments). Actually, government as we know it does not exist—there is no property ownership to cause dispute, murder is almost unheard of, as is stealing (there is nothing to steal). Everyone does his share—the guiding precepts deal with that: 'Do not be lazy, nor be a vagabond of the earth to be hated by all men.' And, there is a healthy respect for following them because 'After death, the spirit of one who did not observe the precepts would wander the earth always, and go hungry, and never find the road to Tchi-bay-kon—The Happy Place.' Tom said he is working on enlightening them about the 'road to The Happy Place,' which is not that big of a problem, since being able to keep all the precepts all the time is worrisome. Who could keep all of them all of the time? Is keeping them half the time good enough? Almost all the time? All but one, is that good enough?

"For now, Tom is concerned that when newcomers become part of the community, they concur with the values of the community and their rituals. They should not indoctrinate or contaminate the community with opinions that contradict the core values that have served it well. He is determined to put an end to this appeasement of evil spirits as soon as possible. Tom asked us to do something to help end these needless sacrifices. I am surprised he appealed to us. Tom has taken this very seriously; it must have taken great courage or confidence, as we might have laughed at him, but he did not know the full extent of our respect for him. Tom is not to be taken lightly! Who could let him down now? We have nothing to lose. The Indians will not think we have lost our senses. They have a healthy respect for spirits and are regularly engaged in incantations in this regard . . . ."

At that moment, Mr. Ryan entered the library with steady, deliberate steps and greeted Samantha. "Good afternoon."

"Hi." She acknowledged him with a welcoming smile. She was becoming friendly with all the Ryans, but she knew he wasn't here for a chit-chat session. She detected he was on a mission.

"Mary and Abby sent me. They would like you to come over. Abby has some new books she wants to read to you, and Mary would like you to stay for dinner. Cheesy Lasagna—everybody's favorite—is on the menu. We'd all enjoy having you."

Samantha was pleased to note the "all" in his invitation; it gave her a feeling that he liked her, too. "I'd like that very much.

Lasagna is a favorite of mine, too, and I'm always delighted to hear Abby's stories. I'll walk over in about 15 or 20 minutes. I've a couple of things I want to finish."

"Yes, that's fine. See you then."

Curious about what Tom had in mind, she picked up the diary and hastily read through the pages but could not find the conclusion to his proposal. It was getting too late to continue searching, so she would have to pick up where she'd left off tomorrow. She placed a bookmark and put the diary back on the shelf, leaving it protruding slightly so she could easily find it later.

As she was about to leave, Steve came into the library. He was on a mission, too. "I've been talking to a police detective who has been trying to connect the Doyles with several crimes for years. He'd like to talk to you, even though there has been, in your case, no crime—so far, that is." He smiled and reassured her, "And there won't be, as long as you are under my protection."

She returned a pathetic smile.

"Without a crime, we agreed to keep it off the record and confidential, but he only wants to see if he can get some more insight into Bruce Doyle and his methods. He also wants you to look at some pictures. If it's okay with you, we can leave here Thursday morning at eight."

She nodded. He left the room, and she hurried upstairs. While she was changing and regrouping in her room, her mind was mulling over the possibilities of Tom's proposal. *Was he going to emulate Elijah's confrontation with the prophets of Baal? That was pretty dramatic. Probably not . . . well, maybe,* she debated with herself. She suppressed her curiosity for the moment as she hurried to the Ryans'.

* * *

The following morning, Samantha was in the kitchen helping Abby with her pancake project when a frail little girl walked slowly from the back of the kitchen to Abby and greeted her in a shy, childish way.

Abby introduced her to Samantha. "This is my friend, Isabella. She's almost six years old. Juanita's her mom."

"Hi, Isabella. I'm Samantha. I'm very pleased to meet you," Samantha greeted her kindly.

"Hi," she replied shyly.

Abby wanted to make Mrs. Hoffmeyer's recipe for Cranberry Pancakes with the maple syrup she'd helped collect last spring. Juanita and Isabella were already in on the undertaking, and Samantha had just recently been recruited. Invitations had gone out to 12 people on the estate to come for breakfast this morning.

As Abby and Samantha set up the table in the grand dining room, Abby was all chatter, explaining how the children from her school had gone to collect the sap for the syrup. "Mr. Hoffmeyer drove the tractor with a wagon right up to our school. We all sat on the wagon, and he pulled us through the woods."

"That sounds like fun," Samantha commented.

"It was! Really fun! There were little shiny pails with sap in them hanging on the maple trees."

"Oh, I see," Samantha said and smiled to show her interest.

"He showed us how to tell which trees are maple trees—well, you know, when little pails aren't hanging on them." She giggled at her little joke. "We took the pails to Mr. Hoffmeyer and his helper on the wagon, and they poured the sap into a huge container. Then we put the pails back on hooks on the trees. The little kids stayed near the wagon. The big kids ran way back in the woods. This was my first time! The big kids did it before. But they still like to go."

"With all that help, I bet you filled up that big container fast," Samantha responded.

"Yes, we did! Then we took all that sap to a building. There was a big boiling pot on a big stove. Mr. Hoffmeyer said they use wood to make the fire. It was so hot in there! We had to stay outside. We could only look over the door. They had a funny door. It was cut in half. The bottom was shut, but the top was open. But it was very wide. Some kids had to be picked up to see over it. Even standing on my toes and stretching out, I couldn't see. Harry Browne from the eighth grade helped me—he's tall. ome of the big kids came to help the little kids."

"Well, that's nice. That's a good idea."

"I guess so. Harry Browne is very nice. He has lots of sisters. His mom makes him be nice to them."

"I hope his sisters are nice to him."

"They are, but a couple of sisters my age are always arguing with each other."

Deliberately changing the subject, Samantha smiled and asked, "What was your favorite part of the outing?"

"When Mrs. Hoffmeyer made Cranberry Pancakes. We had'm for lunch because that's what time it was. We put on lots of the maple syrup—yum, really, really good! I've wanted to make them for breakfast for a long time," she rattled on.

"I'm glad I'm here to enjoy them, today."

"Me, too!"

Isabella and Juanita, having finished organizing the accompaniments, brought them into the dining room on a cart. Abby left to check with Alice on the progress of the pancakes in the kitchen. Samantha made a special effort to engage Isabella while they were putting the finishing touches on the table, and the two became instant friends.

The pancake party was a huge success. The guests arrived promptly at 8:30. Abby and Isabella were perfect hostesses; the pancakes were superb and all went exceedingly well. Real maple syrup always makes a pancake breakfast a gourmet affair.

Isabella was exhausted from all the excitement and needed to rest. Samantha and Abby stayed to help Alice clean up. Later, Abby went home, Alice was redeployed, and Juanita and Samantha sat at the round table in the corner with a pot of tea to revive them. They talked about Isabella. Juanita told Samantha a little about how they'd come to Lake House.

"I was working in the coffee shop of the hotel where Mr. Jones was staying in Houston. He was there for a couple of weeks on business. Very early in the morning—you know Mr. Jones—he came in with his papers. I waited on him. We weren't busy at that time, so we chatted and became acquainted."

"Yes, that sounds like Mr. Jones. He's interested in people and still the early bird."

"Yes, he's a very kind man. Isabella was only a baby then— six months old. I was eighteen. We were pretty much alone. My husband left us—a self-centered man—didn't want the responsibility of a sick child, I think. Well, Mr. Jones took an interest in her illness and offered to help us."

"I'm beginning to realize Mr. Jones has helped a lot of people in a personal way. He helped me, too," Samantha responded, feeling a kinship with Juanita in the "needing help" category.

"I thought so, from the memo we got," she stated. Then, she stood and said apologetically, "Oh, I'm sorry, I have to go. I need to check on Isabella and get back to work."

"Of course," responded Samantha.

"Thank you so much for helping Isabella today and including her. She seems fond of you. Her activities are limited. She can't keep up with the other children," Juanita explained as she lingered for a moment. "They try to spend time with her, but their energy is too much for her. Abby's really the only friend she has near her age. She seems to understand and is very solicitous of her."

"I enjoyed her very much. It was fun for me, too."

Juanita smiled gratefully.

"Really, I had twin nieces. They died in an accident. They were seven years old then," she confided quietly, looking down into her tea cup. "I loved playing games and spending time with them. I miss them very much. Abby and Isabella remind me of them in some ways, and actually, they're somewhat of a comfort to me."

"I'm truly sorry about your nieces," Juanita sympathized with more understanding than Samantha realized at the time. Samantha knew Isabella's life was fragile, but the full impact had not yet taken hold. "I know you made plans to play a game with Isabella later today. Would you mind if I run some errands while you're there? Alice or Margaret usually looks after her while I'm away, but I don't like to take them away from their other duties more than I have to."

"Not at all, not at all!" Samantha responded. "Please, feel free to ask me to stay with her any time. I'd be very happy to! We seem to get along quite well. She seems very easy and agreeable."

"She is. Thank you so much. That would be a big help," said Juanita, grateful for the help *and* for Isabella's new friend.

❧·CHAPTER 17

But let justice roll on like a river,
righteousness like an ever-flowing stream!

Amos 5:24

After their interview at police headquarters, Steve and Samantha headed for her house. Since her hasty departure, she'd remembered several things she wanted. Steve had agreed to take her there; however, he had restrictions and went over them carefully and firmly. It had not even been two weeks since she'd left, and he doubted the Doyles had given up on their surveillance of her house. They knew she was gone, but they might still be on the lookout for her return. Steve insisted they stay 15 minutes at the most. She agreed.

It was well past noon, and remembering Samantha's previous performance after her lack of food, he insisted on stopping for lunch first. The service was slow, and it was an hour or more before they were on their way.

Arriving at the house, they pulled into the garage and promptly closed the door. They had passed no cars on the street. Silently, they entered the house, and Samantha began gathering her items. Absorbed in rummaging around in the nostalgia of her surroundings, she became distracted from her mission. It was taking longer than planned. Steve was in the library, loading some books she had identified. Samantha was in the kitchen, looking through recipes (not on her list), as her mother's handwriting took her back to a pleasant time. She could almost smell the Molasses Ginger Cookies baking as she fondly held the well-used recipe card.

Her reminiscing was interrupted when Steve poked his head around the corner and gestured, "Two minutes."

She nodded, and he returned to the library to get the cartons he had packed.

She remembered something she wanted from the Buick and hurried that way. Still preoccupied with her mother's notes on the recipes, she entered the garage from the kitchen. The SUV was parked so close to the garage door that she could not get by, so she pushed the button on the wall, and the garage door opened. As she was returning from the car, she noticed a newspaper about halfway down the driveway. It was in a plastic wrapper—one of those free editions full of advertisements. Without thinking, she started down the driveway to remove it.

As she bent down to pick it up, a hand grabbed her arm, and a familiar voice said, "Hi, Samantha! How've you been?" She recognized it as Joe's voice, and as terror overtook her, she became speechless. "How about going for a ride? We can get some coffee and talk over old times."

Samantha pulled away, trying to retreat to the house. She knew Steve was in there somewhere, but she couldn't call out. Nevertheless, Steve noticed the van in front of the house and hurried through the kitchen. Not finding Samantha, he rushed into the garage—too late.

Joe tightened his grip on her wrist and grabbed her other hand. Then, gripping both of her hands with his large left hand, he pulled out a knife with his right. He started pulling her toward the van at the end of the driveway. "You'd better come along nicely, or I'll start cutting you."

Samantha resisted, and he cut her across the back of the hand. As she felt the sharp sting of the knife and saw the blood starting to flow, her panic heightened. Even so, she continued to resist, and he sliced her on the upper arm.

Joe noticed Steve waiting for his chance. "And *you* stay right there, or I'll cut her good!"

In spite of the wounds, Samantha braced her feet and tried to step back.

"Come along! I don't have time for this nonsense! Next, I'll cut your pretty face."

Repulsed, she leaned away, trying to keep as much distance between them as possible. Her opposing weight temporally brought their progress down the driveway to a standstill. Just then, she heard an explosion and felt a spray of warm liquid hit her cheek. Joe loosened his grip on her hands, and she fell to the cement. She sat up and saw Joe fall in front of her. Bright red blood was pulsing from a hole in his neck. Horrified, she stared at the bloody puncture and his face. Unable to turn her eyes away, she watched the blood drain away, his face become white and lips pale purple, and his body go limp and dead. At that moment, she heard shots coming from the van. She saw policemen wrestling a man from the driver's seat. Steve came running down the driveway and knelt beside her; the policeman in charge came walking rapidly up the driveway to assess her status.

"Hey, Pete, get the first-aid kit," the officer ordered. They pressed some white gauze on the oozing wounds on her hand and arm to stop the bleeding. They wiped the blood off her face and found no wounds there. "Pete will give you an escort to the emergency room."

Steve effortlessly picked her up and carried her to his SUV. Samantha heard the officer in charge say in a cynical voice, "Dead. That'll save the State a lot of trouble—he's been enough trouble already. Good shot, Reilly! Call in the report! Tell'm to send a mop-up crew to . . . ."

Pete stayed to give the report to the hospital admitting attendant. "Knife wounds—that's all. We have the rest. Consider it reported to the police." Then he signed a form.

At the emergency room, Samantha was treated for shock, and she received seven stitches in the back of her hand and

twelve in her upper arm. The nurse helped remove her torn
and stained clothes, wash the blood off her skin, and put on the
simple light blue cotton dress that was provided. When she had
sufficiently recovered—color in her face and vitals normal—she
was discharged into Steve's care.

When they left the hospital, Steve drove a short distance to
a hotel in a better part of town. She stayed in the vehicle while
he went to the registration desk. Returning shortly, he helped
her out of the SUV and led her to the elevators. The elevator
stopped at the 14th floor. They continued to the end of the hall
to a room with double doors. He closed the suite's doors behind
them and slid the chain bolt in place—more from habit than
necessity. They crossed the sitting room to the bedroom on
the right and proceeded through another set of double doors.
Samantha remained silent and groggy; she walked methodically
with his support.

"You need to rest and recover from your ordeal. I didn't feel
you were up to a long car trip yet. Lie down here and rest. The
medication the doctor gave you should make you sleep. I'll be in
the sitting room or in the bedroom on the other side."

She nodded in agreement, barely processing the information.
She had felt drowsy in the car when they'd left the hospital. Now,
it felt good finely to lie down in a comfortable bed and sleep,
forget everything for awhile. He took her shoes off, pulled back
the covers, and tucked her into the smooth, snow-white sheets.
With a deep breath, she inhaled the sweet scent of the clean
sheets and within seconds was asleep.

While Steve was in the sitting room reading a newspaper,
he received a call on his cell phone. Bruce's father had been the
driver of the van, and his wounds were not serious; nevertheless,
he'd died of a massive heart attack at the hospital. Betty Ann and
her mother had fled to Mexico. Although the police had no hard
evidence on which to convict them of a crime, apparently they
sought a place where they would feel safer. The police would
be watching for their reentry and inform Steve if that occurred.
He was relieved to hear that the Doyles were no longer a threat

to Samantha, but he would wait for the right time to pass this information on to her.

"How did the police happen to arrive on the scene so fast?" Steve asked the sergeant.

"The detective you talked to earlier was worried and ordered that you be followed to the house. Luckily, our best marksman happened to be one of the officers dispatched."

"Lucky, indeed! Thank the detective for us."

"You bet," the sergeant responded. "The police record reported the incident as a 'romance gone wrong,' and they'll try to keep it out of the newspapers."

"Thanks again," Steve said. He silently consoled himself. *If this is reported at all, it'll be buried in a back page. The news events today are considerable—three terrorist attacks in Europe, significant escalation of the Palestinian-Israeli conflict, a bizarre drug raid at a Grosse Point mansion, and the suspicious death of a popular rock star. Comparatively, this little "romance gone wrong" isn't very newsworthy. The reporters will be too busy to do any digging into this. It shouldn't make it past local TV news; if at all, it'll be a five-second blurb.*

For now, they both could relax. Steve was concerned for Samantha's emotional condition and how she would react when she woke up. Nevertheless, for the moment, they both needed the relief—a quiet, peaceful moment.

*   *   *

Samantha slept through the night and into the afternoon. When she woke, she was disoriented, but then it all started coming back, and she muttered, "Oh, no."

Steve heard her, came into the room, and sat on the bed. "How are you?"

She just shook her head. After a long pause, she said with a steady voice, "I'm all right."

The color in her face looked good; Steve was relieved. "I was worried about you. I *am* sorry about all this." He didn't reproach her for disobeying his orders.

Actually, she felt bad for him, knowing how conscientious he was about his job. She had done something stupid and made him look bad. As she started apologizing for not following his orders, he interrupted and rattled off a series of reassuring comments to calm her anguish. "Don't be concerned about any of that. You're safe now. That's all that matters. We have to get you beyond this. You've had quite a shock."

"I'm all right," she said quietly. "Really."

"How does your arm feel? Do you want some of that pain medicine they sent with us?"

"No, it feels okay. It really doesn't hurt—just a little sore to touch."

"I am going to order you something to eat. It's afternoon. Do you want breakfast, lunch, or supper?"

"Breakfast."

"Okay, then I'll go back to your house to get you some clothes and the things we were packing up. Do you think you will be okay alone here for about 45 minutes?"

"That's fine—I'm fine, thank you."

"Is there anything else you want?"

"No, I can't think of anything."

Breakfast arrived—a huge breakfast. He guided her to a table in the sitting room. "Now, you eat a good breakfast, and I'll be back by the time you're finished. Stay put!" he ordered.

"Yes, sir," she said with a smile that reassured Steve she was on the mend.

He was back before she finished eating. They sat for a while, and she sipped her tea. She started asking questions, and he related what he knew about the Doyles.

"Perhaps we shouldn't dwell on it now," he said. "I don't want you to get upset."

"It's okay. Today, I feel sad more than anything. For some strange reason, I'm not angry with Joe. Actually, I feel sorry for him. What a worthless, wasted life—nothing constructive, no worthy purpose to it. All the Doyles—wasted, evil lives. How does that happen? Could I have said anything that would have made a difference in his life? I had no clue—no insight—no wisdom."

Steve shook his head. "It's in the past. I think it's best to leave it there."

She nodded.

"I'm going to fill up that bathtub with some warm water. You can have a relaxing soak. Do you think you can keep those bandages out of the water, or do we need some plastic wrap?"

"I can manage."

"After you get dressed, we'll do something fun. We can go to a ball game or a movie or something. You have been confined for so long, you need to get out."

"That sounds very nice."

While Samantha was in the bathroom, Steve found an advertisement for a concert in the park that evening. *Perfect,* he thought.

She finally emerged, looking refreshed and bandages undamaged.

The park was near the hotel, so they walked. Strolling through the acres of the park, with gushing fountains and abundant gardens filled to the edges with late-summer flowers in full bloom, was just the therapy she needed. They said very little at first, but after all that had transpired and Steve's kindness toward her, she was somewhat curious about him. Knowing the mandate of confidentiality Mr. Jones imposed upon his employees, she was quite sure if she asked about him, he would not ask about her. Besides, after all this, she suspected he knew more about her than he would ever say. If not, he was smart enough to put two and two together.

Since he spent time at my house, he must know I have no parents and have been living alone in their house, she thought. *Since he knew that Joe was a con man after something, he must have known it was money or was connected with money in some way. The only other thing he might have speculated was that they were trying to get at influential family or friends— that was unlikely! He knew it wasn't a "romance gone wrong."*

She felt obligated to tell him some of the truth about her. She knew it would go no farther. But, first, she was curious about him, so she decided to venture some conversation and see where it led. She wondered if he had ever been married, as he seemed to know something about the needs of a woman.

She didn't know quite how to be tactful about asking the question, so she blurted out, "Have you ever been married?" And when the answer came, she felt terrible.

"Yes, I have. My wife and four-year-old daughter were killed in an automobile accident about four years ago—a drunk driver," he replied calmly.

The answer stabbed her through the heart. "I, I . . . I'm terribly sorry. I'm so sorry . . . how awful," she stammered, not quite knowing what to say or how to handle the situation. Knowing firsthand the pain and trauma of the experience, she was on the verge of tears as memories of her own feelings came rushing back. She took a deep breath, got hold of her emotions, and focused her thoughts on him. She went on apologizing, hoping she wasn't making the situation worse for him. "That was thoughtless of me. I'm *so* sorry I brought up such a painful subject." She went on to tell him that she really did know how he must feel. "Everyone in my family was killed in an accident about four years ago—my mother, father, sister, brother, his wife, and my two nieces—everyone! I'm really quite alone in the world."

"I thought it might be something like that. You've suffered a tremendous loss. I guess we are more or less in similar circumstances."

She nodded, feeling relieved that he seemed to understand.

"And then all this . . . you've had a lot to deal with in your young life. You seem to be holding it together quite well, though."

Samantha found it easy to talk to Steve. She felt more relaxed and less guarded. They went on talking about dealing with the reality of their situations, the paralyzing feelings, the shock of the suddenness of it all, their worlds being turned upside-down in a day—a moment—and finally, the difficulty of moving on and trying to find a new direction in life. Sharing their hurts brought them into a new relationship of friendship. Nevertheless, Steve was always mindful of his position. He was carrying out a job for Mr. Jones, and he was responsible for the very young, naïve Samantha.

She went on to tell him that she had inherited some money, and that was what the Doyles were after. Steve said that was what he had surmised, but he thanked her for telling him and reassured her that all this information was safe with him. She told him she had confidence it would be, or she never would have told him.

"I have been so careful! I didn't want anyone to know about it. I was thinking more about how the money might influence people's perception of me—I might not know who my real friends would be, if I ever get past this and make some. And, I guess, instinctively, I thought there might be some risk to me if someone knew, but never in my wildest imagination did I think it would be this dangerous. Mr. Jones is the only other person I've told. As far as I know, the stockbroker and the lawyers are the only other people who know about the money. I don't know how the Doyles found out."

"They probably read something in the paper when the accident happened. Con men make a habit of reading the obituaries, checking out court cases, and things like that—looking for victims," he explained.

They continued walking around the park, enjoying the mild weather and the brilliant flowers. Later, they sat on the grass and listened to the symphony. Not being in a hurry, they waited a while for the crowd to disperse. Steve sat quietly; a shadow of sadness fell over his face. Samantha sensed that he was thinking of his wife and daughter. Perhaps he had heard that music with them, or *they* had gone to a concert in the park, and it brought back melancholy memories. She wanted to say something comforting but, after weighing what she might say, felt it unwise to trespass into that painful territory or shatter a lovely reminiscence.

✧·CHAPTER 18

"The better part of valor is discretion . . ."

William Shakespeare: *Henry IV*

They spent another night at the hotel. Samantha slept late and was beginning to feel much better. Steve had been up for hours. She found him in one of the comfortable chairs, typing on his laptop.

"Good morning," he said. "You're looking better. Do you want me to order you some breakfast here or go out?"

"Here," she said matter-of-factly, as she was not fully awake. "I do feel better. I want to take a bath and get dressed. Will you help me change the bandages?"

"Nurse Steve at your service," he said with a smile. "I've been exchanging e-mail with some of Mr. Jones' staff in Australia and have some things to discuss with you. We can do that while you're having your breakfast. Do you want the same as before?"

"Yes, thank you. Okay. I won't be long," she responded, a little perkier.

*   *   *

As Samantha was eating her breakfast, Steve started relating news of Mr. Jones and his son. Somewhat overstating his case, he encouraged, "Mr. Jones wants you to continue to stay at his house, at least until he gets back. He feels, and I agree, that considering your recent ordeal, you need a safer place. Although the current danger is over, considering your age and circumstances, you're vulnerable. Besides, you need your injuries looked after. You appear to be doing well, after the shock and trauma of the other day, but we *don't* want any relapse."

Samantha didn't put up any objections. Actually, she felt relieved. It had been a struggle, dealing with her emotions alone, trying to find her place and make some sense out of it all. She felt comfortable with Steve—someone looking out for her—not being alone. She felt that way about Edmund and was now looking forward, more than ever, to talking to him. "You're right. I won't object. Thank you very much for your kindness. I know it's your job, but you've been very kind."

"Good! Then it's settled," he replied, with a slight smile of "mission accomplished."

∗   ∗   ∗

They were busy organizing their things for departure when Steve asked, "Would you mind if we stopped to visit an old friend of mine? We're so close to their house, it would be hard to drive by without stopping."

"Well, it's all right," she agreed, hesitantly

"We won't stay long."

"It's okay." Samantha was somewhat apprehensive about this detour, but she didn't want to disappoint Steve and felt that this must be important to him. Besides, she knew he wouldn't put her into an uncomfortable situation.

Steve gave her some background before their visit. He explained that Ralph was a friend and colleague from his former job as a detective in the police department. He'd met Ralph's wife, Jane, for the first time a few years ago, just prior to their wedding; he'd been the best man. This was the first time he had been to their house, and he hadn't seen Jane since the wedding. Sometime before Ralph's marriage, Steve had moved up in the department and had been assigned a high-profile case involving a series of murders in the high-rent district of their city. He and Ralph had been working night and day. Understandably, there was much pressure to get it solved.

*   *   *

It was indeed a short distance—a ten-minute drive. Ralph and Jane were on the porch when they arrived and welcomed them. Steve introduced Samantha as a friend of the Jones family whom he was taking to Lake House for a visit, which was true as far as it went. That seemed plausible, and no questions were addressed to her about that. Maybe Steve had said something to Ralph about confidentiality to spare her any questions. They were ushered into the family room where a pitcher of iced tea, tall glasses, and a plate of cookies were waiting for them on a large, round coffee table. Samantha avoided the sofa and chose a chair on the opposite side of the table. They engaged in some small talk; Samantha was not good at holding up her end of that. She liked them, and in respect for Steve said little, not wanting to risk expressing any opinion that might offend them. Previously, her peers had been teenagers. Now, she was an adult. In Edmund's gathering at the Grand Hotel, his friends had made her feel quite comfortable, but this situation was different. Having been relatively isolated since she was eighteen, she had not experienced social situations with adults near her age.

By nature, she was somewhat shy and by circumstances guarded. Normally, it took her a while to size up people and feel comfortable with them—especially in a social context. But, what was normal now? She was better with one-on-one relationships. She'd enjoyed eavesdropping on her parents' gatherings at home and listened intently when she was included in an outing with adults. On these occasions, she'd kept quiet and just listened and observed her parents, who'd always maintained a tactful, pleasant atmosphere. In her youthfulness and inexperience, she could be blunt and opinionated at times, but this had been in the safety of the family discussions. She knew this did not go over well with some people. Strangely, she rather liked a blunt, opinionated person, if he or she showed intelligence, had a good grasp of the subject, had good arguments to support a position, and didn't sink into bullying, shouting or spewing out irrational questions he never wanted answered.

Anyway, she wasn't ready yet to dip her toe into conversation—not just yet; she had been reserved and subdued for a long time now. She wondered if she would ever have the courage to venture an opinion again to anyone except Edmund. With these new acquaintances, she felt it wise just to listen and evaluate their worldviews. They weren't *there* yet—no heady discussion on the meaning of life, politics, or philosophy. Well, what did she expect? This was definitely mundane but pleasant conversation: the honeymoon—what a beautiful wedding—nice to see old friends—laughing over Steve's toast . . . .

Samantha was almost shocked at Steve's thoughtfulness when he apologized to her. "I'm sorry about going on and on about people you don't know. We're being rude. We should change the subject to include Samantha."

She politely said something about looking at the wedding pictures, so she could put faces to the names. This went over very well.

After taking some time to view the wedding pictures and tossing in some honeymoon pictures for good measure, Jane started commenting on the notorious murder case Steve had been in charge of solving prior to going to work for Mr. Jones. Even though it had been several years ago, it was still talked about. It had dominated the local news and was something unusual for their modest-sized city.

Jane started making general, flattering statements about the case being in Steve's most capable hands—the department had done well to promote him, she was sure. "Ralph always has such good things to say about you," she said. She asked innocuous questions such as, "How do you like your job?"

"I like it very much," he replied.

"Did you join the police department right out of college?"

"Yes," he answered.

"What's your new job like?" she pressed

Subsequently, her questions eased into more specific questions about Mr. Jones. "What's he really like?" Then, trying to lure him into giving her some inside information, she started with statements like: "Just among us—your best friends—you know we would never say a thing . . ."

Samantha almost laughed out loud and was amazed at the woman's curiosity. Perhaps she had gotten results with these tactics with others, but Steve wasn't going to be manipulated into divulging anything confidential about his job.

He said to her, "You wouldn't respect me if I divulged anything that compromised the trust my employer has placed in me. I can tell you that Mr. Jones is a remarkable man, very intelligent and thoughtful, and a very good employer."

Wow! Samantha thought, with a slightly visible approving smile she thought Steve picked up on. *An honorable man, and tactful too!*

She liked Steve a lot, but she had to remind herself that keeping her safe and well was his job, and his attitude toward her was friendly and pleasant, but sometimes firm, and always professional. He was at least ten years older than she was—maybe as much as fifteen years older. He was much more experienced than she was. He had seen the darker side of life, but, to her, he didn't seem jaded or cynical.

Gradually, Samantha's mood changed. Surprisingly, in spite of all that had taken place, she felt relaxed sitting in the couple's family room in the soft chair to which she had retreated after the wedding pictures. Perhaps she felt a release from the tensions of the past weeks, or Jane's rambling on and on in a boring monotone lulled her into a semiconscious state. Her attention wandered in and out of the conversation. Considering it unnecessary to say anything, she sat quietly, enjoying her tranquil moment.

One never knows what word or fleeting incident will influence an invasion of a soothing moment, add to the contentment, or shatter the peace. Memories come suddenly, stimulated unexpectedly . . . or perhaps a *déjà vu* moment floods over one's being. Stirred by something Jane said, her thoughts drifted away to a happier time. Her thoughts were interrupted when she heard Steve announce that they had to leave, as they were expected at Lake House before dark. They made their departure with cordial goodbyes.

*   *   *

As they drove north, Samantha felt quite content to be returning to Lake House and leaving the past behind her.

❧·CHAPTER 19

I was glad when they said unto me, "Let us go into the house of the Lord!"

Psalm 122:1

It was about 10:30 in the morning, exactly two weeks after returning to Lake House. Her wounds, physical and psychological, were healing well in this safe, caring environment. Steve was the only one who was aware of the physical wounds, as, in spite of the warm weather, Samantha kept these hidden. On this particular August morning, the air was still and hinted at another warm day. Samantha was in the library, reading, when she looked up and saw Abby, dressed in a white terrycloth jumpsuit and flip-flops, coming toward her.

"Hi, Samantha," she greeted her with her big smile.

"Hi, Abby."

"We're going swimming. Would you like to come?"

"Who's *we*?"

"Mommy, Isabella, and me."

"I'd love to. Oh, but I don't have a swimming suit." Samantha hesitated.

"Do you have shorts and a T-shirt?"

"Yes. Well, yes—that should do. I'll change and meet you on the beach. How about that?"

"Oh, yes, yes, yes, yes," Abby said in a sing-song voice, as she energetically skipped out of the room, trying to keep her flip-flops under control.

Samantha was happy not to have to wear a bathing suit. She chose a dark-colored T-shirt with a sleeve almost to her elbow; this covered the fresh scar on her upper arm. The stitches were out, but the scar was still a prominent, discolored mark on her white skin. She could hide the scar on her hand with a large, flesh-colored plastic bandage.

Shortly, Samantha was on the beach with Mary, Abby, and Isabella. The girls were running in and out of the waves that were breaking on the shore, and Mary was watching closely.

"The water is tolerable. The waves shifted during the night and are coming from the southwest—not too cold for the girls," explained Mary.

"Time to get wet!" announced Samantha.

Enjoying the sparkling, clear water, the girls squealed and giggled as they ventured farther out and then ducked down under an incoming wave. Abby was a good swimmer and started paddling around, bobbing up and down on the waves. Struggling, Isabella could keep herself afloat for a few seconds before she sunk down under the water and struggled again to regain her footing. She was thin and frail—no excess fat. Besides no fat, her feeble muscles made it especially difficult for her to deal with the water. Nevertheless, she was fearless and kept smiling and laughing. It wasn't deep, and the waves were small, but she was so weak that the next one knocked her down. To Isabella's delight, Samantha picked her up, held her tight, and started playing with her in the waves. Abby joined in the fun, splashing around Samantha and Isabella. Mary finally ventured in and swam out a short distance.

When Mary rejoined the group, she noticed Isabella's blue lips and announced, "Let's go play on the warm sand."

Thoroughly enjoying splashing and playing in the water, Abby protested, but Mary took her aside and explained, "Isabella needs to get warm. It would be helpful if we all join her on the beach."

Disappointed, she agreed.

On the beach, Mary took off Isabella's soaked suit, rubbed her vigorously with a towel, and blotted her hair until it was almost dry. Then she put her into a terrycloth jumpsuit similar to Abby's and a sun hat that tied under her chin. While her mother was tending to Isabella, Abby remained in her bathing suit, running around, collecting pebbles, and putting them in a pile. Soon she was dry enough to put on *her* jumpsuit. Then Isabella joined Abby in her pebble-collecting. When they had a sufficient number of pebbles, sticks, feathers, and whatever else intrigued them, they started smoothing out the sand and making designs. Mary and Samantha sat on beach towels nearby.

Mary explained, "Isabella is so fragile, we have to keep careful watch over her."

"I see," said Samantha. "Juanita told me that Isabella has a heart condition that cannot be cured, in spite of Mr. Jones' willingness to pay any expense for surgery or treatment."

On the beach, Isabella and Abby were noticeably different. Abby had dark Asian skin; black, straight hair; a sturdy, healthy body; a round, full face, and large, dark brown eyes. Isabella was pale and anemic, with slender, bony extremities; light brown eyes, and fine, sandy brown hair that tried to curl on humid days. Isabella had a pretty face, but it was drawn, and her high cheekbones were a bit too prominent. Abby was bouncy, energetic, and strong. Isabella did not exhibit much energy for a five-year-old (almost six—according to Abby) and looked as if a gust of wind could blow her over. She was a sweet shy little girl—pleased by any attention paid to her. She stayed closed to her mother or adults she knew well. Abby ran far afield and had to be reined in by her mother.

Samantha was lying on the warm sand, watching the girls play and thinking about how conflicted she was when it came to Isabella, so pleasant and lovable. She seemed to have a particular fondness and attachment to Samantha. Perhaps she saw her as an older sister to look up to. Samantha could not help but become emotionally involved with her, but she knew her heart would be broken again when she would have to part with her little friend. She was important to Isabella, and she could not reject her affection and trust for her own self-interest.

Just then, Isabella came over and gently pulled on Samantha's hand. "Come and help us make designs and find some more pebbles."

"Of course. Yes, let's find some more pebbles and decorating supplies."

Abby, Isabella, Mary, and Samantha started off along the shore. As Isabella started to walk slower and slower, Samantha asked, "Isabella, would you like to ride on my shoulders so you can have a good view and spy some pretty feathers and tiny pieces of driftwood for Abby and Mary to pick up?"

With a big grin and with as much excitement as she could manage, she replied, "Oh, yes! Yes, I would."

Samantha lifted her onto her shoulders easily, and the four started down the beach, Isabella spotting items for their artistic creations and Abby running to retrieve each one. They all seemed to have an unspoken willingness to accommodate Isabella's fragility and to make life easy and normal for her. Even Abby sensed something special about Isabella's situation and didn't envy her ride on Samantha's shoulders. She was content with her role in collecting the items.

They remained on the beach awhile longer; however, as it was approaching noon, appetites were getting keen, and they proceeded to Lake House to deliver Isabella to Juanita, who was working in the kitchen. When they entered, the girls started chattering to Juanita about the events of the morning—rather ordinary to the adults, but special to the children.

Juanita, anticipating their need for food, insisted they all sit at the corner table and declared that lunch would be provided promptly. Mary tended to the children, and Samantha helped Juanita with the sandwiches.

"We have fresh blueberries for lunch. One of the farmhands brought two large pails filled to the brim with beautiful berries," Juanita announced.

"Wonderful!" Mary and Samantha responded in unison.

With all the food items placed on the table, Juanita joined them and gave her full attention to the ramblings of the children.

* * *

After lunch, Mary, Abby, and Samantha walked toward the front door.

"I want to play my new computer game. Can I go home now?" Abby asked.

"Yes, you may. Stay on the path. Go directly home. I'll be there in a few minutes."

"Okay," she promised. Reenergized from lunch and unable to contain her impatience, she was out the door in a flash, jumping off the last step of the porch, and running across the lawn—a mighty little blur of white in her terrycloth jumpsuit as she disappeared behind the pine trees lining the path to the Ryan house. Samantha and Mary smiled, watching her eager progression.

Mary turned to Samantha and remarked, "It's been a nice morning. I'm glad you're here."

"Me, too. You've all been very kind. It's meant a lot to me."

Mary acknowledged her comment with a friendly smile, then proposed, "Tomorrow is Sunday, and we go to the church down the road. We would like you to come with us. Church is at 9:30—a short fellowship time after, with coffee and doughnuts, then Bible study."

"Thank you. I'd be pleased to go."

"If the weather is agreeable, we usually walk. It's a few hundred yards down the road that goes east, starting a little bit south of the entrance."

"I've never seen it."

"There's a rise in the road and then a little valley past that. You can't see it from here or the entrance. It's a fairly large, traditional-style church—stained glass windows, and a very nice pipe organ in the back. The congregation is small. We barely fill half the church on a regular Sunday. Three or four generations back, an ancestor of the Jones family built the church. Actually, they own the property and the church. The congregation rents it for a nominal sum. They've all belonged. I expect they make up any shortfalls in the budget, but no one ever knows just what. There's also a school—four classrooms, K through eight, with some combined classes. Abby goes there. Children from the farm and the estate go—they're older. They walk together on nice days, or someone takes them in an estate vehicle. The school was very important to Mrs. Amanda Jones—she put a lot of time and effort into it. I must say, the children receive an excellent education. The church has always been an important part of the Jones' family life."

"I got that impression from the nobody-works-on-Sunday-except-security rule and the cold do-it-yourself supper at the main house on Sunday," Samantha mused.

"Yes," Mary said with a grin. She explained that the pastor's wife was one of the teachers. "They have five children. The pastor teaches religion and history classes. A rather lovely, large house is provided for them near the church. The church's music director teaches music classes. He and his wife have five children, who also attend the school. There are two other teachers: a young couple with four children—the two older children are twins—that's a handful. They live a couple of miles north toward town."

"Sounds like the teachers supply a good share of the students," Samantha said, amused.

Mary smiled. "There are about 45 children in the school. The preschool and daycare attendance varies—probably from 14 to 18. For the school, there's no tuition for the members' children, but they do expect parents to contribute what they can to the church to meet the cost, and the parents are expected to volunteer to help with activities or wherever their talents lie—it's a cooperative effort between teachers and parents."

"Sounds like a good plan."

"School will be starting in about two weeks. The children put on little plays and concerts. Be warned, I'm sure Abby will be inviting you to every performance."

"And I will be very pleased to come."

"I don't know if you're acquainted with the Lutheran church . . . ?"

"Yes, I am," Samantha interjected. "Our family went to a Lutheran church, but I never went to school there."

"Oh, it'll be familiar, then. That's good." Mary continued, "Music is an important subject at the school. Frequently, the children's musical contributions are part of the church service. Well, I always say that the order of importance of subjects in a Lutheran school is: religion, music, reading, writing and arithmetic."

"I can believe that," Samantha replied, remembering her family's interest in music.

"Well, I'd better see what Abby's up to. See you tomorrow. We'll come over to the house and meet you in the front sitting room. Juanita and Isabella will probably go with us, if Isabella is up to it. We pull Isabella in a special oversized stroller."

"Okay, see you then," Samantha responded, then went back into the house.

❧·CHAPTER 20

*"For I know the plans I have for you," declares the LORD,
"plans to prosper you and not to harm you,
plans to give you a future and a hope."*

Jeremiah 29:11

It was Tuesday morning. Mr. Ryan entered the kitchen and informed Samantha that Howard Tyler, the archivist, would be coming for three or four days the following week to work on the family records and the library. "I've organized a small dinner party for him on Monday and invited a few of the staff who are interested in history. Steve, Mary, Abby, and a couple of others—you haven't met them yet—will be there. He has agreed to tell us some of his Indian tales after dinner. I told him you're interested in Michigan history and have been reading about the 17th-century Will Jones and the Indians. If you'd like, Howard will make some time for the two of you to talk."

"I *am* definitely interested, and I'd be honored. How thoughtful! Thank you!"

"Mr. Jones suggested it."

"Oh, how thoughtful," she said quietly. "With all that's on his mind, he was concerned about me."

"He hoped it would cheer you up and help pass the time while you're waiting for him to return."

"When did you hear from him last? How's his son?"

"Paul is about the same, but they do expect him to recover. However, he may be left with some limitations. Mr. Jones plans to bring him here to convalesce as soon as he's stable and can travel. Paul and his wife will be coming here to stay—probably indefinitely. The doctors expect it will take many months for him to recuperate and build up his strength. He'll need lots of therapy with special equipment. You'll be seeing workmen coming in and out. They're installing an elevator at the end of the south wing and making other modifications to the family section of the house on the second floor in that area."

*　　*　　*

Monday evening, Mr. Ryan escorted a man in his fifties with thick, wavy salt-and-pepper hair into the library and introduced him to Samantha. Howard Tyler had a ready smile and a cheerful way about him.

"Do you maintain all of this?" she asked, motioning to the bookshelves.

"I do. I have some helpers I send from time to time. Robert Jones, Mr. Edmund Jones's brother, and his wife, Elizabeth, were avid readers. Robert was a student of history—a hobby, I'd say. Although he had a degree from MIT in electrical engineering, his interests were diverse. He started the library at Lake House and set up a sizable endowment to maintain it."

"I've been reading Will's journals, or your translation of them, as my attempt at 17th-century English wasn't very good. For me, any Shakespeare I've read needed to come with a lot of footnotes. I noticed your name in the preface and was happy you translated the journals into 21st-century American English. It made them much easier to read—well, I should say possible to read. Besides the words I didn't know, "s" looks like "f," and some words are spelled differently."

"Yes, it's interesting how the language has changed over the years. Actually, I did it quite some time ago, about 20 years ago, and that would be the 20th century," he clarified with a twinkle in his eye. Being a historian, it was his nature to be precise when possible.

"I'm anxious to hear more about Will. His journals stop after about six years. Do you know what happened to him?"

"Yes, there's a brief history of the rest of Will's life that I was able to piece together from other sources. That's farther down on the same shelf. It seems he stopped writing a journal in about 1642. It appears he started writing when he joined up with the five friends—you know about that episode. He may have written something about his sea voyage to America, but if he did, those writings were lost or destroyed. Why he stopped when he did, I'm not sure. Perhaps they got too heavy to carry around." He chuckled. "Perhaps he was too caught up with family life. Perhaps events were too personal for him to write about, and later, with tragedy that disheartened him, possibly he lost interest."

"I liked Will a lot. I'm sorry to hear he faced tragedy. His life started out so positive and interesting."

"Will and his young wife had what I would call unfinished lives. They had so much promise. But, I'm getting ahead of myself. I'll relay what I know of their story to you tomorrow morning, when we have a chance to talk—don't want to bore little Abby, and the others know the story already. Abby loves the Indian stories. I have some new ones I think everyone will enjoy."

Mr. Ryan, Mary, and Abby arrived first, and one by one the others joined them in the library. Then, on schedule, the young lady who would be doing the serving announced that dinner was ready. Samantha followed her to a pleasant room with a tastefully set round table near an expanse of windows overlooking the terrace, the lawn, the lake, and a cloudy, windy day. As she waited for the others, who had stopped momentarily to admire a piece of artwork in the hall, she looked briefly through the telescope in the corner of the room. She was fascinated by the long strands of coarse grass along the slope to the beach, being beaten down and drawing deep circles in the sand around the base of each clump, and the white-capped waves rolling high onto the beach, making their wet patterns along the shore.

The house was solid and indifferent to whatever nature hurled against it. It had turned chilly, unusually cool for the end of August, and a pleasant fire was consuming real wood and sending sparks up the fireplace. The spent pieces of apple wood dropped from the grate and gave up their scent. The room was cozy, perfect for the conversation with a historian and his tales of the past.

*   *   *

The next morning, Samantha met Howard in the library as planned. Instead of Samantha asking him questions, she was the subject of interest. "I'm interested in your family name—S-c-h-w-e-r-i-n, you pronounce it—Sher'in."

"That's not really our name," she interjected. "The story I was told is that Schwerin is a town in northern Germany in the duchy of Mechlenburg-Schwerin—anyway, that's what it was called in the 19th century, when my father's ancestors, Ida and her son, left. Charles was 12 when they came to America in 1869. Ida's husband, father, brothers, other sons—all the men in the family—had been killed in wars. She wanted to save her last child—Charles. The immigration officers got things mixed up and put down S c h w e r i n for the last name. They hardly spoke any English and didn't realize the mistake until later. Rather than complicate matters trying to straighten things out in a foreign language and a strange country, they stuck with the name. Actually, my name should have been Samantha Sophia Karsten."

To say that the historian looked amazed and astonished was an understatement. He was rendered speechless by her relation. There was a long pause.

Samantha finally said, "What's the matter?"

"Well, I don't know where to start, and that's a first for me. I'm dumbfounded."

Samantha could not imagine what had happened or what she could have said that was so shocking. While she was waiting for him to collect himself, strange thoughts flashed through her mind. *I hope my ancestors weren't fugitives from the law or anything like that. But, what does it matter now? What is there about this seemingly straightforward sequence of events in my family history that produced such an astonished expression?*

Then he explained, "Will's wife's name was Sophia Karsten, and she was from Mechlenburg-Schwerin, in northern Germany. That's why I was curious about your history when I saw your name written in Neville's memo. I knew Sophia Jones was from a village of that name and Will spent some time there. Apparently, it's the same place."

Now, Samantha was stunned. After a pause to assimilate the information as best she could, she responded, "My parents never said they named me after anyone in particular. They said they had a friend named Sophia and liked the name—they hoped I'd be wise, I think."

"Then you never knew of any relatives there?"

"No, I've never heard of any there now. I guess we were never very curious about family history."

"Even if you were, it's unlikely you would have been able to find any information. Few family records can be found, as many public buildings containing the records were burned during the wars. Also, as you told about your ancestor, many families were wiped out or displaced in the war—outright killed, starved, or died of disease—especially the men."

"How did Will get to that town in Germany?"

"Well, after about ten years of living off the land with the Indians in Michigan, the older men, then in their forties, wanted to settle down. Will was still young, just about twenty-nine, and wanted to go back to England. It was early summer, 1643. News at that time traveled slowly, but he knew England was being torn by civil war and was worried about his family and how things were for them. So, he made his way up the St. Lawrence River to a port on the Canadian Atlantic coast. For some peculiar reason, he found a German ship. This was extremely unusual, as Germans were not known to be in this part of the world. It seems they were blown considerably off course and were making plans to sail back to Germany. It was getting late in the season. The other ships had already sailed. The Germans had no other choice but to sail immediately or spend the winter in Canada. That was Will's only choice, too, and he took it.

"After sailing across the Atlantic, they sailed through the North Sea and landed at a port there to unload cargo, then into their home port on Mecklenburg Bay. The last day of the voyage, Will became very sick with a high fever. When they reached Germany, Captain Klaus Karsten and one of the young sailors, his son Kurt, took Will home with them. Klaus, his wife, son, and daughter—you guessed it: Sophia—lived near Schwerin. It took most of the winter for Will to recover. However, under the capable hands of Sophia and her mother, he was restored to health."

"It's strange that Will struggled though the wilderness, combating the cold, bears, and the hardships of nature and remained hearty and healthy, but some virus of civilization almost conquered him," Samantha commented.

"Yes, it is. He must have contracted it at the port where they unloaded the cargo," Howard remarked. "The Thirty Years' War[20] was wreaking havoc in Europe. Somehow, the Karstens managed to stay out of it, since they owned a shipping company, the men were away at sea. Also, they were in northern Germany, which was somewhat remote. The house was large and away from the town, in an isolated location. On the farm, they raised most of what they needed for the animals and nine people—the

---

[20] Thirty Years' War: 1618-1648; term used loosely for a series of wars to dismantle the Holy Roman Empire (misnomer: neither holy nor really Roman; now Europe); involved religious struggles among Christian groups—Catholics, Lutherans, Calvinists, other Protestants. Religious focus later became a territorial fight; symbolizes the transitional period of the Renaissance-Reformation era. By the end, Europe was ravaged. Half of the German population was killed, wounded, or displaced; two-thirds of the land and cities were damaged.

family of four, two house servants, and three men who worked in the fields, tended the horses and animals, and did whatever else needed doing around the farm. The servant girls occupied a room behind the kitchen, and the men had living space above the stables. There were enough bedrooms so that Will had one to himself. It was not as grand as his family's estate and manor house in England, but it was a comfortable home.

"The shipping business was their main source of income, and apparently, even in time of war, it was quite profitable. In the spring, Will was smitten with Sophia and was strong enough to propose. They were married early that summer. They stayed at the Karsten homestead. Will helped on the farm and even went on a few cargo runs around the Baltic Sea. In the spring of 1645, Sophia gave birth to twin boys. In June of 1646, things having calmed down a bit in Europe and England, Will took this window of opportunity to return to England with his wife and sons. He found the estate intact and his parents well. Unfortunately, his brothers had been killed—the details of this were unclear. Probably something connected with the civil war in England. Of course, his family was delighted to see him but a trifle dismayed that he'd chosen a German wife. Nevertheless, they treated her with respect and gratefulness for her family's kindness in taking him into their home and nursing him back to health. They doted and fussed over the babies, as these were their only living grandsons. The other sons had married, but their children had not survived more than a few years, except for one frail girl, Emily, who had been there when Will left."

"What an amazing story," Samantha interjected. "How did you find this out?"

"I went to England and found the records. The estate is still there—descendants of that frail little girl live there. It's open to the public for tours. However, it still belongs to the family—actually, Mr. Edmund Jones is the rightful heir. The name of the branch of the family that lives there is Smith. Can you believe that? Emily married a Smith."

Samantha laughed. "Hardly! No wonder my name drew attention."

He pursued, "You're most likely related to Will's wife, since your ancestors have the same name and come from the same town. What plan of Providence brought you here is beyond me."

"I'm stunned. It's more than I can comprehend. That's an astonishing story!" she responded.

"It truly is."

"So, where does the tragedy come in? I hesitate to ask."

"Will, Sophia, and their sons lived at the family estate in England for several years, until his parents became ill and passed away. Emily, Will's niece, grew up and eventually married the-titled-gentleman Smith. He had no money or property—just his title—so they also lived at the Jones estate. Will was heir to the property, as his brothers and all the other family members were gone. England finally attained an effective Parliament, and Will became a member. The king's rule had been limited by the ruling classes. However, in 1649, when Charles I saw it otherwise and tried to assert power, a civil struggle broke out, and he paid for it with his head. After that, England's government went through a succession of experimental ruling authorities.

Will was unhappy with politics and the unrest in the country and wanted to raise his sons in the free, open spaces of the new country he had come to admire. In the spring of 1653, leaving the family estate in the hands of his niece and her husband, he packed up his family and sailed for America. The weather was favorable, and the crossing was relatively routine. Their ship landed in a settlement in New England—it's unclear where. Will was unhappy with the conflict he found there and decided to try to make his way back to Michigan and the peaceful, hardworking community he had respected.

"However, about this time, the Iroquois were brutally attacking settlements, both white and Indian, along the Ottawa River and in Huron territory north of Lakes Ontario and Erie. They had virtually annihilated the Native American population of the Lower Peninsula and cut off the Ottawa River and St.

Lawrence River routes into Michigan. By then, the Iroquois had acquired guns, ammunition, and gunpowder from Dutch traders. They ruthlessly obliterated the Indian villages of St. Ignace and St. Louis. The Jesuit missionaries to the Huron, Father Brébeuf and Father Lalemant, had been viciously tortured and killed by the Iroquois in March 1649. Into the 1650s, the Iroquois persisted in their siege of New France. After destroying the Hurons, they moved on to massacre or drive out the Indians of western Ontario, north of Lake Erie."

"Sounds rather dangerous to be traveling with a wife and two eight-year-old boys," Samantha remarked.

"Will taught the boys well, and they knew there was no nonsense about their endeavor—even at their young age, they had to pull their weight. Sophia could load a musket as quickly and efficiently as anyone and, if absolutely necessary, fire the long, heavy thing and hit the mark. She was tall for a woman of that era, but fine-boned. Actually, she may have looked much like you. She was no wimp! She could maneuver through whatever they encountered on land or water. At eight, the boys were sturdy lads, much like their father, but just too small to fire a musket. Nevertheless, they could load them and keep them coming for Will," he explained. "The family joined up with a group of traders bound for Canada. However, after the tales of the carnage north of Lake Ontario, they headed far south of that territory. Next, Will and his family found a group of missionaries bound for the southwestern part of Michigan. Obtaining a large, sturdy canoe, they traveled north along the Lake Michigan shoreline. Knowing the dangers they faced, Will was well-equipped with guns, ammunition, and gunpowder."

"That Sophia was pretty gutsy. It must have taken a lot of courage. I can't imagine being able to do all that."

"I suppose so. I'm not sure she knew what she was getting into—then you do what you have to," Howard said with a smile. "No doubt, Will made it all sound very romantic when he related his stories to the families in Germany and England. He probably left out some of the tough, unpleasant stuff when Sophia was around."

"I hadn't thought about that. You're probably right."

"After weeks of searching, they found the comrades Will had left. Actually, the Indians found them. A hunting party saw the canoe. Keeping hidden, they followed it. When Will and his family came ashore, the Indians approached them. Will recognized members of the party, and an enthusiastic reunion ensued. The village had moved a few miles north of the original site and was now a mixture of French, English, and various Indian heritages. The Frenchmen couldn't go back. After Will left, Geoffrey had tried to leave, but after being turned back several times for various reasons, he'd remained. Clive became homesick early on and, as you know, left before Will did. Tom was now the chief leading the community with guidance from his Bible—maybe a second Solomon."

"Oh, I never found out what happened when Tom tried to convince the group of refugees that there was no evil spirit to appease or benevolent spirit to sacrifice a puppy to for good fishing," Samantha stated.

"That *was* rather gruesome," he responded. "I wish I knew for sure, but the details were not recorded. However, whatever he did, it looks as though they finally abandoned the practice."

"I'm glad to hear that! I won't have to search for it anymore. It *was* getting frustrating."

"It's not there—I looked," he assured her.

"So, do you know how the group was getting along during Will's absence?"

"Most of the information for this period is from family word of mouth and letters—it's sketchy. However, it seems Tom was able to implement his vision for the community, and it prospered. Protected by the great lake on one side and swamps, a series of lakes and rivers, and dense forests in the interior, they managed to stay out of the notice of the outside world. Some of the Indians traveled south to trade with other Indians occasionally, but they kept their location hidden. They moved from time to time for better hunting but stayed in the same general area in the northwestern part of the Lower Peninsula."

"Oh, yes, I remember reading in Will's journal how they went to great lengths to avoid revealing the location of their village. I think the only time they came in contact with the outside world was when that small group traveled northeast to trade furs."

"That's right," Howard responded. "Also, at that time they were able to gather information from the outside world in the three languages of the society. Actually, you could say four—English, French, and the two basic Indian languages of that region. When they returned, the travelers spent several days telling all they had learned."

"Yes," she responded. "Even though they wanted to stay hidden, they seemed interested in what was going on elsewhere, especially Tom and the Europeans. I remember reading in Will's journal about their taking in unfortunate wanders from time to time. They would all gather to hear the stranger's tales of personal misfortune and life in other communities. Then, for days the newcomer would sit in the council of the chiefs, who would evaluate the information he brought. It was interesting that they became such a varied group—all bringing aspects of their former cultures, but still appreciating the civility, peace, and acceptance they found in this community. It seems they were able to incorporate *some* of the 'technical advances,' of that time, anyway."

"They were always looking for a better way of doing things. It seems their elders had a particular wisdom in regard to sorting out the best ideas."

"Tom and the elders must have been good salesmen for the people to accept the changes," Samantha hypothesized.

"The Ottawa and the Chippewa had respect for the wisdom of the elders and weren't likely to revolt over changes, and it was likely that strangers from other tribes were used to that tradition, too. There may have been a few 'Woe is me,' or, 'Here we go again,' comments mumbled. I'm not sure," Howard speculated with a little grin.

Samantha smiled and recounted, "That reminds me of Tolstoy. When he tried to change things on his estate and bring about efficiency and technology in the farming practices, the peasants resisted vehemently."

He chuckled, "I guess they did—that seems to be human nature. Nobody seems to like change. I don't know if these people did or, just as I said before, accepted the wisdom of their elders. They seemed to make good choices for their people."

"I wish all leaders had that kind of common sense and wisdom, to discern the good from the bad and reason out what the unintended consequences might be."

Howard smiled, nodded, and then responded in a regretful tone. "Well, it's a nice thought." After a brief pause, he returned to his narrative about the Indian community. "Well, the leaders in Will's Indian community were wise enough to prepare to defend themselves if necessary. They acquired guns, and with the Frenchmen's military skills, the Indians' hunting skills, and Tom's intrinsic savvy, they continued developing their own defenses to fend off any stray Iroquois. Occasionally, a small band of Iroquois hunters or raiders with evil intentions ventured that far."

"Excuse me, but I was wondering about the portrait of Will on the wall over there. Why isn't his family in the portrait?"

"Well, that's an interesting story," he started, deviating from his tale. "As I mentioned before—oh, I *am* sorry. I have an appointment in five minutes in the main office, and this is a long story. Time got away from me—I've enjoyed this very much— we'll talk again soon."

"Thank you so much. I've enjoyed it very much, too," she said quickly and sincerely as he rushed out.

For awhile, Samantha stayed in the library, studying the portrait of Will and the other ancestors.

☙·CHAPTER 21

The heavens declare the glory of God.
The skies proclaim the work of His hands.
Day after day they pour forth speech.
Night after night they display knowledge.
There is no speech or language where their voice is not heard
Their voice goes out into all the earth, their words to the ends of the world.

Psalm 19:1-4

It was well into September and signs of fall were about: the sumac was red, the sassafras yellow, and the annuals around the house were growing long and ragged, reaching to grasp the diminishing sunlight of the shorter days The lake was gray, the wind sharp and brisk. Storms still came, and thunder rumbled over the lake as the lightning flashed on the horizon.

One night, the thunder rumbled all night. Finally, at five o'clock, while it was still dark, Samantha got up and opened the shade to observe the spectacle. She lay across her bed, watching the lightning flashes, one right after another, seconds apart, lighting up the whole expanse of water and waves. During her summer at Lake House, she had seen the many moods of the lake, but never anything quite like this display.

At Lake House, away from any city, one could get a true sense of the vastness of the universe—the power of nature and the design of the cosmos. It was intimidating.

* * *

One afternoon while she was reading, a particular subject brought back the memory of an extraordinary evening a few weeks earlier—late in August. A memo had gone out in the afternoon, inviting any interested resident of Lake House or the Farm to a gathering on the beach for a meteor shower. The atmosphere would be right for optimum viewing. Often, a cloudy night would obscure the rare display, but this night, the time and conditions were a go.

After dark, the lights in the houses and on the grounds had been turned off or dimmed. Guided by flashlights, all had made their way to the beach. The organizers had provided hot beverages, snacks, and blankets. The heavens had provided the show—the dancing stars, the choreographed planets, and the bright flashing meteors; the power of the Lord was on display, spilling over them. The waves had cheered and applauded. It had been glorious! The awestruck spectators felt humble and small—"what is man that You are mindful of him, and the son of man that You care for him?"

* * *

Samantha also passed the days playing games with Abby and Isabella either at the Ryan house or Lake House. Abby was trying to build her vocabulary with the words from the Dolch List[21] by using flash cards. Samantha was trying to help, but all were bored to tears with the method. As a result, Mary, being a clever person, made up a board game using all the basic words. They called it Space Trip. It had cute drawings and was intriguing to the girls. It became their favorite game. Samantha monitored the game, and Abby and Isabella memorized the words in a flash. Even after they knew all the words, they loved to play it, so Mary designed another game with more words called Jungle Trip. It was

---

[21] Dolch List: A list of basic sight words learned by first and second graders.

somewhat more complicated and kept them busy, increasing their vocabulary and reading skills.

Samantha and Mary were becoming good friends. One day, the two of them went into a nearby village and spent the morning wandering through shops, deserted by tourists, as Labor Day had passed, ending the season. They drifted into a bookstore specializing in lake lore and local history. They enjoyed listening to its enthusiastic owner, who answered questions with more information than they could possibly process in one hour. Samantha bought a book that sounded intriguing: *Michigan on Fire*. They thanked the owner for her help, left the shop, and walked a few blocks to a cozy little restaurant, where they chatted incessantly over lunch about all sorts of things—nothing too serious.

This was new for Samantha—the first time she truly had an adult woman friend. She felt comfortable with Mary; even so, she would never divulge her wealth—it would always remain her secret. However, she did talk a little about her family. Mary was not the gossipy sort and always spoke well of their shared acquaintances—the family, visitors, and staff at the estate. Mary admired Steve and Mr. Jones. She wasn't well-acquainted with the rest of the Jones family, as she had infrequent interactions with them when they came to visit.

Mary had often invited Samantha to dinner, and wanting to do something nice for the family, Samantha asked them to be her guests for dinner at a restaurant. Mary was a bit reluctant. "Sweetie . . . ." (She often called Abby, Isabella, and her good friends "Sweetie" when she was in a motherly mood.) "Sweetie, you don't have to spend your money on us like that."

Samantha responded with persistence, "Oh, don't worry about that. Don't worry about that at all. I haven't had to spend any money here, and I do have some insurance income." (It was true; she had a small income from insurance her parents had.) "I'd really like to very much. I would be very disappointed if we couldn't."

"Well, all right then. That *would* be lovely, and we would enjoy it very much. How about Monday?"

"Monday it is," said Samantha, very pleased. She had never arranged a dinner party, but she had observed her mother making arrangements at a restaurant many times. She asked around to find out the nicest restaurant with the best food in the area, and all agreed on one overlooking a nearby river. She called and made the reservations.

Mr. Ryan had to drive as Samantha had no car (though he had assured her she could borrow one of the cars belonging to the estate anytime she wanted to go somewhere). She was still apprehensive about going out on her own and was not familiar with the area. Besides, their needing a car seat for Abby was a good excuse for Mr. Ryan to drive.

The restaurant was as charming as described. The hostess guided them to a round table by the window that she had requested when she made the reservation on the phone. She'd been advised to request this table. For awhile, they engaged in some cheerful conversation and studied the menu.

Abby wiggled with excitement and occupied herself with every angle of the children's menu. Finally, she read slowly and deliberately, "'Mac and cheese, an extra-or-din-ary blend of four cheeses.' What's 'extra-or-din-ary,' Daddy?"

Daddy responded with a gentle grin, "In this case we would pronounce it extraordinary. It means very special."

"Then that's what I'm having: mac and cheese! That's my favorite." When she finished it, Abby said it was the best she'd ever had, and she was an expert on mac and cheese as that was the only thing she ever ordered when eating at a restaurant. The food was excellent, and they all had a wonderful time.

The adults lingered over tea and coffee as Abby slowly savored every bite of a huge dish of chocolate ice cream, after which she put her head on the table and immediately fell asleep. Her mother said she did that occasionally after a lot of excitement. The adults carried on their conversation for a while. Then Samantha paid the bill with her credit card, and Mr. Ryan lovingly picked up little Abby, carried her to the car, and carefully secured her in the car seat. Her sleep was uninterrupted—she barely stirred. This gentle scene struck a sentimental note, but a pleasant one, with Samantha; it reminded her of the times she had fallen asleep and her daddy had lovingly carried his little sweetie to the car or to bed.

Samantha and Mary remained in front of the Ryan house, on the path to the main house, while Mr. Ryan put Abby into bed. Shortly thereafter, he joined them to walk Samantha home. As they walked, he informed her that Howard Tyler would be arriving in the morning. "He told me he was unable to finish the Jones family saga and was sorry he had to leave so soon last time. If you're interested and have the time, perhaps the two of you could meet tomorrow morning. Would 9:30 in the library suit you?"

"That would be wonderful! Definitely! I'll be there. Thank you!" she rattled off.

He thanked her again for the dinner. She felt that he'd genuinely enjoyed it; she was sure Mary and Abby had.

As they reached the front door, he opened it with his entrance card, and she went in and said, "Good night. See you tomorrow."

*   *   *

Wanting to finish some of the books Howard had recommended during their previous visit, Samantha entered the library early the next morning.

Arriving right on schedule, he greeted her with his engaging grin and appeared genuinely pleased to see her. After a friendly exchange of light conversation, they walked over to the portrait of Will. "You asked about this portrait the last time I was here. Well, that's an interesting story. This *is* an intriguing portrait, and particularly well-done. As I mentioned before, Clive left the Indian village about a year before Will—about 1642. He made his way back to England and visited Will's family. Will's niece,

Emily, the daughter of his oldest brother, lived at the estate. She was an accomplished artist and intrigued with Will's story. *She painted this picture during Clive's stay with the family.* He was there several months. That was before Will was married and returned to England with his wife and sons. As a child, Emily had painted a small picture of Will—shortly before he'd left home. Between that and Clive's description of Will and their life in the wilderness, she rendered what you see here."

"She was an outstanding artist—at least, I think so."

"Yes, she was, by any standard. However, she only painted portraits of the family, the pets and livestock on the estate, the house, and some landscapes of the grounds. She was frail and never ventured very far from home. One of her tutors taught her to paint, and she had a natural talent for it. All of her paintings still belong to the family, as they are part of the historical record of that era. I brought this one and a picture of the manor house from England."

"Where's the manor house picture?"

"It's over the fireplace in the common room of the family quarters on the second floor. I'm sure Mr. Jones will show it to you sometime."

"I'm sorry I interrupted you, but what happened to Will and his family?"

"Well, I'm sorry to say that Sophia, at about 30 years old, drowned in Lake Michigan. The details are unclear. Will was devastated and inconsolable. He died about two years later."

Samantha went visibly pale at the news that Sophia had drowned in Lake Michigan. The strange saga of the Jones family and her family was more than she could comprehend. *Sophia Karsten, my namesake, drowned! What an extraordinary twist of destiny!*

Howard noticed the change in her mood. "Are you all right?"

"I'm sorry, I feel a little sick. It was a shock to hear that Sophia drowned."

"Oh, I'm sorry," he said.

"My family drowned in an accident on Lake Michigan," she confided.

"I'm really sorry. I didn't know."

"I know—no one does, except Edmund. It's been too difficult to talk about. Somehow, this was very distressing."

"I can see that," he said sympathetically. "Can I get you anything?"

"I'll be okay in a minute," she said, regaining her equanimity. "This has all been interesting, but this turn of events is . . . ."

Just then, Isabella appeared in the doorway and shyly made her way over to Samantha's chair. Standing almost behind it, she whispered to her, "Mommy sent me."

This was a welcomed interruption, as Samantha did not want to dwell on the fate of Will and Sophia, especially Sophia. She put her arms around Isabella and lifted the girl up onto her lap.

"Tell me what Mommy wanted," she said softly.

Feeling more at ease with Samantha hugging her, Isabella started, "Mommy wants to know when you and Mr. Tyler would like lunch and what you want to eat."

"Well, yes, I guess we *are* getting hungry. Have you had lunch yet?" she asked.

Isabella replied, "No, not yet."

"What would *you* suggest we have for lunch?" Samantha said playfully.

"Peanut butter and jam sandwiches," she responded without hesitation, her face beaming. "That's *my* favorite."

"That sounds good to me, too," replied Samantha. "Do you like peanut butter and jam sandwiches, Mr. Tyler?"

"I haven't had them in a very long time. It would be a treat," he answered kindheartedly, with a playful chuckle, "Especially with Juanita's homemade berry jam."

"Well, Isabella, since you have planned the menu, I think you should have lunch with us. Maybe Mr. Tyler will tell us one of his Indian stories while we eat our sandwiches," Samantha urged.

"I would be very pleased," Howard said. "I know one about a brave Indian princess who saved her tribe from disaster. Would you like that one?"

Isabella's eyes widened. "Yes, I would! Yes, I would!"

"Do you like milk and cookies, Mr. Tyler?" Samantha asked.

"Yes, I do."

Samantha wrote on a piece of paper:

> 3 for lunch
> Peanut butter and jam sandwiches,
> carrot sticks (or something like that),
> dishes of mixed fruit (fresh, if you have it),
> Oatmeal Cherry Walnut Cookies, and milk.
> We have asked Isabella to join us for lunch.
> We will eat in the sunroom.
>
> Thanks, Juanita!
> Samantha

"Sweetie, take this to Mommy. Come back and get us when lunch is ready," Samantha instructed.

"Okay."

"I hope you don't mind," Samantha said as she turned to Howard.

"No, not at all. She is a charming little girl. Are you okay?" he asked again. "You look much better."

"Yes, thank you—much better. Lunch will do us good, and Isabella will be a bright spot after that sad turn of events. But, I *am* interested in what happened to the boys. We have a few minutes, if their tale isn't too long."

"I can give you a quick synopsis."

"Okay."

"When Will fell ill, he asked Geoffrey to try to get the boys back to England. Samuel and Albert were fourteen when their father died. Over the next two years, Geoffrey tried to find them passage with English traders, but they didn't make it and returned to the Indian community. The boys stayed there for several years. Then, Geoffrey got sick or had an accident and died. Finally, when they were older, the boys, wanting to return to England as their father had wished, tried again."

"Why do you think Will wanted them to go back to England? He seemed happy in Michigan with his friends."

"Well, I'm not sure, but I think it was getting harder to escape from the struggles. Dealing with the environment was a challenge he was willing to take, but the conflict between the English, French, and Indians was vicious and unpredictable."

"I see."

"Besides that, perhaps he thought they would have better resources there and a more complete education. Although, England was having its difficulties, too."

"They must have eventually married and had children," Samantha commented.

"Of course. They got as far as a mission settlement or a fort somewhere in southwestern Michigan. They had traveled a long way from their Indian friends, and winter was setting in. By then, the boys had no resources to make the trip to England or back to the Indians, so they stayed with a missionary family. They prospered there, married, and had children. Samuel married a minister's daughter; she was much younger than he was. He was 48 when his son, Arthur, was born.

"What happened to the Indian community?" Samantha asked.

"We don't know. I think most of them became integrated into the western culture as the area became settled by Europeans—some, after all, had European and English heritage. Some migrated south and joined the peaceful Moravian Christian Indians in Ohio—that's an unfortunate story, but it's too long to relate now. The story of Will and Sophia was passed down in the family by word of mouth and brief written accounts. Later, when the territory where the community had been—where Will and Sophia are buried—became available for purchase to settlers,

Will's descendant bought the land here along the lake and the farm and built the beginnings of Lake House. The following generations continued to live here and add to it."

Isabella returned, beaming with anticipation, and the trio proceeded to the sunroom. A happier mood prevailed with their modest repast of peanut butter and jam sandwiches and tales of the Indian princess who saved her tribe.

❧·CHAPTER 22

"It was the best of times, it was the worst of times,
it was the age of wisdom, it was the age of foolishness,
it was the epoch of belief, it was the epoch of incredulity,
it was the season of Light, it was the season of Darkness,
it was the spring of hope, it was the winter of despair . . .

Charles Dickens: *A Tale of Two Cities* (1859)

It was well after midnight. The high winds were howling through the tall pines around the house and causing them to squeak and grind. Only the highest-decibel sounds invaded the solid house with its thick walls and insulation. Tonight, the reverberations leaked in, as Samantha had opened a window a crack. Her room was too warm, and she enjoyed the fresh air coming off the lake.

After lying in bed with her mind racing through recent events, she decided to get up and try to put an end to the insomnia. First, she opened her computer, went online, and read the headlines and news stories of the day. That made things worse! She decided to go down to the library. Perhaps she could find some happy fiction that would shift her mind into a better mode.

She made her way through the dimly lit corridor, down the wide main staircase, and through more dimly lit halls to the library. Here, she found the light switch by the entrance; the huge room was illumined, as bright as a sunny day. She started searching the fiction section. Her eyes were drawn to a series of books bound with the same maroon hardback covers—the entire works of Charles Dickens, one of her very favorite authors. She started reading the titles: *Barnaby Rudge, Bleak House,* then stopped at *A Christmas Carol,* a favorite of hers. *It's a long time 'til Christmas, and I'm not in the mood for a procession of spirits, even though it's a good night for a ghost story,* she thought as she continued perusing the succession of books.

Next was *David Copperfield. An orphan! Once was enough for that one.* She laughed as she thought, *Mr. Micawber: large family, faithful wife; philosophy of life: no matter how bad things get, something good will turn up. And Charles Dickens, sooner or later, made sure it did.*

Dombey and Sons—no. Edwin Drood—no. Great Expectations— another parentless waif, a definite no! Miss Havisham's cold, cynical twisted view of life doesn't suit me—that's certainly not the mood I'm in. Hard Times—that was really depressing. Little Dorrit—now, that would be apropos: money and position influencing how people behave and how people behave toward them, or maybe how they perceive it does. That's a maybe. She pulled it out of the row and placed it on the table.

Then, returning to the books, her eyes landed on *The Old Curiosity Shop. Parentless little person, pathetic grandpa, long-suffering little Nell . . . sweet little Nell, dear little Nell, break-my-heart little Nell—no way,* she thought as she continued her mental assessment of reading options in the Dickens category. *Oliver Twist—not in the mood for a whole bunch of unfortunate orphans. Didn't realize what a thing Dickens had for orphans, or at least no regular family with a mom and a dad. I can't think of one. Oh, maybe the Bob Cratchit family.*

Moving on, she stopped at *Our Mutual Friend. Oh, that's one of my favorites. Dickens had a knack for making incredible coincidences seem realistic. That's a maybe.* She pulled it out and set it on the table along with *Little Dorrit* and went on. *Pickwick Papers—I don't know why I've never made it past the second chapter of that one. Don't think I'll try that one again.*

Then she spotted *A Tale of Two Cities. I've read just about every Dickens novel except Pickwick Papers and that one. Hummm, I wonder. That's not exactly pleasant reading, but somehow I think it might do.* Turning the pages, she located the first chapter and started reading the famous first lines: *"It was the best of times, it was the worst of times, it was the age of wisdom, it was the age of foolishness . . . ."* *Well, that's interesting. Dickens sure has a way with words. Actually, I can relate to that. I feel like that!*

After switching on the table lamp next to her favorite reading place in the library and turning off the bright overhead lights, she settled down to see if this choice would intrigue and enlighten her. After about five hours of reading, she noticed the light in the room had changed. She looked up. In spite of the dark clouds over the lake, there was definitely daylight coming through the high west windows, which were wet from the rain. Not wanting to be caught in her robe and pajamas, she hurried back to her room, not passing anyone. She slid into bed and snuggled down under her light, fluffy quilt to read another chapter. She fell asleep for an hour or two, then woke and started reading again.

After several hours, the phone by her bed rang. It was Juanita. It was well after noon, and Samantha had not come down for breakfast or lunch; she was worried. There were a few more chapters to read, but Samantha was getting terribly hungry and thirsty. She thanked Juanita for her concern and informed her that she had been engrossed in reading and had lost track of time. Definitely needing something to eat, she said she would come down to the kitchen in about 20 minutes.

Samantha hastily showered, dressed, and neatly made her bed. For some reason the maid, had not been around to clean her room. Perhaps she had peeked in, seen her still in bed, and left her undisturbed. Then, she remembered that Wednesday was sheet-changing day for her room, and that didn't occur until mid-afternoon. She tucked the book under her arm and hurried to the kitchen.

Lunch was waiting, as Juanita promised. Feeling obligated to explain her tardiness, Samantha ardently gave her a brief synopsis of the book. With an hour or two of reading left, she added that she was anxious to finish. Knowing that it would be unlikely she would encounter anyone at this time of day, she could read undisturbed in the large dining room while she ate.

After thanking Juanita, she put the food on a tray and headed that way. About an hour and a half later, Steve came in and found Samantha sobbing as she read the final pages.

"Must be *some* book," he commented, realizing it was the book that was causing this reaction and not some catastrophic event. "I'll come back later."

"No, no, I'm almost finished. Please, sit down, if you have the time."

"I do need to talk to you. I need some coffee. I'll be back in a few minutes. Want some?"

"No coffee, but tea would be soothing, if you don't mind," she sobbed, saturating another Kleenex. Her emotions were running the gambit. She was sickened to tears by the coldness of the knitting women in their prime seats, immersed in the smell of death, the flow of blood into the gutters, and the sight and sound of the mechanics of the Guillotine as it severed the heads.

How could the crowd cheer when severed heads were raised? she thought.

On the converse, she was touched and moved to tears by Sydney Carton's noble sacrifice and redemption, finally finding a purpose for his wasted and confused life. The scene of the innocent little seamstress and Sydney, her "brave and generous friend" heaven-sent to comfort her, being carted to the Guillotine was heart breaking. They talked about "the better land where . . . both will be mercifully sheltered . . . there is no Time there, and no trouble." As he kisses her and "they solemnly bless each other . . . she goes next before him—is gone . . ." Then Dickens continues, "I am the Resurrection and the Life, saith the Lord; he that believeth in me, though he were dead, yet shall he live, and whosoever liveth and believeth in me shall never die." Reading to final pages, the words distorted by watery eyes, she arrived at the famous last words: "It is a far, far better thing that I do, than I have ever done; it is a far, far better rest that I go to than I have ever known."

Steve returned seconds before she reached those words and set down a tray with a plate of Oatmeal Cherry Walnut Cookies, his large mug of black coffee, two pots (one with tea and one with hot water), a cup and saucer, and some napkins and spoons. Consistent with his detailed nature, he had thought of everything. He knew how she liked her tea and her favorite cookies—his, too.Then he sat next to her, grinning affectionately and quietly waiting for her to conclude her reading.

"Finished!" she said, snatching a few more tissues from the box, wiping her eyes, and blowing her nose. "That was definitely *some* book."

Steve reached over and picked up the book, turning it in his hands and opening it to the introduction, then remarked, "Yes, it is. We read it in high school."

"You liked it?"

"I did, but *I* wasn't moved to tears," he teased. "I like it better in retrospect, as some things are lost on a 17-year-old boy. At that time, I was impressed by the insanity of the French Revolution, the brutality, oppression, and how people can be so evil at all levels."

"Dickens sure made it vivid," she reflected.

"The part I came to appreciate later is how the proclivity for vengeance or revenge is an evil that destroys the soul," he continued.

"That's true! I was disturbed by the obsession for revenge. That's all Thérèse Defarge could think about. She lost all rationality. Her life became useless."

Leafing through the pages, he settled on one near the back and commented, "Dickens gets it. In this part, he portrays a devilish ceremony where he calls the Guillotine 'The Vengeance.'"

"Oh, yes! That's creepy."

He read, "'The Vengeance' descends from her elevation to do it . . . The ministers of Sainte Guillotine are robed and ready. Crash!' I see those knitting women in their 'pews' as possessed, mindless shells around the altar of the church of Satan."

"You really *were* impressed. That's a *very* interesting perspective."

"I didn't come to the conclusion that vengeance is a destructive evil on my own. I have to admit, I wanted revenge when my wife and daughter were killed. It was destroying me, but by good fortune or Providence, Mr. Jones came into my life and showed me how to let go. It turned my life around."

"I'm glad," she said, impressed but not knowing just what to say. She was slightly surprised that he was confiding in her like this. Although they had talked about his circumstances somewhat when he had taken care of her after the Joe episode, he hadn't gone into such personal detail. Maybe her tears gave her an approachable, empathetic aura, and it motivated his need to talk to someone with a soft heart. She didn't want to press him. *Just let him take his time in his own way*, she thought. *I'll just lend a sympatric ear.*

"Mr. Jones is a remarkably wise man," he commented, then reached into his billfold and pulled out a worn piece of paper. "He gave me this."

Romans 12:17. Do not repay anyone evil for evil. Be careful to do what is right in the eyes of everybody. If it is possible, as far as it depends on you, live at peace with everyone. Do not take revenge, my friends, but leave room for God's wrath, for it is written: "It is mine to avenge; I will repay," says the Lord. On the contrary: "If your enemy is hungry, feed him; if he is thirsty, give him something to drink. In doing this, you will heap burning coals on his head. Do not be overcome by evil, but overcome evil with good."

She read the paper and commented, "That's very comforting. I see that. You're right about being freed from the desire for revenge, so you can focus on doing positive things."

"But note," he instructed, "that there's a difference between revenge and justice. Being in law enforcement, it still applies and is a good guideline. We need to bring criminals and lawbreakers to justice but not be blinded by revenge."

"Do you know what the 'heap burning coals on his head' means?" she ventured.

"I think so," he responded with a chuckle. "I always wondered about that, too. It does sound strange. I looked it up, and if I remember right, it means that due to your kindness, he will be sorry for his deed and repent. Also, it may have to do with an Egyptian or Middle Eastern ritual where a guilty person, as a sign of repentance, carries a basin of glowing coals on his head."

"Well, that's interesting." She laughed amused. "Things take on new meaning when you know the history. Who thinks up these things?"

He shrugged his shoulders and smiled in acknowledgement of the rhetorical question, then paused and went on. "Most of the people here have a sad story behind them and have been helped by Mr. Jones. Around here, there are many worn pieces of wisdom tucked into billfolds and many lives changed for the better."

"Yes, I can definitely appreciate that."

"Well, now, that's what I came to tell you," Steve suddenly remarked. "Mr. Jones will be returning sometime early in the morning—sometime before dawn. I'll be picking him up from the airport. He will most likely be sleeping most of the day, recovering from the long trip from Australia, but I'm to inform you that he especially wants to talk with you in the afternoon, as soon as he's rested."

"That's wonderful! I'm really looking forward to seeing him. He's been away so long. I'll be here!"

Steve and Samantha went into the kitchen to return the tray; no one was there. A large, handwritten note was in the middle of the otherwise empty stainless-steel table occupying the wide center aisle.

SAMANTHA,
I HAVE TAKEN ISABELLA TO THE DOCTOR,
WILL CALL LATER.
JUANITA

"I hope she's all right," Samantha said.

"I'm sure she will be," Steve said reassuringly, trying not to show his apprehension.

By this time it was about five-thirty, so Steve suggested they engage in a joint effort and fix their own supper.

Samantha was quite agreeable to that. "I think there's some Blackberry Cobbler left from last night. I'll check."

"Sounds good! I'll see what else I can find," he offered.

"Okay."

At about six-fifteen, Steve received a call on his communication device that Juanita was on the line and wanted to talk to Samantha. Steve picked up the phone and said to Samantha, "It's Juanita."

She took the receiver. "Hi, Juanita. Is everything all right?"

Juanita assured her it was and explained that Isabella had been lethargic all day, not eating and looking dehydrated, so she'd hurried off to the doctor with her. Isabella had been hospitalized so she could have an IV to rehydrate her and build her up. Juanita assured her that Isabella was responding well. Samantha scolded Juanita a bit for not telling her so she could have gone along, but Juanita insisted they were fine and she would be staying the night at the hospital with Isabella.

"Do you need anything?" Samantha asked. "I'll be more than happy to bring you anything you need."

"No, no. Mr. Jones has arranged that Isabella always has a private room, if she needs it, and they are very kind here. The pediatric section is very accommodating to parents who stay with their children. I'm sure we will be back in the morning. Please, tell Mr. Ryan."

"I'll do that right away. Please, keep us informed, and let us know if you need anything."

"Thank you. Goodbye—see you tomorrow."

"Okay, see you tomorrow."

She relayed the message to Steve, and he contacted Mr. Ryan.

Feeling somewhat relieved by Juanita's tone and assurance that all would be fine, they transported their supper to the round table in the corner and enjoyed the fruits of their labors.

❖·CHAPTER 23

A father to the fatherless, a protector of widows,
is God in his holy place. God settles the lonely in families . . .

Psalms 68:5-6

It was late in the afternoon on Thursday when Edmund entered the library where Samantha was reading. She was slightly startled upon seeing him; then she hurried toward him. She extended both her hands; he grasped them, held on tightly, and greeted her warmly. After a brief question-and-answer exchange, they slowly made their way across the room to an area streaked with warm sunlight coming through the tall bay windows and settled into the cushions of wing-backed chairs.

Edmund spent some time telling her about his son Paul's stroke and their time in Australia. She could tell he had been quite worried but was feeling hopeful now. He informed her that the modifications to their rooms in the family quarters had been completed, and he expected Paul and Sandra to arrive in a few days. Edmund had taken a commercial plane, but Paul and Sandra were coming on a chartered plane; some adjustments for the trip were needed to accommodate Paul. Edmund had wanted to arrive early to make sure all was ready.

"I have much to discuss with you. We may be here awhile, and I need some nourishment. My schedule is off since being in Australia. Would you please ask Juanita to have some tea and

193

sandwiches brought out to us, my dear? Dinner is going to be late today."

She promptly set out for the kitchen and found Juanita and her helpers preparing a special dinner for that evening. Juanita and Isabella had returned early that morning, as anticipated. She looked tired from the strain of Isabella's recent collapse and of getting ready for the event; nevertheless, she greeted Samantha with her usual friendly smile. Samantha put in the request.

"How are you and Isabella?

"Isabella is much better today. Actually, we both slept very well at the hospital."

"Do you have enough help?"

"Oh, yes, yes, everything is going well. We have become lazy with no special meals to cook. Now the pace has changed. But, it's good to have a group to cook for again and get into the routine. Even though there are only six for dinner, I want to make everything very special for Mr. Jones's first dinner home after such a long time away. He's provided extra help, especially since more are coming during the next several days—he thinks of everything. His first concerns were for Isabella. He came to see her a little while ago. He said he couldn't stay because he had to meet you in the library. I thought he might want something to eat, so we've set up a tray. Alice will finish it up and bring it in."

"If it's almost ready, I'll help her and take the tray so she can get back to work on the dinner," volunteered Samantha. In a minute or two, the tray was ready.

Samantha wondered what Juanita meant by "more are coming this week." That was probably Paul and Sandra. Edmund had said "in a few days."

I'll find out soon enough, she thought, then smiled and said, "Thanks, Juanita. I'm glad Isabella is doing better. Is it okay if I visit her later?"

"Oh, yes, yes, she would like that very much! She's been sleeping most of the day but was awake when I checked on her a few minutes ago."

"I'll see her after supper." Then Samantha picked up the tray and hurried back to the library.

"That was fast!"

"Juanita is a mind-reader. She knew you'd be hungry and had a tray ready."

Samantha put the tray on the small table; Edmund pulled it in front of them. Then she poured some tea into a large mug and handed it to him.

"Juanita never forgets my favorite mug—no dainty cups for me."

Sipping her mug of tea, noting it was Earl Grey (Edmund's favorite), she soon felt refreshed and at ease as they continued their conversation.

Edmund's voice took a serious tone as he turned the discussion to events surrounding Samantha and her circumstances. Then, Edmund leaned forward and a solemn look came over his face, "Samantha, I'd like you to live here at Lake House with us, as part of our family."

Samantha sat still; her eyes opened a little wider. Stunned and speechless, she waited for him to continue.

"Having a great deal of money makes one a target for the unscrupulous. You're painfully aware that in your situation, unfortunately, it's unsafe for you to live on your own. I've been keenly aware of this threat with my own family—especially as I became better known."

Samantha reluctantly agreed with him and nodded.

"I'm very fond of you, as you know," he continued. "Sadly, you have no family to help you. However, I would be honored to be informally your mentor, grandfather, protector, if you wish." He leaned closer and patted her hand. "What do you think?"

She was overwhelmed and on the verge of tears.

Edmund tried to soothe her. "I'm sorry. It must be painful to confront your circumstances. I didn't mean to cause you distress . . . ."

"No, no, no, no," she interrupted. "You made me very happy, and I'd be honored to accept your suggestion. I've felt very comfortable here. For the first time in the past four-and-a-half years, I've felt safe and cared about. Are you sure?" Besides her feeling of safety at Lake House, it was a comfort, in a way, that someone finally knew and expressed pity for her situation—the heartache and despair she had covered up these past years.

"I *am* sure, my dear. I know people. You have a kind heart. You're smart. You're wise enough to learn from your mistakes. You're willing to listen and learn. You have much potential. Besides that, you have a significant amount of money that you're responsible for, and you'll need help with that. Wealth has a way of entangling one with worldly things. You're so young and inexperienced for this responsibility. You've seen the darker side, but there are also positive possibilities."

"I'll try hard to live up to your faith in me, and I *do* need advice I can trust. I have to admit, it's been a struggle being alone. I *am* very fond of you, too, and admire you very much—you know that."

"Thank you for that," he said affectionately. "It's not going to be entirely easy to live here as part of the family, now that Paul and Sandra will be coming. The family will be expanding at Lake House. My grandson, Will, is also coming. He should be here just before Paul and Sandra. He's had enough of the big city and has always liked it here. He wants to work with us, and I have to say I'm relieved and pleased. He'll be a great asset to our enterprises. They'll be in good hands after I'm gone. Paul's incapacity has left a big void to fill. Not only was I concerned for his health and safety, but all of our enterprises had become a concern, especially since Robert and Amanda have passed away.

"When Will finished his degree in electronics at MIT and then decided to get an MBA, I was afraid he would want to go elsewhere. His fiancée likes the big city. I think she's quite disappointed he settled on coming here, but that's another issue. He tried business, I think, because it was different from his dad, Robert, and me—the family business, that is. I could see it wasn't in his nature, but it wasn't wise to say too much. Paul and Sandra would go along with what he wanted, which was, as it turned out, the best thing. He found out for himself he wasn't cut out for a career in business administration—especially other people's business. Business managers are easy to find, but Will has rare talents in physics, math, and research."

Samantha could tell by the expression on his face that Edmund was especially proud of and happy with Will. It was contagious, and she was genuinely happy for him. "That's wonderful," she interjected. She knew Edmund would benefit from having the family around him again, especially since he'd lost his wife and brother—his closest friends and confidants. In some ways, Samantha had taken on that role, filling in the void. She was a good listener and found Edmund particularly interesting and astute. She intuitively knew he wasn't necessarily looking for advice; he was much wiser and more experienced than she was. He just needed a sympathetic ear—a sounding board for his thoughts. Most of the time after just hearing his thoughts verbalized, he could work out an impasse. She felt honored he had confidence in her integrity.

"Will's a fine young man," he went on proudly. "I'm sure you two will get along. Paul and Sandra will probably be living here indefinitely, as Paul's prognosis for a total recovery is not good. I think eventually he'll be able to work from here, but he won't be able to travel on business as before. Having Will here should be good for Paul. Will is able to motivate his dad into helping him with some projects. Paul is bound to like you. He has an even temperament, which he doesn't seem to have lost, in spite of his illness. He seems to be handling his incapacity well—as well as can be expected. He does get frustrated at times, but he has a good nature and a good sense of humor. Nevertheless, I must warn you about Sandra . . . ."

Alice, Juanita's assistant, entered the room and informed them that the Ryans and Steve had arrived; dinner would be ready soon, if they wished to go to the dining room. Edmund thanked her and said they would be there right away. They stood, and to Samantha he said, "We'll continue this later. We'll have lots of time to talk now. I've invited Steve. He's close to the family. I have a special fondness for him, and I know you two have become acquainted and, I think, friends. And of course, I've invited Neville and his family to join us for dinner. I like to keep up with Abby."

"Me, too. She's a delightful little girl. We seem to be getting on quite well. As a matter of fact, I like all the Ryan family. Mary has been especially kind to me, and a good friend. I stay with Abby now and then when Mr. Ryan and Mary go out. Abby loves to play games. We have a great time. Would you believe, at her age, she's teaching me to play chess?"

"She's a bright little girl. They're very fond of you, too."

She hugged him and whispered, "Thank you for rescuing me." And they went off to greet their guests.

* * *

The next morning, shortly after seven, Samantha arrived in the kitchen for breakfast as usual.

"Good morning, Juanita," she announced as she bounced in and was greeted by the aroma of fresh baked bread and Juanita's warm smile. "Mmmm—smells good in here!"

Juanita rerouted her to the formal dining room for her breakfast. She followed the instructions and found Edmund already selecting foods from a breakfast buffet.

He greeted her cheerfully. "I'm glad to see you. I thought I would have to eat breakfast alone. I've had too many of those here the past couple of years. I used to enjoy starting the day sharing breakfast and conversation with Robert and Amanda. Neville and Steve usually come in for breakfast about seven-forty-five. It's friendly and casual, but we end up talking business and making plans for the day. Don't be deterred from joining us if you get up later. We have other times for business. I'm not one of those people who can't face anything until the first cup of coffee. I'm what you call a *morning person*."

"Me, too. I'm a *morning person*, too," Samantha responded. "And I don't even drink plain coffee, maybe a latté once in awhile."

"Lattés—that's the new generation," he said with a grin.

"Maybe we should go to a coffee house sometime so you can try one." She paused, then teased, "Maybe not! You just don't seem like the latté type." She had gotten quite comfortable with Edmund, and they bantered back and forth with little jokes. Samantha was laughing, something she hadn't done in a long time, and Edmund was chuckling.

"I'm pleased to see you laughing. You seem comfortable here."

"I like it very much. I really appreciate being here. I don't feel so lonely and lost. I don't feel so apprehensive and sad. It's nice to have people to care about again."

"We care about you, too, my dear."

"Thank you," she uttered in a whisper, trying to suppress the grateful emotions that started to well up.

Suddenly, Margaret opened the door. Samantha could see her enter carrying a tray conveying Edmund's favorite mug, a large pot of hot Earl Grey tea, a pot of hot milk, and a pot of hot water. The teapot was of the fine bone china of another era, and the other containers were of handsome gleaming, silver also of a vintage design. Samantha knew he liked his tea the English way, but in a mug, not a dainty cup. Five places were already set with attractive breakfast dishes, including coffee cups and saucers.

"Would you like to share my tea?" he asked while Margaret waited.

"Yes, I would, thank you. That sounds good."

"Will that cup do?" he asked, referring to the one at her place. "Or do you want a mug?"

"This one will do nicely."

"Well, Margaret, thank you, this will do nicely." He echoed Samantha's words with a grin.

"Yes, sir," Margaret replied with a smile and then left the room, closing the door behind her.

The sun coming up on the other side of the house struck a dew-filled maple tree about 20 or 30 feet away from the dining room. The reflected autumn colors burst through the high windows and spilled down the center of the long highly-polished walnut table. The bright reds and oranges reflected into the room, and it glowed like fire. Edmund was sitting at the head of the table, Samantha in the chair on the side next to him. She sat in silence, enjoying the spectacle she knew would pass too quickly as the sun moved higher in the sky. For now, she was content. They sat quietly for a few moments, enjoying their tea and breakfast.

Samantha noticed again that table was set for five. *Edmund, Samantha, Mr. Ryan, Steve . . . and who is the fifth?* she wondered, but quickly dismissed the thought and went back to her cheerful conversation with Edmund.

"Oh, before I forget," he said. "I need to tell you that Paul and Sandra will be coming Thursday. Sandra is an I-can't-face-the-day-without-my-coffee person, and someone from the kitchen will bring it to her room. Don't expect to see her here for breakfast. I'm not sure what Paul will want yet. He can feed himself fairly well now but still may need help. An Amigo is being designed for him. So, with the power scooter and the elevator, he should be able to make it down here. He may want to join us if he's feeling up to it. I've hired a nurse-aid-therapist, a young man, to help him with dressing, therapy, and whatever he needs. His name is Philip, and he'll be staying in the staff quarters on the third floor. I'll introduce you to him and show you how to get in touch with him in case of emergency. He's due here early morning next Wednesday to get settled in and set up before Paul comes . . . ."

Again, the dining room door opened, and Edmund stopped. Samantha was startled as a tall, attractive, healthy-looking young man filled the space. It looked as if the 17th-century Will Jones had climbed down from the portrait in the library, shaved, gotten a haircut, and put on modern clothes. This young man appeared a little taller and thinner, but still, the likeness was remarkable. Samantha knew the features well, as she'd often studied the face and all the detail the artist had faithfully rendered.

"Well, well," said Edmund. "Here's another morning person." Edmund took a swallow of tea. "Samantha, this is Will. He's come home—for good, I hope."

They greeted each other properly, then Samantha, staring, said no more. *That's the fifth place setting!* she thought.

Will helped himself to a hearty breakfast and sat across from her. He addressed a couple of polite questions to her about how she liked it here and politely included her in a brief discussion with his grandfather about his trip. Then he and Edmund started talking about his work. A minute or two later, Neville and Steve entered, and Samantha thought it was time to slip away. She quickly but politely excused herself and left the room, hardly noticed by men engrossed in the affairs of the estate.

☥·CHAPTER 24

There is one whose harsh words pierce like a sword,
but the tongue of the wise brings healing.

Proverbs 12:18

It was Thursday morning, and as had become their routine for the past week, Samantha met Edmund in the dining room for breakfast around seven. Even if she arrived before seven, Edmund would be sitting at his usual place at the table with his large mug of steaming Earl Gray, and all the accompaniments. A phone was on the corner of the table to his right and a laptop computer on the sideboard. Next to the tea were newspapers, journals, and a variety of colored folders. This morning, there was an open green folder and papers spread out to the full reach of his arm. As she entered the room, he hastily put away his reading material, greeted her with a warm smile, as usual, and gave her his full attention. She cherished their morning conversations and his advice.

As it was now precisely seven, Margaret appeared. Slowly opening the door, she asked, "Mr. Jones, is it okay if I set up now?"

"Yes, yes, Margaret, that's fine."

"Thank you, sir," she replied with a pleasant smile and wheeled in her cart laddered with the delicious breakfast items. She quickly switched on the modern, white ceramic hot plates and placed companion covered ceramic casserole dishes on them, plugged in a coffee urn, and set several generous white mugs next to it. Then she placed several pitchers—water, milk, juice—and next a bowl of fruit, a bowl of sugar cubes, a bowl of brown sugar, and a large, covered glass jar filled to the top with bit-sized, shredded wheat. She set out a basket filled with freshly baked muffins, including Juanita's ever-popular Oatmeal Fruity Nutty Muffins. For the Sunny Yellow Cornmeal Muffins, she placed a jar of honey. (There were beehives at the edge of woods at the farm.) Then, she arranged several pretty little matching etched-glass bowls that displayed a rainbow of glistening colors from the variety of homemade jams they contained. Each bowl had an ornate silver demitasse-sized spoon. After that, the crystal dishes full of butter and creamed cheese from the Werneke farm went in their appropriate places. Then, she placed extra bowls, plates, glasses, silverware, and linen napkins at the end of the buffet, accomplishing it all within minutes.

Someone must have put in extra outlets along that wall for those modern electrical serving pieces. Even the breakfast buffet has a mixture of the modern and the traditional—typical of the Jones family! Samantha contemplated while Margaret was setting up. *Looks like more than just five are coming,* she thought, but didn't ask.

While Margaret was carrying out her task, Edmund engaged her in conversation about her plans, her family, and then concluded with, "Looks good, Margaret. Thank you."

Margaret smiled and left with her empty cart.

Edmund turned to Samantha. "Are you hungry?"

"I am."

"Me, too," he said, and they walked over to the buffet and made their selections.

Returning to the table, they sat, enjoying their breakfast and engaging in conversation intermittently. As they were finishing, Edmund turned to her and started speaking in a more serious tone. "Paul and Sandra are arriving today—probably late this afternoon."

"I'm looking forward to meeting them."

Edmund smiled at her affectionately and went on. "I was telling you about the family. Will, you've met—I've told you about him."

"Yes, I met him here last week, but I've not seen him to talk with him since."

"He's been helping me get our projects organized. We've had much to do. Paul's illness and my being away left others struggling to keep up. I can't begin to tell you what a help Will has been, but much of this is new to him, as he's been away for a long time. Actually, he hasn't worked in many parts of our business. He used to help with some things while he was here for a few weeks in the summer during his college years, but now it's different. He will eventually have the responsibility for all of the businesses."

"That seems like a lot."

"After he's settled in, Paul should be able to help guide him. Will is learning fast and has been very conscientious about it. I knew he would. He takes this very seriously. We're responsible for the livelihood and well-being of many families—not just our own."

"I see."

Edmund paused to collect his thoughts. "Well, I've been putting this off, but now that Paul and Sandra are due today, I must get to it. I need to tell you about Sandra."

"Oh?" Samantha said with a puzzled look.

"Yes. Into every family the good Lord sees fit to put someone who tries the soul. It must be to test the character of the others or a character-building experience. Sandra is *that* person. Be careful of Sandra!" he instructed firmly. "She may resent you and can be vicious to those she feels are a threat to her—real or imagined. I believe she has a personality or psychological disorder. She's not logical and has difficulty following a train of thought. You're very young and probably haven't had experience dealing with someone with this type of disorder day after day.

"I only tell you about Sandra because I don't want you to be hurt by her. I want you to know that we are aware of her condition and to put you on guard. Be cautious about what you say to her. She has a way of twisting a person's words. It's astonishing what she can come up with—the twisted depictions she can conjure up. She can be pleasant at times and lure you into an awkward situation, then all of a sudden turn on you. She's not going to like being in this remote place—it may make her more irritable. Let me know if you have a problem. We can talk about it. I've dealt with many people, but Sandra is different. She's perfected her tactics. She's manipulative—uses flattery and praise as a prelude to expecting you to do something she wants that may be uncomfortable for you. Other tactics are bullying, plying you with guilt, selective memory (or a distorted one with her own twist), and the worst—nagging. Her repetition really can wear you down. If she wants something, she never lets it go."

Samantha frowned. "What can I do?"

"Be kind to her. That's always the best approach. Don't let her get you angry. It will be very hard if you are a victim of one of her verbal assaults. Just know we understand. I've made it clear to her that you're here as a member of the family, under my protection. She rarely crosses me. Treat her as you would someone who is ill, but don't be condescending. Don't correct her or challenge her if she says something that's contrary to the truth. You won't win, and you'll only make her angry. Just smile and let it go. If she asks you to do something that makes you feel uncomfortable or you can't handle, tell her that you will think about it, can't give her an answer right now, and you will get back to her shortly or something like that. Then, you can check it out with me."

"I think Aunt Lucy, my great aunt, was someone who tried everyone's patience, but Sandra sounds different. Aunt Lucy seemed to be an expert on everything, even if she had to make things up, and she always had to have the last word. Everyone let her rattle on and agreed with her, no matter what. It was useless to try to present her with facts. Everyone *was* always kind to her, accepting things for what they were. My mother said, 'You can't change a person's nature.' Maybe that's true. I'll try to do my best to get along with Sandra."

"Very good. Sandra will take no interest in running the house. She'll be happy to leave it to Mrs. Andersen, but she will feel it her duty to criticize at least one thing every day. Mrs. Andersen knows her from years ago, when she and Paul were first married and lived here, before they went to Australia. She knows how to handle it. I think she makes a game of it to see what Sandra will come up with."

"That's good," Samantha responded with a slight smile, not knowing what to say and feeling apprehensive about meeting Sandra. She was glad Edmund was there to advise her.

"The good news is Paul will like you—I'm sure. As I told you previously, he has an easygoing personality and a good sense of humor. In spite of all he has been through, he seems to have retained that."

"I'm happy to hear it. I hope we can be friends."

"I know he will appreciate your friendship."

"I'll do my best."

"I know you will," Edmund said with a slight smile. "I want you to move into the family quarters on the south end of the second floor. There is an empty suite there. I arranged to have it redecorated while they were doing work on Paul and Sandra's suite. Also, I'm having Robert's suite refurbished for Will. There was a problem, and we couldn't get that one done earlier. All the family suites have a nice view of the lake. I hope you will be okay with that."

"How very kind. I've come to terms with the lake, and I do enjoy the sunsets and the changing scenes."

"I've always enjoyed it, too. I had bookcases built in the sitting area, so you can bring as many books from your family home as you wish, and perhaps you'd like to bring some furniture. It's ready now. I'll have your things moved there today, if that's agreeable to you. I'd like you to get settled there before Sandra arrives. I think she will accept your position here better if you're already there."

Samantha said little—the deed was done, and that was the way Edmund had arranged it; he wanted all the family nearby.

She thanked him and offered to move her own things "I have so few things I can do it. You don't have to trouble anyone."

"Nonsense!" He picked up the phone and instructed Mrs. Andersen to send someone to help her. He turned back to her. "Can you do it in 15 minutes?"

Samantha nodded.

"She'll be in her room in 15 minutes," he announced into the phone, then addressed her. "Now, what about the things from your house?"

"Yes, I'd like to bring many of the books. I think I'd like to bring my father's desk and office chair, family pictures, and the rest of my clothes, but that's all."

"Okay, I'll arrange for Steve or one of the other men to take you back. You can get the things you want, and we can arrange to put the house up for sale and donate the contents to charity. You will need the deed. If you don't feel comfortable going there, I'll send someone."

"Oh, thank you, I can do it. I know where the deed is."

"Okay, it's settled, then." He picked up the phone and delegated the task to the person on the other end.

*   *   *

Sandra and Paul arrived late that afternoon. Their luggage preceded them and was taken to their suite by an army of housekeepers, with Mrs. Andersen giving precise instructions; all was quickly put in order. After brief introductions, a few comments about their trip, and some mundane polite remarks, Philip was summoned to take Paul to his suite; an exhausted Sandra followed, not to be seen the rest of the evening. Edmund and Will returned to work in the lower level, and Samantha retreated to her new quarters.

They were quite beautiful—professionally decorated, very tasteful in cheerful pastel colors and patterns. She had not seen anyone who looked like a decorator—someone with swatches and that sort of thing—coming and going from the house over the past weeks. This was all a surprise to her. She hadn't been consulted, but that was just as well, as she didn't even have a favorite color and wasn't interested in interior decorating.

Nevertheless, she loved the results. She felt quite happy as she investigated all the rooms—the dressing room, the bathroom, the bedroom, and the sitting area with its bookcases, as Edmund had described. There was even a fireplace. She opened and closed all the drawers (most were empty, she had so few clothes), opened and closed the closet doors in the dressing area (also mostly empty). She pulled the cords closing the heavy draperies and blocking out the rapidly departing daylight, then opened them again. She ran her hand over the smooth surfaces, sat in each chair, and tried out the bed. She felt a bit like Goldilocks intruding in the bears' cottage, but she wasn't a trespasser; she had been invited to be a member of the family. *I wonder if this will all feel natural to me someday,* she thought. *Will I become accustomed to being here as a member of the family? Will it feel familiar, normal? I promise, I will never take it for granted. I have been blessed! I'll try hard to do my part to make it a happy place. All my money could not have bought this—a family.*

☥·CHAPTER 25

*For where jealousy and selfish ambition exist, there
will be disorder and every vile practice.
But the wisdom from above is first pure, then peaceable, gentle, open to reason,
full of mercy and good fruits, impartial and sincere.
And a harvest of righteousness is sown in peace by those who make peace.*

James 3:16-18

After having supper in the great dining room on the main floor, the group gathered upstairs in the common room of the family quarters. There was a cozy fire in the fireplace and an abundance of wood in the bin to carry them into the next day if necessary. Will was put in charge of adding logs as needed. Howard, in a forceful voice and with that impish grin, gave him the title: Fire-Keeper of the Confederation. With that, various little chuckles and laughs signaled the anticipation and set the mood for one of Howard's stories. Will took his position on the sofa next to the fireplace—Sandra next to him. Samantha and Steve were seated on the opposite sofa also situated perpendicular to the fireplace. Philip had placed Paul in a comfortable chair in the back of the room and sat next to him to attend to his needs. Edmund was content in his usual spot.

When all were settled and comfortable, Howard rose and, in the voice and delivery of a polished actor, started his narrative. "After the light was gone, and they could work no more that day, the clan gathered around a great fire." He made a sweeping gesture with his right hand and made momentary eye-contact with each member of the Jones clan. "The masterful storyteller rose and, enhanced by the glow of the fire, he dramatized the history of the people, for they had no written language." One slow deliberate step at a time, Howard moved toward the fireplace. "Long before Europeans ventured into Great Lakes country, various tribes of Iroquois lived in a vast territory south of Lake Ontario. *The Story of the Good and Evil Iroquois Chiefs*[22] is one of the most important in their history.

"The tribes lived by a code of vengeance and engaged in continuous warfare. Cruel battle-hardened warriors reveled in the carnage and devastation they inflicted. They struck fear in the hearts of the people. Nevertheless, the people of the tribe worshiped their conquering war-heroes.

"Chief Tadadaho, a shrewd and mighty warrior-chief of an Onondaga nation—an Iroquois subgroup—was evil. His appearance alone—matted snake-like hair, ugly battle scars, tall powerful build—terrorized the people, and tales of sorcery, torture, and even cannibalism intimidated them into submission.

"Chief Hayenwatha, chief of another Onondaga nation, was a good and courageous leader. His attempts to reform Tadadaho and bring peace resulted in scorn. Even so, he persevered in his efforts to bring peace to the nations. He invited the people of all the Onondaga villages to a council. An attentive hopeful crowd listened to Hayenwatha's plan for peace and cooperation. Suddenly, Tadadaho appeared, looking wild and menacing. Panic struck as his murderous warriors moved among the people. Everyone fled in terror.

"Shortly afterward, Hayenwatha's eldest daughter became sick and died. The people were convinced Tadadaho had conjured

---

[22] There are many versions of this story; however, most of this version was adapted from the book Indians of North America; The Iroquois pages 13-33 by Barbara Graymont. Nyack College, New York, Copyright 1988. Dr. Graymont is a leading authority on the Iroquois and has written many books and articles on the subject. Her book The Iroquois in the American Revolution was cited as a source in a 1985 Supreme Court decision that upheld a land claim of the Oneida Indian Nation..

up a curse. In spite of his profound grief, Hayenwatha felt compelled to continue his mission. He sent out runners to invite the people to a second council. Again, Tadadaho and his warriors terrorized the few who were brave enough to come. Nothing was accomplished. Shortly after that, Hayenwatha's second daughter died in the same way as her sister. Was this a coincidence? Had Tadadaho cast another evil spell? They believed that evil had overcome good.

"In spite of the second tragedy, Hayenwatha felt a responsibility to bring peace to all. When the mourning period was over, he called a third council. This beloved third daughter, pregnant and the only surviving member of his family, went with him. Before the meeting, a magnificent eagle soared over a nearby clearing where she was gathering dry twigs. A warrior shot the eagle. It fell next to the girl. Men rushed to obtain the revered feathers, knocked her down, and accidentally killed her."

A low mummer of disbelief and astonishment went up from the group around the fireplace. Will tossed another log on the fire, and Howard went on.

"His last daughter and grandchild were dead! Emotionally crushed, Hayenwatha descended into the depths of despair and wandered into the forest. Overcome with grief and rage, his mind became distorted. He could find no solace. Evil was replacing goodness in his heart.

"One day he saw some rushes, cut some, and made three strings of beads. Then he cut two forked sticks, pushed the straight ends into the ground, and placed a long straight stick across the angles. Then he placed the three strings of reeds over the pole and sat before them. He thought, *This would I do if I found anyone burdened with grief and wrapped in darkness, as I am: These strings of beads would become words with which I would address him. With these words of condolence, I would lift the darkness from him.*

"Traveling on, Hayenwatha came to a lakeshore. He found some small white shells, strung them together, and put several strings around his neck as a sign of peace because he was entering

Mohawk[23] Country. Then, in view of a village, he sat on a stump at the edge of the forest. A young woman who had drawn water from the nearby spring reported seeing him.

"Previously, Deganawidah, a peacemaker from a Wendot tribe north of Lake Ontario, had been accepted into their community. He recognized the white-shell symbol and sent escorts to bring the stranger to him. As they entered his lodge, Deganawidah rose to greet Hayenwatha. Their eyes met, and their spirits felt a kinship of peace. Overcome, Hayenwatha could not speak. Finally, he related his bitter story. With compassion and understanding Deganawidah—also a lonely wanderer before arriving at the village—invited him to stay. Deganawidah presented Hayenwatha's sorrow to the chiefs. They were touched. Hayenwatha felt welcomed by these Mohawk people, who lived in peace with each other but were feared by others.

"Returning to his lodge one day, Deganawidah saw his guest grieving before the arrangement of the strings of beads. In an effort to console his new friend, he preformed the following ritual:

1. With the first string of beads. 'When a person has suffered a great loss caused by death and is grieving, the tears blind his eyes so that he cannot see. With these words, I wipe away the tears from your eyes so now you may see clearly.'

2. With the second string of beads. 'When a person has suffered a great loss caused by death and is grieving, there is an obstruction in his ears and he cannot hear. With these words I remove the obstruction from your ears so that you may once again have perfect hearing.'

3. With the third string of beads. 'When a person has suffered a great loss caused by death, his throat is stopped and he cannot speak. With these words, I remove the

---

[23] Mohawks: Iroquois subgroup—similar in language and customs.

obstruction from your throat so you may speak and breathe freely.'"

Howard explained, "This condolence ceremony is still observed among the Iroquois today." Then, he continued the story. "The ceremony completed, Hayenwatha's mind became clear. He felt that the Master of Life must have led him to this good friend. Deganawidah saw Hayenwatha as a man of strength and courage—a good man with many abilities. He had been searching for such a man to assist him in his quest for spreading the Good News of Peace among the nations."

Howard definitely had a flare for storytelling and had his audience intrigued. "Now we come to the story of *The Great Peace*," he announced.

"Deganawidah and Hayenwatha discussed their vision for peace, friendship, and unity among the tribes. In his home village Deganawidah was considered abnormal by the elders because he did not hold to the tribe's official philosophy but persisted in promoting a different way of life—peace and love of neighbor— declaring that his message came from the Master of Life. The Wendot/Huron/Iroquois conviction was to crush all enemies. 'Do unto others before they do unto you and seek revenge for anything they did to you' were the guiding principles instilled into them from childhood. Spurned by his tribe, he set out to find distant tribes that might be more amenable. He built a canoe and sadly departed from his mother and grandmother, explaining that his mission in life was to end bloodshed among the people and establish peace.

"He traveled south on Lake Ontario and encountered a small hunting party. Due to trouble in their village, they had journeyed to that area. They asked him his name. 'I am Deganawidah. I have come from the west and am going eastward.' Deganawidah instructed them to return to their village and proclaim to their chief: 'Great Peace has come, and the village will be free of troubles. In a few days, a messenger of the Good Tidings of Peace and Power will come.' As Deganawidah traveled the east-west warriors' trail, he stopped at the small lodge of a woman who was hospitable to passersby. She fed warriors traveling to their hostilities. In the same manner, she welcomed the man of peace. After his meal Deganawidah told her he carried a message from the Master of Life—The Good News of Peace and Power—that would end wars and terror. 'The Word I bring is that all peoples shall love one another and live in peace.'

"The woman was comforted by the message and the first person to embrace the Great Peace. He named her Jigonsasee (New Face), as she reflected a changed mind. He appointed her Mother of Nations[24], the Great Peace Woman. He instructed her to stop feeding warriors on their way to destruction and commissioned her to be the custodian of the Good Tidings of Peace and Power.

"Deganawidah continued through the Flint Country—the land of the Mohawks. He sat at the edge of the forest, within view of a village, and smoked his pipe—a signal that he meant no harm.

"In an interview with the men of the village, he reassured them he had come on a mission of peace. They escorted him to their council of chiefs where he conveyed his message. After that, he was allowed to repeat it to the whole village. His message

---

[24] In Iroquois culture women were honored, especially women with children. The mothers chose the chiefs and could remove them if they were remiss in their duties. Each infant belonged to the linage of the mother; probably due to the questionable paternity of many children. In 1615, after visiting the Huron, Champlain wrote: ". . . when a girl is [between 11 and 15], she will have suitors . . . many . . . according to her attractions . . . after [asking] the parent . . . , although often [not] . . . the suitor will give her a present . . . ; if she finds him to her taste she accepts [it], hereupon he will come and sleep with her 3 or 4 nights without saying a word to her during that time, and there they will gather the fruit of their love. . . . usually . . . after a week or a fortnight . . . she will leave her suitor . . . Afterward, being disappointed in his hopes, he will seek another girl . . . Thus they continue this plan of action until a satisfactory union. Some girls spend their youth in this way, having had more than twenty [short-term] husbands. [Even the young married 'husband and wives'] after nightfall . . . run about from one lodge to another . . . possessing each other . . . wherever it seems good to them, yet without violence, leaving all to the wishes of the women. . . . such being the custom of the country."

appealed to the long-suffering, war-weary people. However, they were conflicted by the Iroquois code: honor required revenge and retaliation. Not avenging a killing was a sign of cowardice and disgrace.

"Deganawidah proposed a plan. Never having been involved in a killing, no man was against him. He was without a tribe. Therefore, he could become a neutral messenger of peace without the stigma of a coward. This satisfied the Mohawks. They welcomed the plan and became the first nation of the Great Peace.

"After Deganawidah's instruction in the way of peace, friendship, kindness, unity, and justice, the people were prepared to welcome Hayenwatha. Now with sound mind, Hayenwatha became a chief of the Mohawk nation.

"The two men continued spreading the Good News throughout the Indian territory. Having lived in fear and suffering for many years, the peace proposal was accepted with great relief. They formed the League of the Iroquois—the tribes that accepted the Good News of Peace and Power. With a sense of security and strength, the confederation became an extended family of clans. Each clan was based on the linage of the eldest mother who was its head.

"The *kayanernh kowa* (Great Peace) established by Hayenwatha and Deganawidah had many governing rules set up by the confederacy. They dealt with issues such as marriage, adoption of strangers, and inheritance. The central theme had three parts, each with a double meaning: *The Good Word*: righteousness in action, bringing justice for all. *Health*: sound mind in a sound body, bringing peace on earth. *Power*: the establishment of civil authority, bringing with it the increase in spiritual power in keeping with the will of the Master of Life.

"Even their old enemy, the nefarious Tadadaho was eventually converted by a delegation from the League using a combination of spiritual power, a sacred medicine ceremony, and political pressure. Tadadaho, his mind now straightened and submitting to the peace, was offered the position of principal chief with the title of Fire-Keeper of the Confederation."

At this everyone laughed and turned to Will.

Paul said, "Looks like we need some more wood in the grate, Fire-Keeper of the Confederation."

Will just smiled good-naturedly, put on another piece of apple wood, picked up the poker, and stabbed at the smoldering logs. Sparks rose, filling the space above and flying up the chimney. Suddenly, the fire flared up with a roar. "Ah ha!" said Will with amusement. "How's that? A little magic from the Fire-Keeper!"

All responded with a round of applause and cheering.

Will countered with a nod and broad smile. Returning to his seat, he asked, "So tell us, did Tadadaho accept the offer of Fire-Keeper of the Confederation?"

Looking pleased with the question acknowledging interest in the story, Howard continued. "After some contemplation, Tadadaho gave his answered. 'It is well. I will now answer. I now truly accept your message, the object of your mission.' The alliance became known as the Confederacy of the Five Nations—the founding date unknown. This story had been repeated orally for centuries. In the 1800s, when white historians began to publish articles and books about Iroquois history and culture, several knowledgeable Iroquois decided to write down the story. Each one told it differently—no two accounts agreed in every detail or even the order of events. Nevertheless, the confederation was important to the Iroquois, as it signified what their ancestors had done to establish peace, unity, and purpose—a meaningful way of life."

After the story, they sat quietly for a while staring into the fire. Then all of a sudden, they started talking about the story.

Paul commented, "That's an interesting story. It illustrates much of the struggles of life: the struggle between good and evil and finding a purpose in life. It seems to have a lot of biblical principles. That's curious. And, Deganawidah talks about his message being from the Master of Life—the Master of Life gave him the message directly."

"Yes, that *is* interesting," Howard responded. "I have a theory about that. In the 1600s, missionaries started to arrive, set up missions among the Indians. They taught them biblical principles. I think these were integrated into their narratives and legends. As I mentioned, they had no written language, and you all know how the *Whisper* game goes. Some tribes were quite receptive to Christianity."

Then Edmund proposed a question; he knew the answer. "Is man inherently good or evil?"

Not following this train of thought, or the meaning of the story, and wanting to sound intelligent, but as usual, with the opposite effect, Sandra interrupted. "Well, all cultures have their myths and legends. Like the Bible—myths and legends."

Samantha thought, *Where did that come from? What brought that on?*

After a minute or two of silence—all befuddled by her comment—Howard responded. In a calm tone with his engaging little grin which disarmed any irritation, he began, "Actually, the Bible is quite different."

In spite of wanting to direct their discussion to Paul's point—the struggle between good and evil and finding a purpose in life—and Edmund's question, they all sat patiently while Sandra went off on her tangent. For whatever reason, she did respect Howard, and they seemed happy when he stepped in to handle it, even though in the end it would be of no avail with Sandra. She didn't like to be burdened with lengthy facts, or even let facts get in the way of her preconceived notions. She liked the one-liner bombshells she'd picked up from who-knows-where. And, she had an arsenal of pat phrases she could throw out trying to hit the target in a conversation. It seemed to be a crutch she used. Apparently, her mental defect blocked any critical thinking. Somehow, everyone in this group seemed to understand and let her go on as they would tolerate any mentally impaired person.

This is bewildering, Samantha thought. *I am so glad Edmund clued me in.*

Howard had an impressive command of information and was always interesting. "As I mentioned before," he went on, "the Indians didn't have a written language until well into the 1700s when missionaries established schools. For example, later, Rev. Asher Wright used the English alphabet to develop a written language for the Seneca. He even edited a newspaper in their language—early1800s. The main point here is that the Indians didn't have a written language until recently—recently, that is, considering the span of their history. When the most knowledgeable of the Iroquois finely wrote down stories that had been passed down orally for centuries, each version was different."

"As I said—myths," repeated Sandra.

"Yes, when there's more fantasy than fact, you could call it a myth," he indulged her. "In contrast, however, the New Testament, for example, was written down shortly after the events by eye witnesses—Matthew, Mark, John, Paul and others." He paused, gazing around the room. His eyes rested on the bookshelves on the other side of the fireplace next to where Edmund was sitting. He asked, "Would someone hand me the Bible from that shelf over there?"

Edmund picked out the NIV Bible and handed it to Howard, who opened it to the Gospel of Luke. "Luke, the physician, was a methodical man of the science. He was an historian looking for original sources of information—people who were personally involved in the events being described. He writes in classical Greek—begins with a formal preface common to historical works of that time: 'Many have undertaken to draw up an account of the things that have been fulfilled among us, just as they were handed down to us by those who from the first were eyewitnesses and servants of the word. Therefore, since I myself have carefully investigated everything from the beginning, it seemed good also to me to write an orderly account for you, most excellent Theophilus, so that you may know the certainty of the things you have been taught.'

Note the words *eyewitnesses* and *investigated everything*. The Indians who finally wrote their history had no one who saw the events first-hand—no eyewitnesses. Besides the historical events recorded in the Bible, other historians of the time have reported many of the same events. These were recorded events of history not myths—"

"Well, enough of this history," Sandra interrupted, repressing a yawn. "I can't think about anything more today. I'm tired. I'm going to bed. Come along, Paul!"

Philip helped Paul transfer to his Amigo, and Paul dutifully followed her to their suite.

Sandra's interruption put a damper on the mood to discuss the point of Howard's story, and it *was* getting late.

Steve said, "See you tomorrow." Then, he left.

Howard and Edmund said their good-nights and departed in the direction of their rooms.

Samantha sat quietly staring into fireplace. Feeling warm and relaxed, she was mesmerized by the glowing remnants of the last log. Will picked up the poker and jabbed at it. Its fragile charred remains broke into pieces and fell through the grate, this time with a feeble flurry of sparks drifting up the chimney. He scattered the embers among the ashes, replaced the screen, and sat opposite Samantha.

He looked questioningly into her eyes. "Who *are* you, Samantha?"

This took her by surprise. She sat still, tightened up, and emitted a blank expression—she said nothing. Searching for some sort of response, disorganized thoughts bounced around in her tired brain—she could come up with nothing.

After a minute or two of studying each other in silence, Will said, "Well, I suppose my question was something between rhetorical and thinking out loud. I wouldn't ordinarily give much thought to a stray grandfather brought home. However, *you* are definitely different. *You* are here, apparently planning on remaining indefinitely, and *I* am here, definitely planning on remaining indefinitely. Howard says you're a distant relative."

Howard would not have given out this information without Edmund's permission, she thought. *Edmund told me that he did tell the family about me—the 'distant relative' part. It's not a big secret. The staff will eventually know. That's no problem. It's general knowledge that I came here initially because I was in trouble through no fault of mine. Will must know that, too, but that was all.*

Samantha wasn't interested in going into her past, present, or future with Will. She liked Will, or wanted to like him, as he looked so much like the portrait of the Will she had come to admire and become so intimate with through his writings and tales of his history. Yet, his attitude toward her was suspicious—perhaps tainted by his mother. She definitely didn't know if she could trust him with her feelings, or with anything. She didn't want to share any information about herself with him. Besides, it was very late, she was tired and wasn't up to any mental sparing. And, she was exceedingly awkward when things got personal.

"A distant relative," he repeated after another period of silence. "Well, cousin—a poor relation, I suppose. Grandfather has picked up unfortunates before, but you're different. No one has wielded her, or his, way into the protected private family quarters."

Samantha continued to sit silently—frozen, without expression.

His tone changed from matter-of-fact to sarcastic. "How did you manage that, pretty Samantha?"

Having had enough and not knowing what to do, Samantha got up, took a deep breath, and blurted out in a soft gentle voice, "Good night, Will. I hope we can be friends." Then she left.

On the way to her room, she reproached herself. *Was that a stupid thing to say after what he said? And, what was all that about?* Mulling over what Will had said, she couldn't get to sleep. She tried to divert her thoughts as it was distressing to dwell on it. Finally, she consoled herself. *For Edmund's sake, I didn't want to say anything to make Will dislike me or cause dissention. What should I have said? It was probably best to say nothing. What could I have said? What mood was he in?*

Exhausted emotionally, mentally, and physically, she fell asleep.

❧·CHAPTER 26

*Having gifts that differ according to the grace given
us, let us use them: If it is prophesying,
let him use it in proportion to his faith; if it is serving,
let him serve; if it is teaching, let him teach;
if it is encouraging, let him encourage; if it is contributing
to the needs of others, let him give generously;
if it is leadership, let him lead with zeal; if it is
showing mercy, let him do it happily.*

Romans 12:6-8.

The next morning Samantha slept late—late for her. Preoccupied with the events of the previous evening, she puttered around her room aimlessly trying to dismiss them, but they kept bothering her. She was sorry to miss her time with Edmund; she didn't feel she could talk to him about it and was afraid of encountering Will in the dining room. She knew that by 9:30 all would be cleared away and cleaned up. The kitchen helper would be on a break or deployed elsewhere, and Juanita would be alone in the kitchen. Having a particular fondness for Samantha, Juanita would take pity on her and prepare something special.

As she entered the kitchen, Juanita greeted her with her generous, friendly smile. Isabella was sitting at the corner table coloring; she got up and greeted her with a big hug. Samantha thought Isabella looked better this morning—more color in her cheeks.

"That's a lovely picture," Samantha said. "I like the colors."

"Thank you."

"You missed breakfast this morning. Are you okay?" Juanita asked with concern. "Mr. Jones was worried about you but didn't want to call your room and wake you. Call him when you get a chance."

"Oh, yes, I'm fine, thank you. I'll call Mr. Jones right away. I wasn't able to get to sleep for awhile." She called Edmund and left a message for him that she was fine, had overslept, and was sorry she'd missed him.

"Something troubling you?" Juanita asked. Although Juanita wasn't much older than Samantha, she had a motherly concern for her.

"Oh, nothing worth mentioning—just a silly little thing."

"Well, I'm going to fix you some breakfast. Can't have you getting sick."

Samantha was famished, and the prospect of a bowl of cold cereal wasn't very appealing so she was grateful for the offer.

"Sit with Isabella, and I'll fix you a decent breakfast," Juanita ordered. "I was about to fix Isabella a snack. You can eat together. How about your favorite—eggs and grits?"

"Can I have eggs and grits, too, Mommy?" Isabella asked enthusiastically.

Juanita said with a laugh, "Well, for goodness sake, yes, you can." Then, Juanita looked at Samantha. "She only ate a few bites for breakfast. You're a good influence on her."

Just then Will entered the kitchen looking for some breakfast. He headed straight for Juanita. After greeting her, he caught a glimpse of Samantha and Isabella at the corner table. Surprised, he said, "Well, good morning, you two." Then turning back to Juanita asked, "What are the chances of getting some breakfast?"

"Pretty good," she responded with her warm smile. "I'm fixing eggs and grits for those two. How about you?"

"Eggs and grits? What's that?"

"That's Samantha's favorite," Juanita responded. "And, it looks like it's going to be Isabella's, too."

"I'm feeling adventuresome. Beside, I'm so hungry I could eat just about anything."

Shortly, Juanita had three plates of eggs, grits, and thick slices of toasted homemade whole-grain bread ready. Samantha helped her bring them to the table along with utensils and napkins. Will pitched in bringing the beverages and setting the table. Then Juanita brought the all important Parmesan cheese.

Samantha informed Will, "We like to sprinkle everything with Parmesan cheese."

Will took his turn with the grater and followed Samantha and Isabella's example. After a few bites Will said, "This is really different."

Isabella was direct and insisted, "But do you like it?"

"Yes, my dear, I think I do," he replied, sounding like his grandfather for the moment.

Isabella smiled as she finished her small portion and said, "Me, too."

"Now, Sweetie Pie, you need a nap," her mother said.

Isabella protested leaving Samantha; however, Samantha supported her mother's decision.

"I'll see you later. We can read books together," Samantha promised and gave her a hug. Satisfied, Isabella went off with her mother.

Will and Samantha were alone; they sat in an awkward stillness for a few minutes—Samantha sipping her tea and Will drinking his third mug of coffee. Then Samantha surprised herself and broke the uncomfortable silence. "You're getting a late start this morning."

"Actually, I've been working since two a.m. I couldn't sleep. To tell the truth, my conscience was bothering me about what I said last night. I'm glad I found you—I want to apologize."

Looking down and staring into her tea, she blushed. She could only whisper, "Thank you."

Nevertheless, he heard her and realized that he *had* hurt her. He went on to say, "My grandfather is a wise man and has always been a good judge of character. He must have his reasons. However, to be honest, I *am* conflicted about this."

"I can appreciate that."

"I'll try to keep an open mind. I'm sure we'll get to know each other and time will tell."

"That's fair," she responded.

"Well, I should be able to stay awake long enough to finish my project. See you later," he said in a friendly tone.

"See you later," she echoed.

*   *   *

Fortifying herself against the chill of an October wind coming off the lake, Samantha bundled up. Then she walked north along the deserted beach. Later she spent the afternoon next to a warm fire in Juanita's suite reading stories with Isabella on her lap.

When Isabella had gotten too heavy for Juanita to carry up the stairs, Edmund had a front parlor converted into a cozy suite with all that was needed for Isabella's care and comfort. This particular room was chosen for its proximity to the kitchen—Juanita could easily check on her throughout the day. Isabella didn't go to school; she didn't have the strength. Also, the doctor was concerned that if she were exposed to other children, she might contract a virus and not survive—even a common cold could be fatal. Everyone was careful to stay away from her if they even suspected they were coming down with something. On one occasion Samantha stayed with Isabella when Juanita had a cold. Juanita slept in another part of the house until she was over it.

Abby loved to come over after school and show Isabella what she had learned and play the little teacher. Learning from her mother, then Abby, Mary, and now Samantha, Isabella was able to read quite well for her age. However, today Abby had an arithmetic lesson for her. She was the only friend she had near her age. If Abby went to an event, such as a birthday party, she always asked for a balloon, piece of cake, favor, or the like for her friend, Isabella. Afterward, she'd hurry to see Isabella and share the experience with her. Having Isabella for a friend, a friend who could not reciprocate except with gratitude, was definitely a character-building experience for Abby.

*   *   *

That evening Samantha had dinner in the grand dining room with the rest of the family, as had become their routine. Today, Steve was there, and Paul was now a regular with Philip to attend to his needs. Finishing at irregular intervals, each excused himself or herself, stating some pressing business. Again, Will and Samantha were alone finishing dessert.

Will seemed to want to linger and talk with her; Samantha had no pressing business. "Did you have an interesting day, Cousin?" he started.

"Interesting? I don't know. Enjoyable, yes. Juanita was very busy in the kitchen, and I spent the afternoon reading with Isabella. Abby came over after school with her usual enthusiasm and a lesson for her. That probably seems dull to you, but I enjoyed it very much."

"You seem very fond of Isabella. What are the popular books for that age?"

"I am very fond of Isabella," she said, then went on to name the books they'd read that afternoon. She didn't know if he was interested or just making idle conversation. However, what she knew of Will, he wasn't one to waste time on frivolous things. Maybe he really did want to get to know her better.

"Surprisingly, I'm a bit taken with Isabella myself," he admitted. "It's a curious thing—having a fatal illness—especially with a child. I wonder what she knows about it. She seems almost ethereal."

"Ethereal?" Samantha noted with surprise. "Well, Cousin Will, there's more to you than meets the eye."

He smiled and changed the subject. "What did you think of Howard's story of the good and evil Indian chiefs and the change of heart of the evil one? Do you think he really recognized that peace and goodness were the better way?"

"I'm not sure. You would think that love, peace and harmony would be an obvious way to live, but human nature doesn't seem to work that way. I tend to agree with your mother on the myth and legend of the Indian story. I think it got better with time."

"You agree with mother? You must be the only one."

"Now, now. The Indian story seemed too neat, and as Howard said, it was passed down orally for generations. When it was finally written down, all the writers had significant variations. No one can verify it from any written account."

"I suppose that's true," he said.

"Something disturbed me about the Iroquois tribes accepting peace and 'love your neighbor'—why did they go on such a killing rampage in the mid-1600s? They almost wiped-out the other Indian tribes. Howard told me that Will and his family had to avoid their wake of carnage when they traveled back to Michigan."

"Yes, that's interesting. I don't know. Did the love and peace thing just apply to the Iroquois neighbors?"

"The Alliance seems to have made the Iroquois stronger, but they were really cruel. They weren't satisfied with just killing their so called neighbors—they tortured them!" she said.

"We'll have to ask Howard about that. However, that makes Grandfather's question more interesting: 'Is man inherently evil or good?' Like you say, living in peace and harmony would seem to be the obvious best course, but that's not what we see. What do you think?"

All this interest in what she thought was unexpected. She hadn't heard this much questioning in a discussion since the days she spent with her family. She couldn't help being a tad suspicious of his motives, especially considering his tone last night. Did he have that much character that he was making an effort to get to know her better? Was he making a sincere attempt to treat her like family? Was he looking for some weakness to use against her? She had seen a gentler kinder side to him and curiosity *was* in his nature. She was family—'Cousin' Samantha—now, not the protected guest with staff following a need-to-know directive. His questions were not restricted; he was third in command of the Jones dynasty—#1 Edmund, #2 Paul, and #3 Will. Nevertheless, his tone seemed honest and straight forward.

Samantha thought for a few seconds. "I can only refer to a wiser source. My dad used to quote the Bible a lot. I was raised on it. I can remember some things that should answer the question."

"Where is your father?"

"He died."

"I'm very sorry," he said sincerely.

"Me, too," she said quickly and went on. "Do you want the quotes?"

"Sure."

"Okay. I never can remember the exact reference. You'll just have to trust me."

"Definitely," he said with a grin.

"'All of us have become like one who is unclean, and all our righteous acts are like filthy rags . . . .' I know that one is from Isaiah."

"That's pretty harsh for starters," he said with a grimaced. "I must have missed that part. Actually, I must confess, I was brought up on the Bible, too. My grandparents saw to that— church every Sunday, Sunday school afterward, and evening Bible study, usually led by Uncle Robert, after a do-it-yourself-cook's-day-off cold supper. We weren't even allowed to do school work on Sunday. Nobody spent money unless absolutely necessary. We stayed home with the family. Grandfather and Uncle Robert tried to be home on Sunday. In spite of all the traveling they did, they seldom missed—even when the family was in Florida. Nobody worked on Sunday . . . ."

". . . . except Security," she finished, and they laughed. "It just occurred to me, and now that I think of it, the fact that Security has to work on Sunday is rather telling. Evil doesn't recognize the Sabbath."

"You're right. I hadn't stopped to think about that either. So back to the Bible quotes—you're not off the hook yet."

"Well, to spare you more quotes, I'll just end it with the one I think is the most conclusive and simplest: 'Jesus answered, "No one is good—except God alone."' That's recorded in Mark, Luke, and Matthew. What else can I say? I can't argue with the ultimate authority on good and evil. I'm not arrogant, audacious, or astute enough to do that."

"I guess that *is* pretty convincing," Will said. "Either you believe the Bible or not. Actually, I do remember the context of that particular story in the Bible. I remember it well because it's about the very, very rich man who asked what he must do to inherit eternal life and was told he had to follow the commandments. He thought he had, but Jesus said that he should sell everything he had and give it to the poor, and then he would have treasure in heaven. After doing that and becoming penniless, he was asked to follow Jesus. Well, he couldn't do it and went away sad. Somehow this came up regularly in church and at Uncle Robert's Bible study. As a boy, I wasn't about to say I followed the commandments entirely—I hadn't murdered anyone yet, and I wasn't into stealing. But I wasn't always nice to my sister, and I sometimes gave my parents a hard time—a very hard time—not to mention the coveting part. I hadn't even gotten the first part right. But that wasn't what bothered me the most. It was selling everything! Eventually there came a time when I knew my family was very rich. I was worried that my grandparents and Uncle Robert would sell everything and take us off to be missionaries in Africa or some remote primitive island. And I was afraid to ask about their plans. I asked about everything else but was afraid they would think me greedy or ungrateful or uncharitable—not to want to be a missionary or minister. And that really wasn't my 'calling.' And then there was the ending about it being easier for a camel to go through the eye of a needle than for a rich man to enter the kingdom of God. In spite of all the Bible study, church, and charity, I was plenty worried about getting into heaven, and I knew the alternative was definitely not good. My one solace was I wasn't rich, just my parents and grandparents and Uncle Robert."

"Does that still bother you?"

"Not really. I think it was Martin Luther who said, 'Man is not saved by faith and works, but by faith that works.' It just reminds me that philanthropy and being responsible are essential when a person is rich. Our family isn't out to change the whole world—just to be responsible for our little corner of it. I think we take that seriously. Grandfather and Uncle Robert have been the role models for running good businesses that provide good jobs for people and helping others in difficult circumstances. They don't just throw money at problems and let someone else do it—they get involved. Now that Grandmother and Uncle Robert are gone, a huge responsibility has fallen on Grandfather. I think Dad will be able to help more as time goes on. There's a lot he can do from here even in his circumstances. He's a little slow and grows tired easily but is improving. Working in these surroundings is helpful—rests frequently, works when he's up to it. We keep the deadline stuff away from him. Even Mother enjoys charity work and has her favorites, but she has to work within my father and grandfather's guidelines—especially no flaunting the wealth and naming things after her or any family member for that matter. My talents lie more in R&D, but I'm gradually learning as much as I can about all aspects of the business."

"But what about the Bible study? Your grandfather has been back since August, and now it's October. Church on Sunday, yes—do-it-yourself meals on Sunday, yes—but I haven't noticed any Bible study after supper."

"After Grandmother and Uncle Robert died, he was alone. I guess the tradition died with them."

Samantha thought she detected a sad tone of regret in his voice.

"Grandfather's question about good and evil was typical and reminded me of old times on Sunday evenings. He wanted us to think about that. And apparently we did! He doesn't put out a thought or a question lightly—it's usually something essential. Uncle Robert led most of the sessions—sometimes Grandmother—sometimes Grandfather. They each had their own style and favorite lessons. I especially missed Grandfather's guidance—his profound questions when he was in an instructive mood."

"I think I understand," Samantha responded. "I have a collection, in my mind, of episodes, quotes, thoughts, and philosophies from things I've read but haven't had guidance on how to put it all together or sift out the foolish from the worthy—the truth. Sort of finding the meaning of life I suppose—well, my life anyway. Your grandfather is a good mentor in that respect. I hope he starts the Bible studies again. I'll ask him."

In spite of the burden he must be feeling, at this moment Will seemed to be in a relaxed pensive mood as he sat deliberating with Samantha. She was interested in knowing more about him, so she ventured, "What did you do about school?"

"We didn't go to public school. We had tutors—Grandfather arranged our education. Grandfather and Dad were opposed to having their children's education turned over to the government."

"I had a goal, last summer, to read all of Tolstoy's novels," she responded. "Well, I didn't realize what I was undertaking and just got through *Anna Karenina* and *War and Peace*. I also read some background information on Tolstoy—his life and philosophy. There was a lot about schools in *Anna Karenina*. Tolstoy would have agreed with your grandfather about turning the children's education over to the government."

"Well, Cousin Samantha, there's more to *you* than meets the eye," he mused, echoing her previous comment about him. "Actually, we did go to public school, for a few months, in about the fifth grade—Mother's idea. We happened to be spending the winter with my parents while Dad was working in Washington, D.C. We lived in Alexandria, and my mother thought it would be nice if we mingled with the children of the other families in that up-scale area. We were way ahead of our classmates and pretty bored. After the experiment, Dad won out. We were sent back to live with my grandparents—we were back to tutors. And, to be honest, having been around adults all the time, we were spoiled. We led very sheltered lives in other respects. Our grandparents were worried about kidnapping—believe it or not! I suppose there was a remote chance. Nevertheless, a youthful looking bodyguard with a gun under his jacket was often our companion. I'm not sure I can explain how that makes a kid feel."

Fear of kidnapping for ransom? Amazing! Who would have thought such a thing happened to people you know? Samantha thought this sarcastically but was not ready to validate his grandparents' fears with a personal revelation. Now she knew why Edmund was so protective and alert in her situation. This had been on his mind for years.

"In our studies at home, we were the center of attention—all our questions were discussed and answered to our satisfaction. I didn't get along with the other kids at all. It was pretty much a disaster. The school put us a grade ahead, and I was smaller than the other boys—I was teased and bullied. I asked questions the teacher didn't like—don't think she liked me either. Paula did better—made a couple of friends—didn't make many waves. I suppose the big argument for public school is socialization—you know, getting along with bullies and avoiding fights." He had a cynical tone; apparently the experience left its scars.

Sympathetically, Samantha frowned and changed the subject. "Paula is your sister?"

"Yes, we were very close, not only because we're twins, but because we traveled a lot and only had each other—I miss her. Since she's taken up this altruistic pursuit of a medical career, she has little time for anything else. She was in California for her residency, and now she's in Oregon. I think she was looking for a change of scene. Although, I think all she sees are hospitals and patients. She's a long way from Boston, and I've been absorbed in my studies so have had no time to visit her. Even Barbara, my fiancée, always complained about how little time I had to spend with her. Well, with my job, MIT and the commute—horrendous traffic—I didn't."

231

"Now you have a short commute to work," Samantha prompted with a smile.

"Wow, it's great! Working whatever hours I wish, as long as I wish—taking breaks when I get mentally and physically fatigued. Don't have to waste time grocery shopping, fixing food, ordering out, eating out, or grabbing junk food. Here I can eat decent meals. Couldn't be better! It's so uncomplicated here—I get tons more accomplished."

"You do spend a lot of time working here."

"Oh, I guess I have since I've been back. When I'm working on a big project, I can get pretty intense. After all the racing around in Boston for the past few years, I'm content just to stay here. I'm not one for night-life—seems aimless. Don't much like jazz clubs—too noisy for anything but drinking—that's not appealing, either. I get my kicks out of solving a big problem. I suppose I'd be called a nerd. I suppose that's why I got picked on at public school—for some reason most kids don't like nerds."

"I like nerds. My brother was a bit of a nerd. We were close."

"Was? Were? Where is your brother now?"

"Dead," she said bluntly.

"You poor kid. Do you have any relatives?"

"No," she said. Then, feeling comfortable enough with him, explained, "All my family died in an accident almost five years ago—it's hard to talk about."

"I can understand why grandfather took you under his wing. We'll change the subject, little cousin," he said sympathetically and in an accepting way, giving credence to her new family status.

"Yes, that's part of it, thank you. It's still very painful," she volunteered as she felt his acceptance.

"How did *you* get on in public school?" he asked changing the subject.

"Actually, I didn't go to public school all the time—more than you, though. I went to private school and had tutors, or my mother and father tutored us. It wasn't because they had a particular philosophy about being educated by the government but because of the nature of their business."

"What was that?"

"They owned a golf course about 100 miles or so south of here. Of course, in the winter, it was closed, and my father, a golf pro, liked to go were he could play golf, so we went to Florida."

"You play golf then?"

"Well, yes, I do."

"I think we still have a membership at a rather exclusive golf club nearby—very nice course. Uncle Robert was an avid golfer, his one vice," he said with an amused smile. "And Grandfather enjoyed playing from time to time. They took guests there—seems almost everyone likes to play golf. Uncle Robert taught Paula and me to play—haven't played in awhile though."

"Neither have I."

"Well, shall we give it a try one of these days? It had better be soon—the golf season's about finished."

"I think that would be fun." Curious, she reverted to the previous subject. "Why didn't you and Paula go to the school at the church?"

"We were too old when it started. Grandmother would have liked that—it was very important to her. I think her experience with us encouraged her to start it."

"Your grandmother would be proud. According to Mary, they have continued to do exceptionally well. She's quite involved and speaks well of it. Abby seems to love it! She's always bubbling with enthusiasm when she comes home. But then again, she's always bubbling. I think she'll grow up to be a teacher—she's a natural. She loves to share what she learns with Isabella. Abby can be impatient, but she's always kind and patient with Isabella. I love to see the two of them together after school."

"I'm glad the school is doing well. I miss my grandmother very much—seems empty around here without her. She was very wise and such a dominate presence. When I was in trouble or had a problem, *she* would be the one I'd go to. She never seemed judgmental and wouldn't say much, just enough to guide me into working out the right solution. She had a knack for that. Then, I'd think it was my idea. I'd be very pleased with myself."

"Some people can do that. My father was like that."

Will did not want to dwell on the dead (the house was full of "ghosts" for him, and he knew Samantha was vulnerable to hers); he quickly shifted to the living. "Abby and Isabella are definitely cute kids."

"You seem to like kids," she remarked.

"Well, let's just say I like Abby and Isabella."

CHAPTER 27

". . . Bring the full tithe into the storehouse, that there may be food in my house.
And thereby put me to the test," says the LORD
Almighty, "and see if I will not throw open the
floodgates of heaven and pour down so much blessing
that you will not have room enough for it.
I will prevent pests from devouring your crops, and the
vines in your fields will not cast their fruit,"
says the LORD Almighty. "Then all the nations will call you blessed,
for you will be a land of delight," says the LORD Almighty.

Malachi 3:10-12

The next morning Samantha arrived in the grand dining room early, as usual. Edmund was there with his tea and papers, as usual. He greeted her warmly, as usual. What was unusual was Will's arrival precisely at seven. Margaret had just finished setting up and was leaving as Will entered. Customarily, his appearance at breakfast was later but irregular—depending on how his work was going. He seemed in a cheerful mood as he greeted them and immediately helped himself to an assortment of breakfast foods, especially a generous serving of his favorite Egg and Cheese Casserole—not a routine item on the breakfast buffet.

He seemed a trifle fidgety, which did not go unnoticed by his grandfather. "How's everything going? How's work?"

"Oh, fine, fine," Will replied, but seemed somewhat distracted. Nevertheless, with less enthusiasm than usual, he briefly reported his progress with various projects.

"I saw you two last night engrossed in conversation," Edmund commented.

"Well, *you* are just the person we need. Actually, you started this," Will commented with a good-natured grin. "Somehow we got to talking about your question about man being basically good or evil. Did you know Samantha quotes the Bible?"

"I'm not surprised."

"From her sources, she decided on evil. I remember Mr. Wayne instructing us about the founders of our government, who were students of the Bible, and who thought men could not be trusted, so they set up three branches of government to check each other. Other countries have a philosophy that man is basically good, but not these guys. I remember Mr. Wayne having us read *The Federalist Papers*—Hamilton, Madison and Jay. Madison—Founding Father, principle author/signer of the Constitution, 4th president—wrote about that in the 51st article in 1788."

"You do have a good memory!" Samantha said in amazement.

"My tutors were big on original sources. They wanted us to be able to find it if we couldn't remember it word-for-word. The library is full of copies of letters, speeches, and documents of that sort. Uncle Robert was interested in that, too. I suppose now we could Google it, but when he started there was no public access to the Internet[25]. I still like to look around in there and read a written

---

[25] The development of the Internet started in 1957 when the Soviet Union launched Sputnik 1, the first satellite. Officials in the U.S. military became concerned that the USSR might be able to launch bombs into space, and then drop them anywhere they chose—thus in 1958 the Defense Advanced Research Projects Agency (DARPA) was established. DARPA's initial role was to start American research into ways to safeguard the U.S. against a space-based missile attack and reclaim the technological lead from the USSR; 18 months later they had developed and deployed the first U.S. satellite—the start of the U.S. Internet. The Internet changed

copy. I can get a source faster from there than on the Internet. Our tutors had us do that. We had a lot of our classes in there."

"That Mr. Wayne was a good man," Edmund commented.

"So, what did Madison say in number 51?" Samantha asked.

Edmund sat quietly looking pleased.

"If you have time, we can move to the library. I'll show you my library skills."

"I do," Samantha responded.

"I do," Edmund echoed. "That should be interesting."

As they entered the library, Will started gesturing to the areas of the shelves explaining the documents or books they contained.

"Very impressive!" Samantha commented. "I hope I can do that someday. I'm very impressed with your library. I've spent many hours here."

"I know," Will said. "You're interested in books."

She wondered, *How did he know that? Steve knew, the security guards reported my whereabouts to him—they knew—Edmund knew—Mr. Ryan knew—Howard knew. Even Abby knew where to find me when she asked me to go swimming. It's no secret.* It suddenly occurred to her how much others were aware of her and perhaps talked about her. *Well, I supposed I am a curiosity. I hope they speak kindly about me!*

"Yes, I am," she answered Will. "So, where are *The Federalist Papers?* Can you find Madison's view on the separation of powers?"

He went directly to the book and pulled it off the shelf and opened it to Federalist No. 51.

"Show off," she teased. "So, what does he say?"

"Here it is! I'll read it." He read extensively on the reasons for the separation of powers and methods for securing them and, in particular: "If men were angels, no government would be necessary. If angels were to govern men, neither external nor internal controls on government would be necessary . . . ."

---

quickly in 1992 when the U.S. government started pulling out of network management and commercial entities offered internet access to the general public.

Then, Will said, "I guess we're no angels."

The three of them sat in the library a while longer engaging in some lighthearted conversation. Samantha mentioned again how impressed she was with Will's library-skills exhibition. Will and Edmund chuckled over some amusing stories about Mr. Wayne and his teaching methods.

"I remember Mr. Wayne getting that look when my thinking would go astray," Will mused with a slight smile. "How many times would I hear him say, 'Now, now, Will, let us focus and reason together in the area under discussion . . . .'"

They all got caught up in the cheerful mood, and, apparently, Will lost track of time as he suddenly jumped up and announced, "I'm really sorry—have to go. Barbara's coming from Boston to see Lake House—her future home. She'll be here about a week. Wish me luck. She likes the big city. I like it here . . . ."

"She's coming today?" Samantha interjected.

"Yup, I have to pick her up from the airport. Oops, I think I'm going to be a little late. I'll tell her it's your fault," he said looking at Samantha.

"Oh, no, you won't!" she ordered, presuming on their new relationship. "I don't want to get off to a bad start. We need to be friends."

"Only kidding," he said, smiling good-naturedly and hurried out of the room.

After he left, Edmund said, "I should have warned you about her visit. I had very short notice—only found out late yesterday. I haven't met her, but Sandra is ecstatic. She speaks of her in glowing terms. Not that that gives a whole lot of insight into her character. We'll see."

"I guess we will."

Then changing the subject, Edmund started, "I'm glad we have this chance to talk. I've been wondering if you've thought any more about a project you might enjoy taking on."

"Well, yes, I have. I know we've talked about it briefly in the past, and I've been thinking about it quite a bit. I've been helping Mary at the school, and I'm very interested in it."

"I'm glad. That was dear to Amanda's heart. I'm sorry to say I've been busy with the business and other things and haven't been able to look into it as much as I'd like."

"You told me not to give so much to the church as to cover all their expenses because it's important that the members assume that responsibility and the blessings it imparts. So I was wondering what you thought of my building up the school. It needs the media center remodeled and expanded, and there are at least ten children from nearby farms who would like to come to the school, but they would need to hire another teacher and perhaps build on another classroom. One of the families has six children, and they can't contribute much to the church to subsidize the school. Also, if the school expands, a van and a driver will be needed to pick up some of the children. If I did that, I could work through the pastor or whoever manages the finances and keep it anonymous."

"You're full of ideas. I think that's an excellent plan. I'm particularly pleased because it was Amanda's project. She'd be pleased to know that her work will be continued by someone who truly has the energy and enthusiasm for it."

"I'll need help. This is new to me."

"I can arrange that. If the school expands to accommodate 60 to 70 or more students, we should probably hire a principal who would teach classes part-time—a good place to start. He could be your go-between and help administer the finances. I have someone in mind, but we can interview a few candidates—I'm chairman of the school board. Well, in fact, I'm the only one on the school board. Amanda was on the school board and a couple of older ladies—they passed away. No one ever called for elections to replace them. I assume everyone is happy the way it is—haven't heard any complaints. I'll help you get started until you feel comfortable enough to go it alone. We can start right away."

"I'm really looking forward to it."

"Me, too," he responded with a reassuring smile.

*   *   *

The days passed—October was almost over. Barbara came and went faster than the leaves off the trees in the last wind storm. Samantha met her briefly. She was extremely attractive; her mannerisms were much like Sandra's. Sandra gushed over her, and they carried on and on about a world of things totally foreign to Samantha. Barbara had nothing to say to Samantha except "Hello" and "Goodbye." She said nothing to her at the one dinner she had with the family the second evening of her visit. Barbara and Sandra went on endlessly smiling at each other, chattering away engrossed in their trivial conversation and trying to impress one another with this and that.

I've never seen anyone with a perpetual smile—it can't be genuine, Samantha thought. *Sandra looks happy—I've never seen her look happy. She rarely smiles, and when she does, it's only for a few seconds and looks artificial. I've never seen her laugh.*

Samantha had a feeling that Edmund didn't particularly like Barbara, although he was gracious and polite at all times. Barbara and Will were out all the next day, and the following morning she was gone.

Samantha had seen Will, briefly, only once since Barbara left. He had asked her if she would help enter and organize some data into spreadsheets on the computer, as two of the guys who usually work on that were ill. One was in the hospital—he had developed pneumonia. They didn't expect him back for awhile. Samantha was more than willing to help and contribute something. She was pleased he had confidence in her ability to do it. Being a math major and knowing her way around computer programs, it wasn't difficult for her, and she was quick to learn. However, she found out later that it was Edmund's suggestion. She had worked in an office on the lower level one afternoon; one of the programmers had shown her what to do. Later, a computer was set up in her suite so she could work from there, and Paul could help her if needed. Actually, she'd had to work intensely at first to organize the data. The work had piled up due to the absence of the others.

∗   ∗   ∗

The next morning, after working late into the night, Samantha entered the dining room for breakfast about ten minutes before Margaret would disassemble the breakfast buffet. Expecting to find it empty, she was surprised to find Edmund still there. "You're a little late this morning—I've been waiting for you."

"Oh, I'm very sorry. I could have come sooner if I had known."

"It's okay, I know. Will told me you were up late entering the analysis data." Will and Edmund would know as the computer enters the time and date for all entries.

"Yes, I was."

"It was there for him when he looked for it this morning at three o'clock—that's when *he* started," he said shaking his head. "What schedules you young people keep, but I remember working late into the night when I was young and being up early the next morning—Robert the same—drinking pots of coffee to keep us going. I suppose Will gets that intensity from us."

"Oh, I wanted to have it for him as soon as possible. I knew he'd be looking for it early, but I didn't expect it would be *that* early. Now, I'm glad I finished it. I know he keeps odd hours. I can't do that too often—the hours I mean. I'll be glad to help anytime you need me."

"He was very happy with it," Edmund praised.

She smiled with appreciation.

✥·CHAPTER 28

So God created man in his own image, in the image of God he created him;
male and female he created them. God blessed them and said to them,
"Be fruitful and increase in number; fill the earth and subdue it.
Rule over the fish of the sea and the birds of the air and over every living
creature that moves on the ground." Then God said,
"I give you every seed-bearing plant
on the face of the whole earth and every tree that has fruit
with seed in it. They will be yours for food.

Genesis 27-28

The next morning, after Edmund left, Samantha encountered Will arriving for breakfast. She hadn't seen him for weeks. Looking scruffy with a good start on a beard, he strongly resembled the picture of the 17th-century Will. Samantha didn't comment; she knew he must be working on a project. They greeted each other pleasantly then sat quietly for several minutes—Will picking at his food (unusual for him, being a tasked oriented person). Samantha, unnoticed, tried to determine his frame of mind by studying his face and mannerisms.

She observed his glasses tucked into his shirt pocket. He had the same problem she had—he had to take off his glasses to read or view close objects, in this case his food. He was forever taking off his glasses and forgetting where he left them; however, he had five or six pair, which tended to accumulate throughout the day in a small basket on the hall table. As he mislaid one pair, he would retrieve another from the basket. As the glasses were found by the maids and family members, they would deposit them the basket.

Will broke the silence. "I've got it!" he blurted out.

"Got what?"

"I've just figured out the last of a problem I've been working on! Are you doing anything later this morning? Would you like to go to the farm? I've got to run and get this in the computer."

"I'm happy you figured out your problem. No, I'm not doing anything special later this morning. Yes, I *would* like to go to the farm," Samantha responded enthusiastically.

"Terrific, I don't know what time—I'll find you when I'm done," he said hastily as he rushed out of the room.

Samantha knew the Jones family owned the farm across the road; however, she had not been to the farmhouse or the farm buildings or even passed them. They were in the opposite direction from any route she would have traveled. The fields across from the estate entrance were part of the farm, but she had never noticed any activity there.

Will appeared later that morning shaved and neatly dressed; Samantha noticed a fresh clean smell about him. They exchanged a few remarks. Then, dressed for the cold, they emerged into unexpected, unseasonably mild surroundings. They walked leisurely down the long driveway, now lined with leafless trees. Brown and dried, the leaves had been blown by the wind into irregular piles, and they crunched and rattled as they waded through them. They walked through the forest of pine trees and finally reached the entrance. With a wave, they passed the security guard who opened the heavy, iron, pedestrian gate from the little gatehouse fortress of native stones resembling those in parts of the main house. They strolled along the last few yards of the drive to a narrow, private road that ran between the farm and the Lake House property.

Enjoying the blissful day, they hiked north. Will's spirits lifted, and his steps became animated and buoyant. He was almost dancing down the deserted road—walking sideways, then backward, then forward, then on the right side of Samantha, then on the left, expending pent-up energy from days of sitting at his computer. He was in a lighthearted mood—at ease and relived to have finished a difficult problem.

"You must have been working mighty hard lately—haven't seen you for days."

"Yes, I've been working all hours. I get pretty intense."

"I've noticed."

"I've finished a big project and badly needed some fresh air, sunshine, and pleasant company. The farm will be a nice change—haven't been there in quite awhile."

Hearing the "pleasant company" part put Samantha at ease. She was content with the "pleasant company," too. It was a sunny, late-fall day; the wind was light, and it was perfectly pleasant—warmer than anticipated. Will pulled off the sweatshirt covering his short-sleeved golf shirt. Samantha noticed that he was quite muscular—more muscular than she'd noticed when they had first met. He was tall with a medium frame and well proportioned, but the extra muscle was quite noticeable. She wondered if he'd been working out.

When would he have time? she contemplated. *I'm terribly curious, but it might be too presumptuous of me to ask—maybe too personal. We are becoming close friends. I wonder . . . ?*

Her curiosity got the better of her, and before she realized what she was saying, she blurted out, "Have you been working out?" Then her face turned red. And he noticed!

"Well," he said with a modest laugh. "Yes, I have. I work out with Dad 20 minutes in the morning and 20 minutes in the afternoon—sometime it goes a little longer—nice break for me. Philip worked out a training plan—one for Dad and one for me. Philip's suggestion—it encourages Dad. I've really never been interested in taking time for that sort of thing, but it's been good and fun. We joke around a little. I keep him filled in on business and what I'm doing. We have a good time. We have a lot to catch up on! Somehow you think your parents will be around forever. In a strange way, it has made me appreciate Dad, and we've become closer. Sometimes something good comes from something unfortunate."

"That's wonderful!" she said dismissing the part about parents being around forever and focusing on his positive experience. "I truly like your dad—he's a fine man." Then she added with a shy smile, "You look great."

"Thanks!"

"I was embarrassed to ask, but my curiosity got the better of me," she confessed.

"I noticed! Your face is red, and I don't think it's sunburn," he teased.

She just smiled sheepishly as they sauntered along quietly for a few minutes.

Then in a more serious tone, Will started explaining, "We do *some* organic farming, but primarily we do common-sense-good-practice farming. We'll use pesticides prudently rather than lose an entire crop, such as strawberries, that has taken several years to establish. Grandfather can't just have a farm—he has to be involved in better farming methods and better crops. He employs a farm manager who works with Michigan State University—experimental plots, that sort of thing. Students come here, live on the farm, and work. They go back to school when the last of the harvest is over and come back in time for spring planting. Grandfather and Uncle Robert developed a model for self-sufficiency. We have our own wells, energy sources, waste disposal, and composting. They've been well ahead of their time for environmental responsibility. Besides communication devices and other things, we do research on electrical generation—windmills and solar panels mainly."

"Solar panels? The sun doesn't shine that much here."

"That's right! We need to be very clever—develop optimum efficiency. It's a big challenge."

"There's certainly a lot of wind here, but I've never seen, or heard, any windmills. I saw a gigantic white one near Mackinaw City. I've never seen anything like that here."

"Well, that's good. That's the goal. For one thing, they're a different design—small cylinder shaped—not the giant airplane propeller look. Also, they're camouflaged—not white. They're painted to blend in with the sky, the clouds, pine trees—whatever the landscape. We really didn't have to do much in the way of research. The military has already done it. Their uniforms aren't just random patterns and colors, but the result of extensive research. We just tapped into it. With robot painting, it's not difficult—we've developed computer programs for it. We contract with factories and businesses to determine placement for optimum efficiency. That's our first consideration. Then, we camouflage them for the site. We try to avoid conspicuous places, and we've worked very hard to keep them quiet."

"You *are* a clever fellow," she praised.

"Actually, the credit goes to Grandfather and Uncle Robert—and Dad, too. I'm just starting to build on their work."

"You're grandfather never ceases to amaze me."

"I come from a long line of inventive people. It's sort of humbling and a lot to live up to. To be honest, I'm rather excited about being here and carrying on the family tradition."

Samantha smiled at him approvingly. His enthusiasm was contagious, and his interest and pride in his family was very appealing.

"Great-grandpa and Uncle Robert, when he was young, before central heating, when the house was heated by fireplaces, worked on ways to make them more efficient. We continue to update them now. I don't know exactly why, but I love those old fireplaces—maybe the link with the past."

"Howard called you 'Fire-Keeper of the Confederation.' But I think 'Keeper of the Flame' describes you, figuratively and literally."

He laughed and went on. "Most of the wood we use is from an old apple orchard—the trees no longer produce adequately."

"I like the smell of an apple-wood fire."

"Me, too. As you can see, the Joneses are never satisfied with the status quo—always looking for a better way of doing things. Fortunately, we've had a lucrative business that produces ample income so we can indulge our passions—our intellectual curiosities. It takes megabucks to fund innovations. We've been blessed with the intellect and resources to do it."

"I'm impressed with your enthusiasm and sense of responsibility."

He smiled slightly and modestly said, "Oh, I guess that's the way we were brought up. Uncle Robert, Grandma, and Grandpa were our teachers—talk about 'teachable moments.' Now when I think about it, our lives here were one long 'teachable moment.'"

"I had a lot of those too," Samantha reminisced. "I don't think I realized it at the time, but now my mother and father's words come back to me—words of wisdom, I guess you'd call it."

"I guess so. There's one more energy project we're working on here. Have you noticed the two buoys in the lake to the north of the house?"

"Now that you mention it, yes, I have."

"That's part of another research project to generate energy from waves. Unfortunately, we can't camouflage the buoys without jeopardizing the safety of boats. That whole thing isn't going well—everything isn't a success. I'm not keen on it, either. It's not worth it. The lake chews up, or buries, whatever we put into it."

Suddenly he stopped, and a worried look crossed his face, "Well, Samantha, I've been going on and on. I hope I haven't bored you with all this family history and work projects."

Samantha smiled as they exchanged looks. She noticed that ever since he had surfaced from his long, tedious project he hadn't called her "Cousin" or "Cousin Samantha."

"Certainly not! Remember, I've been reading the history of the Jones family ever since I got here. Fascinating clan, I'd say, still is."

They reached a rise in the road and, in the distance, they could see a large white picturesque farmhouse, an assortment of attractive white farm buildings, and a large greenhouse. Samantha was surprised to see white buildings; she was expecting red barns.

"There's the farm." Will made a sweeping gesture toward the northeast. "We grow much of the food used at the estate or buy it locally. We have apple, pear, and peach orchards on the northeast section of the property. The rolling hills and valleys there have been an excellent location for fruit trees. We don't grow cherries—no point. We can buy all the cherries we want from numerous nearby orchards. And, there's a cranberry farm nearby—don't do that either—all that tedious harvesting—flooding and wading in water and all that—not interested."

"I know about the dried fruit. Mary and I stopped at the Lakeshore Orchards' processing plant not too long ago. We picked up a case of dried cherries and dried mixed fruit, including cranberries, for Juanita's muffins and cookies. I got some chocolate covered cherries. They're totally addictive."

"I know—the dark chocolates are my favorite. Did you save some for me?" he joked.

"I'm sorry, I just bought a small package. Mary and I ate them all on the way home. They were irresistible. Next time I'll buy some *just* for you—I'll put'm in the trunk so we can't get at them."

"Well, okay," he said with a grin and went on. "Beside local cherries, we buy milk and dairy products from the farm next to ours—the Werneke Farm. Two sisters inherited the property—work the farm with their husbands and children—family's been there for generations—but not as long as ours. They're very good farmers—our good friends as well. That's a tedious demanding business—taking care of all those cows properly. I'm glad they do it and we're not into *that* business.

"Our ancestor, Andrew Jones, bought this land, 640 acres, somewhere in the late 1700s[26] when this territory was being

---

[26] 1785. After the revolutionary war, Michigan was now in the NW Territory belonging to the colonies; colonies took steps to provide a system of land survey and a form of government,

surveyed and as it became available to settlers. According to the Grayson Land Ordinance of 1785, the land was to be sold for one dollar an acre, but the purchaser must buy at least one square mile—$640[27]. Few settlers had that much money. Speculators bought the best land in large amounts. After the price went up, they sold sections to incoming settlers. We still have the original 640 acres. Andrew Jones bought this land because he was the grandson of Samuel Jones, one of Will and Sophia's twins. He wanted this land because his father had shown him where his grandfather had lived with the Indians and where Will and Sophia are buried. His father, Arthur, died in 1786, and he wanted to bury him here too. There's a cemetery about 200 yards behind the church. You can't see it from the church because of the trees, and it's down in a small valley. All the Joneses are buried there."

"That's remarkable. Where did Andrew get the money?"

"He got it from England—somehow from the estate. I'm not sure just how the money was transferred. After that Andrew and his son, Henry, bought more land,[28] then sold it and started to make some significant money. That seems to be the start of our prosperity. Later, the family was in the Great Lakes shipping and lumbering business and made the first real fortune. When they saw lumbering and shipping waning, they were smart enough to get out and had enough money to risk farming."

"Will you show me the cemetery sometime?"

"Sure. If we're not too long at the farm and the weather holds up, we can walk back that way."

They reached the farmhouse. Introductions were made. The manager, Keith Hoffmeyer, Molly, his wife, four boys and hired

---

which included Michigan. They developed a system of land title deeds. Continental Congress passed Grayson Land Ordinance and surveying the land began; it was to be sold to settlers.

[27] Because 640 acres was too much for a farmer to manage in the 1700s, the entire state was again divided.

[28] 1820. Settlers started occupying land in the northern part of the Lower Peninsula. April 24, 1820 an Act of Congress made provisions for public lands to be sold for $1.25/acre.

helpers were all genuinely happy to see Will and greeted Samantha warmly. Will introduced her as his cousin. As they had all assembled for lunch, Will and Samantha were invited to join them.

After lunch, Keith gave Will and Samantha a tour around the greenhouse and various barns with an explanation about the function of each. "We raise mostly crops," the manager explained. "We have a few chickens for eggs and eating—just enough to supply the farm and the estate. We raise a few true bison—part of the experimental component of the farm. Bison need a lot of space for grazing, so we only keep four—five at the most. We seed their pasture to replicate the grazing lands of the Great Plains and rotate them to maintain a good stand of grasses—the Great Plains had hundreds of different native grains and grasses, you know."

"No, I never thought of that. Interesting," Samantha responded.

"We rarely butcher our bison. When we do, we have a lot of meat—a male can weigh up to 2,000 pounds," he continued. "Molly has a great recipe for Bison Bean Chili."

"Very tasty! I've had it," Will said.

"Most of us like fishing and hunting. Juanita and Molly have 101 recipes for lake fish—salmon, whitefish, walleye, perch— and wild game of all sorts—deer, duck, goose, pheasant, turkey, partridge, quail. We get plenty for the estate and farmhands," Keith went on.

"I've noticed. I'd never had venison before I came to Lake House. I like the Sweet Sour Meatballs Juanita makes," Samantha commented.

"That's my favorite, too," remarked the manager. "Molly has the same recipe. The venison should be pretty good this year—those deer have eaten enough of our corn."

"Do you go hunting, Will?" asked Samantha.

"I have. In my teenage years I used to go with some of the security guys—haven't been since. Deer season starts soon. Maybe I'll go one day. How about you?"

"No, I've never been hunting," she replied as a mater-of-fact. "I think I'll pass on that activity. I'll just enjoy eating the Sweet

Sour Meatballs—don't really want the details on how they got to the skillet."

*   *   *

After the farm tour, they headed toward the cemetery. There was still enough daylight, and the mild weather was holding. They walked over the stubble of a harvested field and then passed through rows of gnarled trees with a mixture of spindly shoots and thick, sagging branches. Will commented, "This old orchard is a good place to find Morels in the spring."

"Are you good at identifying edible mushrooms?"

"Well, just Morels. There're the best."

They continued on into a small valley. Near the base of the southern slop, Samantha saw the gravestones surrounded by a black iron fence of tall spears—each impaled with a small iron ball. Will opened the sturdy wrought iron gate, and they entered the well-cared-for interior. Dominating the center of the graveyard was a mausoleum of substantial size; chiseled in large letters above the entrance was:

JONES

Under that in smaller letters was:

> *Jesus answered them, "My sheep hear my voice, and I know them,*
> *and they follow me. I give them eternal life, and they will never perish,*
> *and no one will snatch them out of my hand. My Father,*
> *who has given them to me, is greater than all, and no one is able to*
> *snatch them out of the Father's hand. I and the Father are one."*

John 10:27-30

Huddling next to the side of a nearby tombstone, protected by the dead siblings in front of them, a few chrysanthemums had survived the frost. In the late afternoon sun, the yellow flowers glowed against the black marble—a hint of life among the bare, gray trees.

Samantha braved a question to Will. "Your mother sometimes talks about ghosts at Lake House. Has anyone seen ghosts there?"

"No," he said, appearing amused. "Mother just likes to use the term figuratively to dramatize the fact that we don't indulge in the so-called pleasures and lifestyle of the modern world very much. Technologically we might be far ahead, but we hold on to values and traditions passed down by our ancestors."

"I see. This place looks like it might have a ghost or two hanging around."

"I suppose it looks that way this time of year, especially this time of day with the sun starting to fade behind the clouds. But, no, no one has ever mentioned seeing any apparitions. And then, the people buried here were blessed with full lives and were devout Christians—redeemed souls. They wouldn't be hanging around lamenting their earthly life or trying to hold on to it. I'm sure they went off to a much happier place."

"No ghosts! That's good to hear."

"If there were spirits with unfinished lives, with a sad ending, it would be the 17th-century Will and Sophia. That story had a depressing ending. Well, I guess you know all about that from reading the diaries and from Howard. When we were children, Paula and I used to enjoy Uncle Robert's stories about the ancestors, especially Will and the Indians. We liked to imagine our great—great—and so on—grandfather and his twin brother living with the Indians as boys right on this very spot. You can imagine—our fantasies would run wild. Uncle Robert is the one who established the library and hired Howard. He had a strong interest in the family history."

"Yes, I know. How do you feel about that? Keeping the record of the family history, I mean."

"Oh, I appreciate it. I don't think I'd have had the patience for it, but I'm glad someone did it. Sure glad there weren't any horse thieves in our genealogy. *They* might have left a few ghosts."

"Maybe so," she agreed with a little laugh.

"At least I don't think there were. I'm sure Uncle Robert would have been honest enough to point out any shady characters."

Samantha smiled. "Somehow I can't picture the Jones family with horse thieves and shady characters. No black sheep—remarkable."

"Maybe a few strays now and then, but we all seem to come back to the fold."

"That's good. I'm glad you came back to Lake House," she gathered the courage to express.

"Me, too," he said with a slight smile, looking directly at her. "There isn't much daylight left, and if there's a moon, it'll be behind those clouds that have started to come up. We'd better hurry back to the house, if we don't want to be stumbling through the dark."

❧ CHAPTER 29

*"Whereas it is the duty of all Nations to acknowledge
the providence of Almighty God, to obey
his will, to be grateful for his benefits, and humbly
to implore his protection and favor—"*

George Washington: *Thanksgiving Proclamation 1789*

It was Sunday afternoon, and as usual, the family was gathered in the common room. An apple-wood fire, blazing in the fireplace, expelled the icy, chill of a gray December. The room was spacious; however, it was arranged tastefully into cozy areas for conversation, playing cards or board games, or reading. Samantha was sitting on the sofa by the fire reading a book, or rather holding it in front of her eyes, as she intermittently observed the family from around the edges and contemplated their natures.

Edmund was sitting in his favorite chair under a bright floor lamp catching up on *Wall Street Journal* articles and various periodicals. Initially, the housekeeper had organized his reading materials neatly in a sizable, walnut end table with several open shelves. On top was a laptop which he took up after the paper products had been read and transferred to a less neat stack on the floor, on the other side of the oversized chair. The computer was not for work but to read the news he had missed in the paper articles. The family subscribed, electronically, to many newspapers and literary services. Edmund also corresponded with friends via e-mail. He was as astute with the computer as any college student.

Paul and Will were in the corner alcove halfheartedly watching a football game—a Lions' game. However, there appeared to be more conversation going on than TV watching; they had the sound off. Will and his dad were alike in many ways—both good natured and friendly. With Will it was "what you see is what you get." There were no pretenses or illusions in his makeup; Paul seemed the same. Samantha could see Paul's personality emerging as he was better able to speak without hesitating or grasping for words.

It seemed that since Will's grandmother was gone and Paula was away, Samantha had become his confidante and sounding board. He was becoming especially comfortable with her after their rocky start. Keenly aware of it, she took this responsibility seriously—that is, to maintain confidentiality and never reveal any vulnerability or use unkindly any weakness she saw. Will was open with his dad. Of course, Will always looked up to his grandfather but was a trifle reserved with him; maybe he was somewhat intimidated by him because he saw him as such an awesome figure to live up to.

As for Will and his mother, Samantha felt they were talking on different levels. Sandra talked while Will listened politely, agreed with her on trivial matters, changed the subject, or made an excuse to leave if things got seriously sticky.

Samantha wondered what had happened to Barbara. Will hadn't mentioned her, and Samantha wasn't about to ask. He hadn't gone to Boston, he hadn't even been away for a whole day, and Barbara had not returned. No one ever mentioned her name. What *had* happened to Barbara? That question was answered, earlier that afternoon, when Samantha happened to overhear a conversation between Will and his mother. Will was occupying a room across from Samantha's while his suite, on the other side of the common room, was being remodeled. She felt slightly guilty about eavesdropping, but, then again, she was in her own room and the doors happened to be ajar. Her curiosity got the better of her; she suppressed her guilty feelings and listened, being on guard to close her door quickly if they emerged.

The voices were low, but she recognized Sandra admonishing Will. "You've been such a serious, studious, sheltered boy. You've had no experience with a fine, sophisticated woman of Barbara's status. If you had only followed my advice, Will, this wouldn't have happened. It isn't too late, I'm sure. You don't realize of how fortunate—"

"Mother." He spoke firmly, but respectfully. "Please, excuse me, but you don't understand. Barbara and I are too different. She said she couldn't possibly live in this remote place and she'd feel buried here. She didn't like it and—"

"Well, I can certainly understand that! You wouldn't have to live here all the time. You can have an apartment in Boston. You could build a business there."

"*I* don't like Boston! *I* don't like big city life! *I* like it here! I like the family traditions here. She likes being with her family in Boston. She likes trips to New York, Paris, London. She likes shopping, plays, nightlife. I can't do that. And, I don't love Barbara. I don't think I even like her. She's superficial—shallow. I don't think she even likes *me* that much! I think she liked the way of life she thought I could provide for her. This wasn't it!"

After calling on every adjective she could conjure up to vent her distain for her circumstances, Sandra continued with, "You'll never find a decent wife buried in this remote, eerie, spooky castle. A strange, disturbing fortress—that's what it is—the wind howling through the pines like supernatural voices and those waves crashing, crashing, crashing! That incessant lap, lap, lap water torture is enough to drive anyone insane . . . ."

At that, Samantha closed the door; she'd heard enough. *I wondered if that was a true expression of how Sandra feels or just melodrama.* Samantha waited; she heard the door across the hall close and someone walking away. *Light fast steps—must be Sandra.* Before long, there was another opening and closing of the door. This time the footsteps were heavy and steady. They moved toward the common room. *Sounds like Will.*

Sometime later, carrying a book, Samantha entered the common room and took her place on the sofa by the fire. As she gazed around the room, she thought, *How lucky I am to be in this wonderful place with these kind and interesting people. Sandra's concept of this lovely home—"remote, eerie, spooky castle, a strange disturbing fortress"—is bewildering.* Words like howling, torture, insane, and supernatural were perplexing to Samantha. Samantha's concept of this place was the opposite, in every way. *I don't understand what Sandra wants out of life. I feel safe and happy here.* She didn't know anything about the sort of lifestyle Barbara wanted, either; Samantha could not relate to it.

Well, now, at least Samantha knew what had happened to Barbara. Will definitely did not mourn her loss—no sulking or looking sad or depressed. Will only displayed cheerfulness. Maybe he was relieved it was over.

Seemingly undisturbed by her earlier conversation with Will, Sandra was curled up on the other sofa next to the fire across from Samantha. Sandra was engrossed in her favorite fare; she had uncharacteristic tastes in reading. She never read fiction. Her tastes ran to accounts of true sensational crimes—the mad-slasher or serial-killer type.

Maybe that's where she got her vocabulary—spooky, eerie, supernatural, insane, thought Samantha almost laughing out loud. Then she reproached herself. *It really isn't funny. Sandra is seriously unhappy. I wonder why? She has a son who's kind to her, and he's here. Everyone here is respectful and kind to her. Her son is bright, accomplished, successful. I think so. Does she? She's with her husband. He's ill but well cared for and making progress. They're together. She doesn't have the burden of his care as do so many wives. She has no financial worries. She can travel as much she likes, anywhere she likes. She visits her friends, family, and daughter when she likes. She has a successful, intelligent daughter. She's involved in worthy interesting charity projects. I think so. Does she? She has so many blessings. Why does she just see the negative side of things? Edmund thinks it's just in some peoples' nature—they can't help themselves. Maybe so.*

Sporadically, Sandra would read the biography of a celebrity or famous person, such as the late Diana Princess of Wales; no book about her was unread by Sandra. Her taste in biographies never gravitated toward those who had a great role in history—Abraham Lincoln, Alexander Hamilton, or someone who made contributions in medicine or technology. Instead, she was interested in Paris Hilton and the like. Who knew? Now and then, Samantha would see one of Sandra's books on a table or footstool. She'd peek inside, thinking it might be an opportunity for conversation with her, but it turned out to be of no advantage. Samantha couldn't appreciate that type of book and hardly knew the subject of most of the biographies. Occasionally, there would be a scandalous, dicey biography about a president or otherwise respectable famous person.

Sandra obtained her books from the public library. She complained, "The library, here, is too creepy, full of ghosts, and I can't tolerate those eerie, portraits staring down at me." Sandra never went into the Lake House library. There wasn't anything in there that interested her—no books by Kitty Kelly could be found.

Surprisingly, Sandra had been polite and pleasant to Samantha; however, they never had a conversation of more than two or three sentences. Samantha wondered, *What's behind those eyes that never meet mine or that smile that flashes too quickly, then fades?*

* * *

Paula had not been to Lake House since Samantha had arrived. Her position on the medical staff being the lowest, she had little time off and regularly worked on holidays. She hadn't come for Thanksgiving and would not be coming for Christmas, either.

She would have time off in January; however, as Will said, "Getting to this part of Michigan on schedule in the middle of winter is iffy, and she's opted for Hawaii with friends. Which would you choose?"

I wonder if Sandra knows Will and I spent time together. Does she know we are becoming close friends? Samantha reflected. *What would she think?*

The times Will and I spend together are when Sandra is away. Curious! Is it just a coincidence?

Samantha's thoughts drifted back to Thanksgiving Day last week. There were eight for dinner; two of the security staff, on duty for the weekend and with no family, were asked to join them during an hour break. She had been seated next to Steve at the table; Will was at the other end. Samantha had noticed, out of the corner of her eye, that no matter who was speaking, Will kept looking at her but quickly turned away when his mother looked his way. Will avoided Samantha and barely spoke to her that day. After dinner, she and Steve had gone for a walk around the grounds. Will and Paul expressed interest in the football game, and Edmund expressed interest in a nap. Sandra disappeared for the rest of the day.

* * *

Thanksgiving morning had been delightful. Edmund had decided to revive an old tradition. When Amanda and Robert were alive and the children were here, they gave the staff the day off to be with their families. The Jones family cooked its own Thanksgiving dinner. Afterward, they washed the dishes and cleaned up the kitchen. This year, Sandra volunteered to coordinate the dinner. Each person had submitted a special recipe, or two, or three, to Juanita, and the ingredients had been ordered. When asked what her contribution would be, Samantha remembered making pies with her mother—Pumpkin Custard and Apple Raisin. Also, she knew how to make a simple, but festive, family favorite—Cranberry Fruit Salad. The pie crust was unusual but easy.

Earlier that week Juanita had shown her how to use the oven she needed for her project and where she could find the supplies. The pies had to be made the same day as the meal, because the crust was best when fresh, and Samantha appeared, as scheduled, at five o'clock Thanksgiving morning. She was surprised to hear the rattling of pans. Who could have been there before she was?

With flour on his face and covered with a white, cook's apron, Steve emerged from behind the pot-and-pan storage area. "You look very cute!" Samantha had remarked with a laugh.

Steve had offered to make Cloverleaf yeast rolls from scratch, so he had to start even earlier. He, also, made Irish Pub Soda Bread—the recipe provided by his grandmother in Dublin. Edmund had been in charge of the wild turkeys, shot at the farm by Mr. Hoffmeyer and his farmhands; he had arrived a little later. She'd had fun rattling around the kitchen and working on the culinary masterpieces with Steve and Edmund. They had been undaunted by the early hour and were in high spirits as they engaged in the hands-on-change-of-pace tasks.

The meal had been a huge success. Sandra had decorated and set the table beautifully with crystal glasses, elegant fine china, real sterling silverware, white linen napkins and tablecloth, and a gorgeous centerpiece that consisted of the rich colors of fall flowers, leaves, and artistically twisted narrow long stems with small white and red berries.

White and silver serving dishes were heaped full of mashed orange squash, whipped potatoes, and crispy herb dressing. There was the deep red of the Cranberry Fruit Salad in a white bowl, their traditional Green Bean Casserole, silver bowls with brown gravy, and two white linen-lined silver baskets—one with perfect golden brown rolls and the other with the crusty whole-grain Irish Pub Soda Bread. And, finally, the platter of sliced wild turkey beautifully garnished and presented by Edmund.

After a humble and exquisite prayer of thanksgiving had been offered by Edmund, they all enjoyed the accomplishments of the morning. Samantha's pies had received the praises of all, including Sandra.

Following the dinner, as was their custom, they read the first Thanksgiving Proclamation of the new nation written by George Washington as president. Samantha had her copy tucked in her book; she wanted to keep it. Edmund had been in charge of the project and had assigned a part to each person. She took out the Proclamation and read it again.

Intro: *Edmund*

THANKSGIVING PROCLAMATION
By the President of the United States of America,
a Proclamation.

Will: Whereas it is the duty of all Nations to acknowledge the providence of Almighty God, to obey his will, to be grateful for his benefits, and humbly to implore his protection and favor—and whereas both Houses of Congress have by their joint Committee requested me "to recommend to the People of the United States a day of public thanksgiving and prayer to be observed by acknowledging with grateful hearts the many signal favors of Almighty God especially by affording them an opportunity peaceably to establish a form of government for their safety and happiness."

Sandra: Now therefore I do recommend and assign Thursday the 26th day of November next to be devoted by the People of these States to the service of that great and glorious Being, who is the beneficent Author of all the good that was, that is, or that will be—

Harry: That we may then all unite in rendering unto Him our sincere and humble thanks for His kind care and protection of the People of this Country previous to their becoming a nation; for the signal and manifold mercies and the favorable interposition of His providence in the course and conclusion of the late war;

Steve: for the great degree of tranquillity, union, and plenty which we have since enjoyed; for the peaceable and rational manner in which we have been enabled to establish constitutions of government for our safety and happiness,

Brad: and particularly the national one now lately instituted; for the civil and religious liberty with which we are blessed, and the means we have of acquiring and diffusing useful knowledge; and, in general, for all the great and various favors which He hath been pleased to confer upon us.

Samantha: And also that we may then unite in most humbly offering our prayers and supplications to the great Lord and Ruler of Nations, and beseech Him to pardon our national and other transgression; to enable us all, whether in public or private stations, to perform our several and relative duties properly and punctually; to render our national government a blessing to all the people by constantly being a government of wise, just, and constitutional laws, discreetly and faithfully executed and obeyed;

Edmund: to protect and guide all sovereigns and nations (especially such as have shown kindness unto us), and to bless them with good governments, peace, and concord; to promote the knowledge and practice of true religion and virtue, and the increase of science among them and us; and, generally, to grant unto all mankind such a degree of temporal prosperity as He alone Knows to be best.

Paul:

> *Given under my hand, at the city of New York,*
> *the third day of October in the year of our Lord*
> *1789*
> *Go. Washington*

Awakening from her day dream, Samantha remembered that she had promised to read books with Isabella and Abby this afternoon. Announcing her plans to the group, each nodding or acknowledging her with barely an interruption to his or her current pursuit, she left and made her way to Juanita's suite. She found Abby and Isabella sitting on the floor by their own cozy apple-wood fire. Juanita was busy folding clothes.

"Hi, Samantha!" they greeted her in unison.

"Hi! You look cozy!"

Juanita told Samantha that she wanted to finish the laundry, catch up on some personal business, and then visit a friend in another part of the estate. She asked Samantha if she could stay until she returned. Samantha readily agreed.

Samantha joined the girls on the floor where they were making up little games around the story in the book. They each took the part of a character—each one reading her part with dramatic expression. This went on for a while; however, there were more characters than girls, and they would get mixed up, which would send Isabella and Abby into self-conscience giggling. Finishing the first book, they started a board game, and, about an hour later, chose another book, assigned parts, and started their dialogue.

They were startled by a knock on the door. Abby skipped over and opened it. It was Will. "Hello, Mr. Jones, come in!"

"Well, hello little Misses and little bigger Miss."

The girls giggled.

"You can call me Will."

"Okay, you can call me Abby!" She laughed, delighted to be honored with his presence.

"Okay, thank you," he said.

"And you can call *her* Isabella," Abby instructed, pointing to Isabella. Then, pointing to Samantha. "And *her* Samantha."

"Is that okay with you?" Will asked.

"Yes, it is," chimed Isabella and Samantha in unison.

"So, what's happening?"

Abby explain, "We're reading a story about a princess, a bear, a frog, and a gopher. I'm the princess, Isabella's the frog, Samantha's the gopher, and you are the bear. It's perfect! We really need a bear."

Samantha smiled at Will with an "Oh, well, hope-you-are-okay-with-this" look.

He confirmed it with a good-natured smile and a nod, and they all sat on the floor in front of the fireplace—Samantha on the left, Will on the right, and the girls in the middle. They started their story, each reading with great expression, and the girls giggling and laughing as they portrayed their characters.

❧·CHAPTER 30

"A soft answer turns away wrath, but a harsh word stirs up anger.
The tongue of the wise commends knowledge, but the mouths of fools pour out folly.
The eyes of the LORD are in every place, beholding the evil and the good.
A gentle tongue is a tree of life, but a deceitful tongue crushes the spirit."

Proverbs 15:1-4

From time to time, the pastor, his wife Laura, and two or three of their older children would come to dinner. Pastor Schafer was a scholarly man. Besides graduating from the seminary, he had a Ph.D. in ancient history and an excellent knowledge of Greek and Hebrew. Edmund was forever asking him to expand on a particular word from an American English translation of the Bible. He came to this small congregation so he could continue writing. Edmund's estate provided a business manager for the church; therefore, the pastor could do what he did best—preach, teach, care for the congregation, and write. Of course, he would have time to spend with his large family. The parsonage provided ample space for his family of seven and Lili Logan, Laura's troubled sister, now just 17 years old, who came to live with them a few weeks ago.

On this particular afternoon, before dinner, the adults had gathered in a large sitting room. Isabella was becoming weaker and spent most of her time in her room resting; two of the older children had been dispatched to read stories and play board games with her. Juanita was invited to joined the family and her good friends—the Schafers.

Edmund and Pastor Schafer were sitting by the tall windows overlooking the water and the sky. The unusual cloudless sky sent the late autumn sunlight streaming across the water, bursting through the great windows, and encircling the two men in an aura of light. Samantha felt as if she were witnessing St. Paul and Dr. Luke discussing eternal life. For the time being, she sat silently intrigued by every word; soon, she noticed the whole group silent with their eyes fixed on the two men.

Then an awful thought came to her, *Was this amazing scene a prelude to something else?* The conversation gave her an overwhelming fear that Edmund might die soon. She could not tolerate the thought a moment longer and turned her attention elsewhere; she focused on the other people in the room.

She could observe Sandra unnoticed, and her attention turned to her. She was very beautiful and looked tranquil at the moment—a peaceful exterior to a troubled interior. Generally, they had been getting along well, as Samantha had followed Edmund's advice. However, one was never sure what Sandra was really thinking. Once she'd overheard Sandra saying to Paul something about her being a penniless waif Edmund had picked up someplace.

Paul had come to Samantha's defense and told Sandra, "Treat her well. This is still my father's house and helping people is his nature. You need to honor your father-in-law's wishes in the matter."

The result was civility toward Samantha, but how Sandra perceived it was unknown. Nevertheless, it made Samantha feel grateful to Paul. She felt that he must truly like her—well enough to risk whatever Sandra's retaliation might be. Surprisingly, Sandra said nothing and walked away.

Sandra and Paul hadn't known each other very long before they were married. Paul came from a caring family. From what Edmund told her, Samantha supposed that Paul had been much like Sandra had described Will, "a serious, studious, sheltered boy . . . no experience with a fine, sophisticated woman . . . ."

Edmund had explained, "Paul brought Sandra home just once, before their marriage. She appeared charming and attentive to him. Paul was unwittingly flattered and manipulated into marriage. After their marriage, Paul was devastated by her behavior. Her actions baffled us, or more precisely her reactions toward simple, seemingly innocuous, statements. Anyone, Paul most often, could become a bewildered target of her strange, cruel words."

Apparently, like Barbara, Sandra thought Paul could provide her with security and whatever lifestyle she chose for herself. At first, Paul had turned to his mother. Then, Edmund got involved. Always the analyst, he suspected there was more to this than just a nasty person and consulted a psychiatrist—for sure, Sandra would not have admitted she had a problem. The psychiatrist was invited to the house for a few days to observe Sandra. Indeed, he felt she had a rather pernicious psychiatric disorder—cause unknown and cure unknown. He could not be precise. For some reason she liked him, and she was on her best behavior. She could be terribly charming and endearing at times. The psychiatrist felt that there would be no physical danger to her personally or others. However, her irrational tongue lashings aimed at Will and Paula, and her sudden, sharp tirades against Paul were unhealthy for the children; therefore, they were left with Amanda and Edmund.

The stress of being around children made Sandra worse. She wasn't interested in the children as people and invented things about them that had never occurred. She pretended to be the expert on children when that attribute suited her fantasy or made her look good. Perhaps, in her defective mind, she believed it was true. She didn't know their strengths or vulnerabilities; she didn't know them as unique individuals—when they were little or grown. She bragged about their achievements, which she had no part in nurturing.

Edmund told Samantha, "Will was particularly troublesome for Sandra, as he had been energetic and inquisitive. She could not endure his challenging her and constantly questioning things. When he was small, he couldn't understand her behavior and became extremely upset by his mother's crushing words. Sandra was frequently away—travelled with Paul on business, visited her family, and took trips with friends. When she was at Lake House, she hardly spent any time with the children. Their care fell to nannies, tutors, and Amanda. Paul, Robert, and I tried to do our share—making as much time for Paula and Will as our busy schedules allowed."

Samantha sank farther down into the soft chair that surrounded her. The room was warm, and she felt relaxed and sleepy. Now, her attention turned back to Pastor Schafer and Edmund, who were continuing their discussion on eternal life. Ordinarily, she would be listening with interest, as she admired them both. She heard them mention something about the immortal soul, free will, and eternal life being different from eternal existence.

Pastor Shafer said, "I'm surprised people aren't more interested in finding out where they will spend eternity . . . ."

As interesting as that was, Samantha couldn't gather her concentration to follow that thought, and her mind drifted again—this time to Paul. Philip was not with him this evening, as Paul was now able to fend for himself quite well. He could walk with canes but still used the Amigo for long distances. He could transfer from the Amigo to a regular chair and back again. He seemed to be able to sit longer and had more stamina for activities. On this particular occasion, Sandra was sitting next to Paul on a small upright sofa—a loveseat. They looked like a normal devoted couple. In her way, as much as she was capable, they—Edmund, Amanda and Paul—came to believe that she loved Paul.

Samantha remembered her parents—how they cared for, respected, comforted, and talked to each other. What sympathy she had for Paul and what admiration, never to have had a real wife—someone with genuine feelings and emotions—someone to share his heartaches, disappointments, frustrations, joys someone to share his life honestly—someone capable of working through problems in an open and truthful way.

How difficult it must be always to have to guard every word and then be harshly punished for a misspoken one, she thought. Sandra stored up any little weaknesses she perceived or errors he made to pull out later. She had an arsenal of these to take subtle or blatant shots at him, to put him down or manipulate him, even in his helpless state. *Had she no sympathy for him? Was she just used to treating him this way? Was she incapable of modifying her behavior?* Angry about being here fueled her emotions; somehow, in her mind, it was Paul's fault.

Samantha particularly admired Paul for his willingness to stay with Sandra and do his best for her. What a blessing he had insightful and understanding parents, and *they* had been willing to accept her and do *their* best for her.

It must be doubly difficult for Paul to be here now without his mother, she thought. Samantha was sorry she had not known Amanda— everyone loved her and spoke highly of her. It was fortunate for Will that he had his grandmother for a substitute mother. Samantha was happy to see Paul and Will becoming close— making up for lost time, as it were. She was pleased that Paul had this joy in his life, at this difficult time, and admired Will for the time and effort he put into building a relationship with his dad.

Thinking of Paul and Sandra prodded thoughts of the men who came to the golf course. She had heard every chauvinistic comment contrived against women that some men enjoyed making, thinking they were smart or trying to make a joke. Then they would end by saying, "I can't understand women!"

Brilliant! she thought.

Her dad had remarked, "You're right! That's too big a job. There's only one woman I want to understand—my wife." He said that, not as a joke, but, in all sincerity. He had the courage to show that he respected his wife. He was interested in his family— understanding the needs of his wife and children, understanding them as special people with their own characteristics. He had not lumped them into some contrived categories.

Paul certainly had his work cut out for him understanding his wife. Those "cleaver" men should be grateful for the wives they have. Would any of them last a week in Paul's shoes? she wondered.

Samantha was getting to know Paul better. He had been helping with some of the projects, using the computer in her suite. He was a good teacher, and they were getting along well. Besides that, he was teaching her the finer points of chess, and, sometimes Abby would come up and play with them. He seemed to enjoy his new students. At times, they would just play cards—some simple game that Abby liked. Paul was a good sport about it and seemed to enjoy it as much as Abby.

Occasionally, Samantha would find herself alone with Paul in the common room or in the dining room, after the others had hurried off. They had some uncomplicated conversation about how he felt about being back at Lake House—he was enjoying it, how he felt about Will—he was very proud and appreciated the time they spent together, news of Paula—he was proud of her too and missed her, his parents—he had a great deal of admiration for them and missed his mother. He also talked about Uncle Robert, with fond memories, and the things he remembered at Lake House when he was a boy. However, he never mentioned Sandra during their conversations—no mention of their travels together, their time in Australia, what they did together with the children, no part of his life he shared with Sandra—nothing.

❧·CHAPTER 31

In winter's tedious nights,
sit by the fire with good old folks,
and let them tell thee tales of woeful
ages long ago betid.

William Shakespeare

The endless lake effect snows of January and February buried Lake House to the first floor window ledges—the lower level windows were no longer visible. The walkways and driveways were diligently plowed leaving paths cut through the snow like little sheer-sided canyons. The thunder of the summer storms was exchanged for the rumbling and grinding of the thick ice along the shore being broken and heaved by the swelling and ebbing of the massive volumes of water under it.

The occupants of Lake House passed their days as usual—well, not quite as usual. One person was missing. Sandra rented a condominium near family and friends and left for Florida before the threat of being snowbound became a reality. The last piece of luggage loaded, the SUV departed down the snow-lined driveway, and a peace settled over Lake House.

Edmund and Samantha met as usual for breakfast. Edmund had told her that he would have George Reynolds investigated. "I have the information on George. He is reputable," Edmund assured her. "I've instructed the Jones estate financial advisors

270

to review your portfolio. They've made a few minor suggestions. All in all, your assets are being well managed."

"Thank you so very much!"

And now, plans for the additions to the school were foremost in their conversations. The new principal, Gilbert (Bert) Pfeiffer, had been hired—another man with a large family. With five more grade-school children, they would definitely need an ample addition. Samantha purchased a large vacant house on ten acres across from the school. She planned to renovate it according to the needs of the Pfeiffer family, and then rent it to them for a nominal sum. They were delighted with the arrangement. Julie, Bert's wife, was especially pleased to be involved in the plans and thrilled to have such spacious modern accommodations for their large family—two natural children and three adopted boys (one in a wheelchair). Samantha was thrilled she could help (unknown to them) this generous family and their commitment to three previously unfortunate children. She also purchased a new vehicle with a lift to accommodate little Jimmy's wheelchair and make transporting the family easier. This was part of the benefits package, plus the best health insurance that could be attained (fortunately, Edmund, could provide this for all his employees). This was to entice Bert to take the position, as he was a talented sought-after school administrator, and the "school board" was set on obtaining him. A principal at a Christian school was not as generously paid as his counterpart in the public sector, but then pay wasn't a primary motivation for church workers. Nevertheless, he still had to support his family. Since he was a called church worker, he needed to be commissioned at one of the church services, and the "school board" had to make his employment official—he approved whole heartedly.

The Pfeiffer family settled into temporary quarters—two adjacent apartments on the Lake House grounds. Bert and Samantha and occasionally Edmund met with the architects, contractors and various people getting ready for the expansion project to start as soon as school was out. Bert, having a handicapped child, was particularly valuable in seeing that the renovations accommodated his son's needs and those of other children in similar circumstances. Later, in their long-range plans, they wanted to consider a special-needs room and teacher. *Excellent—an excellent idea*, Samantha thought, excited about how this was all coming together.

Arranging small luncheons and get-togethers, Samantha personally took it upon herself to introduce Julie and the children to all the school families—one-by-one. Bert visited each family—one of his duties as principal.

* * *

From time to time Howard came and stayed a few days, and "in winter's tedious nights," they sat "by the fire with good old folks" and "tales of woeful ages long ago" were told.

One evening while Howard, Edmund, and Samantha were alone by a good fire in the common room, Samantha asked, "Mary and I were visiting our favorite bookstore the other day, and I saw a book containing a story about Archibald Jones and the Crystal Lake disaster of 1873. I didn't have time to read it. What was that all about? Was Archibald Jones a relative?"

"No—thank heavens, no, definitely not!" Edmund responded emphatically with an amused look on his face and then looked at Howard. "Do you want to tell her the story or shall I?"

"I will." Then in his characteristic style, Howard started. "It was late summer 1873. Archibald Jones, from Illinois, and local backers invested heavily—labor and capital—in the Betsie River Improvement Company. Its major project was to link Crystal Lake with the Frankfort Harbor and Lake Michigan via the Betsie River. This would allow medium-sized vessels to transport logs and wood products from the interior of the forests. The task was undertaken with horse-drawn equipment and a great number of men with shovels.

"While *this* was going on, Archibald contemplated an even more grandiose plan. He envisioned Platte Lake, to the north, connected to Crystal Lake through a series of canals linking small lakes. Boats could swiftly transport logs from an even wider area to the lumber mills in Frankfort. For this project, he hired a surveyor. As he walked uphill from Platte Lake, it was obvious that the water would be flowing the wrong way—Crystal Lake would have drained into Platte Lake.

"No one had bothered hiring an engineer to assess the Betsie River project. Instead of being a couple of feet above Lake Michigan, it was later found to be more than 30 feet.

"After months of arduous digging—to deepen and straighten the shallow mile-long creek that connected Crystal Lake to the Betsie River—only a levee held back Crystal Lake. Before the planned opening of the channel, a windstorm swept over the lake and crumbled the levee. Everything broke loose! Seeking its own level, water from Crystal Lake started coursing down the creek, carving out a deeper, wider channel as it gained speed and power. The sounds of chaos—rumbling, crashing, breaking—could be heard for miles. When the surge hit the Betsie River it made churning lakes out of the lowlands. It busted up the piles of cut logs along the banks and swept them into the swamps and downriver.

"Three boys were putting the finishing touches on their raft. They'd planned to ride the rush of water when the Crystal Lake damn was opened. Not quite prepared, and at the whim of the erratic flow of water, they got hung up on an island where they spent the night.

"A local minister, in his horse-drawn carriage, noticed the rising water at the ford. Nevertheless, throwing caution to the wind, he urged his horse through the deep water—they were washed into the river. The good reverend miraculously and with the help of the angels, no doubt," Howard continued, flashing his signature grin, "managed to swim to shore, but the poor horse and carriage were swept away. Farm animals and wild animals were killed by the logs or drowned in the torrent, causing an unsightly mess as bloated carcasses sporadically popped up and floated down the river."

Getting caught up in the telling of a good story, Howard was into the drowning scene before he realized what he was saying. He glanced at Samantha and cautiously waited for her reaction.

She spontaneously interjected, "Oooh, how awful!" Noticing his look of self-reproach and sensing his concern for her, she paused a moment to clear the miserable scene from her mind and redirected the story. "What happened to Crystal Lake?"

Noting her I'm-okay look, he appeared relieved. "It lowered the lake, probably about 20 feet, in just a few weeks—a quarter of the lake's water was lost. Eventually, the hole was plugged, but it never went back to its former level—turned out to be not all that bad—now there're beaches and a 21-mile road around it—before there was minimal access to the lake."

"What happened to Archibald Jones?" Samantha asked

"Seems that shortly thereafter, he slipped away—returned to Illinois. I've never read about his making any retribution for all the damage he caused. Fortunately, he never returned to meddle with Michigan again."

"That's good! Well, the part about his not returning to Michigan—that's good," Samantha said. "He certainly doesn't sound like any Jones in this family, that I know of—past or present—in fact, exactly the opposite."

"True, true," Howard agreed.

Edmund just had a pleased look on his face. They all sat quietly enjoying the warm fire. The "tale of woeful ages long ago" lingered in their thoughts, and the companionship of good folk made a winter's night less tedious.

* * *

Samantha still made plenty of time for Isabella and Abby—playing games, reading stories, and joining in on whatever else their youthful imaginations and ingenuity came up with.

She had a penchant for making pies from time to time. Using her mother's recipes gave her sentimental remembrances of her and a chance to spend time with Juanita. Her most recent endeavor was her recipe for Very Berry Blueberry Pie—an awesome success. The blueberry harvest had been exceptionally good, and the freezer was well stocked with them.

During this particular pie-baking session, Juanita disclosed her feelings about her decision not to pursue surgery for Isabella. "It was a slim hope—that she could be restored to a normal, longer life, that is. The doctors couldn't say. Money was no issue—Mr. Jones would have paid for anything. I just wasn't willing to take the risk."

"I see," Samantha expressed.

"And who's to say what a normal, full life is?" Juanita went on. "We could have lost her immediately during the surgery—the odds were *not* in her favor—not good at all. Even if she made it through the surgery, there would have been weeks in the hospital— so much discomfort and pain—so much distress through every procedure—unpleasant side effects from strong medications— risk of infection. She was just too little to understand. So, I made the choice—we brought her here. Everyone is very kind. Mr. Jones has been wonderful. She's doing better than anyone expected. Most of all, she's happy. That's what I wanted for her. We're so blessed. I think I made the right decision. I feel in my heart it was the right thing."

"You've always done your best for her. You've had difficult choices," Samantha affirmed.

Juanita smiled slightly with a look of acquiescence, and Samantha gave her a reassuring hug.

*   *   *

On one rare, mild, bright, and sunny day, toward the end of February, Mary and Samantha, finally, took their trip to a *dim sum* restaurant.

Paul was doing much better. He was working more and was in quite a joyful mood. Samantha thought he'd improved by leaps and bounds after Sandra left. Paul's therapy room on the lower level was quite large. More exercise equipment had been brought in, and the office employees were invited to use it on their breaks, when Paul wasn't there. With Paul becoming more independent, Philip's duties had been reduced. However, since Will and his dad had experienced such good results with their exercise plans, they decided to keep Philip employed to maintain an exercise room for the employees. He planned a worked-out schedule for whoever was interested, and interest was, indeed, high. Samantha decided this would be a good option for her—too many days, this time of year, were not fit for outside activity.

Occasionally, Samantha went to the lower level offices for assistance with the computer data—she filled in when they were short-handed—and become acquainted with the employees there. She particularly liked Janet who kept all the computers in working order. She and her husband lived in an apartment on the grounds. Karl was on the general maintenance crew. They had two boys, nine and ten. Samantha remembered that Janet and Karl had expressed a desire to adopt a handicapped child, but they were deterred due to their work schedules and time spent with the boys' activities. The boys were becoming more independent and willing to help with the project, but, still, the obstacles were too challenging. Samantha was delighted to tell them about the plans for the school and to offer help. They agreed to meet with her and Edmund to see if they could do it. All was successful. With Edmund and Samantha's help, they enthusiastically decided on the adoption, and plans were set in motion.

Edmund seemed more relaxed now as more of the responsibility for the business was taken on by Will, Paul, and other capable persons. Nevertheless, he kept informed—knew everything that was going on in the business and lives of the employees—and ever ready to help when the need arose.

Will seemed to find some part of each day to seek out Samantha and spend time with her. Occasionally, he would join their school planning sessions and was rather proud of her involvement. Yet, he was bewildered by it—especially the funding. The costs were not going through his records. Edmund satisfied him by telling him that they'd received a large donation, and he was taking care of it through the church and the "school board." This was out of Will's domain, for the most part, as long as they were meeting their expenses. Will was smart, but he didn't connect Samantha with the "large donation" part. He just thought it was sweet that she was following in his grandmother's footsteps with the school.

Samantha and Steve continued to be good friends and spent time together occasionally. In her zeal to turn Lake House into a place for ex-orphans, she tried to talk Steve into adopting a young boy of about six or seven. She promised much help and went on and on about the plans for the school. He wasn't sure about taking on the responsibly of a child—he was a hard sell. Nevertheless, she would keep trying.

*   *   *

Another project Samantha took on was Lili Logan, Laura Schafer's sister—troubled and beaten down by her unfortunate choices. Lili had a desire to rebuild her life and help with Laura's children, especially, while she taught school. Wanting to get her high school diploma and go to college, Pastor and Laura were homeschooling her. They asked Samantha if she would tutor her in geometry and algebra; she was glad to do it. Lili and Samantha were closer in age (Laura was in her late twenties). Their sessions not only consisted of math problems but Lili's problems. Samantha was a good listener and understood that Lili needed a trustworthy friend—she was willing to take on that task too. Lili, feeling comfortable with Samantha, confided in her.

It wasn't that Lili was trying to hide anything—she had a garrulous open-book nature. It seemed that admitting her mistakes and lamenting openly gave her a catharsis. Of course, her sister and brother-in-law knew her whole history by now, at least the sordid aspects of the past two years. Her family had been frantic; she had not contacted them—not even once—to let them know she was alive. In spite of loving, conscientious parents, Lili ran away when she was fifteen with a man who was thirty. She got into drinking, marijuana, some hard drugs, and became pregnant. She wouldn't get an abortion—was afraid morally and physically. After months of arguing with her about getting an abortion, the man deserted her. For days she was in a stupor—drinking what was left of the alcohol and eating nothing.

Finally, the motel owner came to investigate. He found her in a terrible state and took her to a local mission where they took care of her. She couldn't stay if she were drinking. Withdrawing from alcohol seemed a minor inconvenience considering the discomfort of being pregnant and having no money. And, she was barely able to function due to depression.

Six weeks early, she delivered an undernourished boy with Fetal Alcohol Syndrome. In the hospital, while she was holding him, he went into uncontrolled seizures. "I just watched him shake," Lili told Samantha. "I just sat there—I couldn't move. I let him die. I know I did. I couldn't have the abortion, but in the end, I kill him. No one knew—I knew."

Samantha sat quietly listening, then reached over and held her hand for a moment.

After the death of the baby, Lili continued to be hospitalized for several weeks due to her fragile state of health and mind; with guilt heaped on her, Lili couldn't function or speak. Through medication and an organization called *Healing Hearts Ministries,* she was able to find forgiveness and make progress toward recovery. Finally, she gave the social worker the name of her sister—Laura Shafer. She had been unable to face her parents, and the Shafers had taken her in to help her readjust.

Lili may have suffered some permanent loss of brain function due to the alcohol, drugs, and malnutrition compounded by a neglected pregnancy, but Samantha was patient with her and was challenged to think up new ways to present the information. Apparently, Lili did have some learning pathways intact and made it through geometry and algebra with acceptable grades. This took a lot of concentration, resolve, and hard work. Samantha admired Lili's determination and felt she was definitely on the mend—both physically and mentally—and hoped she could find peace among sympathetic friends.

On the surface, Lili, with the remnants of purple at the ends of her long, dull, sandy hair and a tattoo on her lower arm, looked like an ordinary teen in an innocuous rebellious phase. Looking at her silly, external indulgences, one might not have taken her seriously.

It's surprising what you find when you take the time to care, Samantha thought. *Sooner or later, I suppose, I may know everyone's story around here. But, are there any as sad and misguided as this one? I'm learning that there are no just ordinary people. Everyone has a story of heartaches and joys. I truly admire Edmund. He takes the time to look beneath the surface, find the soul of the person, and value it as a work in progress—as God would.*

And so the winter passed.

☩·CHAPTER 32

*[Jesus] said to them, "Let the little children come unto me,
and forbid them not; for to such belongs the kingdom of God . . . ."*

*And he took the children up in his arms,
put his hands upon them, and blessed them.*

Mark 10:14&16

Easter morning was especially splendid this year. Nature was offering the promise of a glorious spring. The birds were fluttering about the treetops, stopping now and then on the high branches to do some chirping and singing—calling to one another. All nature was harmonizing in a major key. Samantha breathed in the fresh, cool air and started the long walk, through the Lake House grounds, through the maple arches with buds waiting for the next warm day to start opening, through the pine trees with patches of snow still lingering on the north side with the scent of sap rising, along the white fence on the south side of the farm, up the slight incline, and over the hill to the church. It was effortless. It was that kind of a morning. She was in that kind of a mood.

The great church was magnificent, with its traditional architecture and native stone expertly incorporated into the design. The still air carried the full chords and arpeggios of a glorious hymn from the carillon over the countryside. Wonderful people ascended the steps; handsome, well-behaved children accompanied their parents. Never looking lovelier in her Easter

280

egg colors, the perpetually pessimistic Mrs. Pentwater with her permanently furrowed brow was actually smiling. It was that kind of a morning.

Samantha thought the service was beautiful; the organist had never played better, and the choir hit every note of the "Hallelujah Chorus" perfectly. All of God's children were making music in a major key. The stained-glass windows vibrated with color. Pastor Schafer had never preached a better sermon. It was that kind of a morning.

She sat between Edmund and Will in a pew near the front of the church. Sandra sat near Paul, who was in the space reserved for wheelchairs and Amigos. Toward the end of the service, Will reached over and took her hand in his. Firmly holding it, he slid their two hands into the narrow space between them, resting them on the pew cushion. Surprised, she wondered what he meant by this. Was he moved by the beauty of the morning and wanting to make a connection with someone, and she happened to be there to share it, or was it something more? She was pleased for the bond, no matter what the intention, and did not pull away. Then he smiled at her. She smiled back, thinking he was the handsomest, most brilliant, kindest young man she had ever met—but then, it was that kind of a morning; everything was the best. When they stood for the last hymn, he did not let go of her hand, and they made a cooperative effort to share a single hymnal.

After the service, Will stepped out into the center aisle and, as gentlemen do, allowed her to step in front of him. As they moved slowly with the crowd toward the exit, he protected her from jostling. Edmund followed. Having come from a front pew and stopping briefly to wish fellow parishioners a happy Easter and exchange a few remarks, they were the last to leave the sanctuary. All were making their way to the fellowship hall for the Easter brunch. Will put his arm around Samantha's shoulders and led her in the opposite direction—near the entrance to the coatroom. Everyone was gone by now, except a couple of ushers engrossed in checking the pews for stray service folders and pieces of paper with youthful scribblings. To her astonishment, Will put his arms around her, held her tight, and kissed her right under the life-size picture of *Jesus Blessing the Children*, and Samantha kissed him back and *meant* it.

Putting his arm around her shoulders and leading her out of the nearest exit, he said, "Let's not stay for brunch. Let's walk back to the house. I want to talk to you."

Being somewhat puzzled and at a loss for words, she responded with, "Sure."

Then Will started, "I had a plan. I thought if I held your hand in church and you didn't pull it away, and if I kissed you and you didn't slap my face or give me the 'let's be friends—'or cousins, in this case—speech, I would build up enough courage to ask you to marry me."

Samantha was astounded. This was all happening incredibly fast. Their relationship was moving to a new level at the speed of light. Walking to church this morning, they had been friends, never having exchanged a kiss or the intimate words of lovers; walking home, they were in love and engaged to be married (she *would* say yes).

"Will you marry me, Samantha? I do love you."

"Yes, yes, I will. I love you too, but I never thought . . . ." Then he kissed her as Edmund drove by with a big grin on his face.

"You know," he said, "I think that wise old man had this in mind from the start."

"I have a feeling you're right," she responded.

They walked on arm in arm, chattering away, confessing all the feelings they had been storing up. *It is, indeed, a splendid morning!* Samantha thought.

*　　*　　*

Their hearts sank when they saw Dr. Abbott's car parked in front of the house. Their joy would soon turn to sorrow, and all their excitement to share their news would need to wait.

Samantha's first thoughts turned to Edmund. *We saw him drive by. He didn't stay for the brunch. Was he feeling ill? He looked fine when he drove by, and we caught a glimpse of him with that big grin on his face. I saw Dr. Abbott in church when we arrived. I didn't see him leave during the service. I didn't see him after the service—there were so many people, we could have missed seeing him.* Countless thoughts rushed through Samantha's mind, and then, they turned to Isabella. *Juanita and Isabella weren't in church, but that's not unusual—Juanita doesn't like to take her out in the cold. She had been getting weak, but she always rallied.* She and Will rushed to the front door, and as they entered saw the door to Juanita's suite open and Edmund there. It *was* Isabella!

A tearful Juanita came to meet Samantha. "She's waiting for you. She said she wanted to say goodbye to you."

Choking back the tears and collecting herself, Samantha followed Juanita to Isabella's bed. She looked so pale and small. Juanita sat in a chair near the head of the bed and gently stroked the little girl's forehead. Samantha sat on the bed, held the small, frail hand, and quietly said, "Hi, Isabella."

"Hi Samantha," she responded feebly, then glanced toward the other side of the bed. "The angel over there explained everything to me. I have to go. I asked him if I could say goodbye to you. He said, 'Yes, but it will be a few minutes. Will is asking her to marry him.' I'm *so* glad."

Amazed, Samantha smiled. "I'm *so* glad you waited."

"Thank you for being my friend, Samantha," she said slowly and softly.

"Thank you for being *my* friend, Isabella."

Will had his hand reassuringly on Samantha's shoulder and felt the convulsions in her body as she repressed the sobs.

Isabella closed her eyes; she looked peaceful. Her breathing was irregular. Samantha's hand overlapped Isabella's tiny one. She could feel her pulse—faltering and faint. They sat there for about half an hour, Juanita caressing Isabella's head, Samantha holding her little hand, and Will now sitting on the bed behind Samantha with his arm around her shoulders. Their eyes were fixed on Isabella, hoping for any sign of a change that would bring her back. Then Isabella's head turned slightly to the right, barely noticeable. The muscles in her right arm tightened as if she were trying to reach out, and the muscles in her shoulders tightened as if she were trying to get up. Then all went limp, and the life drained out of her. The change was clear; there was no mistake. The lovely, bright spark of life that was Isabella was gone. Isabella was gone.

*   *   *

It was early morning, the Wednesday after Easter. Warm for April, the wet air full of pewter-colored fog made the atmosphere oppressive as Will and Samantha emerged from the front door of Lake House. It was a miserable morning.

The dwarf ornamental trees scattered around the lawn were shrouded by the mist. Not yet in bloom, their bleak, bare branches spawned eerie aberrations. A pair of mourning doves were perched on a low branch emitting tones distorted by the dampness. Nature was moaning in a minor key. It was a miserable morning. It was a melancholy morning.

The walk, through the Lake House grounds, through the bare maple arches, through the dark pine woods, through the black iron pedestrian gate, along the fence on the south side of the farm, up the incline, and over the hill to the church, seemed endless.

The great church gradually materialized out of the vapor; the ghostly shapes of the people rose slowly up the shrouded steps and became visible as they passed though the haloed glow of the lamps surrounding the massive, high-arched entrance. The grand carillon was silent. The quiet, well-behaved children were wearing muted colors instead of the Easter-egg colors of last Sunday, and Mrs. Pentwater had exchanged her bright colors for gray ones. Her head was down, her eyes red. It was a miserable morning.

Samantha sat in the first pew between Juanita and Will. Edmund was next to Will. The small coffin in front of them was draped with white flowers. The light in the church was dim. No sunlight came through the stained-glass windows. Their colors were dark. The organist played a solemn hymn beautifully in a minor key.

Pastor Schafer reassured and comforted his flock with an appropriate homily. Samantha's attention drifted between her thoughts and his words.

"We occupy such an infinitesimal portion of time and space in this world . . . ." she heard him say.

She thought about her family. *How fast the time had passed. I was so young. Wouldn't they always be there?*

Then her attention returned to his words: "The angels came and carried her to a place where she will run through days of endless peace, joy and perfect love . . . ." Her mind drifted to her nieces playing in the park. She could see them playing with Isabella now. "She is happy. We're sad . . . ."

Her thoughts drifted to Will—she noticed a tear in the corner of his eye, Edmund's, too. *They loved her, too. I've been selfish thinking only of myself and my loss.*

She reached over and held Juanita's hand. Surprisingly, she seemed at peace. A person's grief comes in surges at different times; when one member of a family is immobile with grief, others have moments of strength to give support and carry on the tasks required. This time, Samantha had a "family" to comfort her. She wasn't alone any more. She could comfort them; she knew from experience what they needed.

She looked at Pastor Shafer and heard him say, "Our heavenly Father rejoices over Isabella. 'The LORD your God is with you, He is mighty to save. He will take great delight in you, He will quiet you with His love, He will rejoice over you with singing.' Zephaniah 3:17. God loved Isabella before we knew her and has blessed her. 'Behold, what manner of love the Father has bestowed upon us, that we should be called children of God!' 1 John 3:1. And, 'Before I formed you in the womb I knew you.' Jeremiah 1:5. God asks us to trust Him. 'And we know that in all things God works for the good of those who love him, who have been called according to His purpose.' Romans 8:28."

Samantha looked at the stained-glass windows. The dim shapes in the glass started to emerge. She vaguely saw an angel with a sword in one panel and Jesus reaching out His hand in another. As she studied the panels, she heard the pastor's words. "The angel of eternal death sheathed his sword as Jesus reached out His hand to Isabella and guided her to eternal life. We would say, 'Come back!' She would say, 'I'll be watching for you—I'll be waiting for you. Come here!'"

* * *

As they retraced their steps home, the fog began to lift. Reaching the end of the fence bordering the farm, Samantha spotted a Red Admiral perched on the last white post. She stopped abruptly and whispered to Will, "The first butterfly I've seen this spring."

"Me, too," he whispered back.

Suddenly, the cheerful little creature flew up and landed on Samantha's arm, evoking a startled laugh—suppressed so as not to frighten it away. Motionlessly, they studied its intricate design and beauty. Then, abruptly, it rose up in front of their faces, paused a second or two, then darted off in an erratic flight pattern over the fence and into the meadow.

Samantha and Will walked on, arm in arm, with smiles emerging, lighter steps, and spirits soothed by the manifestations of renewing life.

As they came out from under the maple arches and entered the grounds, the sun shone brightly around Lake House. Water droplets dripped from the house and trees with their progressing yellow-green bud, sparkling and emitting a prism of color—an aura that seemed to forecast a bright future. When one life goes, new life comes. Their future full of the hope, Will and Samantha would raise their family, carry on the traditions of Lake House, and bring new life to it. They would be protectors of the whole family of Lake House—protectors of the faith, continuing to pass down its precepts to the next generation.

Love the Lord your God with all your mind, heart, soul, and strength
and love your neighbor as yourself.
There is no commandment greater than these.

ABOUT THE AUTHOR

Sally Faubel is a registered dietitian. She started her career in dietetics as Pediatric Dietitian at the University of Minnesota Hospitals. Later, she worked for a food management company and then as a clinical dietitian. Subsequently, she became self-employed as a consultant dietitian, contracting with hospitals and long-term-care facilities. After writing patient assessments, policies and procedures, she has written a novel.

Her parents owned a golf course in Saugatuck, Michigan where she grew up. She has lived in Michigan most of her life and now resides in Western Michigan with her husband, Jerry. They have a daughter and son-in-law, both are physicians in Colorado, and a granddaughter.

*   *   *

Books by Sally Faubel, RD

Favorite Lake House Recipes

Breakfast at Lake House

The recipe books features foods from Michigan farms and game from Michigan streams, lakes, meadows, and woodlands. Nutrition and production information are included.

CPSIA information can be obtained at www.ICGtesting.com
Printed in the USA
LVOW101850300712

292191LV00003B/76/P